Countdown . . .

They had about ten and a half minutes yet, give or take a bit, before the expanding blast wave of the nova reached them. Plenty of time *if* nothing unexpected happened.

"Skipper! I've got a bender coming through dead ahead!"

She checked the ID. The call was from second lieutenant Traci Wayne, only thirty kilometers off Lee's port wing. A *bender* was something warping space, possibly one of the Euler triggerships . . . but there was a chance it was something else.

It was. She saw the brilliant flash of twisted starlight, saw the Xul Type IV materialize out of empty space fifty kilometers ahead. Like humans, the Xul used the Galaxy-spanning network of stargates, but their ships also possessed FTL capability which sharply warped local space.

And the alien warship had dropped into the normal space time matrix directly between most of Lee's squadron and the stargate.

They were going to have to fight to get through.

By Ian Douglas

Books in the Inheritance Trilogy

Books in the Legacy Trilogy

Books in the Heritage Trilogy

GALACTIC CORPS

BOOK TWO OF THE INHERITANCE TRILOGY

IAN DOUGLAS

An Imprint of HarperCollinsPublishers

This is a work of fiction. Names, characters, places, and incidents are drawn from the author's imagination or are used fictitiously and are not to be construed as real. Any resemblance to actual events, locales, organizations, or persons, living or dead, is entirely coincidental.

EOS
An Imprint of HarperCollins*Publishers*
10 East 53rd Street
New York, New York 10022-5299

Copyright © 2008 by William H. Keith, Jr.
Cover art by Fred Gambino
ISBN 978-0-06-123862-8
www.eosbooks.com

First Eos paperback printing: November 2008

HarperCollins® and Eos® are registered trademarks of HarperCollins Publishers.

Printed in the U.S.A.

10 9 8 7 6 5 4 3 2 1

As always, for Brea. My light. My life. My muse.

Timeline of the Inheritance Universe

Years before present

50,000,000–30,000,000: Galaxy dominated by the One Mind, sentient organic superconductors with hive mentality. They create the network of stargates across the Galaxy, and build the Encyclopedia Galactica Node at the Galactic Core.

30,000,000–10,000,000: Dominance of Children of the Night, nocturnal psychovores. They replace the One Mind, which may have transcended material instrumentality.

10,000,000 TO PRESENT: Dominance of the Xul, also known as the Hunters of the Dawn. Originally polyspecific pantovores, they eventually exist solely as downloaded mentalities within artificial cybernetic complexes.

Circa 500,000 B.C.E.: Advanced polyspecific machine intelligence, later called variously the Ancients or the Builders, extends a high-technology empire across a volume of space several thousand light years in extent. Extensive planoforming of Chiron, at Alpha Centauri A, of Mars in the nearby Sol System, and of numerous other worlds. QCC networks provide instantaneous communications across the entire empire. Ultimately, the Builder civilization is destroyed by the Xul. Asteroid impacts strip away the newly generated Martian atmosphere and seas, but Earth, with no technological presence, is ignored. A Xul huntership is badly damaged in the battle over Mars; it later crashes into the Europan world-sea and is frozen beneath the ice. Survivors of the Martian holocaust migrate to Earth and upload themselves into gene-tailored primates that later will be known as *Homo sapiens*.

10,000 B.C.E.–7500 B.C.E.: Earth and Earth's Moon colonized by the Ahannu, or An, who are later remembered as the gods of ancient Sumeria. Around 7500 B.C.E., asteroid strikes by the Xul destroy An colonies across their empire. Earth is devastated by asteroid strikes. One colony, at Lalande 21185, survives.

Circa 6000 B.C.E.: Amphibious N'mah visit Earth and help human survivors of Xul attack develop civilization. They are later remembered as the Nommo of the Dogon tribe of Africa, and as civilizing/agricultural gods by other cultures in the Mideast and the Americas.

Circa 6000–5000 B.C.E.: N'mah starfaring culture destroyed by the Xul. Survivors exist in low-technology communities within the Sirius Stargate and, possibly, elsewhere.

1200 B.C.E. [SPECULATIVE]: The Xul revisit Earth and discover an advanced Bronze Age culture. Asteroid impacts cause devastating floods worldwide, and may be the root of the Atlantis myth.

700 C.E.: The deep abyssal intelligence later named the Eulers fight the Xul to a standstill by detonating their own stars. The astronomical conflagration of artificial novae is seen in the skies of Earth, in the constellation Aquila, some 1,200 years later.

The Heritage Trilogy

2039–2042: *Semper Mars*
2040: 1st UN War. March by "Sands of Mars Garroway." Battle of Cydonia. Discovery of the Cydonian Cave of Wonders.

2040–2042: *Luna Marine*
2042: Battle of Tsiolkovsky. Discovery of An base on the Moon.

2067: *Europa Strike*

2067: Sino-American War. Discovery of the Singer under the Europan ice.

The Legacy Trilogy

2138–2148: *Star Corps*
2148: Battle of Ishtar. Treaty with An of Lalande 21185. Earth survey vessel *The Wings of Isis* destroyed while approaching the Sirius Stargate.

2148–2170: *Battlespace*
2170: Battle of Sirius Gate. Contact with the N'mah, an amphibious species living inside the gate structure. Data collected electronically fills in some information about the Xul, and leads to a Xul node in Cluster Space, 30,000 light years from Sol. A Marine assault force uses the gate to enter Cluster Space and destroy this gate.

2314–2333: *Star Marines*
2314: Armageddonfall
2323: Battle of Night's Edge. Destruction of Xul fleet and world in Night's Edge Space.

The Inheritance Trilogy

2877: *Star Strike*
2877 [1102 M.E.]: 1MIEF departs for Puller 659. Battle of Puller 659 against Pan-Europeans. Contact with Eulers in Cygni Space. Battle of Cygni Space. Destruction of star in Starwall Space, eliminating local Xul node.

2886: *Galactic Corps*
2886 [1111 M.E.]: Raid on Cluster Space by 1MIEF. Discovery of stargate path to major Xul node at Galactic Core.
2887 [1112 M.E.]: Operation Heartfire. Assault on the Galactic Core.

GALACTIC CORPS

Prologue

They were not omnipotent.

Throughout their multi-million-year period of galactic dominance, they'd been known by many names. The Destroyers. The Hunters of the Dawn. The Enemy. The Xul. They called themselves by a thought symbol that might translate as We Who Are.

Perhaps ten million years ago, give or take some few hundreds of thousands of years, We Who Are had possessed organic bodies; as such, they'd been a species, like all heirs of flesh, shaped and constrained by the impersonal forces of evolution. In common with all products of the evolutionary process, they'd possessed a marked will to survive.

What most clearly distinguished We Who Are from most other species was simply the extremes to which that will carried them.

Early in their history, they'd survived—barely—a traumatic encounter with another species upon their home planet. That encounter left them shaken, brutalized, and monomaniacally mistrustful of the motives of anything Other.

It left the other species extinct.

That ancient struggle for dominance, ultimately for survival, imprinted itself upon the psyche of We Who Are. When, in due time, they began moving out into the Galaxy, they carried that imprint with them. No other species posing a threat, however remote, to We Who Are could be permitted to survive.

Over the course of some millions of years, We Who Are extended and expanded the range of their lonely suzerainty over the Galaxy. Eventually, however, they encountered the far-flung bastions of another starfaring species, nocturnal psychovores who styled themselves as the Children of the Night. Like We Who Are, the Children possessed as a racial trait the need to exterminate all competition. Unlike We Who Are at that time, perhaps eight million years ago, the Children were already ancient, their line extending back into a murkily remote past when they, in their season, had wrested dominance of the Galaxy from a still more remote species, a self-aware congeries of organic superconductors that called themselves the One Mind.

Young, fired with righteous ambition and an instinctive determination to crush all competition in order to be alone, and therefore safe, within their Galactic fastnesses, We Who Are eventually triumphed after a savage no-quarters war that scoured a hundred thousand worlds of life. The Children of the Night passed into the ultimate Night of extinction, as had the One Mind before them.

And with that victory, the We Who Are became the new xenophobically senticidal caretakers of the Galaxy.

More millions of years passed. Eventually, like the majority of technically oriented species before them, We Who Are chose to discard their organic bodies, uploading their consciousnesses into nearly immortal cybernetic shells. They carried with them, however, the racial traits of mind and awareness that had distinguished them as organic beings— including the blatantly Darwinian imperative to eliminate all possible competitors, all possible threats to their existence.

In fact, this radical form of natural selection had dominated the galactic scene ever since sentient life had first emerged, some eight billion years before. In any given epoch, it took only a single intelligent species with technic aptitude and a lack of empathy for anything Other to emerge from the cauldron of its birthworld and insure its survival by eliminating all possible rivals. Galactic civilizations rarely overlapped perfectly in terms of their scientific and technical levels; with each encounter, one species tended to be older than the other, usually by many thousands or tens of thousands of years, and hence far more technically advanced.

As new civilizations emerged and achieved technical capabilities permitting space flight and long-distance communication, most wondered why the skies of their worlds, which should have been humming with the signs of advanced civilizations, seemed so silent, so empty. Each time new races, new civilizations took their first tentative steps out beyond the worlds of their genesis, We Who Are, sooner or later, detected their efforts from their scattered bastions, descended upon their worlds, and relentlessly exterminated them. Hence, the silent sky.

But like the Children of the Night, the One Mind, and so many others who'd come before, We Who Are were not omnipotent. The vast, sprawling spiral of the Galaxy, possessing some three hundred billion stars, is far too large, with far too many worlds, for any one race to monitor every possible lifeworld, every emerging sentient species.

And there were so many of these. . . .

In the outlying regions of the Galaxy's Perseus Arm, within the dense polar jungles of the warm, inner world of a class-G5 star, a race of brachiating mollusks—morphologically, at least, they somewhat resembled certain members of that terrestrial phylum—swung from the interwoven branches of sessile thermovores not unlike Earthly trees. The species was young, as yet, but had developed an elaborate philosophy based on mating calls, territoriality, music, and mathematics. One day, they might have much to offer an evolving Galactic polylogue, but they hadn't yet developed electronics or radio, much less the instantaneous magic of quantum-coupled communications. The huntership-communes of We Who Are had passed through this star system several times within the past ten thousand or so years, but not noticed the species' thriving, arboreal cities.

Not yet.

Closer in toward the galactic core, within the teeming star clouds of the Sagittarius Arm, on the rugged, tide-strained volcanic moon of a superjovian gas giant, a race of armored paraholothurids built water's-edge hive-cities of compacted excrement and composed palendromic epics celebrating their having been chosen as slaves of the sky-disk they saw as the eye of God. Natural radio emitters, they broadcast the glory of the one true religion to the stars. We Who Are had detected those signals and searched for their origin; so far, they'd not found the holothurids' world, for they tended not to think of planetary bodies outside of the star's liquid-water habitable zone as a possible abode of life.

That particular blind spot had given them trouble more than once in the past, and likely would again.

Closer in still toward the galactic hub, near the merging of the Norma and Scutum-Crux Arms, a fiercely radiating type A star blasted its unusual coterie of rocky worlds with intense radiation. Bathed in abundant radiant energy, Life had emerged on the innermost world and, borne by the local stellar winds, had seeded the other, outer planets of the system as well. Sentience had arisen here a few million years before, rising among several of the numerous, fast-evolving taxas of selenium-germanium chelated crystalline chemovores that constituted the local biosphere. Here, again, the manipulation of naturally occurring radio waves became the basis for communication, and, again, those manipulations had been detected in the depths of space, light-years distant.

The pace of crystalline life, however, tends to be slow, too slow for We Who Are to distinguish that life from the inorganic chemistry of accreted minerals. Those received artificial signals had caused the local We Who Are node some considerable concern, but it was clear that the problem soon would take care of itself. Type A giants are short-lived stars, their lifetimes on the main sequence lasting less than half a billion years. The local star already was showing signs of instability, and soon the abundant radiation that made life and sentience possible here would become that life's executioner.

Twenty-three thousand light years from the Galaxy's center, within the smear of stars and nebulae known as the Orion Arm, a world called Chiron by its most recent inhabitant, represented two distinct threads of civilization within the Galactic scene. Bathed in the yellow and orange hues of a double star, the world's continents were battered and cratered by an intense celestial bombardment of half a million years before, and everywhere stood the somber and silent ruins of a golden civilization swept away by the firestorm. They were known by those who'd come later variously as the Ancients and, so numerous were the crumbling shells of their hell-blasted world-cities, as the Builders.

The Builder civilization had been a brilliant concord of machine intelligences arisen and evolved from various organic precursors; the asteroids that had destroyed Chiron had been flung into the planet by We Who Are, whose hunterships had sought out the Builders' colony worlds scattered widely across perhaps a third of the Galaxy and in like manner, relentlessly and methodically exterminated each one.

Chiron was also known to its more recent colonists as Alpha Centauri A-II. Just four and a third light years away lay the G2 star called Sol, and the homeworld of an ambitious, carbon-based, oxygen-metabolizing species of sexual mammals that called itself Humankind. Within the past thousand years, an eye's blink against the span marking the rise and extinction of myriad expressions of galactic life and sentience, humans and their artificially sentient machines had left the world of their birth to venture to the worlds of nearby stars, beginning with Chiron, and going on to assimilate numerous star systems scattered throughout an oblong realm measuring perhaps eight light centuries across at its greatest extent, four at its smallest. They'd encountered other intelligent species—the primitive An, the advanced but retiring N'mah, and the benthic species of brilliant mathematicians known to them as the Eulers—all three the shattered remnants of past encounters with We Who Are.

And, more than once within the past handful of centuries, Humankind, too, had attracted the xenocidal attention of We Who Are, and the destructiveness of those encounters was rapidly escalating. Most recently, a human battlefleet had used an ancient system of stargates to reach an important node of We Who Are near the Galactic hub, and there used Euler technology to detonate the star.

The resultant nova had finally caught the full attention of the Galaxy's overlords.

And they moved now with blatantly uncharacteristic haste to obey their racial hard-wiring and eliminate once and for all this new and potentially serious threat to their survival.

The final clash, the final Armageddon would come soon, and, when it did, it would do so on a scale unknown since the extinction of the Builders.

1

Gunnery Sergeant Aiden Garroway wiggled a bit deeper into the bottle's embrace as the armorer swung the dome canopy down over his head and sealed it in place. "Link check," he heard, the Navy chief's words forming in his mind.

The canopy was opaque, a nanosurfaced ceramic-iridium laminate impervious to almost anything up to a direct hit by a 100-gigawatt laser, but the bottle's electronics fed the external view directly into Garroway's brain, channeling the data through his cerebral implants. The armorer's face leered down at him, distorted by the feed's fisheye effect, and by the reflections from the fishbowl helmet of the man's vacwear utilities.

"Link is on-line," Garroway replied. "You're going to have to fix that, though, Chief. *God*, you're ugly."

The man laughed. "Not as ugly as the Xulies. Good luck, Marine."

"Ooh-rah." With a thoughtclick, Garroway switched the data link to an external view, fed from the *Ishtar*'s outer hull.

The view here, high above the stargate, was stunning, spectacular. . . .

Carson was a nondescript double star near the fringe of Commonwealth space, a planetless pair of cool M-class dwarfs circling one another in a tight embrace. Two light hours out, so distant that the two suns themselves were merely bright ruby points of light against the background scattering of stars, the local stargate drifted in slow orbit, an immense, slender-rimmed hoop twenty kilometers across, gleaming silver and red in the somber light.

The Marine transport *Ishtar* was drifting slowly toward the gate belly-first, some fifteen kilometers above the structure's center. Her ventral hatches were open, her forward dropdeck exposed to hard vacuum—hence the need for the armorer's helmet and sealed utilities.

He switched the feed back to his pod's external optics. Around him, caught in the glare of overhead lights, were the launch racks holding other bottles, and Navy and Marine personnel—armorers, deckhands, and technicians—were moving among them, prepping each for drop.

"Be sure to bring back some good suit vids, okay, Gunny?" the armorer told him. "I hear it's real pretty over there."

"I'll see what I can do, Chief. But I imagine we're going to be too busy to get anything artistic."

"Shit, I didn't say artistic. I just hear the view's nice, is all. What I really want to see is some after-op combat footage of a bunch of dead Xulies!"

"You and me both, Chief."

"Bravo Company," another voice said, cutting in. The dry, staccato tones were those of the company commanding officer, Captain John "Blackjack" Black, though the actual speaker would be Smedley, the company AI. *"Squad and section leaders, check your Marines and report status."*

Garroway was the gunnery sergeant assigned to the company HQ, and, as such, was the senior NCO in charge of the seven other enlisted Marines in the unit, under Captain Black himself. He ran through the electronic links with the other HQ personnel—two riflemen, two comm officers, two Navy hospital corpsmen, and a tech specialist/observer. All feeds showed green and ready, systems charged and go, weapons safed and ready.

"Green Tower," he said over the company net, using the HQ section's code name to link through to Smedley. "This is Tower Two. All Tower platforms report ready for drop."

"Copy, Two," Smedley replied.

Garroway chuckled. The AI was named after Major General Smedley Butler, one of the Corps' heroes from the ancient, pre-spaceflight era of almost a thousand years ago. According to the histories, though, the original Smedley had been quite a character, often in trouble with his superiors because of his rough manner. Somehow, Garroway doubted that the guy had been quite as laconic as his artificial namesake.

There were historical simulations of the original Butler on file back on Mars, and in the library on board the *Hermes.* He decided he would link in some time, just to see how the two compared.

"First Platoon, ready to launch," 2nd Lieutenant Cooper, the platoon's commanding officer, announced over the Net.

"Second Platoon, ready to go." That was 2nd Lieutenant Hamblet.

"Third Platoon, ready," 2nd Lieutenant Costigan added.

"PryFly, Bravo Company," the captain's voice said. Garroway thought he heard some stress there. If so, it was the old man himself speaking, and not his electronic proxy. "We are ready for launch."

"Very well," another voice said, this one from *Ishtar's* primary flight control center, or PryFly. "Bravo Company release in five . . . four . . . three . . . two . . . one . . . *release!*"

Garroway felt the sharp jolt as magnetic grapples released his bottle, and then the *Ishtar's* ventral hull was receding against the stars. From his perspective, it appeared that the transport had suddenly begun accelerating away from him; in fact, *Ishtar* had just halted its gateward drift, allowing a cloud of M-CAPs to emerge from her belly and continue drifting toward the gate at a steady kilometer per second.

M-CAPs, Marine Combat Assault Pods, were only the

most recent means of transporting individual Marines into battlespace, an upgrade to the Space Assault Pods, or SAPs in wide use until only a few years ago. Somewhere between a very large, bulky, and powerful unit of heavily armed space armor and a very tiny, lightly armed, underpowered one-man space craft, a CAP carried a single Marine within its claustrophobic core. A gravitic drive allowed the device to accelerate at forty gravities—about four hundred meters per second per second. It responded directly to a Marine's thoughts, through his cereblink, and provided him with constantly updated information on his surroundings and the tactical situation.

For self-evident reasons, Marines called them bottles, among other nastier, more vitriolic names.

"Okay, people," Blackjack's voice told them over the Net. "We're doing this by the book. We want to maintain the element of surprise for as long as possible, so do *not* engage your gravitics until I give the word. Power at ten percent only. Magnetic shielding engaged. Optical benders on. Everyone copy?"

A chorus of voices came back over the Net, mingled calls of "aye, aye, sir" and "copy that" and "ooh-rah." A display open to one side within Garroway's mind showed the telemetry from each pod, all green and go.

The assault force, one hundred fifty Marines of Bravo Company, First Marine Assault Battalion of the First Marine Interstellar Expeditionary Force was going to war.

Falling . . . falling . . . the bottles drifted into the opening of the stargate unpowered, with just enough power trickling through their drives to keep them from running afoul of one another, and to keep the magnetic shields charged and ready. Around them, unseen within the distant rim of the gate, a pair of Jupiter-massed black holes circled along their ancient tracks in opposite directions, at a velocity approaching that of light. The stresses on local spacetime were somehow—the technology was still well beyond the capability of human physics—focused at the gate's lumen. The frequency of those rotating singularities had already been tuned to connect this gate with one particular other gate . . . one some twenty thousand light years above the plane of the Galaxy.

For the briefest of instants, Garroway felt the sharp, inner twist of tidal forces, and then he was through.

The sky wavered . . . shimmered . . . then blinked.

And he was somewhere else, somewhere . . . *astonishingly* else.

Not for the first time, Garroway wondered why you couldn't see through an open gate to the other side, or why radio or lasercom signals could not be passed through, while solid things like starships made the passage *almost* unimpeded. The physicists said that had to do with a kind of flicker or stutter effect due to the period of the rotating singularities that allowed mass through in discrete, quantum chunks, but which interfered with the wave aspect of energy. Even so, he'd once seen the flash from a nova pass through an open gate, and do so with power enough to destroy a Xul huntership.

So much Humankind had yet to learn.

He looked around, studying ambient space with all the rubbernecking fervor of a first-time tourist in EarthRing City. An ancestor of Garroway's had been here once, centuries before. The place was known as Cluster Space, and it was located, so far as AI navigational programs could place it, some twenty to twenty-two thousand light years above the plane of the Galaxy, and at least thirty thousand light years from Earth.

From out here, of course, the microscopic yellow speck of Earth's sun was quite invisible, utterly lost within the vast and milky swirl of pale light hanging in the sky, a spiral that looked oddly like a pale-colored whirlpool frozen in an instant of time. Most individual stars at this distance were lost; only novae or the very brightest of giant suns were visible as separate stars out here. What remained was a kind of graininess or digital noise to the light. In fact, it looked much like the pale glow from the Milky Way seen on a pellucidly clear, dark night on Earth or, better, Mars . . . and for an obvious reason. It was the same glow, but seen from

the outside against the black emptiness of the intergalactic voice, rather than from within one of the Galaxy's spiral
arms.

Here, the Galaxy stretched across half of the sky, tilted at
a slightly oblique angle. Garroway could distinguish the
slight differences in hue, blue and blue-white in the spiral
arms, reddish in the swollen bulge of the central core. The
smear of nebulae, some coal-black, other emission nebulae
showing pale glows of green or red, wove among the stars
like ragged streamers in an unfelt wind.

Opposite, against the ultimate void of the intergalactic
abyss, a solitary globular star cluster hung in isolated splendor, a teeming beehive of suns, spanning a breadth of sky
perhaps sixteen times as large as the full moon when seen
from Earth, glowing with an almost undetectable reddish
hue identical to the ruddy glow of the Galactic Core.

In a different direction lay the local star, a class-M red
dwarf visible solely as a bright red spark against the night.
That star, catalogued simply as CS-1, but nicknamed Bloodlight by the Marines, was the primary target of the op,
which had been tagged Clusterstrike by the mission planners.

Behind the Marines was the stargate . . . but not the gate
into which Bravo Company had just fallen. The tidal stresses
of the gate back in Carson Space had linked across the light
millennia with the gate here, allowing the swarm of Marine
bottles to come through, gate-to-gate.

A flood of radio-frequency noise washed through his bottle's exposed sensors, and Garroway set his personal AI to
screening it, sifting through for hard data on enemy positions. The enemy was here. Humankind's ancient enemy, the
Xul . . .

Among other threats, a trio of Xul fortresses orbited here,
only a few hundred kilometers away, and those fortresses had
to be eliminated if Clusterstrike was to succeed. Trans-gate
probes had already slipped through and located each of the
three, along with every other enemy ship and station within
this system. Those probes had managed to return, apparently

unnoticed, but Marine bottles were larger and noisier than AI probes, and they were in this instant terribly vulnerable to attack.

Unlike the earlier Space Assault Pods, each M-CAP was effectively invisible, the coating of nano covering each one serving as uncounted trillions of optical relays, pulling light from one side of the bottle around to a carefully calculated point on the opposite side before releasing it. The effect was to make the bottle almost invisible so that light, radar, and other radiation was curved past the bottle rather than reflecting from it—optical bending. The various patches in each bottle's hull not shielded by the benders—which allowed the Marines to see out and to communicate with one another and with the company AI net, among other things—were so small they were nearly invisible at any range greater than a few meters.

Still, the illusion was not perfect, and things like radiated heat or the spatial distortion caused by a gravitics drive could cause enough of a ripple against background stars to reveal their presence to a careful and watchful enemy. At Captain Black's command, and under Smedley's precise control, the school of invisible fish shifted vector as a unit, moving now slantwise across the opening of the stargate, each platoon angling toward a different target, the three Xul bastions guarding this gateway into Cluster Space.

So far, their entrance appeared to have gone unnoticed.

It would have been a mistake, though, to assume the Xul were careless or less than alert. Intelligence had reported that their defenses had been tightening up at all of their known gate outposts over the past few years, as the Xul Mind as a whole began, slowly, to react to Humankind's attacks.

For almost nine years, now, 1MIEF had been playing a deadly game, one absolutely vital to the survival of Earth and Humankind. With both military and civilian intelligence services certain that the ancient enemy, the Xul, had learned the location of Sol and of the existence of humanity, Lieutenant General Martin Alexander, acclaimed Hero of the Battle of the Nova, had for almost a decade, now, been wielding the 1st Marine Interstellar Expeditionary Force like a personal weapon. Again and again, a Xul bastion outpost, either long-known or newly discovered, would be targeted by 1MIEF for a lightning raid. Usually, the Xul bastion would be located within a system containing one or more of the ancient stargates.

Those gates were still mysteries. Human xenosophontologists and intelligence officers all agreed that the system of stargates scattered throughout the Galaxy and beyond were not, themselves, the product of Xul technology, but were leftovers from some other, much more ancient civilization, now long vanished. But the Xul, like the N'mah and humans, used the gates to their own advantage with other technologies for crossing the long, empty light years. The Gatenet provided a transport web spanning tens of thousands of light years—*if* you knew where each gate attunement led.

The Xul appeared to be very much at home with the Gatenet, had woven it into the fabric of their empire. Humans were still learning the shape and dimensions of that Net. But one by one, human forces continued to secretly find, note, and then attack every Xul gate outpost they could find. By keeping up a relentless assault, the hope was to keep the Xul preoccupied with tracking down and destroying 1MIEF, rather than with moving into the star systems occupied by Humanity—including Sol—and obliterating them.

Clearly, the Xul could send Humankind into extinction if they set their considerable assets toward that goal; the trick was to keep them so off balance with constant raids, each one a pinprick on its own, that they never got around to that final genocidal thrust at the worlds occupied by humanity.

How long could 1MIEF keep up the pinpricks? No one knew, though the topic was a favorite during off-watch bull sessions in the Marine squad bays on board each of the fleet's transports. Marine and Navy sim-warriors and armchair generals made elaborate bets as to how long the task force could stay on the offensive, whether or not they'd be recalled to Sol, and how long it would be before the Xul empire collapsed.

Garroway had participated in a few of those sessions, but had refrained from joining in on the betting. If he'd started making wagers, he would have been betting against his own survival . . . a distinctly uncomfortable position in which to find oneself. He believed in the Marine Corps and in the Corps' indomitable fighting spirit, but he also knew just how large the Xul presence in the Galaxy must be. Conservative estimates said the Xul hunterships outnumbered *all* human starships on the order of several tens of thousands to one. The Galaxy was that large.

Not good odds. Not good odds at *all*.

His bottle was rapidly approaching one of the Xul fortresses now, a massive, squashed sphere five kilometers across. The surface showed a platinum-silver sheen that appeared smoothly reflective from a distance but which, as his M-CAP fell closer, was revealed to be a maze of geometric shapes, angles, protrusions, towers, squared-off valleys, and raised blocks. Weapons ports and turrets revealed themselves everywhere, plasma guns and magnetic accelerators and other weapons that affected the very nature of matter itself—and which were still sheer magic in so far as human technology was concerned.

Smedley announced that they were passing through the first of several magnetic screens. The surface nano on each pod adjusted to let it slip through without disturbing the field and announcing the Marine assault team's presence. Garroway found he was holding his breath, wondering when something would trigger, when surprise would be lost and the battle would begin. . . .

M-CAPs were superbly stealthy, as close-to-invisible as modern military technology could make them. Though bottles could accelerate at forty gravities, their approach so far had been deliberately low-key and unobtrusive, too slow for the automated Xul defense systems to recognize a threat.

They hadn't been seen so far. That, or the Xul targeting sensors already had them locked in, and were simply waiting for the order to fire.

Closer now . . . fewer than five kilometers. His personal AI took over full control of the small ship, identifying the best place for touch-down, coordinating with the company AI and the other fifty bottles in First Platoon, slowing Garroway's bottle with precisely timed bursts of its gravitics drive until it was hovering motionless a few meters above the surface. Gently, then, the craft lowered itself against the small but distinct gravitational attraction of the Xul fortress, until the two kissed.

"Contact," Garroway reported. Within his mental tacsit display, other Marines were reporting a successful touchdown all around him.

According to plan, the Headquarters element had grounded with First Platoon, which had as its target the largest of the three Xul bastions. Second and Third Platoons were deploying to the other two fortresses. Each Marine element was now on its own.

Still under AI control, Garroway's bottle extended its boarding cutter, a cylinder extruding nano-disassemblers from its business end to eat through the ceramic composites that made up the Xul structure's hull and create a tightly sealed docking collar. The bottle should be able to eat through the outer layers of armor within a minute or so, allowing Garroway and the other Marines to drop down into the interior of the fortress.

"*Incoming bogies!*" a shrill voice called over the tactical net. "*We've got incoming bogies!*"

So the Xul had finally adapted to this form of attack. The pods must have triggered some sort of alarm or defensive system as soon as they'd started touching down. On Garroway's mental tac display, a cloud of red targets was now emerging over the Xul fortress's close horizon, bearing down on the Marine assault platoon like an angry swarm of bees.

"Perimeter defense!" Captain Black called. "Take 'em down!"

The thirty M-CAPs of First Platoon and the HQ section had set down on the Xul fortress in an AI-controlled pattern, with an outer ring along the perimeter of Marines with heavy weapons, and two inner rings intent on tunneling into the fortress. Garroway snapped on his targeting link, and felt his bottle spin within the boarding collar to bring the target cloud under his weapon.

The AP-840 M-CAP mounted a single weapon at its stern—the part of the bottle opposite the boarding collar, still raised three meters above the Xul hull. After latching on and digging in—"taking a bite," as Marine slang put it—the M-CAP essentially became a mounted turret weapon. The gun, depending on the mission load-out, could be a V-90 Striker missile launcher, a rapid-fire magnetic pulse gun, or a Starfire plasma weapon.

Garroway's bottle mounted the V-90. The Striker was a smart weapon that could carry a variety of warheads. The missiles filling Garroway's ammo bins each were fitted out with ND-4 nanodisassembler pods. Tracking the incoming cloud in his mind, nudging the selector to full auto, he thoughtclicked the firing control and a stream of forty-centimeter missiles snapped from his weapon mount. The missiles co-ordinated with one another to disperse into the cloud, ignor-ing the leading elements of the enemy force and detonating deep within the attacking formation.

Each exploding pod released a cloud of its own—millions of molecule-sized nanodisassemblers traveling at high speed and programmed to begin taking apart whatever they hap-pened to strike. Working on an atomic level, they were fast; almost immediately, red-highlighted targets on the tactical display began winking out, as though black cancers were eating through the formation from within, the decay begin-ning at a dozen different starting points and swiftly working its way out.

Other Marine M-CAPs around the perimeter began firing as well, adding their own clouds of nano-D to the general destruction, or lashing out with man-made bolts of plasma lightning.

Then the cloud reached the Marine perimeter.

Each target was a Xul warrior—a machine, actually, that was apparently grown within the hulls of their hunterships and forts. Two to three meters long, egg-shaped, but with smooth convolutions and bulges, each extruded a number of tentacles at seemingly random points on their shells, each possessed glittering lenses, also randomly positioned over their bodies. Some of those lenses would be eyes. Others . . .

Laser fire snapped across the outer hull of Garroway's pod, generating a silvery puff of expanding vapor. *Damn!* The Xulies weren't supposed to be able to *see* the Marine bottles with the optical benders on . . . but, then, no one was certain what wavelengths the Xul warriors used for vision, or what other senses they might possess.

He snapped off another burst of nano-D in response, but the Xul that had nailed him had already vaporized an instant before, caught by a flash from Sergeant Colby's plasma gun.

"Thanks!" Garroway called to her over the tactical net.

"Don't mention it, Gare!" was her response. She was already tracking another Xul warrior, as was Garroway. As the enemy swarmed over the Marine position, he'd switched to single shots and shoot-to-hit; the enemy was widely enough dispersed now that the Marines could no longer wipe out large numbers of the enemy combat machines with area fire. His bottle spun wildly, tracking a Xul as it streaked past low above the surface of the fortress. Garroway held his fire until his targeting cursor tracked past several nearby Marine bottles, then slammed a nano-D pod squarely into the now-fleeing machine from behind. The Xul warrior fell to pieces, a spray of dissolving parts, seconds later.

Local nano-D levels were rising sharply in the immediate battlespace. Drifting motes of disassembler were striking his pod, now, then rebounding. They were programmed to recognize the outer nano coatings of the M-CAPs and ignore them and seek other targets, but a few were beginning to burrow into his bottle at points scoured clean of nano by the Xul laser bursts. The automatic defenses on Garroway's pod were growing erratic, and would soon fail.

"Smedley!" Garroway called, loosing another barrage at a pair of incoming Xul combat robots. "I've got nano-D on my pod, friendly fire! Tell the bastards to go chow down on something else!"

The company AI tweaked the electronics in Garroway's bottle, and the errant nano-D drifted away into space like a puff of vapor, repelled by the brief, coded signal. A lot of the stuff was starting to work on the Xul fortress's hull around the bottles, too. That might cause problems later, but there wasn't much that could be done about it. Modern battle-fields tended to soften and sludge down as random traces of nano-D, both friendly and enemy, began to accumulate in the area.

Then there was a sharp jolt, and Garroway's bottle dropped by a meter, sliding down hard into the boarding collar. The deck he was standing on dilated open. He didn't immedi-ately fall in the microgravity of the Xul fortress but, setting the pod's combat initiative on auto, he triggered a pair of battlespace drones, launching them into the emptiness at his feet.

A firefight was raging down there, as other Marines en-tered the enemy bastion. Garroway's drones uplinked to his helmet, showing him images of Marines in heavy armor struggling in a low, broad passageway with Xul fighterbots coming at them tentacle to metallic tentacle. He charged his suit's weapons, then gave a hard shove down through the open deck. Passing through the boarding collar, he entered the fight.

The passageway was two meters tall and ten to twenty wide, and the Marines were forced to stoop slightly because a Marine in Type 664 combat armor stood at nearly two and a quarter meters.

It was a Dantean scene, a circle of Hell, with Marines and Xul fighterbots struggling at knife-fighting range. It looked as though it should be unbearably noisy, but the in-terior of the Xul fortress was in hard vacuum and each bolt of plasma, each detonating grenade, each ripping or explod-ing alien shell did so in eerie silence. When Garroway's boots touched the deck, though, he could feel the noise, a kind of steady, pounding thrum in the bulkheads and deck as the vibrations were transmitted through Xul ceramic to his combat armor.

The one advantage possessed by the Marine assault team was that they were physically shorter than the Xul machines, which, in that low corridor, were coming at them horizontally, pulling themselves along with powerful flicks of their tentacles against the deck and the overhead. As a result, the only weapons the enemy could bring to bear were those set into the tops of their egg-shaped bodies. After a few moments, the Marines, too, began leaning forward, lifting their boots off the deck, dropping prone to minimize their cross-sections as targets as they poured a devastating and concentrated fire into the attacking hordes.

Garroway mounted an MPPG-40 on the right arm of his combat armor, a rapid-fire mass driver on his left. He shouldered forward about twelve meters, taking up a firing position next to Corporal Gerad Kukovitch, a massively built fungie in the company from Spokane, Washington. Kuk was mounting a 20mm full-auto grenade launcher on his suit; he was one of the few people in the company big enough to pack one. The Marine was floating horizontally, taking partial cover behind one of a number of pillar-like structures scattered through that alien hall. They looked like massive, meter-thick bundles of rope or ceramic cabling growing like tree trunks between deck and overhead. Garroway stretched out beside him, firing from the other side of the pillar.

Side by side, the two Marines coordinated their fire, 'Vitch's grenades silently flashing as they ripped through the enemy ranks, Garroway's MPPG sending blinding bolts of blue-white energy arcing down the corridor, ripping deep into everything they touched. Sergeant Larissa Colby joined them a second later, adding her plasma weapon to the melee. One by one, other Marines began locking in with the growing phalanx of Marines while their suit AIs linked in with one another under Smedley's guidance to coordinate their fire.

Together, as a unit, they were far more effective in concentrating their fire.

And then, almost magically, the enemy horde vanished, seeming to melt away into deck, overhead, and the far bulkheads of the chamber.

"Keep alert!" Captain Black called over the company Net. "They'll be back! Special weapons forward!"

Two Marines moved up the debris-filled space, hauling massive tubes with them. Tripod legs unfolded as they planted the mounts against the deck and activated them.

For some centuries, Marine tactics against Xul ships and bastions had involved boarding the enemy and lugging backpack nukes into the structure's depths. Nuclear explosions on the outer hull of one of the immense Xul hunterships or the even larger enemy fortresses did little permanent damage, and the resultant craters generally were patched over within a matter of minutes by flying clouds of fist-sized repair robots. A nuke detonating deep inside a Xul ship, though, tended to cause terrible damage, hampered automated repair efforts, and often loosed the microsingularities these monsters used as their power sources, and *that* was almost always fatal even to the largest Xul ship or structure.

Backpack nukes had been standard Corps issue until a few years ago. Now, however, the Marines had something a little better in their arsenal. . . .

2

First Platoon, Bravo Company
Cluster Space
0635 hrs, GMT

"Enemy targets bearing ahead and behind," Smedley reported in maddeningly calm tones.

"Here they come again, boys!" Captain Black warned. "Let 'em have it!"

"Ooh-rah!" Second Lieutenant Cooper yelled over the Net. *"Kill* the bastards!"

The defenders of Xul ships and bases tended to act and react in predictable ways. Assaults were *en masse*, wave attacks with thousands of units moving forward as one in an attempt to overwhelm Marine perimeter defenses. Once the Marine defenders had killed enough of the oncoming Xul combat units—estimates suggested the number ran around twenty-five to thirty percent of the total number of the attackers—the remainder would break off and disappear, usually by vanishing back into the walls of the structure's interior passageways and compartments. Some minutes would pass while the Xul built up their numbers once again, bringing in fresh combatants from deeper inside the target, and then the assault would be renewed.

That was what was happening now, as the passageway once again filled with black metallic egg shapes and flickering, writhing tentacles, coming in from both directions. Garroway crouched behind the pillar and aimed his weapon, thought-snapping the firing command, the plasma gun's link with his armor electronics triggering bolt after searing bolt of man-made lightning.

Garroway let himself settle into the rhythm of combat, picking out targets and burning them down. The riflemen needed to buy a few precious minutes for the special-weapons boys, and then they would be able to withdraw.

Xul ships and space fortresses had often been compared to organic structures, like the physical bodies of immense living organisms kilometers across. While no one knew how true this might be, the comparison was unavoidable. The masses of alien circuitry making up much of their internal mass appeared to have been *grown* rather than constructed, and there were nothing like crew compartments or quarters on board these things. Rather, the Xul appeared to be electronic life forms uploaded into the circuitry of a titanic computer. When any part of the structure was damaged, robotic devices the size of a human fist appeared in clouds swarming through the damaged area, appearing to extrude themselves into new circuitry in the same way that medicos used nanochelation to plate out circuitry inside the human brain and nervous system, but on a *much* larger scale.

These tentacled combat robots the Marines were engaging now appeared to be analogues of white cells and other immune-defense systems in an organic system. If that was so, the passageways like this one, which seemed to riddle all Xul structures with labyrinthine complexity, could reasonably be compared to a body's circulatory system, to blood vessels and lymphatic ducts serving as conduits for robotic devices designed for a variety of tasks including both repair and defense.

And to carry the uneasy comparison just a bit further, that meant that the Marines of 1MIEF were microbes, invaders penetrating the Xul's giant circulatory system with the intent of killing it.

At least in the human organism, bacteria didn't come in

the form of platoons of Marines, heavily armored and carrying plasma and antimatter weaponry.

As with armchair discussions of 1MIEF's strategy and tactics, the topic was often discussed in Marine squad bays during off-duty hours. For now, Garroway's thoughts touched on the image only briefly: *Let's give this fat bastard one hell of an upset stomach!* The rhythm of targeting and firing fell into an almost automatic process, guided by his training and the mental conditioning of weiji-do.

The two heavy gunners, meanwhile, rapidly completed setting up their weapons, one aiming forward, into the advancing mass of Xul warriors, the other aimed into the attackers in the opposite direction. A moment later, the weapons rocked in their mounts, and a pair of silvery shapes, each roughly the size of a big man's forearm and fist, flashed from the muzzles and, accelerating on their microgravitics, streaked into the surrounding darkness. One slammed into the side of an advancing Xul warrior, knocking it aside and continuing to accelerate as it flashed out of sight.

Designated RD-260, the weapon was popularly known as the RAM-D, for Remote Antimatter Detonator. Each round contained nearly a kilogram of antimatter suspended in hard vacuum and an electromagnetic bubble, preventing it from coming into contact with the containment cylinder's polyceramic and steel walls.

The gunners began reloading, hauling new RAM-D rounds out of the carry-satchels mounted on the hips of their armor. Tactical doctrine called for loosing three rounds apiece . . . *if* the enemy gave them that much time.

Sergeant Dixon, meanwhile, was laying down the back-up, a Mk.17 backpack nuke. He had it up against the overhead close beside one of the chamber's pillars, holding it firmly in place while the nano coating on the device's back formed an unbreakable bond with the surface of the alien composite. Dix's nuke was the mission's back-up guarantee . . . just in case the Xulies intercepted the other packages.

Garroway kept up a steady fire, frying Xul combat machines as quickly as he could target them. The microgravity environment within the confines of the passageway, however, was becoming clogged with drifting bits of debris, everything from glittering particles the size of grains of sand up to the three-meter shells of almost-intact Xul warriors burned out by Marine marksmanship. Clouds of nano-D adrift in the area were dissolving the larger pieces, but left behind a gritty, clinging dust that illuminated the enemy's laser beams as they flashed and probed through the gloom.

The Marines' armor was deflecting most of the incoming lasers, the outer layers of nano redirecting and scattering each flash harmlessly in a cascade of brilliant iridescence. Laser bolts repeatedly struck the pillar Garroway was half sheltering behind, striking with sharp, silent flashes and puffs of white vapor.

Some of the enemy fire was getting through, however, striking Marine armor on bare patches not covered by nano—on sensors and joint lines and link connector pads. Corporal Tomkins was down, air and boiling blood spraying from a severed lower arm until the suit's autosealers and nanomedibot injectors could kick in. *"Corpsman! Corpsman front!"* In seconds, Doc Huston was with the wounded Marine, dragging him out of the line of fire, putting his own armor between the wounded man and the enemy as he hauled the man back toward the pods.

Then PFC White was hit, half of her visor charred, cracked and leaking air. Doc Billingsly had her in seconds, slapping a sealant patch over her visor before it could crack further, and pulling her back out of the firefight. The Marines continued putting down a devastating defensive fire, drawing closer to one another as their defensive perimeter tightened up.

The special-weps gunners loosed their second rounds, firing almost together. The leading Xul machines reached the Marine perimeter at almost the same moment, colliding headlong with Marine riflemen in a confused tangle of armored legs and arms and whiplashing tentacles. Suddenly, the defensive perimeter was broken, with dozens of the gleaming combat machines smashing through the line and grappling with the armored Marines. In an instant, the battle went from a firing line drill to a knife fight.

One of the massive warrior robots collided with Garroway as he burned down a Xul machine alongside it, and the impact drove him back like the blow from a sledgehammer. The enemy was too close for plasma weapons now, too close even for his flamer. As Garroway tumbled over backward in the embrace of a Xul attacker, he thought-clicked his slicers into place—squared-off plates extending from his suit gauntlets over the backs of his hands thirty centimeters beyond the tips of his fingertips. Each plate was nano-grown from a carbon-niobium alloy in a sheet with edges feathered down to just an atom or two thick, rigidly anchored in a quark-quark substrate. They were monofilaments made rigid, sharp enough to slice cleanly through any solid matter less dense than neutronium.

Garroway's right arm came up and around as he shifted in his mind to weiji-do, the martial art form modern Marines trained in extensively in boot camp. Weiji-do, the Way of Manifestation, was a set of mental conditionings and downloaded training related to more ancient forms like t'ai chi. The imagery was of the essential chaos at the root of all existence out of which matter and energy were summoned, a deliberate tie-in with the principles of quantum physics that pulled energy from the base-state Quantum Sea.

Mentally drawing on the chaos of unformed reality, he focused a savage thrust of mental energy into the slicer blade as he rotated his suit sharply, sending the blade like a scalpel through the ceramic-plastic laminates of the Xul machine's shell. Pivoting, he arrested his rotational energy and came back with his left blade; the Xul machine's tentacles dropped away as the machine's body gaped open with mirror-smooth surfaces at the cuts. A final thrust, and the machine snapped into two pieces, lifelessly inert. Electricity snapped and flickered across exposed alien circuits, the bolts grounded out by Garroway's armor.

Continuing to rotate, he brought the mass driver mounted

on his left arm to bear on another Xul machine as it grappled with PFC Nikki Armandez. BB-sized pellets accelerated to ultra-high velocity slashed across the machine's shell, ripping open a fist-sized gash in the black sleekness. The machine bucked and jerked, like a living thing, as Armandez twisted clear of flailing tentacles.

Around him, the other Marines were fighting hand-to-hand—or, rather, hand-to-tentacle—as well, firing into enemy combat machines when they were a meter or two away, slicing them into tumbling, drifting chunks when they closed to within an arm's reach.

Garroway was forcibly reminded of an ancient adage drilled into all Marines in boot camp: *the* most dangerous weapon in combat was a Marine. It didn't matter whether he was armed with a plasma weapon, a mass driver, antimatter drone, forearm-mounted slicers, or his bare hands. It wasn't the Marine's high-tech toys that were dangerous. It was the *Marine* that wielded them.

In seconds, the breakthrough had been stopped, the alien machines inside the perimeter literally cut to pieces, while the rest withdrew as suddenly and as silently as they'd appeared. Four more Marines were down, their armor burned open, air and blood leaking into the chamber as a thin, icy pink haze.

Garroway did a quick mental rundown. First Company and the HQ element together totaled fifty men and women, five of them corpsmen. That left thirty-nine combat effectives on the line, now, and that included the specialist comm and computer personnel who had other things to do besides burn down enemy robots.

"Four AM-drones away!" 2nd Lieutenant Cooper reported over the Net.

"That'll do it," Captain Black said. "Everyone start falling back to the entry point. Bring the wounded!" A tiny point of light began winking in Garroway's mind—the recall beacon, indicating the direction of his waiting M-CAP.

Garroway and Corporal Kukovitch held their position

behind the pillar, covering several other Marines as they fell back past them toward the waiting M-CAPs, dragging along the bodies of fallen comrades.

That was a point of pride. *No* Marine was left behind, living or dead, and no Marine or corpsman serving with the unit assumed *any* Marine was dead in the field, no matter how bad the wound appeared to be. Unless someone had been smoked—literally turned to vapor by an enemy weapon—the possibility remained that they could be retrieved, even if large parts of their bodies had to be regrown or replaced.

Hell, Garroway had experienced that himself nine years back, at the Battle of Nova Space. They'd come after him, too, pulling him from a derelict alien spacecraft as a nearby star exploded. If they hadn't, he would have been an irrie—an irretrievable—himself.

They leapfrogged back, section by section, one group of Marines providing cover as the rest fell back in moves of several meters at a time. Within a few minutes, they closed in around the tight cluster of M-CAP pods, where they'd broken through into the Xul base's interior, creating a new, much tighter perimeter. For the moment, the Xul warrior robots were not in evidence—not out in the open, anyway, but sensors wired into Garroway's external armor were picking up motion—vibrations detected through the Xul hull metal each time he touched it. Each Xul wave attack tended to be larger, usually by an order of magnitude, than the last.

They were gathering. The next assault on the Marines was going to be a big one.

"Medical Ontos now on final approach," Smedley's voice said.

"Heads up, people," Captain Black warned. "Medevac coming in!"

A portion of the overhead flexed, suddenly, directly above the center of the new Marine perimeter, then began breaking apart in a swirling storm of disintegrating chunks. In the next instant, *something* broke through, ten meters wide and massive, chewing its way through the tough Xul hull armor in clouds of nano-D.

For a moment, it was difficult to see exactly what was eating its way down through the overhead. Something was there, a dark bulk that appeared to swirl and shimmer, becoming at times translucent, almost transparent, and which seemed to reflect the surrounding darkness of the passageway.

Then the effect faded, and the mass solidified into a dark gray surface displaying the Commonwealth emblem and the word MARINES prominent on the curved hull. A ramp was already lowering. That rear entrance couldn't open wide in the narrow confines of the fortress passageway, but light from the vehicle's interior spilled through a narrow opening into the dark space, reflecting from drifting debris.

The craft was an MCA-71 Ontos, one of the bug-like 383-ton Marine workhorses that had served with the Corps for twenty-some years. This one had been designated for medevac. More Navy corpsmen were already descending through the open cargo bay hatch into the Xul fortress, helping to move Marine casualties out of the Xul passageway and into the comparative safety of the rugged little transport.

Garroway held his defensive position with the other Marines on the perimeter. Briefly, he tapped into the telemetry from one of the RAM-D pods—RAM Two; a schematic animation opened in a side window in his mind, showing a drone's-eye view as the device steered itself swiftly through twisting corridors into the bowels of the Xul fortress. RAM-Ds possessed extremely sophisticated on-board AIs that allowed them to operate with considerable autonomy, and gravitics sensors that let them home on the microsingularities orbiting within the heart of Xul structures.

The image flared in a burst of static snow, then winked out.

"RAM Two has been intercepted," Smedley's voice reported. *"RAMs One, Three, and Four are proceeding on course."*

Garroway braced for a possible shockwave. If whatever had snagged RAM Two broke the magnetic containment field isolating the antimatter charge, in just a moment there was going to be a very *large* explosion. . . .

But seconds passed, and there was no blast. Much Xul technology was still mysterious, and at times seemed unevenly applied. Telemetry indicated that the other three charges were continuing on course, moving swiftly into the fortress's depths. Perhaps the Xul hadn't noticed them yet. Or perhaps they didn't yet know what they were, and had just snagged the one in order to find out.

And *that* meant the explosion could come at any time. Tampering with a kilo of antimatter was never a good idea. . . .

Marines and corpsmen began loading the strike force's dead and wounded onto the medevac Ontos. Still moving section by section as their squadmates covered them, Marines began scrambling up into their waiting M-CAPs. Corporal Fitzhugh yelled a warning at the same time Smedley flashed a new alert—targets emerging from the passageway bulkheads in all directions. Again, Garroway chose a target and commenced fire, burning down one oncoming Xul machine . . . then another . . . then a third as the shadowed distance seethed with black movement. The Marines were pumping out an incredible volume of fire—plasma bolts, lasers, nano-D rounds, high-velocity mass-driver slugs, pounding and slashing away at the advancing wall of Xul robots, filling the broad two-meter space between overhead and deck with spinning chunks of metal and ceramic. Garroway's plasma gun flashed an overheat warning to his helmet display, and he switched to his mass driver to let the primary weapon cool. How long, he wondered, could they keep this up? . . .

Well, it wouldn't, it *couldn't* last much longer. With the RAM-Ds well on their way into the fortress's interior, it was, as the ancient adage put it, time for all of them to get the hell out of Dodge. Garroway wasn't sure what "Dodge" was, but he knew the sentiment behind the expression well.

The open ramp on the Ontos was closing, the slender gap of light visible from the cargo deck narrowing to a slit, then winking out. The shielding nano on the transport's surface created a shimmering effect and, once again, the massive intrusion of the Ontos' hull became, not invisible, but eye-wrenchingly difficult to look at.

"Everyone clear!" 2nd Lieutenant Cooper called over the Net. "Medevac lifting off!"

With a jarring vibration felt through the deck, the Ontos lifted clear of the Xul fortress, leaving a swirling tumble of debris in its wake. In twos and threes, the M-CAPs were pulling free of their entry holes, following the Ontos into the void.

There were only a dozen Marines left on board the Xul station now. This was the most deadly part of any board-and-destroy op, with most of the assault force already off the target, and the last few on board trying to make their escape as the bastion's defenders closed in.

PFC Armandez was still a bit ahead of the main Marine line. She'd been falling back toward the M-CAPs when the Xul attack had begun anew, and dropped down behind one of the sheltering pillars to fire on the enemy. "Nikki!" Garroway called. "Get the hell back here! We'll cover you!"

She was starting to turn toward Garroway when a pair of Xul lasers struck her low in the back, at the seam between her torso armor and her power pack. Part of the energy was dissipated by her armor, but he saw a puff of vapor and that was a sure sign her suit had been breached and was leaking air into vacuum. She slumped and went into a tumble.

The medevac Ontos was already gone. Garroway pushed off from the deck, diving in a flat trajectory through the narrow space to snag Armandez and awkwardly grapple her into his arms. Triggering his suit gravitics, he propelled the two of them together back past the Marine perimeter.

A solid wall of Xul warriors surrounded the handful of Marines. "Everyone get out!" Garroway yelled. According to his helmet electronics, he was the senior man present, and it now was up to him to get the last of them out.

"How are we gonna get Nikki out?" PFC Lauden yelled, slashing at the oncoming tide with his mass driver.

"Never mind, damn it! Just clear out! Now!"

"Aye, aye, Gunny!"

The other Marines began clambering into their pods.

Marine histories were full of stories of valiant last stands, of a last Marine who stayed behind to cover his squadmates as a tide of enemy fighters rolled over his final position. Garroway had no intention of becoming another.

He also wasn't leaving Armandez behind. Towing her along, following the homer beacon flashing in his mind, he made his way to his M-CAP, still imbedded in the passageway's overhead.

The problem was that M-CAPs were definitely one-Marine vehicles. Two people might squeeze into one together, if they were real friendly . . . and if neither was wearing their bulky Type 664 combat armor.

Working quickly, Garroway stuffed the unconscious form of the wounded Marine up into his M-CAP, literally stuffing her as far up the narrow opening as he could manage. The nearest Xul warriors were almost on him. . . .

Again, he triggered his slicers, extending the ultra-hard, ultra-thin blades to their full extent. Positioning himself directly under the opening to his pod, he slashed hard with his left arm . . . then his right . . .

His own legs, severed high up on the thighs, spun to either side, trailing globules of rapidly freezing blood and lubricant. The pain didn't hit him immediately, *wouldn't* hit him, he didn't think, for a few precious seconds, if he didn't let it. . . .

He did immediately feel the shock of falling pressure, like a hammer blow to his lungs. Air shrieked out of his armor into the surrounding hard vacuum until his suit's inner layer, reacting automatically to the falling pressure, sealed over the gaping stumps of his legs. Garroway was already pulling himself up into his pod, as biting cold and lung-searing decompression threatened to drag him back into unconsciousness . . . and death. He had to struggle to work his torso up past Armandez's legs; even minus his own legs, he wasn't sure there was enough room inside the bottle for two.

It was starting to hurt now. A *lot*. . . .

His armor's built-in medinano dispensers were already firing swarms of microscopic healers into his bloodstream, however. Anodynes began dulling the sharp shriek of pain; fluorocarbons began picking up where the near-vanished oxygen had left off; artificial coagulants began sealing off the wounds, stopping blood loss while cerebral monitors blocked the onset of shock.

It was a near thing. The inside of his helmet visor was iced over, and he was having trouble seeing. By feel, he found the pod's linking plate and slapped his open palm across it. Numbers and status readouts flickered through his mind, but he ignored them, triggering the hatch seal.

He felt the hatch iris shut just below his sealed-off stumps, the scraping sensation threatening to override the anodynes. A warning light flickered on in his mind, followed by a verbal readout. *"M-CAP hatch seal failure. M-CAP hatch seal failure."*

Damn. Even with his legs gone, he wasn't in far enough to let the bottle's hatch seal shut.

The hell with it. The bottle wasn't supposed to accelerate with a hatch open, but he overrode the watchdog circuit and thought-clicked the launch command. There was a grating rasp, then a sudden shock as the pod broke free, accelerating clear of the Xul fortress.

For a moment, he half feared sliding out an open hatch beneath him as the pod accelerated on its way, but he appeared to be well wedged into place. Exploring with his gloved hands, he decided that the bottle's outer hatch had, indeed, cycled closed; it was the inner hatch that was blocked open by the stumps of his legs, and that was what was causing the alarm. The bottle's rather narrow-minded AI didn't think the craft was sealed and ready for flight unless *all* hatches were shut, sealed, and locked.

He dismissed the irritating alarm. There was nothing he

could do about the cause, and he appeared to be safe for the moment.

Well, safe from the threat of being left behind, at least. His warning indicators showed enemy fire passing close by his craft.

He goosed it, ordering full acceleration and praying the inertial dampers were working well enough to shunt aside the fearful pressures of a high-G boost. There was no time, no place for subtlety in the escape. With the fortress fully alerted to the Marine incursion, there was no hope of sneaking away unseen. The M-CAP's nano coating lowered the craft's visibility at all electronic wavelengths, making it tough to see and track, but at point-blank range it was hard *not* to pick it out, by the distortion it caused against the background starfield, if nothing else.

Through his interface with the tiny craft, he could see the fortress, looming huge as it receded astern, and a sky filled with streaks of white fire. Weapons fire—whether human or Xul—was in fact invisible in vacuum, but the pod's computer painted the tracks in as a flight aid. With a thought, he banished the special effects; there was nothing he could do in the way of actively dodging incoming fire, and seeing those bolts was both distracting and terrifying. If his pod was hit in the next few minutes, he would never feel the blast that killed them.

He ordered the pod's computer to establish a course consisting of random jinks that would continue to bear on the stargate.

Without the flashing lights and energy bolts, surrounding space took on an almost surreal aspect of beauty, majesty, and peace. The Xul bastion continued to dwindle astern, as the stargate slowly grew larger ahead. In the distance, the glowing spiral of the Milky Way Galaxy stretched across half of heaven, as beautiful, as insubstantially delicate as a dream. Green icons floated between him and the gate, a scattering of pinpoints marking Bravo Company's other M-CAPs.

One pinpoint flared for an instant, a dazzling star, then

vanished. Corporal Levowsky's pod, according to the read-out. PFC Hollander's pod went next. *Damn!* . . .

He forced himself to ignore the ongoing roll call of Marines who would *not* be retrieved. Some of the escaping Marines were going to get nailed just by sheer chance, judging from the volume of hostile fire, and those Xul laser and plasma bursts were hot enough to reduce an M-CAP and its passenger to thin, hot gas in an instant.

At this point, it was down to sheer chance. The Marine pods all were jostling and jinking their way toward the stargate. Some percentage of them would not make it. Which ones were hit, which ones made it, that now was entirely in the laps of the Gods of Battle.

Garroway had another alarm to contend with as well, and, once again, it was something he couldn't do much about. He'd lost much of the air inside his armor when he'd breached his own suit. In the moments since, his armor had been struggling to replenish internal pressure from the life support system in his backpack. He was no longer chewing cold vacuum, which was a distinct improvement . . . but by tapping the rebreather source gases in his tanks, he'd sharply lowered his stay time. His armor's on-board computer estimated that he was down to another hour or so before his oxygen supply went critical.

And according to the telemetry from Armandez's armor, her LSS had been damaged as well, leaking a good eighty percent of her gas supply to space before it had sealed off the damage. Their rebreather filters would continue to pull oxygen from exhaled carbon dioxide and water vapor as they breathed, but there would be less and less free O_2 available with every breath cycle as more and more of it was locked up by his metabolism.

Again, he killed the warning.

What he couldn't kill were the growing physical problems brought on by his self-inflicted wounds. The pain was manageable for the moment, thanks to the nano-anodynes, but it was growing steadily worse. Shock and blood loss both had brought him close to unconsciousness, and he'd severely compounded that threat with the abrupt loss of pressure in his suit. Again, the problems were being held at bay for the moment—fluorocarbons were far more efficient at oxygen and CO_2 transport in the circulatory system than were red blood cells, so you didn't need as much of the stuff as you'd lost, but his blood volume was dangerously low and threatening still to drag him into shock, despite the medinano churning away in his brain.

He hoped the bottle's AI was bright enough to get them through the gate, because he didn't think he was going to be awake for very much longer. . . .

"Hey, Gare?" a female voice called over the combat Net. "Gare, you okay?"

"Yeah." The word felt fuzzy on his tongue. He was having some trouble focusing now. The com ID said the voice belonged to Sergeant Colby.

"Cut your random guidance," Colby told him. "We're trying to rendezvous for a pick-up!"

Garroway thought-clicked the guidance control, resuming a straight-line course. If the Xul were watching closely, they would be able to nail him in seconds . . . but somehow that just didn't seem important any longer.

"Hang on, Garroway," another voice said, a man's voice, this time. His helmet identified it was 2nd Lieutenant Cooper. "We've got you, buddy."

The downloaded visual showed three other Marine bottles closing on him from three sides. Magnetic grapples emerged from their hulls, latching on. Despite the inertial damping, he felt the slight jar as they grabbed him, then began accelerating again, four pods moving randomly now as a single unit.

He could also hear another voice in the background, an AI reciting a running countdown. *"Eight . . . seven . . . six . . . five . . ."*

It took him a moment to realize the count was for the antimatter charges left on board the Xul bastion.

That woke him up, shaking off the growing lethargy, at least for the moment. He looked back at the Xul fortress just as the numbers ran out. *"...three...two...one...* *now...now...n-"*

White light filled heaven.

The blast was soundless, of course, in the vacuum of space, but the Xul bastion, shrunken now to something the size of a football held at arm's length, blossomed along one side as three kilograms of antimatter came into direct contact with the normal matter surrounding them. In an instant, the five-kilometer-wide structure vanished, engulfed by the deadly white bloom.

The image winked out, then, as the M-CAP's optics shut down to preserve the bottle's electronics and Garroway's optical centers. His eyes were safe, since the image was being downloaded directly into his brain, but too much energy in the input could make his brain *think* it had just been blinded, and at a certain safe level, the input was cut automatically.

For a long moment, he rode in darkness, seeing now with his own eyes, but with nothing to look at but the darkness of the pod's cramped interior, and Armandez's armored legs and boots pressed up against his visor.

He felt the shockwave as it passed, a distant, rumbling thunder felt rather than heard against the pod's hull. Radiation counters soared, and more warning lights flashed in his mind and on his helmet display. He, Armandez, and the three Marines hauling him to safety had all just received lethal doses of hard radiation.

Well, that wouldn't be the first time. If they got back to the hospital ship *Barton* in time, they could do something about that. His legs, too.

If ...

The outside optic feed was restored as light levels fell to acceptable levels. Garroway was fading fast, but he was able to see not one, but three brilliant suns now shining in an uneven embrace of the approaches to the stargate. All three Xul fortresses had been successfully reduced.

And almost directly ahead, the first starships of 1MIEF were emerging from the stargate, *Ishtar, Mars,* and *Chiron,* followed by the fleet carriers *Chosin* and *Lejeune,* already loosing their swarms of Marine aerospace fighters. Surrounding the vanguard was a small cloud of destroyers and light cruisers, followed by the immense MIEF flagship *Hermes*.

Three small, purple icons were trailing along beneath the *Hermes'* lee, but as the flag completed its transit of the gate, those icons accelerated sharply, arrowing into the Cluster Space system and swiftly flashing into the faster-than-light invisibility of their Alcubierre Drives.

Those, Garroway knew, were Euler Starblasters, alien weapons of incredibly destructive power. He tried to twist around to follow the line of their flight, in toward Bloodlight, the distant red sun of this system . . . but within the next second or two, everything—the M-CAPs, the distant sprawl of the Galaxy, the trio of short-lived suns guarding the stargate and the stargate itself—all were lost to a vast, swelling blackness as unconsciousness claimed him at last. . . .

3

1506.1111

UCS Hermes
Stargate
Cluster Space
0717 hrs, GMT

Lieutenant General Martin Alexander, CO of the 1st Marine Interstellar Expeditionary Force, was linked into *Hermes'* tactical command net, and from his mind's-eye vantage point high atop the data stream he could see the unfolding of the entire battle. Bravo Company, chosen to spearhead this op, was pulling out, the individual M-CAPs hurtling at maximum acceleration for the safety of the stargate, as three brand-new and short-lived stars burned behind them.

The virtual icon of Vice Admiral Liam Taggart hovered next to Alexander's awareness, backlit by the stars of the Galaxy. "Battlenet is reporting multiple targets accelerating toward our position," Taggart's voice said in Alexander's mind. "I'd rather not let them get too close. If I may? . . ."

"Of course, Admiral. Get those damned things out of my sky. . . ."

Technically, the two men shared command, Taggart commanding 1MIEF's naval forces and actions, while Alexander commanded the Marine units, both in space and on the ground, while supreme authority was vested with the Commonwealth Senate.

In fact, Alexander held overall command of the entire expeditionary force. The Senate was some tens of thousands of light years distant, now, and it was up to Alexander to determine how best to carry out the civilian command authority's directives. The 1MIEF was an extension of Alexander's determination and will, whatever the chain of command might look like charted.

If Alexander was in overall command, Taggart's request for permission to engage the enemy was still little more than a polite fiction. The two long ago had arrived at a flexible and efficient compromise in military authority, and Alexander trusted the older man's experience with naval tactics. The two men worked well together, had been working well as a superb team now for over nine years.

Usually, Alexander preferred to stand back and give Taggart free rein. But Cluster Space was important, the biggest and most strategically vital Xul node yet encountered, and Operation Clusterstrike had been conceived as a major body blow against the Xul.

They would take this one down by the book.

The MIEF fleet was dispersing now as it cleared the Gate, the ships bathed in the intense glare from the exploding fortresses. Xul ships were approaching from the system's heart, but *Ishtar*, *Mars*, and *Chiron* were already directing their long-range weaponry against them, slamming them with long-range mass-driver fire. A cloud of smaller warships—cruisers, light cruisers, and destroyers—accelerated rapidly, spreading out both to present more difficult targets, and to allow them to put the enemy vessels into a crossfire. As the big carriers came through behind the lead battlecruisers, swarms of Marine fighters and AI combat drones began streaming from the launch bays, filling Alexander's virtual sky with hurtling, gleaming shapes.

Traditionally, Marines were intended to secure an invasion beachhead, emerging from the sea to seize and hold a landing area until regular Army troops could arrive and take over. That, at least, had been the Corps' tactical dogma as far back as the twentieth century, when the Marines had ceased being purely naval troops and come into their own as an independent fighting force. Over the next few centuries, the major combat role for the Corps had been as elite infantry, tasked with a variety of missions, from boarding, search, and seizure to hostage rescue to combat assault.

Most recently, however, in the escalating war with the Galaxy-wide empire of the Xul, the Marines assigned to 1MIEF had been tasked with gate-clearing, a euphemism referring to ops like this one, requiring Marine elements to melt their way into the interior of one or more enemy bastions guarding a stargate's approaches, planting nuclear or antimatter charges deep within the structure's bowels, then fighting their way clear as the fortresses exploded. The moment the forts were destroyed or crippled, the main naval elements of 1MIEF could pour through the stargate and secure the gate approaches.

And then the Euler ships would come through.

"Your people did a hell of a job," Taggart said, indicating the burning, new suns of the three Xul fortresses. They were fading now, though local space was still bathed in the harsh, 511 keV radiation released by the annihilation of positronium. A kilogram of antimatter detonated in each of those Xul bastions made a hell of a bang.

"Thank you, Admiral. I'll be happier when we know the bursters hit their target."

Alexander watched the straight-line trails marking the inbound course of the three Euler Starbursters on his internal display, arrowing toward the distant pinpoint of Bloodlight. Two more minutes . . .

"I'd still like to know how a species that evolved in a deep ocean basin could even have an idea of what the stars are," Taggart said, "much less develop the technology to reach them. Doesn't make sense."

"Given enough years," Alexander replied, "damned near anything is possible. Just be glad the Eulers and their technology are on *our* side!"

The Eulers were the benthic inhabitants of several star systems in Aquilan space, some twelve hundred light years from the worlds of Sol. Contacted nine years before, during the first incursion by the Marine Interstellar Expeditionary Force into the region of space near Nova Aquila, Eulers was the name humans had given them. Their name for themselves, it seemed, was a mathematical equation, an indication of their intensely mathematical worldview, and the humans studying them had named them after the human mathematician who'd developed that particular equation for humankind.

After nine years of study, there was still no other way to transcribe the thought-symbol they applied to themselves, or even to be sure they possessed *language* as humans understood the term. The massive, tentacled beings appeared to communicate with one another by changing colors and patterns visible in their mottled skin and by the taste of chemicals in the water, though direct telepathy among their own kind had not been ruled out.

Remarkably, for an oceanic species, they did possess sophisticated computer implant technology, and that was how they were, in fact, able to communicate with humans, through shared virtual realities. Their technology, their industry, and their material fabrication sciences all were quite advanced, despite the apparent disadvantage of living in the ocean deep at crushing pressures.

Like the N'mah, the Eulers defied the old xenosophontological dictum that had once declared that an intelligent species evolving in the sea would never develop technology because they could never make fire. Eons ago, they'd gene-engineered crab-like creatures to serve as their symbiotic extensions, first into the shallows of their home world, then onto dry land and, eventually, into the depths of space, to other worlds. Through their symbiotes, they'd developed fire, and industry, and a faster-than-light stardrive identical in its physics to the Alcubierre Drive employed by the Commonwealth. And the Eulers had traveled far.

Thousands of years ago, they'd encountered the Xul. The details still weren't well understood by human xenosophontologists, but there'd been a war, perhaps several. The Eulers had learned how to use their FTL ships as shockwave triggers to make stars explode.

The Marines had learned that little trick from the Eulers nine years ago, at the Battle of the Nova. The Alcubierre Drive worked by encapsulating the starship in a bubble of severely warped space-time. Space ahead of the vehicle was sharply contracted, while space behind was expanded. The ship itself didn't move at all relative to the space-time matrix around it, but the *space* moved, and carried the ship with it, accelerating to a fair-sized multiple of the speed of light.

So far so good. Humankind used several different techniques to travel FTL, now, including the mysterious stargates scattered across the Galaxy and beyond, and the matrix transition employed by very large carriers like the *Hermes*.

The weapons potential, however, arose when you slammed a bubble of Alcubierre-warped space through the core of a star. When the already incredibly dense mass of fusing hydrogen at the heart of a sun was suddenly condensed by the passage of an Alcubierre bubble, it triggered a partial collapse that sent a shockwave rebounding out from the core that blew the outer layers of the star into space in a titanic explosion—an artificially generated nova.

Three thousand years ago, the Eulers had fought the Xul to a standstill, albeit at horrendous cost, scorching many of their own worlds to lifeless cinders in order to vaporize the foe's fleets of titanic hunterships. Now the Marine and naval forces of 1MIEF were using the same weapon, but carrying the attacks to the enemy in long-range strikes of annihilation. A young Marine named Garroway had piloted an Euler starcraft through the star warming a Xul-controlled system at the Battle of the Nova nine years ago. Since a ship under Alcubierre Drive was not, technically, in the usual four-dimensional matrix of space-time, it could pass clean through the target star without actually colliding—or vaporizing. The shockwave trailing behind it, however . . .

Since then, 1MIEF had continued using Euler technology. Human FTL ships were much larger and, therefore, easier for the enemy to intercept, and the Euler version of the Alcubierre

Drive was far more powerful, warped space more tightly, and therefore made a bigger ripple when it hit the core of a star.

The three Euler Starbursters now streaking toward the Bloodlight, the Cluster Space sun, were piloted by sophisticated artificial intelligences, however, rather than humans or Euler-symbiotes. It was easier that way. Unlike most humans—those who weren't religious fanatics, anyway—AIs could be programmed to welcome death.

Victory required that only one Starburster reach the local star; sending three was for insurance. Since the Euler craft could not transit a stargate faster-than-light, however, and since they possessed nothing in the way of defenses except their speed, the fleet first had to move through and seize a volume of battlespace on the far side of the gate. To do that, of course, it was necessary to destroy any sentry fortresses the Xul had placed nearby . . . and that was where the Marines came in.

Someday, Alexander thought with wry amusement, someone might create an AI combat machine smart enough, compact enough, and deadly enough to go into Xul forts and sentry ships and plant antimatter devices . . . but so far, at least, that particular dirty job was still best given to the Marines. Flying an Euler Starburster into the heart of a sun was child's play compared to fighting your way into the interior of one of those Xul monsters and planting a bomb where it would do the most good.

Ninety more seconds. Bloodlight, however, was ten light minutes away, farther than Earth was from her sun. If . . . no, Alexander corrected himself, *when* the star detonated, it would be eleven and a half minutes before the Marine-naval expeditionary force knew the op had been successful.

Which was a good thing, actually. It should give them time to get clear.

Not for the first time, Alexander wondered if this particular raid could succeed. There were so many unknowns . . . not least of which was whether the Euler nova triggers would even work on a red dwarf star. Suns targeted by the Starbursters over the past few years all had been larger, more massive stars. An M-class dwarf possessed only a tiny fraction of the mass of stars like Earth's sun, and there was some debate within the expeditionary force's scientific and technical circles as to whether such a small star as Bloodlight could even be induced to go nova.

Well, they would know one way or the other in just . . . he checked his inner time readout again . . . another ten minutes, twenty-five seconds.

For now, the ships of 1MIEF continued to pass through the stargate into Cluster Space. Over the course of the past nine years, the 1st Marine Interstellar Expeditionary Force had changed and evolved as human tacticians and strategists studied past actions and tried to determine the best mix of firepower and maneuverability for dealing with the Xul giants. The emphasis now was on faster, more maneuverable ships than the lumbering battlecruisers like *Mars*.

The *Planet*-class battlecruisers massed 80,000 tons each, but 1MIEF now numbered some two hundred starships, and most of them massed under twelve thousand tons. Compared to the one- and two-kilometer-long behemoths favored by the Xul, they were minnows nibbling at the flanks of whales.

But with enough of them firing together, they could bite hard. Smaller still, but still deadly, were the fighters of the four Marine Aerospace wings currently embarked with the Expeditionary Force. Launched from the Fleet's flotilla of aerospacecraft carriers, those fighters—F/A-4140 Stardragons and the newer F/A-4184 Wyvern—were small, fast, and highly maneuverable. With antiship loadouts, they were deadly as well, especially when attacking in a swarm, like now.

Focusing his attention on one of the aerospace fighter icons moving within his inner display, Alexander began tracking the attack run of the Aerospace Squadron 16, the Reivers, as they closed on the nearest of the Xul monsters.

Brave people, he thought. *Brave* Marines.

If capital ships were minnows attacking Xul whales, the fighters were mosquitos.

And they were already taking a hell of a lot of casualties. . . .

Green One,
AS Squadron 16, Shadow Hawks,
Cluster Space
0718 hrs, GMT

Major Tera Lee relaxed into the pilot link, watching the mental image of the Xul warship expand within her awareness from a bright star to a monster, now just two thousand kilometers distant. A Type III, the enemy vessel was one of the Xul huntership behemoths designated as a *Nightmare*-class, a flattened spheroid two kilometers across, the largest mobile Xul vessel yet encountered by the Commonwealth.

Lee was squadron CO of VMA-770, the Shadow Hawks. A twelve-year veteran of Marine aviation, she was tucked into the claustrophobic embrace of an F/A-4184 Wyvern, one of the sharp-edged single-seaters only recently delivered to the Shadow Hawks. This would be the Wyvern's first test of actual combat, although Lee had been practicing in simulation for a year before she'd ever strapped on one of the machines for real. Technically, she had over a thousand hours of virtual flight time on the beast.

She knew better than to put too much reliance on simulations, however. Sims were good, but *nothing* matched the realities of combat. As she expanded her consciousness through the Wyvern interface, however, she noted that everything was green and wide open. So far, so good. . . .

"Green Squadron, this is Green Leader," she called. "Everyone check your phase shift frequencies and cloaking. I don't want anyone getting their souls eaten in there."

The other fifteen pilots in the squadron came back at her with electronic confirmations—seven humans, eight AIs. That would be another first this morning—going into combat with half of the Shadow Hawks' pilots consisting of sophisticated software instead of flesh and blood. She didn't care for the idea at all—and neither did the others in her squadron—but orders were indisputably orders. It could be that the coming scrap would settle the old issue of live pilots versus electronics once and for all.

Twelve hundred kilometers. The scale in her downloaded imagery shifted. The Xul warship was still invisible to unaided, Mark I eyeballs, but the battlenet continued to feed high-definition imagery to the AIs controlling this phase of the engagement.

Nine hundred kilometers. She hoped that she was still as invisible to the Xul as the enemy would have been to her unaugmented vision. There were horror stories about what happened to ships' crews engulfed by the monsters—about people having their souls eaten, as the darker tales liked to put it.

In fact, the Xul rarely made use of their patterning technology as a weapon, though it wasn't unknown. Since the first human encounters with the Xul centuries ago, however, there'd been reports of Xul hunterships somehow devouring human vessels and so completely scanning their contents that humans and AIs alike were somehow transferred to the bowels of the Xul vessels as living, self-aware programs even though the ships and bodies of the crew were destroyed. That had happened to a human explorer vessel, *The Wings of Isis,* at Sirius in 2148, and to the *Argo,* an asteroid colony vessel hundreds of light years from Sol just nine years ago, and there were rumors of other electronic abductions as well.

The scuttlebutt shared among Marines in late-night barracks bull sessions said that humans uploaded into Xul computer nets were kept alive—if that is what their virtual and bodiless existence could be called—for centuries as they were continually interrogated and emotionally dissected by their captors.

By enabling a spacecraft to shift slightly out of phase with the normal four-D plenum of space-time, Commonwealth ship designers had found a means to make the vessel both more difficult to detect going in and harder to scan for the patterning and uploading process. That, Lee thought, was a considerable comfort. Better to go out in a bright flash of hard radiation than wake up as an eternal captive within the virtual hell of a Xul huntership. Even if the "real" her died with the destruction of her body, *something,* an electronic duplicate would awaken to that hell, and she was unwilling to give the Xul demons another human analogue to torture. Even worse from a purely personal point of view was the possibility that her mind, her living awareness, would somehow be transferred to the immense virtual reality computers that seemed to be the bulk of the Xul starships, that it would be she who awakened in the Xul hell.

Better not to think about *that* possibility at all. . . .

The one advantage in an aerospace fighter lay in the fact that the Xul never seemed to think *small*. Fighters and one-man boarding pods appeared to be beneath the notice of the behemoth hunterships, and a swarm of one- or two-Marine fighters could get in close and loose the equivalent of a capital ship's broadside.

Even so, casualties in this type of operation tended to be heavy. A lot of her brother and sister Marines in the squadron would not be coming back.

Better not to think about that, either.

She was closing with the Xul huntership at just under fifty kilometers per second. $Pappy_2$, a simplified iteration of the MIEF AI, was doing the actual flying at the moment, jinking and turning the hurtling Wyvern in random patterns to avoid the patterns of antimissile fire filling the sky now to every side.

The Wyvern was a smaller, nimbler fighter than the older Stardragon, massing only seventy-two tons, and with fewer hardpoints for weapons load-outs. It was faster and more maneuverable, however, and could phase-shift more completely, which gave it better protection against Xul defenses. Like the Stardragon, it drew power through a non-local entrainment link from its home-base carrier, in this case the Marine assault carrier *Samar*, and used quantum field-drive acceleration, so fuel was not an issue. Within her weapons bay, she carried four AM-98 missiles, each with an AI brain and a 1-kilo antimatter warhead. Those missiles had a powered range of ten thousand kilometers; the idea, though, was to get them so close to the target they could be released inside the Xul huntership's defensive screens.

The trick, of course, was getting clear in time after releasing the missile.

"Okay, Shadow Hawks," Lee said over the squadron net. "Form on me, left echelon. Maintain three hundred kilometer separation." Their AIs would be jinking them all over the sky on the way in, and in those circumstances, it didn't do to get too close to your formation neighbor.

Her link with her fighter's sensors were painting the enemy fire across her mental display, her IHD, or In-Head Display, as the link was properly known. The enemy ship continued to expand smoothly in her mind's eye, the jitters and jinkings of the hurtling Wyvern edited out by the AI as they were transmitted.

To her left and astern, a dazzling sun winked on, the expanding fireball of an exploding fighter. Green Three . . . Lieutenant Costigan. A plasma bolt from the Xul huntership had released the magnetically pent-up antimatter within Costigan's four antiship missiles, loosing a storm of raw energy, and his Wyvern had simply vanished in a fireball equivalent to a fair-sized nuclear warhead.

At least it had been quick. There were worse ways to go than fighting the Xul, at least according to the scuttlebutt.

One of the AI-piloted fighters flashed out next—Green Nine. But then the remaining fourteen ships of the squadron were past the red line at five hundred kilometers from the target, putting them inside the mathematical zone promising fifty percent survival for missiles loosed at the enemy.

Another AI-piloted Wyvern flashed into dazzling brilliance, Green Twelve, the flare fading swiftly astern. Xul plasma bolts and laser beams crisscrossed the sky, weaving a constantly shifting net through which the surviving Commonwealth fighters twisted and dodged.

"Hold with me!" Lee called over the net. "Just a little deeper in. . . ."

At less than one hundred kilometers, they plunged through the Xul monster's outer layers of magnetic screens, designed to let the enemy fire-control systems pinpoint course and speed data of incoming projectiles. Here, Lee was convinced, was where flesh-and-blood pilots held the advantage over AI software. Her tiny fighter's controls were linked in with her mind, taking commands both from her intent and from Pappy$_2$. Organic pilots might not have reflexes fast enough or precision sharp enough to fly a high-performance aerospace fighter, but software lacked the flexibility and the scope to maneuver through this kind of maze. The two working together provided the best chances of survival—and a completed mission.

At fifty kilometers, she thought-clicked the missile firing command, kicking two of her antimatter killers into open space. Their drives ignited automatically, sending them streaking toward the Xul target. She'd already applied full lateral drive, a high-G maneuver that would have killed her if not for the inertial dampers cocooning her within the narrow confines of the Wyvern's cockpit. Behind her, the other ships in her squadron broke formation, the better to loose their warshots in an unpredictable cascade.

Pulling nearly two hundred gravities now, Lee swung wide, killing her forward thrust and angling back toward the stargate in a series of rolling, twisting maneuvers.

Her attack run had carried her deep into the volume of space occupied by the approaching Xul hunterships. Two more Xul vessels, both lean, needle-slim Type I's, swung past her prow nearly three hundred kilometers distant. She snapped them both with targeting cursors, locking in her two remaining AM missiles. She was *not* going to endure the indignity of returning to the *Samar* with missiles still in her weapons bay.

A thought-click, and her last two missiles flashed into the night.

It was a night, she saw, illuminated by innumerable pulses and flashes of light. Fighters, the Shadow Hawks and the other attacking squadrons, were scoring hits. The main Commonwealth fleet was adding to the display as their long-range weapons began striking home. Space around her was filled by the deadly flicker and flash of short-lived suns, and awash with the radiation of matter being annihilated.

In the far distance, the Galaxy hung in silent repose, unmoving, cold-lit, and remote.

As happened sometimes, the memories returned. . . .

Lee had been offered a memory edit, but she'd refused. Her memories, she believed, were a part of what she was, of who she was, and she would no more willingly part with them than she would with one of her legs. Hell, a leg could be regrown. . . .

Nine years ago, just before 1MIEF took the war against the Xul to the enemy, she'd taken a small reconnaissance spacecraft through a stargate to a Xul node. The place had been code-named Starwall, and was located somewhere along the outer reaches of the Galaxy's core.

She'd been trapped there for hours. Radiation from the core had burned her terribly before her ship's AI had managed to return her to a Marine listening post on the other side of the gate. They'd had to regrow much of her body after that, using medinano to excise the radiation damage cell by cell.

Later, and despite the surgery, she'd learned she would never have children.

That had been the worst part of it by far. For a long time afterward, she'd not been sure she even wanted to live. She'd grown up in American Saskatchewan as part of a large family—four fathers, five mothers, and twenty-three sibs. She'd always expected that after her hitch with the Marines was done, she'd marry into a big line family and have children of her own.

Gradually, though, she'd come to grips with the issue. The Corps was her family, and the men, women, and AIs in her squadron her kids.

Her battlenet link painted new volleys of high-energy fire from the expeditionary force, streaks and lines and hurtling spheres of green light rendering the invisible visible in her mind.

"Shit, skipper!" Lieutenant Daniels called over the tactical channel. "We're gonna get fried by our own people!"

"Follow procedure and trust the system," she told him. "Pappy knows what he's doing."

Indeed, only a massively parallel AI like the MIEF primary AI could coordinate the incredible volume of fire and moving spacecraft now filling the operational battlespace. No merely human mind could have kept track of so many variables, so many targets and energies.

"If everything is on sched," Lieutenant Garcia's voice put in, "we're going to get fried by that nova pretty quick!"

"Follow procedure," Lee replied. "The triggerships haven't even reached the sun yet. There's plenty of time. . . ."

In fact, a countdown was ticking away in a side window open in her mind. They had about ten and a half minutes yet, give or take a bit, before the expanding blast wave of the nova reached them . . . assuming everything was on schedule. Plenty of time *if* nothing unexpected happened.

"Skipper! I've got a bender coming through, dead ahead!"

She checked the ID. The call was from 2nd Lieutenant Joanna Wayne, and she was only thirty kilometers off Lee's port wing. A *bender* was something warping space, possibly one of the Euler triggerships . . . but there was a chance it was something else.

It was. She saw the brilliant flash of twisted starlight, saw the Xul Type IV materialize out of empty space fifty kilometers ahead. Like humans, the Xul used the Galaxy-spanning network of stargates, but their ships also possessed FTL capability through something like the Commonwealth's Alcubierre Drive, which sharply warped local space.

And the alien warship had dropped into the normal space-time matrix directly between most of her squadron and the stargate.

They were going to have to fight to get through.

4

UCS Hermes
Stargate
Cluster Space
0719 hrs, GMT

In General Alexander's mind, 1MIEF's battle array resembled a kind of spreading haze of discrete ships, darting and shifting from side to side as they moved. Fleet movements were coordinated by the AI-controlled battlenet, which jinked individual ships to make them harder to target without running afoul of one another. The battlenet could coordinate fire, too, concentrating the volleys from a hundred ships on one Xul monster at a time. Under that kind of intensive bombardment, even the largest, thickest-skinned whale would be whittled down to a cloud of tumbling debris before long.

At the moment, the fleet's heaviest fire was concentrated on a single Xul Type III, a monster code-named *Nightmare*-class, a flattened spheroid two kilometers across. White flares of light popped and strobed across the Xul vessel's hull, pounding at it, battering it, sending gouts and streamers of gas and vaporizing metal spraying into space. A squadron of aerospace fighters were closing with it as well, slamming antimatter warheads into its shuddering bulk.

The vessel was still thirty thousand kilometers off, invisible to the unaided eye, but visible in crystalline detail through the battlenet datafeed, which was drawing in image feeds from several hundred drones spreading through battlespace.

The Nightmare was hurt, trailing plumes of escaping vapor that froze as it hit vacuum into glittering clouds of minute ice crystals. Craters gaped in the monster's hull, glowing sullen red and orange within the shattered interior. *Burn, you bastard,* Alexander thought with a silent, fierce intensity. The war with the Xul had been unrelenting and without mercy on either side, a literal war to the death.

A moment later, something inside exploded with savage violence, blowing out a quarter of the Xul warship's flank. What was left began to fold and crumple in upon itself. Xul ships generated micro black holes as part of their power and drive systems, and when their drive containment fields failed, those singularities tended to eat their way through the ship's structure, devouring everything with which they came into contact and releasing a flood of hard radiation in their wakes.

Alexander could hear Taggart's thoughts as the admiral gave orders to the fleet. Another large Xul huntership was being targeted now, as the massed weapons of 1MIEF's warships shifted to another target—a Type II huntership a kilometer long and thirty-eight thousand kilometers distant. The fleet's weaponry ran an impressive gamut—high-intensity lasers at both optical and X-ray frequencies, gigavolt plasma discharges, and a wide variety of projectiles and missile warheads—from kinetic kill projectiles to nukes to antimatter charges, with calibers ranging from a few millimeters to several meters. A high-energy storm of devastating warshots began slamming into this new target, scouring and ripping at its ceramic armor like a lightning-charged hailstorm.

However, more and more Xul vessels were moving and beginning to converge on the 1MIEF fleet.

"Ten seconds to expected detonation," a new voice intoned within Alexander's head. Then, *"Five ... four ... three ... two ... one ... mark."*

Alexander glanced toward the local star. Bloodstar, the red sun of Cluster Space, continued burning as before, of course, a sullen ember, little more than a pinpoint of ruby light. It would be another ten long minutes before the light from the exploding star reached them.

"Okay, Pappy," Alexander told the disembodied voice. Pappy was the senior artificial intelligence in 1MIEF, named after an early Marine aviator named Gregory "Pappy" Boyington. "Give me observational data as soon as it's available. Tag? You heard?"

"I did, General."

"I suggest we start falling back to the stargate."

"Affirmative, General." Alexander heard him begin giving orders, sounding the tactical recall.

This was the tricky part of the operation, getting the forty-two Commonwealth warships that had already come through the stargate, along with over a hundred aerospace fighters and minor combatants, back through to Carson Space without being overwhelmed by the Xul counterattack. The Xul, as the Commonwealth had learned over the years, tended to be cautious. Swat their noses hard enough, and they might not follow up on an enemy raid for years. Still, the toughest part of any op, whether in space or on a planet's surface, was in the withdrawal phase, when the last few ships or men covering a retreat were left to face overwhelming numbers alone.

The Marines were used to that situation, the Navy less so.

The Xul Type II was collapsing upon itself, now, dwindling with eerie rapidity as the black hole within swallowed it from the inside out. But AI scans of battlespace data indicated that there were as many as two *thousand* Xul warships in this system. Cluster Space, as was well known, was a major Xul node and operations center.

At the moment, the biggest question was whether or not the Xul would try to follow 1MIEF back through the stargate to Carson Space.

Hermes, largest of the ships of the human fleet, as well as the slowest and most clumsy, completed her reversal maneuver and began making her way back toward the gate.

About her flashed swarms of smaller craft, including the

retreating Marines of the initial assault force. Alexander
flashed an order to Pappy. "Make sure you track every
damned one of those M-CAPs," he said. "Coordinate the
withdrawal with Smedley."

"Affirmative, General," Pappy's calm voice replied. *"We
will leave no one behind."*

Of course, how the hell did you guarantee something
like that? Battlespace was a bewildering soup, of ships
large and small, of retreating M-CAPs, of aerospace fighters, Ontos transports, drones, sensor and communications
probes, missiles, and drifting chunks of white-hot wreckage. Many of the fighters and Marine assault capsules were
damaged, some disabled completely and adrift in emptiness.

But they had to try.

Green One,
AS Squadron 16, Shadow Hawks,
Cluster Space
0722 hrs, GMT

"Pull out, Skipper! Pull out!"

Wayne's voice shrieking in her mind wasn't helping. Lee
blocked it off and focused instead on urging her Wyvern to
exert maximum lateral thrust, and then some, as she flashed
toward the loom of the Xul monster.

It was a Behemoth, the code name for the Xul Type IV
huntership. It had been noted and photographed at several
Xul node-bases, but for a long time the assumption had been
that it was a fortress, immobile.

In fact, Commonwealth Intelligence wasn't sure whether
the Xul themselves differentiated between fortress and warship. All that really was known about the Behemoth was
that it was *big and deadly*—a slightly flattened spheroid five
kilometers across—and that it was often posted as a sentry
near Xul-controlled stargates or worlds, but that it *could*

move under its own power when necessary. The Xul equivalent of the Alcubierre Drive gave it FTL capability, and there was evidence that it possessed a space-matrix translation capability akin to that of the MIEF's *Hermes* and other extremely large Commonwealth ships.

Moments ago, this Behemoth had dropped out of FTL almost directly between the Shadow Hawks and the stargate, emerging into normal space with the signature burst of light bent and focused along its wake of warped space. Lee had ordered her surviving fighters to disperse and accelerate, getting past the Behemoth by using antimatter missiles as screens.

Major Lee's weapons bays were empty, but she could go into an attack approach anyway, seeking to draw off some of the defensive fire from the enemy batteries.

Thank God, she thought, *for the AIs. . . .*

AI-piloted aerospace fighters never stretched the envelope. They flew conservatively . . . and fought conservatively as well, and here was a perfect example: the Shadow Hawks' AI fighters still had missiles left in their weapons bays. Expending antiship missiles on distant targets with a low probability of hitting with them just so you didn't need to take them back to the carrier was a *human* way of thinking and fighting, not one of intelligent software.

She was damned glad three AI-piloted Wyverns in her formation had survived, though. Their remaining missiles probably wouldn't destroy the enemy vessel, not without some extraordinary luck, but they would give them a chance to get past the Behemoth. Antimatter explosions blossoming against the Xul hull would screen the hurtling fighters from enemy sensors. She had ordered Green Five to loose its two remaining AM-98 ship-killers going in. Seconds later, twin blue-white flares of light had erupted against the Xul hunter-ship's hull like a close pair of hot suns just ahead. Now, Lee's Wyvern was hurtling toward the fast-expanding bubbles of plasma and vaporizing debris as her wingman screamed at her to pull up.

Her Wyvern hit the shell of fast-moving plasma with the shock of striking a solid wall, but her inertial dampers cushioned her through the worst of it. She could feel the burn of hard radiation, though, as it seared through her shields, and then she was in a tumble, spinning nose-for-tail a few meters above the tortured metal and ceramic landscape of the Xul Behemoth as alarms shrieked and flashed over the Wyvern's link with her brain.

The jolt had been enough to knock her out of a trajectory that would have sent her slamming into the huntership's hull, however. In an instant, she was past the alien vessel's bulk, struggling with her ship's mind-linked thrusters to bring the tumbling fighter back under control. Damage alerts shrilled at her, and with a thought-click she silenced them. She *knew* she was in trouble, damn it, and didn't need the irritating reminder. . . .

The universe spun past her awareness. "Pappy!" she cried. "Let's have some help, here!"

The AI was already helping, and she knew it. She considered, then rejected, the idea of having him stabilize the wildly spinning view of her surroundings being fed into her brain. $Pappy_2$ had enough on his electronic mind at the moment. She concentrated instead on trying to slow the fighter's spin, letting Pappy work through her to precisely balance the firing of her thrusters.

Two of her stabilizing thrusters were off-line, which made it tricky. Her comnet, her connection with the other ships in her squadron, was down as well. Other electronic systems were beginning to fail in cascade.

And then, without further warning, Pappy went off-line as well. It took her a few moments to realize that he was down, and when she did, she bit off a sharp curse. Without the AI's help, she was going to have a hell of a time navigating to the stargate, *if* she could get her essential ship's systems on-line and working again.

The damaged Wyvern continued its nose-over-tail tumble into the night. . . .

UCS Hermes
Stargate
Cluster Space/Carson Space
0727 hrs, GMT

The distant curve of the stargate flattened as *Hermes* approached the oddly distorted space at the gate's center, until it was a golden straight line bisecting the encircling sky. An instant later, Alexander felt the faint, internal shiver and disorientation as *Hermes* passed through the stargate.

The flattened pinwheel of the Galaxy, the reddish beehive of the globular cluster, the advancing Xul armada all vanished, wiped from the sky.

The Marine expeditionary force was back in Carson Space.

Or most of them were, at any rate. Fighters and Marine assault pods were still coming through. Alexander opened a channel to the commanding officer of CVW-5, *Samar*'s fighter wing.

"How many fighters did we lose, Reg?" Alexander asked.

COCVW-5 was Colonel Regin Macalvey, a tall, lanky Marine from EarthRing's Skyholme Sector. He was currently in his F/A-4140 Stardragon, regrouping his squadrons as they came back through the gate.

"All together, General? Or are you asking about the Shadow Hawks?"

"Both."

"We're still tallying, sir. Losses for the whole wing might be as high as twelve percent. We're still waiting for some stragglers to report in."

"And the Shadow Hawks?"

"Four ships have reported in so far, General. Out of sixteen. There may be some more, though, still on the other side of the gate."

"I see."

"We'll want to go back across and have a close look, General. Once this little dust-up is settled." He didn't add that fighters stranded on the far side of the gate were going to have some trouble when the star over there blew. *If* it blew. . . .

"If we can, CAG," Alexander replied. "CAG" was an ancient term for a carrier's aerospace wing commander, a relic of the days when he was called "Commander, Air Group."

An assessment probe was going to be vital after this op, Alexander reflected . . . but that assumed that the red star went nova, that the Xul node on the other side of the gate was destroyed, and that 1MIEF wasn't going to have to destroy the gate to keep the bad guys out.

A lot of assumptions. The next few minutes were going to be very busy indeed.

"Sir, we have Marines and AIs both still on the Cluster side of the gate. *Alive*. We can't leave them, there."

"I know that, CAG. And you know there are no promises."

"But—"

"Get your people squared away, Colonel." Alexander was watching the data feed update itself. Every few minutes, another reconnaissance drone would slip through the gate with a tactical update to the fleet communications net. As the data flowed through Alexander's link, he could see the Xul fleet massing on the other side, still approaching the gate. "We might have some visitors very soon, now."

"Aye, aye, sir."

Macalvey sounded bitter. Like any good Marine CO, he genuinely cared about the men and women under his command, cared even about the AIs. His personnel record mentioned that Macalvey was a member of the Church of Mind. It explained a great deal, not that explanations were required here. Alexander himself was a long-lapsed Neopag, but he had the Marine officer's deeply ingrained concern for his people.

In any case, there were sound practical reasons for getting back into Cluster Space when this was all over. The three Euler Starblasters were still on the other side of the gate, if they'd survived, along with a large menagerie of smaller probes and drones. He wanted to recover them if at all possible. The more the Commonwealth could learn about the ways and means of blowing up stars, the better. It was their primary weapon, now, against the Xul hordes.

He sensed Admiral Taggart's awareness. "Our fleet is in position, General," Taggart told him. "If they come through . . ."

"With luck, they'll wait to think things through," Alexander told him. The slowness of Xul tactical responses was proverbial, though it never did to rely too much on their past performance. The enemy *had* been known to pull a surprise move from time to time in the past.

"Yeah. The question is whether that pipsqueak sun over there will pack enough of a bang to get them all."

"Or if they'll be warned by their friends closer in." The Xul, it was known, possessed FTL communications. A base or ship close to the exploding sun might have time to transmit a warning to other Xul vessels farther out before it was engulfed.

So many unknowns.

Alexander checked the time. One minute more until the big question was answered. *If* the star had exploded on schedule, the nova's wave front was nearly to the gate by now.

The last recon drone imagery showed seven of the massive Xul hunterships less than a thousand kilometers from the gate, and still closing with it. The red dwarf star continued to burn in the distance, casting a bloody glare across their sunlit surfaces. Deeper in the system were hundreds, no, well over a thousand more, pinpointed by the X-ray and gamma radiation loosed by their black-hole power plants.

If that entire enemy fleet managed to come through the gate into Carlson Space, 1MIEF would be finished.

Space within the ring of the stargate shimmered. Abruptly, with the suddenness of nightmare, the long, slender prow of a Xul Type I, gleaming gold in the light of the Carson sun, emerged from the empty space inside the gate's ring.

"All ships!" Admiral Taggart commanded over the combat link. *"Fire!"*

Still emerging from the warped space of the stargate, the Xul huntership was caught in a web of high-energy beams and exploding missiles. Taggart had positioned the retreating Expeditionary Force fleet to take maximum advantage of the tactical bottleneck; the Xul ships could only emerge into Carson Space through the twenty-kilometer lumen of the stargate ring, and over a hundred combatant vessels of 1MIEF could focus all of their fire on that one tiny region of space.

The incredibly tough ceramic and metal alloy of the Xul warship's outer hull withered, rippled, and peeled away beneath that blast, as high-velocity kinetic-kill projectiles slammed into it at an appreciable fraction of light speed and plasma bolts seared into it at star-core temperatures. Moments later, the first nuclear and antimatter warheads began slamming into it, and the area immediately in front of the gate opening was blotted out by expanding spheres of plasma.

Under that ferocious onslaught, no material substance could remain intact for long. The Xul ship's fiercely radiating, needle-shaped hull continued moving into Carson Space, but its drive and weapons systems were dead. Pieces of its internal skeleton were visible now, and the remnants of its hull cladding were softening and streaming away as metallic vapor.

But even as it drifted clear, four more Xul ships were emerging from the gate interface.

Thirty seconds to go . . . an eternity in the lightning-quick stab and parry of space-naval combat.

Major Lee,
AS Squadron 16, Shadow Hawks,
Cluster Space
0731 hrs, GMT

It had taken several minutes, but at last she'd been able to stabilize her tumbling spacecraft. The vast sprawl of the Galactic spiral was at last no longer sweeping across her mind's eye. Behind her, the local sun, a ruby pinpoint, continued to burn in the far distance.

The situation was damned bad. Com and nav systems both were out, as was her link with $Pappy_2$. And there was worse. When she oriented her Wyvern to line up with the stargate and thought-clicked her main drive, nothing happened.

Stifling the sharp surge of fear, she began running diagnostics. Like other aerospace fighters, the Wyvern's main drive drew energy from a ZPF quantum power transfer unit, using quantum entanglement to transmit power from one point to another without actually having to cross the space between. Enormous zero-point field taps on board large capital ships sucked potentially unlimited power out of the sub-fabric of space itself and routed it directly to field-entangled power receivers on board individual aerospace fighters.

The advantage, of course, was that fighters didn't need to carry their own power generating systems for drives or weapons. The down side was that the carriers and big Marine transports had to be closely protected, since the destruction of a carrier would shut down all of her fighters. Briefly, Lee wondered if the *Samar* had been destroyed, and that was why she wasn't drawing any juice.

But . . . no. *Samar* was back in Carson Space. She'd come through the gate, released her fighters, then returned—safely, so far as the battlespace telemetry could report. The problem, obviously, was on her end of things.

It was tempting to assume that something was blocking or intercepting the energy transmission, but Lee knew that wasn't the way things worked. She shook her head, frustrated. It still felt a bit strange to her . . . knowing that she *should* still be drawing energy from a Marine transport some thirty thousand light years away.

That was part of the technological magic of zero-point energy taps. The energy wasn't so much transmitted as it was simultaneously co-existent in two separate places, on board the transport and inside the QPT receiver of her drive. Some day, the techies claimed, that bit of quantum-physics magic might make possible the ancient dream of teleportation from point to point; in the meantime, it was enough that her fighter could draw energy from her mothership even at this range. When it didn't work, the human mind tended to fall back on what felt like common sense. If energy wasn't coming through, something must be blocking it.

The truth was that some essential component in her own quantum power tap receiver must be down. She might pick up the cause through her diagnostics, but the system was complex and a full set might take hours.

Damn it. If Pappy$_2$ had been up and running, he'd be able to track the information down in no time. Her own personal AI was little more than a secretary, able to sort through incoming data and present it in a way that made sense, but unable to show much in the way of initiative or creativity.

She hated feeling this helpless.

She considered the Wyvern's suicide switch.

All Commonwealth fighters carried the things, a means of exploding a small antimatter warhead located beneath her seat. There were five steps to go through before the thing could be unsafed and triggered, but once she made the final connection—a manual button accessed underneath a lockdown cap rather than a thought-click—she would never feel a thing. The system had been installed in all fighters and most small military craft as a means of avoiding being patterned by the Xul . . . or for situations such as this one, where battle damage had rendered the craft inoperable and there was nothing to look forward to but suffocation or radiation poisoning.

She discarded the thought. She wasn't ready to make that decision, not just yet.

The situation was bad, but at least some of her systems were still running—life support and, thank the gods, her ship's sensors, which were still feeding data over her cerebral link. That meant she was picking up battlespace data from the far-flung net of drones and probes still adrift on this side of the gate. From the look of things, a *lot* of Xul ships were gathering, moving toward one of several stargate icons extending across her IHD in a broad, sweeping curve.

Cluster Space was a very special target, she knew. She

and the other members of her squadron had been thoroughly briefed before this op, and had downloaded a lot of data going all the way back to the 22nd Century.

In 2170, a Marine strike force had entered this system, sometime after the first encounter with Xul ships at the Sirius Stargate. Backtracking on the path followed by the Xul force, they'd discovered the Cluster Space system, far out among the halo stars at the outer fringe of the Galaxy, at least thirty thousand light years from Sol. They'd emerged from a different kind of stargate, a broad tunnel drilled into the heart of a twenty-kilometer-wide planetoid. According to the records, the Marines had recovered a damaged fighter that had fallen through the gate during the battle, planted antimatter charges, and escaped back through to the Sirius Gate before the charges had detonated, destroying the asteroid gate in Cluster Space and erasing the path back to Sirius.

That raid, quite possibly, had prevented the Xul from discovering Earth—less than nine light years from the Sirius Gate—for another century and a half, buying Humankind precious time. Not until 2314 had the Xul discovered Sol, launching the devastating bombardment against Earth that now, almost six centuries later, was still called Armageddonfall.

The idea now was to keep that from ever happening again. The next time the Xul visited Sol, they might well finish the job. *They* could destroy stars as well.

Elint—electronic intelligence—acquired by 1MIEF nine years ago during the battles in Aquila Space and at Starwall had revealed a wealth of various stargate connections, and the intelligence services both of the Humankind Commonwealth and of the Marines specifically had been mining that data ever since, trying to assemble a useful map of gate interconnections.

There were, it was estimated, some millions of stargates scattered across the Galaxy, and each gate could be tuned to connect with as many as several thousand other stargates. The web of interconnections was extraordinarily complex and farflung, and human explorers and their AI analogues had thus far visited only a tiny, tiny fraction of all of the possibilities.

But intelligence gathered during a gate reconnaissance at Sirius four years ago had led to the discovery of the Carson Gate, and that, in turn, had led *here,* to a major Xul node in Cluster Space. Probes sent from Carson to the Cluster had verified that this was *another* route to the Cluster Node; in fact, there were no fewer than fifteen stargates in orbit around that single tiny, red-dwarf star, making this system a major communications and travel hub. The destruction of that one gate in this system over seven centuries ago might have temporarily delayed the Xul discovery of Sol and Earth, but it probably hadn't even inconvenienced the Xul, who appeared to use the gate network to maintain their xenocidal watch over the teeming worlds of the Galaxy.

This time, the Commonwealth possessed the technology to close *all* of the gates. From experience, they knew that a nova probably wouldn't destroy them outright. Each gate was distant enough from the local star that even a nova wouldn't seriously affect it. But the nova *would* destroy all or most of the Xul ships, fortresses, and other structures orbiting in the local star, as well as annihilate any bases located on the worlds of the star's planetary system. When 1MIEF went back through the Carson/Cluster gatelink, Marine assault teams could be dispatched to each gate in the system with antimatter charges that would finish the job once and for all.

Those icons appearing in her In-Head Display represented a few of the local system's stargates, along with hundreds of red icons marking Xul warships within the range of the MIEF's battlespace sensor drones. It occurred to her that she was about to get a ringside seat on just what happened to Xul vessels on the nova side of a stargate during an MIEF raid.

Of course, she didn't expect to survive the experience. Any blast wave that seriously damaged a Xul huntership would sweep her little fighter away like a dust mite in a hurricane.

She checked to see that her recorders were going, however. The MIEF would be sending assessment teams through afterward, and if there was anything left of her Wyvern, the automated beacon transmitted by its rad-shielded storage unit would bring them in for a recovery. Of course, all of the unmanned battlespace drones had the same sort of storage, but there might be something unique to her viewpoint. Standard operational procedure required her to take steps to preserve the electronic record of what happened, just in case.

It also gave her a chance of recording a message, with a chance that it would reach family and friends back home in Saskatchewan.

Of course, she'd not had much to do with them since her radiation exposure at Starwall nine years ago. Somehow, knowing she would never have children again, she'd drifted apart from her blood family. The last time she'd linked with them had been . . . when? During one of 1MIEF's returns to Sol for resupply, certainly. But not four months ago, the last time she was there. Maybe two times before that, early last year. . . .

She would have to consult her personal memories, currently inaccessible in her implant hardware, to be sure. Even though it was her choice, she tended to follow Marine guidelines when it came to family memories, locking them into hardware storage during a mission to avoid complicating distractions at an inopportune moment. Like they always said, "If the Corps had wanted you to have a civilian family, they'd have issued you one in boot camp."

Hell, right now she couldn't even remember any of her parents' faces.

Fuck it, she thought. *Just like you've been saying. The Corps is your family, all the family you'll ever need. . . .*

Tears were drifting between her eyes and the inside of her helmet visor, tiny, silvery spheres floating in microgravity.

How much time did she have? If everything was on sched, the blast wave from the local star should be very nearly—

Without preamble, Bloodstar began growing brighter.

5

UCS Hermes
Stargate
Carson Space
0731 hrs, GMT

"Minus three . . . two . . . one . . . mark!" The AI's voice in Alexander's mind said, counting off the last seconds. If Bloodlight had indeed gone nova, the shock wave should just now have reached the stargate. Depending on how the gate was tuned, the blast could pass through an open gate, emerging from another gate light years away.

That didn't appear to be the case this time, however. Four Xul huntership were drifting just in front of the Carson Space gate, wreathed in lances of plasma and detonating nuclear and antimatter warheads. But nothing had emerged from the other side, no light, no hard radiation.

Had something gone wrong over there?

It was entirely possible that red dwarf stars were simply too low-mass for a Euler triggership to affect. That had always been one of the possibilities, one of the dangers of this mission.

Or perhaps the triggership had been delayed.

There was no way to tell, not from *this* side of the gate, or at least not until another battlespace drone emerged to update the combatnet.

One of the four Xul hunterships in the kill zone, a Type I newly emerged from the gate, was beginning to break up under the hellacious, focused bombardment. Under the concentrated fire of every capital ship of the MIEF, even a kilometer-long Xul warship couldn't hold up for long. A portion of the needle-sharp prow broke away, spinning rapidly end over end. The rest of the Xul vessel was beginning to crumple, and intense radiation was bathing the area. The black hole inside its engineering spaces must have broken free, and was now eating its way through the Xul ship's bowels.

But the Xul ships were firing back, sending a storm of laser energy and plasma bolts back at their tormentors. Three destroyers, *Foster*, *Johnson*, and *Mevernen*, had been destroyed just within the past couple of minutes, and the light cruiser *Yorktown* had been badly damaged, savaged by a concentrated volley of Xul weaponry. Now the heavy cruiser *Maine* was coming under fire, staggering as high-velocity mass-driver rounds slammed into her in a devastating fusillade.

The Commonwealth vessels continued firing, however, with unrelenting determination. As Alexander watched, the hull of the Type I twisted and dwindled, falling in upon itself. There was a final flash of radiation, from visible light through X-ray and gamma wavelengths . . . and then there was nothing remaining but drifting debris.

"Target Alpha destroyed!" someone called over the tactical net. "Pour it on, people!"

Two more Xul ships, another Type I and a Type II, were receiving the brunt of the expeditionary force's fire now. The fourth of the group, a Type II, was limping now after receiving a barrage of antimatter warheads across its dorsal surface, with streams of hot gas gushing from several gaping rents in its hull and freezing almost immediately into clouds of glittering ice crystals. It appeared to be trying to reverse course back through the gate.

"Let Charlie go," Taggart's voice said over the net, identifying the retreating vessel. "Concentrate on Bravo and Delta."

Bravo, the Type I, was starting to come apart under the heavy barrage, but it was also accelerating now, pushing deeper into Carson Space. A suicide attack? Or simply a breakdown in communications on board the stricken vessel? The Commonwealth firing line tracked it, continuing to pour fire into its shuddering, crumbling hull. It swept past the PanEuropean gunboat *Delacroix* at a range of less than ten kilometers. *Delacroix*'s turrets spun as they followed the Xul warship, slamming round after round of nano-D shells into the enemy's flank.

Alexander had strongly protested the integration of the PE, Chinese, and Russian squadrons into what was supposed to be a *Commonwealth* naval-Marine expeditionary force, but the Commonwealth Senate had been . . . insistent, primarily because of the high losses among the Commonwealth forces over the past few years. Opposed or not, Alexander believed in delivering praise when it was appropriate. He made a mental note to mention *Delacroix*'s deadly accurate fire when he composed his after-action report.

Assuming he survived to write it, of course. If the star next door had not gone nova, 1MIEF would shortly be in *very* serious trouble.

AS Squadron 16, Shadow Hawks,
Cluster Space
0731 hrs, GMT

Something had happened to the red dwarf. That much was clear simply through the Wyvern's optical inputs. But the effect was not what Lee had been expecting.

Within the past several seconds, the star had visibly grown much brighter. Lee's radiation sensors were off-line, but she suspected there was a strong UV, X-ray, and gamma component to the brightening as well, enough to give some teeth to that flare of visible light.

The increase in energy was more gradual than it should have been, however. Xul ships appeared now in sharp relief between their sunlit and shadowed surfaces, but their hulls weren't softening and melting, weren't boiling away under the assault.

Lee knew from the pre-mission briefings that there was a chance the local star could not be triggered into going nova. Like other typical red dwarfs, the local star was comparatively low-mass—about twenty percent the mass, in this case, of Earth's sun. In nature, only massive stars could go nova, and traditional novae were thought to occur only in binary star systems, when matter from one star fell into the other. The Euler triggerships, moving within a bubble of sharply warped space, distorted the core of a star as they passed through, inducing a rebound effect, it was thought, that generated an explosion of the star's core. The question was whether a red dwarf, which could be anywhere from forty percent down to about eight percent of the mass of Earth's sun, *could* be physically induced to explode. There'd been talk of testing the theory on a red dwarf within Commonwealth space before actually launching this raid, but the thought of blowing up a star, even a tiny one, simply to test theory had been too much for a majority of the members of the Commonwealth Senate. The request, put through by 1MIEF's science team, had been denied.

Still, it *should* have worked. Red dwarfs were smaller and cooler than other stars on the main sequence, but they were still stars, working fusion magic in the transformation of hydrogen to helium. There was another consideration as well. The Cluster Space sun was not a typical halo star—one of the thin haze of extremely ancient, cool red stars surrounding the Galaxy, but must instead be a straggler from the Galaxy's spiral arms. Its lone attendant planet proved that much. Stars from inside the Galaxy—Population I stars, as they'd been designated since the 20th Century—possessed heavier elements besides the usual stellar components of hydrogen and helium and therefore could form planetary systems. They were considered to be metal-rich, the word *metal* in this instance referring to any element heavier than helium whether it was chemically considered to be a metal or not. Population II stars, the halo stars surrounding the Galaxy, were ancient survivals from an earlier galactic epoch; without heavy elements in their make-up, they couldn't form planets.

The spectrum of the Cluster Space dwarf showed lots of carbon. Likely, Bloodlight possessed a core of carbon, a by-product of stellar fusion that must have been accumulating for tens of billions of years. The MIEF science teams felt that the rebound effect within a carbon core should result in the detonation of a nova—at least a small one—despite the star's low mass.

Lee watched the star for a full minute, looking through her cockpit's transparency with her naked eyes, now, rather than using the Wyvern's electronic feed. Despite the increase in overall brightness, she could look directly into that ruby spark without discomfort, without her helmet's optics dialing down to preserve her vision.

Possibly what had been triggered was a stellar flare; red dwarfs, especially small ones, often were unstable enough in their radiation output to earn the name flare stars. Such stars—Proxima Centauri, just 4.3 light years from Sol, was such a star—could increase in brightness by as much as two or three hundred percent, in some cases.

Whatever had happened, it was bad. The Xul fleet hadn't even been inconvenienced by the brightening of the sun, and was continuing to move toward the stargate. The MIEF would be arrayed on the far side, now, in Carson Space, and fighting for its life. Once General Alexander decided that the Xul were going to cross over to Carson Space in force, he would detonate a number of antimatter charges on the Carson Space stargate. That would stop more Xul from crossing over.

It would also strand Lee and any other survivors from the MIEF fighter wings that might still be on this side. Again she tried to engage her ship's auto-repair functions, tried to bring Pappy$_2$ back on-line, tried to fire up the main drive.

Nothing.

She elected to focus all of her energy on reviving Pappy. The AI could handle electronics repairs better than she.

And it would be nice to have someone to talk to, especially someone who might be able to make sense of the screwy data coming in from the Cluster Space star. It looked like—

Abruptly, the brightening star exploded, growing *much* brighter, and then still brighter, until the cockpit transparency went black.

Something must've delayed the explosion, she thought. *That, or the Euler triggerships took their sweet time getting to the star.*

She tried shifting back to her Wyvern's electronic feed, and got nothing but static. Shit! She was cut off now from the outside, unable to see with her own eyes or through the Wyvern's electronic senses. Apparently, the radiation from the exploding star had knocked the rest of her sensors off-line. She'd been helpless before; now she was helpless *and* blind.

At this point there was nothing she could do but wait. She noted that the temperature of her outer hull was rising now—at minus thirty degrees Celsius, up over one hundred degrees in the past thirty seconds. She didn't know for sure how hot it would get. Her Wyvern's hull integrity might well hold up, and she would survive this initial pulse. The killer in a nova, at least this far away from ground zero, was the cloud of charged particles lagging behind the speed-of-light radiation front by several hours. *That* would kill her, no doubt about it.

She considered the suicide switch again. It would save the waiting . . . and possibly some pain. She wasn't sure just how bad a dose of radiation she was getting right now, but it might be bad enough to kill her relatively quickly, over the course of several hours, say.

If she started vomiting, she would know.

She was determined not to be trapped adrift again, helpless and doomed to a slow death. Once had been enough, nine years ago, at Starwall. The similarity of that incident to her situation now was shrieking at her in the back of her mind.

It would be very easy to end things. Now.

On the other hand, she was a Marine . . . and Marines didn't give up, not *that* easily, anyhow. There would always be time to use the switch later, if things got too bad.

Almost fifteen minutes later, something hit her Wyvern's hull.

She felt the jar, and heard a sharp, metallic clang through the hull from somewhere aft. It startled her so badly she almost started the suicide switch enable procedure. If the Xul had grappled her fighter and were taking her on board one of their huntcrships . . .

But she also knew that the Xul patterning procedure happened quickly and electronically.

There was another clang, and a sound like metal scraping metal. What the hell was going on back there? Damn it, she wished she could see.

Something banged against her blacked-out canopy. She flinched, then braced herself. If they were coming for her through the canopy . . .

What she felt next, though, was a surge of acceleration. Zero-gravity gave way to a definite sense of weight, pushing her back against her acceleration couch.

Okay, someone had grabbed her and was taking her someplace. She wondered if the Xul took prisoners in ways other than patterning them and uploading them into a virtual reality within their computer network.

Then her canopy transparency cleared and, once more, she could look out into the emptiness of space. Three large, utterly black shapes surrounded her Wyvern, two just off her bow, one to port, one to starboard, and a third above and slightly behind. That third shape, seen only in dead-black silhouette, had positioned itself between her canopy and the exploding sun; riding in the object's shadow, her canopy had once again become transparent.

The shapes, she saw with a surge of heartfelt relief, were Wyverns—needle-prowed forward of the cockpit bulge, flat and disk-shaped aft. She could just make out the hull number on the Wyvern forward and to port—identifying it as 2nd Lieutenant Traci Wayne's ship. The wave of relief nearly left her trembling. Three of the Wyverns in her squadron had come after her. The noises she'd heard were tow cables; fired from special ports in a Wyvern's hull, several meters of their free ends were coated in nano sheaths that, on contact, welded themselves to the target hull. She was inextricably bound to the two Wyverns forward, now, at least until a signal from the towing vessels deactivated the nano-binder's programming.

Her first thought was a surging rush of joy. *I'm not alone,* she thought. *I never was. . . .*

Her second was one of anger. *Idiots! They should have returned through the gate, not hung around looking for me!*

Still, she knew she would have remained.

And she was going home.

Assuming her entourage could get her through the gate, of course. Xul ships were continuing to crowd up close to the gate, anxious, perhaps, to escape the doomed star system. Or anxious, perhaps, just to get at the Commonwealth fleet waiting on the other side. Xul psychology was still largely a matter of guesswork. They were not human, and they did not think in the same ways humans did.

In any case, the three operable fighters and their dead-weight tow would have to thread an unpleasant gauntlet to get through. She could see a Type II making the passage now, moving through the interface at the center of the ring, vanishing from existence as it entered the opening. Five smaller hunterships and one huge Type III hung near the gateway.

Her escorts were beginning to fade slightly as they switched on their phase-shift gear. While not true invisibility, the fighters were just enough outside of normal space-time that they appeared indistinct and somewhat blurred. Her own phase-shift gear, like nearly everything else on board her damaged fighter, was inoperable. At least, though, the Xul would be tracking only one fighter on its way to the stargate, not four.

Acceleration continued to push her back into her couch. Along with so much else, her inertial dampers were off-line. She hoped Wayne and the pilot of the other towing Wyvern had guessed that, because if they started boosting at a hundred gravities, they would be taking her off the couch with a sponge back in Carson Space. It felt like they were keeping it low, though. She guessed they were pulling about five gravities now, maybe a bit more. Her flight suit was re-conforming to provide pressure in her extremities and gut to keep blood from pooling there.

The acceleration increased. How much? Eight gravities? Ten? At around ten Gs, she knew, she would black out.

Well, it wasn't absolutely vital that she stay conscious, but she wanted to if for no other reason than that she wanted to see. The stargate was expanding rapidly now as the quartet of fighters hurtled toward it. Wayne and the other pilot, she saw, were angling toward one rim of the stargate. Smart. It would keep them clear of those last few Xul warships jockeying for position near the gate's center, and she doubted that they would open fire on the fighters and risk damaging the stargate.

She wondered why the Xul weren't firing on them now. Phase-shift gear wasn't *that* good at hiding a fighter, not at knife-fighting range, like this. Then she realized that the enemy might well be filling the sky around her with volleys of high-energy weapons fire and she would never know it, not without the software that painted incoming beams and attached icons to missiles. Without computer enhancement, she wouldn't see a thing until something actually hit her, and then it would be too late.

Lee wished she could talk to Wayne and the others . . . then thought better of it. They were very busy right at the moment, and needed full concentration for a maneuver that made threading a needle at arm's length child's play by comparison.

Closer, now, and faster. Her vision was narrowing now, her peripheral field going black, and her arms were too heavy to move. She wished she could have another look at the Galaxy sprawled across heaven, but she could no longer turn her head. All she could see was directly ahead—the rapidly expanding stargate, with a Type III Xul huntership approaching the gate's center.

Well, the nova light was probably so bright by now she

wouldn't have been able to see it, anyway. Stargate and Xul vessel both had taken on a hard-edged, blue-white glare where they reflected the glow of Bloodlight coming from behind her. Come to think of it, that provided the four fighters with another advantage—coming down out of the sun. Any Xul sensors looking back that way must be fried by now.

She caught a glimpse of one curving arc of ring-surface flattening out just to the left of dead ahead. And then . . .

UCS Hermes
Stargate
Carson Space
0748 hrs, GMT

"Four more fighters coming through, General," Colonel Macalvey reported, his voice tight with excitement. Every remaining MIEF fighter was in space, now, swarming about the incoming Xul hunterships as they drifted in an immense and untidy clot at the center of the stargate. "Tough to see them in all that crap."

Alexander didn't reply. The debris cloud in front of the stargate was so thick now that it was tough to see anything, but three of the fighters were broadcasting their transponder signals at full intensity—hoping to ward off so-called friendly fire as they came into the kill zone—and battlespace drones emplaced on the stargate ring itself were picking up and boosting those signals. The transmissions revealed the tightly grouped icons of three . . . no, *four* Wyverns flying scant meters off the inner side of the stargate's ring as they streaked through into Carson Space.

Good. A few more Marines had made it back. . . .

And with them came a burst of signal-boosted telemetry, updating the battlenet. Alexander felt the stream of raw information flowing into *Hermes'* computer network. From the little he could grab, unanalyzed, Bloodlight *had* exploded on the other side, though not as soon as, and not with the violence, expected. As soon as the data were downloaded, the science team AIs would be fine-combing it, updating the available information on Xul warships coming through the gate.

The big question, of course, was whether the violence of the exploding star had damaged the enemy vessels, hurt them enough to stop them from coming through into Carson Space.

So far, the battle was going well, and at least vaguely according to plan. In any battle, the key determining factor is the terrain. Open space *has* no terrain, and tactics must be dictated by the relative technology possessed by the combatants, and by numbers.

The stargate, however, impressed a type of terrain on battlespace, a bottleneck, specifically, that allowed only a few ships to pass from one side to the other at a time, and that only slowly. In open space, the Xul possessed staggering advantages in technology and firepower, but the stargate bottleneck allowed Admiral Taggart to mass the weaponry of the entire MIEF against a single, tiny area and focus it all on the Xul ships as they passed through into the Carson Space kill zone.

That kill zone was visible now, even to the unaided eye, as a thick fog and a tangle of wreckage adrift in front of the Carson stargate. As volley upon volley of high-energy beam weapons gutted each Xul ship coming through the gate, gouts of internal gases and molten hull material erupted into space, freezing in seconds into glittering droplets and creating a dense haze. Nuclear and antimatter warheads added expanding spheres of hot plasma to the haze, and throughout were tangled bits of debris, much of it still glowing white-hot.

The stargate was twenty kilometers across, and already the nebula of debris covered a volume of space much wider than that. It was actually becoming difficult to see what was going on at the cloud's center. The radiation there was intense enough to scramble most sensors, though the ring-emplaced sensors were still doing a good job of spotting most of the stuff coming through.

The Xul warships continued to emerge, visible only as large shapes half-glimpsed through the debris cloud. They were coming through at low speed—at eighty to ninety kilometers per hour—and colliding with the drifting wreckage. While they weren't moving fast enough to cause significant damage to their outer hulls with the collisions, they appeared to be disoriented, as though they weren't expecting space to be so crowded with wreckage and debris.

Fire continued to rain down upon each in turn, tearing great gashes in ceramic-metal hull material that glowed red and orange with the intensity of the bombardment. The space in front of the stargate pulsed and strobed with the silent flashes of detonating antimatter warheads, and the debris haze was thick enough that plasma bolts and laser beams had become visible to the unaided eye, illuminated by the trails of vaporizing particles of dust and ice.

Those Xul warships that worked their way clear of the man-made nebula found themselves at the focus of long-range bombardment from nearly one hundred Commonwealth warships, and by the short-range jab and sting of Marine aerospace fighters.

Over the past twenty minutes, the battle had slowly transformed into a slaughter. From his vantage point, he could watch the Xul craft emerge from the gate, struggle to orient themselves, and come under that highly focused, devastating fire.

And, under that assault, one by one, the Xul hunterships died.

But the plan called for *saving* one of the monsters, a big one, if possible. . . .

Penetrator Team Savage
UCS Hermes
Stargate
Carson Space
0804 hrs, GMT

First Lieutenant Charel Ramsey brought the palm of his hand down on the link contact, and, with a heady surge of energy pulsing through his conscious mind, he became a god.

Ramsey was newly arrived on board the MIEF's flagship. He'd joined her after a passage through from Earth on the heavy cruiser *San Diego* only four weeks ago, part of the reinforcement and resupply convoy operation designated Starlight III. As a new graduate of the Navy and Marine Corps Intelligence Training Center at Sinus Medii, on Luna, he'd been assigned to the expeditionary force's N-2 division, answering to General Alexander's command constellation directly and based here on board the *Hermes*. As an N-2 intelligence officer, he'd been assigned to a penetrator team.

And he was going in hot.

Integration complete, a voice—partially his own—said over the Intel net. *Ramsey-Thoth now ready for launch.*

Ramsey's body was lying on one of the link couches inside *Hermes'* Combat Ops Center, or COC, but his mind was . . . elsewhere. Linked by his neural implant system into *Hermes'* computer network, with all other input signals blanked by his software, his mind's eye was now residing within a narrow, tightly bounded virtual space representing a K-794 Spymaster probe.

Ramsey's thoughts were integrated now with a powerful artificial intelligence given the name "Thoth," an apt enough name, since the original Thoth had been the ancient Egyptian god of science, writing, knowledge . . . and magic. Designed to operate in this curious blend of human and artificial intelligence, Thoth provided Ramsey's viewpoint with the speed, power, precision, and data acquisition functions of an AI. Ramsey provided purely human talents of flexibility, creativity, and intuition not yet possible for even the most powerful AIs.

The subjective effect was to give Ramsey a thrilling, deep-centered sense of truly godlike power and control, a feeling utterly unlike any other. It felt . . . wonderful. Addictively so.

"Probe Ramsey-Thoth is clear for launch," the voice of Lieutenant Karen Hodges said in his mind. She would be his link with COC Control. "At your discretion, Gunny."

"Copy that," Ramsey replied.

"Be advised that a Type III is now transiting the gate," Hodges added. Images built themselves up in an open window in Ramsey's mind. He could see the two-kilometer Nightmare slowly emerging from the gate, its hull beginning to sparkle with the impacts of incoming fire. "Could be a good target of opportunity."

"Copy that, COC Control. See you all back at the farm."

With a thought-click, a powerful magnetic field hurled the probe clear of *Hermes* and into empty space. The probe's N'mah-derived space drive switched on, and the Spymaster, with Ramsey's viewpoint on board, hurtled toward the fizzy, nebular haze gathered in front of the stargate.

Targeting the emerging Type III, Ramsey locked onto the huge vessel and accelerated. . . .

Nine years ago, Ramsey had been a Marine gunnery sergeant, an enlisted grunt with twelve years of active duty behind him. He'd been part of the assault team that had gone into a planetoid hollowed out by the alien Eulers, and been the first human to establish direct mind-to-mind contact with them.

For another year, he'd served with the MIEF Contact Team, helping to establish the protocols and translation software that let humans communicate freely with the deeply alien, benthic species known as the Eulers, and worked as well on the design of Euler triggerships, adapting them for human use. At the end of that year, he'd been approached by the Office of Naval Intelligence and given the opportunity to come on board full-time as an e-spook. His experience with the Eulers, he'd been told, had demonstrated the levels of flexibility and mental adaptability the intelligence services were looking for.

Over all, it had been an interesting tour. The only downside was that as part of his training, he'd been sent to OCS and emerged as an officer.

As a former non-commissioned officer, Gunny Ramsey had been absolutely convinced that the *true* backbone of any military service was its NCO corps, a statement that likely had been a truism in the army of Nimrod. Becoming an officer had been a little like defecting to the other side. He still carried the nickname "Gunny," and endured the good-natured teasing of his fellow commissioned officers.

Part of the problem was that he was now in his mid-forties, and literally twice the age of most of his associates. His other nickname, though not one usually used to his face, was "Grandpap."

Damned kids . . .

The Spymaster probe, one of some hundreds loosed by the MIEF capital ships, dropped through the man-made nebula, homing now on the emerging Nightmare. The probe's outer shell was growing hot now in two ways, from friction with dust particles and from the sea of radiation bathing the kill zone. He felt Thoth increasing the probe's magnetic shielding, and begin jinking the two-meter-long dart in order to avoid Xul antimissile fire.

At the last possible moment, the Spymaster decelerated sharply, hitting nearly two hundred gravities. Ramsey didn't feel that, of course, since he wasn't physically on board the probe. Artfully arranged patterns of electrons, fortunately, were not subject to such inconveniences as gravity or high acceleration.

Or radiation, for that matter, so long as the probe's hardened circuits were shielded from EMP. One second before impact, the probe's bow shielding fired, transformed by an antimatter charge into a spear of raw energy stabbing down into the Xul ship's armor. The probe struck a seething opening filled with searing hot plasma and tunneled in, its lead element revealed now as a nano-tunneler.

The Spymaster probe vanished, swallowed by the narrow-mouthed crater of its own making.

And moments later, Ramsey-Thoth began to hear the Nightmare's Song. . . .

6

UCS Hermes
Stargate
Carson Space
0810 hrs, GMT

"The first wave of Penetrators is away, General."

"About damned time."

Alexander watched the green threads of the tiny missiles extending from *Hermes* and other ships in the fleet toward the most recent Xul ship to cross the gate interface. The first were already impacting on its hull.

This was the real heart of Operation Clusterstrike. He'd wanted to launch the incursion earlier in the battle, but various factors had conspired to delay things. In particular, the Intel people—N-2 in the Navy and Marine lexicon—had needed to analyze the electronic screens now being used by the Xul fleet in order to give the Penetrators a better chance of getting past the enemy's defenses, both passive and active. They'd also been holding out for a Type III or one of the newly identified Type IV's as a target, on the theory that the larger Xul huntships would have more complex, deeper, and more valuable electronic infrastructures to tap.

And, finally, they'd needed an updated picture of what was happening on the far side of the gate. The arrival of those last four fighters and the data they'd uploaded to the battlenet had revealed that the Xul assault was tapering off. As they'd come through the gate, there'd been only a half-dozen hunterships on the other side, and only one large one—the Type III now being targeted by the Penetrators.

Alexander allowed himself a small—a *very* small—release of the stress that had been riding his shoulders throughout the battle. There'd been so many unknowns with this operation, and one of the largest and most deadly had been whether they would be able to contain the Xul fleet. With as many as a thousand Xul warships in Cluster Space, no one had been able to guarantee that the MIEF line on the Carson Space side of the gate wouldn't be overwhelmed.

Expendable munitions stores were running low throughout the fleet. Lasers and plasma weapons alone would not have been enough to slow that onslaught if they'd chosen to keep coming.

Both Alexander and Taggart possessed mental triggers keyed to detonate a number of antimatter charges already placed around the Carson Gate's circumference. If the Xul had been able to push through the bottleneck, if both Taggart and Alexander had been convinced that the MIEF line would not hold, they would have destroyed the gate.

Carson Space was located, as near as the astrographers could determine, some eleven thousand light years from Sol, on the outskirts of the Galaxy's Perseus Arm, a pinpoint in the vast spiral of four hundred billion stars chosen both for its remoteness and for the fact that a careful search of the region had failed to turn up any signs of a Xul presence.

Of course, with the gate destroyed, the surviving ships of 1MIEF would have to be translated back to Sol a few at a time within the vast hangar deck of the *Hermes*, a slow process that wouldn't even work with the larger ships in the fleet. And if *Hermes* had been damaged or destroyed, the journey would have taken a lot longer—a number of years under Alcubierre Drive.

It would have been worth it however, to keep the Xul from

discovering the origin of the attack, but there would have been a terrible danger, too. Alexander knew that 1MIEF needed to keep moving, keep threatening the Xul from as many different directions as possible. If the task force lost the initiative, the Xul might recover enough to find Humankind's world of origin, and *this* time, Earth and all her colonies would be obliterated.

Maintaining the initiative in this war was absolutely vital to humanity's survival, but it was a balancing act that was growing more and more difficult, more deadly, with each passing month. By now, the ancient enemy was aware that *somebody* in the Galaxy was out to kill them, and given their peculiarly paranoid way of thinking, they would be frantic by now in their efforts to track down the threat and destroy it.

In fact, the only thing that had kept Humankind out of the Xuls' xenophobic eye had been the size of the Galaxy, the sheer vast number of suns and worlds and emerging civilizations. As it was, they'd learned of Earth and its attendant cluster of tiny interstellar communities several times already over the past few centuries. Armageddonfall had come within a hair of annihilating Earth herself, and the Xul capture of an asteroid colonizer ship, fleeing Sol at sublight speeds after the bombardment of Humankind's homeworld, apparently had given them more precise information about humans, their origins, and their history.

That discovery had prompted the creation of 1MIEF, the Battle of the Nova in 1102 of the Marine Era, and the subsequent near-decade of raids and strikes at Xul nodes across the Galaxy. The joint naval-Marine expeditionary force had been tasked with the seemingly impossible—keeping the Galaxy-wide empire of the Xul reeling and off-balance. If the Xul were bending all of their considerable resources toward finding 1MIEF instead of Earth, perhaps Earth would be able to come up with . . . something else, a weapon, a strategy, an alliance, *something* that would enable Humankind to survive.

A lean and desperate hope.

Survival would have been a lot less likely had 1MIEF been destroyed this morning . . . or if Taggart and Alexander had been forced to destroy the gate and return to Sol Space by other means. But the gamble appeared to have paid off well. According to the ongoing tally, twelve Xul hunterships had been destroyed so far in the hellfire unleashed in front of the Carson Gate. That had come at a high price; 1MIEF had lost thirty-one ships of various classes, and a large percentage of the aerospace fighters. After this one, the expeditionary force would need to rearm and re-equip, either back at Sol or at one of the other major Commonwealth bases, at 36 Ophiuchi or New Earth, perhaps.

But then it would be back into the battle line again.

Perhaps information taken by the Penetrators would pinpoint the next objective.

The fleet's fire was raking the newly emerged *Nightmare*-class huntership now, but carefully, with exacting precision. Certain areas of that immense, quasi-spherical hull had been set aside as targets for the Penetrator swarm, and it wouldn't do to vaporize the Penetrators before they could eat their way into the Xul hull.

A pair of Type II huntersihps were emerging now, and much of the bombardment shifted over to them. Fire continued to rain down on the Type III, however. That one Xul ship, over two kilometers across, could wreck the Commonwealth fleet if it got close enough. Naval gunfire hammered away at the monster, concentrating on weapon banks, sensor arrays, and drive blisters. If possible, they would immobilize the Nightmare, allowing the Penetrators to do their job without the dangerous distraction of haste. Some Penetrators would be destroyed, no doubt, but hundreds had been fired into that monster precisely so that a few, at least, might survive.

And after that would come the really tricky part of Operation Clusterstrike. . . .

* * *

Penetrator Team Savage
UCS **Hermes**
Stargate
Carson Space
0812 hrs, GMT

Lieutenant Ramsey wasn't *really* a fish. It was important, however, to create metaphors that seemed as real and true-to-life as possible if the Penetrator team was going to be able to work with them.

What is software, after all, but patterns of information? Electric charge and lack of charge, gates permitting or refusing trickles of current, a flow of electrons guided this way or that, entire networks of interconnected processors and relays, the whole organized into complex arrays of movement, storage, and potential, all according to carefully designed schema and encodings meaningful to the designers.

Information.

Xul and human technology had that much in common, at least. Human computer systems used binary logic coded into electrical charges moving across microscopic threads of gold, copper, osmium, hafnium-carbide, and other elements and compounds layered on wafers of silicon or boron-carbon nanolaminates; the Xul used a trinary logic generated by triple gates etched into ceramic substrates or suspended in gels of organic polymers.

More, Xul minds were not even remotely human, existing as nested hierarchies of intelligence and communication within vast networks of awareness, myriad minds in a kind of chorus of thought blending layer by layer into a metamind directing each huntership, the metaminds in turn interconnecting into higher and more remote layers of awareness and organization.

Still, since the recovery and dissection of a Xul huntership within the frozen world-ocean of Europa, in Earth's home solar system over eight centuries before, human and human-designed AIs had probed, analyzed, and mapped numerous examples of Xul technology. Software, and entire artificially intelligent tech-genera, had been developed to allow human computer systems to interface with alien.

And at every opportunity, those software systems were used to probe and penetrate Xul technologies, seeking that most powerful, that most vital of all weapons in any war.

Again, *information*.

But where patterns of charge and electron flow can be meaningful to an intruding software program, those patterns are meaningless to human awareness without some fairly high-level and sophisticated translation. In short, a kind of computer animation was playing out a movie within Lieutenant Ramsey's mind, through Thoth's connection with the hardware implanted within his brain and nervous system.

To Ramsey's mental viewpoint, he was moving through an ocean.

He was used to virtual spaces set to replicate marine environments. This time, though, it wasn't the lightless abyssal depths favored by the alien Euler, but something like the warm shallows of a coral reef, a sparkling clear, blue-green translucence filled with myriad swarms of brightly colored fish representing moving patterns of data, with vast and tortured landscapes of coral, seaweed forests, anemones, and other marine life representing storage areas, quiescent memories, and hardware infrastructure.

Ramsey had been born in EarthRing, but most of his childhood had been spent in the Florida Reefs, not far from Lost Miami. He'd done a lot of diving both there and in the nearby sunken Bahama Banks, and even worked for a time on the Atlantis Project. He'd chosen the undersea metaphor as his preferred means of interfacing with the alien Xul system.

As the Penetrator chewed its way deeper and yet deeper into the alien armor, its sensors had been alert to electron flow and magnetic moment. Eventually, nearly forty meters down, it detected a bundle of thallium-niobium-bromide threads in an induced high-temperature superconductive state and changed direction slightly to intercept it. Once the Penetrator's access tip had been exposed and brought into contact with the superconductor cable, Thoth had begun insinuating himself into the alien network.

And Ramsey's mind was piggybacked with Thoth, along for the ride.

He could hear the Chorus . . .

Once, in a virtual reality diving simulation at the Bimini Oceanarium, Ramsey had heard whalesong, the deep, eerie, and echoing tones of the long-vanished humpback whale. This was like that, a low, throbbing, and utterly compelling pulse through his VR surroundings more felt than heard. And with Thoth's ability to decode the signals for him as they came through, he could hear them as words, *intelligible words.* . . .

9021:   >> . . . *threat* . . . <<

7365:   >> . . . *failure* . . . <<

4643:   >> . . . *cessation* . . . <<

CHORUS: >> . . . *this is not possible!* . . . <<

7365:   >> . . . *possibility is self-evident* . . . <<

1549:   >> . . . *ending is the way of existence* . . . <<

CHORUS: >> . . . *but Mind must endure! . . . but Mind must endure!* . . . <<

8575:   >> . . . *but Mind must endure . . . but the Threat is grave* . . . <<

The phrases were fragmentary and incomplete, the connection like listening in on less than half of a complete conversation. It felt as though individuals were singing thoughts, then joining in a chorus with other individuals to blend ideas and, perhaps, generate new concepts.

He'd heard this type of sing-song before. There were recordings of Xul exchanges from The Singer, the Xul Type III frozen for half a million years in the ice of the Europan ocean, and from other Xul ships electronically "boarded" by AI probes during encounters over the centuries since. All intel officer trainees listened to those recordings endlessly, seeking to familiarize themselves with the strange timbre and layered, roundabout reasoning that passed for Xul thought.

Individual speakers in the conversation were identified by

four-digit numbers, *felt* rather than seen or heard, through a
kind of electronically enhanced intuition.

8947:	>> ... *the Mind has encountered* ... <<
4641:	>> ... *We Who Are have encountered this species before* ... <<
3399:	>> ... *this species* ... <<
8947:	>> ... *Species 2824* ... <<
8571:	>> ... *Species 2824* ... *System 2420–544* ... <<
8947:	>> ... *has been a Threat before* ... <<
2255:	>> ... *to We Who Are before* ... <<
CHORUS 1:	>> ... *the Threat must be eliminated* ... <<
CHORUS 2:	>> ... *Species 2824 must be eliminated* ... <<
CHORUS 1:	>> ... *System 2420–544 must be eliminated* ... <<
CHORUS ALL:	>> ... *We Who Are must endure* ... <<

Dream on bastards, Ramsey thought. The Xul had been
trying to eliminate Humankind for a long time.

Bit by bit, modern Humankind had been piecing together
the complete history of his ancient encounters with the Xul,
a history, it turned out, that reached back to the very begin-
nings of Man as a species.

Ages ago, the Xul had wiped out the Builders, an interstellar civilization—possibly a machine intelligence, though details were sketchy—that had terraformed Mars perhaps as
much as half a million years ago, left mysterious artifacts on
Earth's moon, and apparently tampered with the genome of
Homo erectus in order to create not one but two new hominid
species ... *Homo sapiens* and *Homo neanderthalensis.*

The Martian colony had been destroyed and the planet's
artificially generated atmosphere had been blasted away, but
somehow the Xul had overlooked the Builders' genetic laboratory on Earth. Humans and Neanderthals had survived.

Sometime around 7000 B.C.E., the Xul had all but annihilated the An, a technically proficient species with an interstellar empire consisting of several dozen worlds, including

Earth, where Neolithic human tribes had been enslaved, trained, and interbred to serve the colonizing masters as farmers and as miners. The An and a few of their human slaves had survived on the Earthlike moon of a gas giant at Lalande 21185, but only by losing most of their technological know-how. Though Earth was bombarded by asteroids and the An population centers destroyed, the human survivors on Earth had struggled back from the brink of extinction, helped openly by the alien N'mah. Something of the encounter with destroying monsters from the stars had lingered on, though, in myth, legend, and religion. It was the ancient Sumerians who provided their word for "demon" to the destroyers—*Xul*.

The Xul had almost certainly been alerted to Humankind's existence sometime in the 21st Century, when The Singer had been uncovered on Europa. A group mind housed within the enormous spacecraft's computer network had sent a signal starward. That fragment of the Xul overmind, however, after half a million years of isolation beneath the Europan ice, had been hopelessly insane. Attempts to retrieve and translate data stored there had been less than completely successful.

In 2148, a human explorer ship, *The Wings of Isis,* had been patterned and stored by a Xul huntership at the stargate orbiting Sirius A. In 2170, Marine and naval elements had fought the Battle of Sirius Gate, destroying a Xul ship, and also making contact with the alien N'mah living a low-tech, survivalist existence inside the stargate structure itself.

And since then there'd been repeated isolated contacts and encounters with the Xul, repeated clashes and raids. The arrival of a Xul ship within the Sol System in 2314 had very nearly destroyed the world of Humankind's birth. Only the destruction of the intruding Xul ship, made possible by a Marine assault force actually entering the monster with backpack nukes, had saved Earth and, quite possibly, all of humanity.

Xenosophontologists—the researchers, human and AI—who studied alien intelligences, had been studying the Xul since the recovery of The Singer on Europa. Each electronic penetration of a Xul ship-network taught them a little more. According to them, the Xul—who apparently referred to themselves as *We Who Are*—possessed a kind of hardwired Darwinian paranoia triggered by any encounter with non-Xul intelligence. For uncounted ages, they'd watched and listened from their base-nodes scattered across the Galaxy, noting the emergence of life and of Mind, and eliminating that life once it appeared to pose a threat—which generally was defined as developing technology, especially star travel.

At the same time, however, it was difficult to get their attention. They appeared to react strongly to the arrival of starships in areas under their control, but they did not appear to do much in the way of active patrolling. They also tended to overlook species existing in environments outside the expected. That An colony at Lalande 21185, for instance, had escaped the general destruction of the An's interstellar empire because it wasn't in the so-called habitable zone encircling its star. The world called Ishtar was the moon of a gas giant in the frozen realm far from the system's red-dwarf primary, but parts of its surface were kept habitable by gravitational tidal stresses. The N'mah were amphibious, with their adult phase living underwater; the colony contacted by Earth had escaped Xul notice by colonizing flooded portions of the interior of the Sirius Stargate. And then there were the Eulers. . . .

The point was that the Xul did not think, did not react the same way humans would to something perceived as a threat. Their paranoia was over-the-top, a species-wide overreaction that saw *anything* different as a threat, but their physical reaction to that threat tended to be measured and slow, even dilatory, and often fragmentary. Human xenosophontologists were as yet uncertain why this might be so; all intelligence officers, however, had been repeatedly instilled with a kind of mantra when it came to spying on the Xul: we don't yet understand them; *any* scrap of information, however small, is vital.

And so Ramsey and Thoth entered the Song, listening and recording. Using data brought back from previous penetrator raids within other Xul hunterships, the Ramsey-Thoth cooperative had woven a software emulation shell about itself, the digital equivalent of donning camouflage. From Ramsey's perspective, he was another of the brightly colored fish flashing above the reef. The Song itself, besides playing out in his thoughts as words, was echoed by the movements of schooling fish around him. As one of the numbered voices sang its piece, one of the fish would brighten and dart, followed an instant later by a swarm of its fellows. When the chorus sang, *all* of the fish pulsed and throbbed and flashed in unison.

Unnoticed, Ramsey-Thoth settled in with one of the lesser swarms. The software shell reflecting the surrounding thoughts like nanoflaged body armor rendering a Marine invisible.

6223:   >> . . . *threat* . . . <<

7118:   >> . . . *serious threat* . . . <<

7472:   >> . . . *the local Mind faces disruption* . . . <<

8571:   >> . . . *disruption is ending/evil* . . . <<

6223:   >> . . . *is ending/evil/wrong!* . . . <<

8947:   >> . . . *but Mind will survive* . . . <<

CHORUS: >> . . . *Mind* must *survive* . . . <<

7472:   >> . . . *query—what of MIND?* . . . <<

8947:   >> . . . *MIND is* . . . <<

7472:   >> . . . *MIND must be informed, lest the[?cancer] spread* . . . <<

9335:   >> . . . *unprecedented* . . . <<

CHORUS 1: >> . . . *unprecedented* . . . <<

CHORUS 2: >> . . . *unprecedented!* . . . <<

2221:   >> . . . *the threat offered by this species is unprecedented* . . . <<

5294:   >> . . . *the Hub should be informed* . . . <<

CHORUS: >> . . . *the Hub will be informed* . . . <<

CHORUS 1: >> . . . *that MIND may live even if Mind should dissipate* . . . <<

CHORUS: >> . . . *that We Who Are survive . . .* <<
CHORUS: >> . . . *We Who Are will be/endure/survive . . .* <<

Ramsey had been listening with an intuitive openness of mind. All Marines underwent extensive training in certain mental disciplines while in boot camp and in OCS, disciplines such as weiji-do that increased the flexibility, adaptability, and psychic strength of the human mind.

Weiji-do, developed back in the 22nd and 23rd centuries and based on some of the stranger, reality-generating aspects of Quantum Physics, was sometimes called the Way of Chaos, but a better translation would have been the Way of the embodiment of the chaotic potential of creation and reality. The skill-set helped Marines function with confidence within the virtual realities and downloaded sim-worlds of computer-generated combat networks and information feeds, but it also sharpened innate intuitive and psychic abilities. The training allowed the Ramsey portion of the Ramsey-Thoth mental fusion to relax into a deeply altered state and follow individual threads of the alien exchange—in effect backtracking on some of the movement patterns woven by those flashing, colorful fish around him.

He was curious about two particular concepts overheard in the alien conversation—the reference to the hub, and the thought-symbol translated as MIND. Both ideas had rich associations within the substrate of the Xul mentality. He felt himself sinking into the structure of the reef itself, felt the pulse of life around and within him.

He recorded everything, of course—images, listings of data, sounds . . .

The Hub, he was almost certain, was an astrographical reference. If so, it could only refer to the Galactic hub, the very center of the Galaxy. Some of the side links and associated data stores appeared to relate to another Xul node—a very large, very important Xul node—somehow connected with the deep Galactic core.

The concept of MIND—his own mind supplied the sense of all capitals—had been hinted at by other incursions into other Xul networks. Though poorly understood, the idea appeared to hinge on the notion of nested hierarchies, or meta-gestalts.

The species humans knew as the Xul were generally thought of as a type of hive mind, though that phrase suggested similarities to anthills or beehives on Earth, or to the *kadje* nests so common on the cold, wet world of Cerridwen that were misleading at best. Electronic sigint carried out on Xul structures in the past, though, suggested that the lowest, simplest components of the Xul mentality were individual software components running Xul warriors or individual weapons. All of those "minds" grouped together, working together, and linked with patterns of information that might well have been uploaded into the system from living organisms eons ago, comprised the "Mind" resident within a single Xul huntership.

All of the ship-Minds resident within a single Xul node, one of the gated star systems where dozens or hundreds of hunterships, fortresses, and base elements were networked together into an metamind, usually referred to in N-2 circles as the Node Mind.

There was a sense, here, of something higher. Logically, if Xul mentalities were built up in hierarchic data structures, a metamind made up of the thought processes of all Xul ships and nodes throughout the Galaxy might form a yet higher-level gestalt.

MIND.

But there was no time, and there were no resources here, for analyses. The data were recorded within the molecular computer circuits of the Spymaster probe, still sheathed deep within the huntership's armor.

Something else was happening as well. For an eternity in electronic terms—but actually something on the order of eight to ten seconds in objective time—the Xul huntership had been under fire by the massed MIEF fleet. While the Commonwealth's targeting AIs were being careful not to hit areas probed by the cloud of Spymaster penetrators, they'd been bombarding other parts of the Xul Nightmare, if only to keep it from engaging the Commonwealth fleet at close range and destroying it—a necessary tactical trade-off.

A part of Ramsey-Thoth was aware of cascades of data washing through the realm of the simulated coral reef like an incoming storm tide. Portions of the Nightmare's hull were failing, and the main engineering core had been seriously damaged. The black hole at the heart of the hunter-ship's power systems would be released from its magnetic containment at any moment. When that happened, the ship's structure would very swiftly fail.

Mind—the Mind of the ship—was maneuvering the huge vessel back through the stargate.

No one knew for certain what would happen when the bodies of fleet intelligence officers were on one side of a stargate, and their disembodied minds were on the other. The physics of the stargates were not well understood, but it *was* known that the orbiting of pinpoint-sized microsingularities within a stargate's ring created the special discontinuity that allowed passage across the gate interface, that matter passed through easily, but that radiation—including radio signals and visible light—did not. The only way to communicate from one side of a gate to the other—other than through the physical passage of message drones, of course—was to use field-entangled QCC communications which, theoretically, could connect with one another anywhere in the universe *without* traversing the space in between. Quantum-Coupled Comm units were large and complex, however, suitable for larger starships, but too large for fighters, to say nothing of the slender, 2-meter length of a K-794 Spymaster.

If they wanted to get their intelligence treasure-trove back to the *Hermes*, they would need to transmit it before they completed the passage back to Carson Space.

As he emerged from the depths of the reef, he was aware of a new and ominous component of the virtual reef . . . shadowy gray shapes circling the flashing schools of fish.

Sharks. The Xul were aware of attempts to penetrate their data structures and networks, and had evolved means of dealing with those intrusions. Within the symbology evolved within Ramsey's personal net, those defensive routines appeared as large and hungry sharks.

It was definitely time to withdraw.

Rumor and popular myth held that when an operator linked into an enemy system was discovered, or if the alien network itself were suddenly destroyed, or, indeed, if the mind crossed to the other side of a stargate interface, the shock of being cut off from his organic brain could kill him. That was simply not true; his body was alive and well protected back within the intelligence center of the *Hermes*. If his link with the Xul computer was cut off, he would simply wake up back there, as if emerging from a deep and dream-filled sleep.

But there *was* a danger. The organic brain could not tell the difference between virtual reality and Reality, could not know the difference between illusion, memory, or a data feed and the actual input from the body's natural senses. The human mind required a bridge to safely extricate itself from the alien mental environment. Sudden destruction of the target, or an attack by enemy defenses, could so shock the human psyche that serious damage was the result. Intelligence operatives *had* suffered serious emotional trauma when things went wrong on a Penetrator op.

Insanity or, at the very least, serious neurosis, was always a possibility.

Ramsey usually tried not to think about the possibilities. He highly valued his mind, its sharpness, its responsiveness, its clarity, and, for him, at least, death was preferable to insanity.

The sharks had identified him. Somehow, he must have given himself away within the embrace of the data storage reef.

"We need to withdraw," he told Thoth. "*Now. . . .*"

"The threat has been noted," the Thoth part of his mind replied. "I'm initiating—"

The sharks never reached him. Instead, the Xul ship itself, pounded by volley upon volley from the Commonwealth fleet, had finally begun to collapse.

Worse, he could feel the odd sense of discontinuity as the
huntership crossed the stargate interface.

"Transmit!" he yelled, ignoring the need for stealth.
"Now! . . ."

And then his conscious world came crashing in upon
him.

7

1506.1111

UCS Hermes
Stargate
Carson Space
0816 hrs, GMT

From General Alexander's electronic viewpoint on board
the *Hermes*, it appeared that the tide had definitely turned.
As the Xul *Nightmare*-class huntership began to crumple,
folding itself into its own rogue microsingularity in a burst
of hard gamma radiation, he allowed himself the exhilara-
tion of knowing the Commonwealth had won.

"There he goes," Taggart's voice said.

"I see him, Liam. Did our penetrators get clear?"

"Not sure yet, Marty," Taggart replied. "Lots of telemetry
coming through." The admiral paused, studying the streams
of incoming data. "Yeah . . . I think we hit the jackpot with
this one!"

"I want verification that our people are out of there."
Sending human minds in virtual reality into the very bowels
of Xul hunterships seemed to Alexander to be an incredibly
high-risk proposition. If the Xul could pattern the minds of
humans on captured starships and upload them into their
own virtual realities, they could do the same with human
emulator software penetrating their own networks. Only two
factors made the idea worthwhile in his mind—the amount

of sheer data these raids could return, and the fact that the target ship, by his express order, was about to be destroyed in any case. Alexander would not allow humans—even downloaded human copies—to endure that kind of imprisonment, that kind of terror and pain.

"No information yet, General. We'll need to wake them up, take them through the usual post-mission debrief. It'll take time. . . ."

"Just make damned sure we get them back," he snapped. "Their minds as well as their bodies! And I want to see an analysis on what they managed to pick up as soon as one is available."

"Right, Marty." Taggart had that whatever-you-say-General tone to his mental voice, one Alexander had heard plenty of times before. It was the tone of voice one reserved for a micromanaging CO, or an officer who was telling his people how to do jobs that they knew damned well how to do.

The hell with it. He didn't care what Taggart thought, or anyone else, for that matter. Operation Clusterstrike had been *his*, suggested by him and largely planned by his command constellation. He wanted to be in on the pay-off, wanted to know what the Penetrators had gleaned from the Xul Nightmare.

He also needed something to show Yarlocke and her crowd back at Defense, something positive.

If he didn't, 1MIEF would be recalled, and that would have some very bad consequences indeed.

Senate Committee Deliberation Chamber
Commonwealth Government Center,
EarthRing
1025 hrs, GMT

Cyndi Yarlocke always enjoyed the view from this largest of the deliberation chambers within the Government Center. The walls were opaque, of course, but the entire surrounding viewall and the room's vaulted ceiling were set to transmit seamless imagery from optical scanners mounted on the Ring's outer framework.

The effect was that of transparent walls looking out into space. High on one wall, Earth hung against a backdrop of stars, impossibly beautiful, impossibly fragile, a marble, illuminated now from the right and showing only half its surface, of ocean-blue and intricate swirls of cloud-white. Beyond, its half-full phase mimicking Earth's, the Moon hung in silvery splendor.

If you looked closely, the scattered lights of cities could be picked out on the dark sides of both. It was dawn over eastern North America; the megopoli of Vancouver, Portseattle, and the two Californias drew the Pacific coastline in myriad points of cool, white light, strung together on a luminous, tightly woven net, like shining drops of dew on a spider's web.

Since the very first tentative voyages to the Moon, that view of Earth seen from space had been an icon of fragile and delicate beauty, of oceans and clouds, of ocher deserts and green plains and wrinkled mountains and bright-lit cities all gathered together in a single, tiny sphere of intense color no larger than a fist held at arm's length.

More delicate still, though, were the Rings. . . .

They encircled Earth at roughly Geosynch, some 35,700 kilometers above the planet's equator. Beginning as an accretion of artificial space habs and modules and orbital stations, the ring complex had been under construction since the middle of the 24th Century, shortly after the Armageddon incident with the Xul huntership. Likely it would *always* be under construction, as more and more of the infrastructure of Earth's civilization moved off-planet and into space, as more and more manufactories and power stations and shipyards and planetoid mining centers and ecohabitats were wired in.

The Rings were not solid structures, of course. Human technology had not yet reached a stage where it could even contemplate the construction of a single ring-structure over seventeen billion kilometers in circumference! Like the far vaster rings of Saturn, EarthRing consisted of individual units orbiting Earth in Geosynch; an invisible web of nano-extruded diamondthread, each strand only a few carbon atoms thick, held many of the different sections together, motionless relative to one another, though others were free-orbiting. Some of the units, like Commonwealth Government Center itself, were huge, sprawling in labyrinthine complexities across hundreds of kilometers; others were the size of a single small living unit, or smaller.

Together, in their billions, their lights and reflective surfaces created EarthRing, just visible as a wispy streak of light, thread-thin where it bisected Earth, brighter—like a tightly ordered, extremely narrow Milky Way—until it seemed to double back upon itself, growing into an immense arch to connect with Government Center. Four space elevators connected the Ring with the surface, but those were too slender to be seen with the naked eye; Commonwealth Government Center was close to the orbital terminus of the Quito elevator, less than eighty kilometers away, in fact, but even at that distance the 36,000-kilometer sky-to-ground thread was quite invisible.

As always, Yarlocke was moved by the overwhelming sense of *fragility* presented by the vista stretched across the Deliberation Chamber's walls. More than once, EarthRing had been called the single greatest wonder of Humankind, a summation of the richness of human civilization and technology rendered visible.

Both as a senator of the Human Commonwealth and as the Chair of the Senate Defense Appropriations Committee, Yarlocke considered human civilization to be her special and personal responsibility. The seeming delicacy of that vista, of world and far-flung gossamer Ring set against the backdrop of stars, was far more objective than most citizens were willing to admit. It was up to her, and a few of her fellow senators, to keep that fragile globe and its ecosystem safe, a charge she regarded as a sacred trust.

And that meant reining in certain senior military personnel, men and women who meant well, certainly, but who did not understand the terrible danger currently faced by all of Humankind.

The counter to that danger, she knew, was not military force, not Marines and warships . . . and certainly not blowing up distant suns as though the very stars of heaven were disposable!

No. The Xul threat could *only* be countered by understanding and diplomacy. Cyndi Collins Yarlocke was as certain of that one fact as she could be of anything.

"The other members of the committee are beginning to link in, Cyndi." Harry, her personal AI, spoke within her thoughts.

"Let them wait," she replied. She did know how to make a proper entrance.

"And Senators Armandez and Tillman are waiting outside."

"Go ahead and let them in," she said after a moment. She preferred having this glorious room to herself, but there would be time for rubbernecking later. Word would be coming back from the Marine expeditionary force very soon now, she knew, and she needed to make sure the other members of the Appropriations Committee knew what she was about to do.

The Senate Committee Deliberation Chamber was dominated by a long, oval table and deeply cushioned link chairs, though the whole assembly could sink back into the floor and be replaced by ranks of chairs in an auditorium setting for meetings requiring a quorum to be physically present. A door slid open, and Jon Armandez and Lester Tillman walked in. "Hello, Cyndi," Tillman said with a grin. Armandez merely nodded, cold.

"Gentlemen," she said. "Is anyone else going to be here in the flesh?"

"I don't think so, Senator," Tillman replied, shrugging. "Bad timing. Most of the committee is off-Ring right now. Summer holidays, you know."

She made an unpleasant face. "Holidays. Our world faces utter destruction, and the people charged with her protection go off on vacation."

"Some would say, Madam Senator," Armandez said evenly, "that the Marines are doing a pretty fair job of that already."

"Save it for the debating floor, Jon," Yarlocke said. "When you have an audience that might care."

She watched as the two senators took chairs at the table, leaning back and placing the palms of their left hands on the link pad embedded in each chair's arm. Both men appeared to be asleep.

Armandez, she thought, could be a problem. Most of the other senators on the Appropriations Committee could be reasoned with, but Jon Armandez had a kid in the Commonwealth Marines. The guy had always been a militarist—he represented *Ishtar*, for God's sake!—and had squared off against Yarlocke more than once in debates over appropriations intended to keep 1MIEF up and running, but the problem had become significantly worse since his daughter had enlisted.

Damn it, the Senate ought to enact a law excluding people with close relatives in the military from running for public office. It constituted a conflict of interest, and ought to be prohibited. She'd never get a bill like that past the pro-military clique, though. Right now, the military—especially the Marines—were popular. If she was going to ram her proposal through, she was going to need to get more of those people on her side, and that was going to be tough.

She wished Marie Devereaux were still here. The former senator from Quebec had been a vehemently outspoken critic of the militarists, a powerful speaker, and a persuasive advocate of the cause of peace.

Not persuasive enough, perhaps. Despite her opposition, the Senate had approved sending 1MIEF into Xul-owned space, and later cheered the news of the wholesale destruction of entire star systems. Devereaux had been voted out of office six years ago, in the elections of 2880, and had run as a candidate for Commonwealth President in both '80 and in '84.

As if any Québecois could ever attain *that* office. There
were still too many sectarian divides within the patchwork
of states that made up the Commonwealth. Too many citizens resident in the old United States mistrusted the Québecois and their political agendas, and too many Québecois
remembered—or thought they did—the occupation of parts
of Quebec by the then-U.S. back in the 21st Century. National memories, it seemed, took a long time to die.

Still, she thought, it might be worthwhile to support Devereaux's presidential bid in exchange for some political favors. *Especially* in terms of moving some of the fence-sitters
in the Senate chambers over to her way of thinking. She
made a mental note to arrange a virtual meeting with the
woman, perhaps later, after the upcoming meeting.

Eight more senators wandered into the Deliberation Chamber, greeting her with nods or a few words, and settling into
the link chairs. Durant. Hartov. Stevens. She knew them all.
Many were fence-sitters, uncommitted, as yet, to either side
of the debate. She needed to reach them, somehow.

Yarlocke took a last look at Earth, suspended in space in
fragile glory.

She needed their votes in order to save the Earth, and all
of human civilization.

It was time. She'd kept them waiting long enough. Taking
one of the empty chairs, she sat down, dropped the backrest
almost flat, and placed her hand over the link plate. Instantly,
the vista of Earth and Ring vanished, replaced by an inner
menu selection. At her mental command, Harry opened an
electronic door for her and she stepped into a virtual assembly.

The assembly room appeared to be in deep space, the
spiral of the Galaxy aglow with gentle light hanging in emptiness. Twenty-four senators were waiting for her, visible as
a constellation of gleaming icons, each tagged with tiny
windows displaying biographical data and her personal notes
on each.

"Sorry I'm late, people," Yarlocke said as she entered the
icon swarm. "I was in conference, couldn't get free."

If any in the swarm doubted her excuse, they didn't make

it public. As she merged with the assembly, taking up a position at the swarm's center, each of the twenty-four icons revealed itself as a single bright star surrounded by hundreds of lesser points of light.

The Senate Defense Appropriations Committee was a small government within a government, consisting now of several thousand humans and AIs, working out of their own hab physically attached to Government Center. Out of almost five hundred representatives in the Commonwealth Senate, forty-one sat on the committee. The rest of that small army was made up of aides, Senate staffers, AI secretaries, and the swelling bureaucracy that attended any organization of this type. Each senator had an entourage of his or her own, from human assistants down to personal data-mining netbots, as well as communication channels, many of them self-aware, that extended throughout both EarthRing and the cities of Earth herself. Those assistants were represented here by the lesser points of light, the senators by the brighter stars.

There were also several star clusters representing non-voting members of the committee, notably General Dorrity, the senior liaison officer with Defense. Dorrity was trouble . . . another Marine, and therefore invested with an inflated sense of loyalty to Alexander and his vandals.

With all of that communications technology, Yarlocke thought, it ought to be possible to get a better showing at these meetings. The Commonwealth Senate, she knew well, tended to be a peripatetic bunch, and it could take—she smiled inwardly at the thought—an act of Congress to get them to show up for a physical vote. In fact, over half of those attending this session were present within Government Center only *electronically,* rather than physically. Most were elsewhere within the Ring. A few were on Earth. This was an election year, and most of the members of the Commonwealth Senate were absorbed in the necessities of getting re-elected, and that meant actually being personally present within their districts.

Yarlocke understood campaigning and the attendant demands of politics, but sometimes it was difficult to get anything constructive done. Only a relatively small minority within the Senate actually recognized the danger now threatening Humankind. It would be up to her to convince, first, the Appropriations Committee . . . and then present the full Senate with a *fait accompli*.

But . . . it could only be done one step at a time. At least this time she'd been able to strong-arm enough of her fellow senators to attend—electronically, at least—to comprise a quorum. Twenty-five out of forty-one was a clear majority of the voting body.

The question now, though, was how many of those other twenty-four would be siding with her this morning?

"A quorum being present," an AI voice said within the minds gathered in the virtual chamber, *"the Senate Defense Appropriations Committee, meeting this fifteenth day of June, 2886 of the Common Era, is now in session. The honorable Senator Cyndi Collins Yarlocke presiding. . . ."*

"Thank you all for coming," she said, addressing the group. "By now, most of you will have seen the initial reports from Cluster Space. General Alexander, Admiral Taggart, and the 1st MIEF are reporting another victory over the Xul."

She sensed a stir through the gathered assembly, and smiled to herself. Only a few had seen that news item. Good. Perhaps she could use their surprise to her advantage.

"Gentlemen, ladies, fellow sentients . . . by now all of you know my position concerning the current war. It is a war we have been prosecuting now for nine years, and with little to show for the staggering investment in money, ships, and lives. It is a war, unfortunately, that has numerous supporters, thanks to misinformation and certain misconceptions. Even more unfortunately, electronic polls demonstrate conclusively that the majority of Humankind cares little one way or another about this war. They do not feel threatened by the Xul. And, indeed, why should they? The last time the Xul posed any threat to humanity whatsoever was in 2314, some six centuries ago, near enough.

"Gentlemen, ladies, fellow sentients, I submit that it is

time at last to end all funding for 1MIEF. It is time to make peace with the Xul. And it is time to bring our young people home from the stars." She paused for a moment, anticipating the storm. "The Chair will now entertain debate. . . ."

And there was a storm, as dozens of star-icons vied with one another for the Chair's acknowledgement. Harry indicated to her that Senator James Witter, of North California, had been first off the mark, but Witter was already solidly in Yarlocke's pocket. His constituency was nestled in between the military-heavy senatorial districts of Portseattle and South California, and he owed her a number of favors for her support in the Alameda Scandal two years ago.

Instead, she decided to get the worst over with first. "The Chair recognizes the Appropriations Committee liaison with the secretary of defense, General Dorrity."

"Madam Chairperson," Dorrity's voice said. "Just how in hell do you plan on getting the Xul to sit down with us at the peace table?"

Rather than give the answer herself, she decided to let one of her supporters provide a response. That way, she could maintain the image of . . . not neutrality, not when her views on the issue were so well known . . . but of fairness. Balance. Even-handedness.

"The Chair recognizes Senator Ralston."

"General Dorrity," Ralston said, "how do we know they won't talk peace until we ask them? The Xul are intelligent beings, members of an extremely old and sophisticated species, one that was star-faring before the engineering of humanity half a million years ago. As rational beings, they will surely see the advantages of peaceful coexistence, now that we have, ah, more than adequately demonstrated our ability to defend ourselves."

"Senator, with all due respect, the Xul are not rational, not as humans define the word."

"Racist paranoia, General."

"If by 'racist' you mean I possess a human viewpoint, then I plead guilty. If there's one thing we've learned about the Xul, it is that they are not human, and do not in any way *think* like humans. In fact, 'racist paranoia' is a decent description of how *they* think. Any intelligence not of the Xul must be exterminated. That simple concept appears to be a fundamental trope for them: non-Xul are dangerous, and must be exterminated for the survival of the race. We can *not* reason with someone who has such a fundamentally different way of looking at the universe than we do."

"Again, General, we have not tried! When did we last make a genuine attempt to *communicate* with these people, as opposed to going in and blowing up one of their suns?"

"The Wings of Isis attempted to communicate, Senator," Dorrity said coldly. "The *Argo* attempted to communicate. There have been others."

"Ancient history, General. That was before we demonstrated that we can defend ourselves with the Euler triggerships. They know we can hurt them. Now it's time to talk with them."

"What passes for communication with those monsters is to reduce the person trying to talk to a pattern of electronic information inside one of their computers."

Yarlocke listened with only half her awareness. The arguments were old, familiar, and age-worn, the continuation of a debate that had been going on for the better part of a decade. Indeed, she suspected that a search of the congressional records would turn up the same tired arguments going back five hundred years or more. The militarists, conservatives both in the government and in the military, were convinced you couldn't reason with the Xul, that they were more programmed machine than rational and sentient lifeforms. More liberal wings of the government, the Pax Astras and others, liked to point out that even human-designed AIs, many of them, were sentient and self-aware beings, and that, except where they were deliberately restricted by their programming, often were capable of self-determination and could rewrite their own code. They could be convinced, in other words, by a rational argument, just like humans. If that was true of AI software, why wouldn't it be true of the Xul as well?

Of course, Yarlocke had to admit that many *humans* in

her experience, unlike the more advanced AIs, could not be convinced by rational argument. Dorrity, for instance, was driven by sentiment for his beloved Marine Corps, and by such intangibles as *duty, loyalty,* and *honor.* Not that those were bad things in and of themselves, necessarily. But they could be damned inconvenient when the person you were arguing with couldn't let go and see the bigger picture.

Yarlocke absolutely believed in loyalty, but she never let such niceties interfere with her duty as she saw it.

Nor was she about to let someone else's sense of duty or loyalty get in her way.

As the debate ground on, Yarlocke had one of her personal data hunters move through the network, polling current vote probabilities. Out of twenty-five voting members on the committee, ten were either committed to the Pax personally, or had promised her their vote in return for other favors. That left her three short of a majority if a vote were called now.

Eight in the assembly were solidly militarist, and five short of a majority. The swing votes would come from the seven remaining members of the committee who had not yet declared for either side. Calling up the files and voting records of those seven, she studied them closely. Two, Donahue and Hernandez, were Social Democrats, with voting records that tended slightly toward the liberal side. One, Raynor, was an outspoken member of the Church of Mind. While religion wasn't supposed to enter into senatorial deliberations, Yarlocke knew that religion shaped the man. The C of M put a heavy emphasis on the unity of all thinking creatures, and on that basis alone Raynor might be open to reason.

The other four were Independents, and which way their vote would go was anyone's guess.

The data were encouraging, though. Three of the seven might well be induced to vote her way, given the proper inducement, and that would be her majority. She could reasonably assume that two of the four Independents might vote her way simply out of chance, which gave her a decent margin.

She would not allow herself to feel complacent, however.

A lot of work remained before she could declare victory in this issue.

But she did feel confident of final victory.

The 1MIEF would be brought home and disbanded. The unjust war with the Xul would be ended. Humankind would enjoy the blessings of peace for the first time in centuries.

And Senator Cyndi Collins Yarlocke would at last have her chance at her *real* goal. . . .

UCS Hermes
Stargate
Carson Space
1445 hrs, GMT

"Congratulations, General."

"Eh? For what, Cara?"

"On your victory, of course. The data are . . . promising."

Alexander leaned back from his desk, breaking palm contact with the battlenet link. He'd been going over the casualty and ship loss reports for three hours straight, now, and he needed a break.

Cara was the name of his primary EA, or Electronic Aide, a personal secretary responsible for sorting, manipulating, and storing the blizzard of downloaded electronic information, official and personal calls, and virtual meetings he faced each and every day. She'd been with him, through numerous upgrades, ever since his days at the Academy, when he'd been a snot-nosed j.g. with more enthusiasm than sense.

A long time ago . . .

"Thank you, Cara. That may be premature, however."

"The final tally lists fourteen Xul huntership destroyed by direct combat," Cara said, a crispness to her mental voice. *"Given the strength of the enemy forces, that compares very favorably with the loss of thirty-three Commonwealth and allied ships, of all types. And the probe data suggests that the enemy has withdrawn from Cluster Space."*

"Withdrawn, possibly," Alexander replied. "But not destroyed. Nova Bloodlight was a fizzle."

"The nova's yield was not that of a larger main sequence star, certainly," she told him. *"But our BDA probes have picked up evidence of considerable damage in the Cluster Space system. At least two hundred Xul hunterships appear to be adrift and lifeless over there. And the others have fled."*

"Correction," Alexander told her. "The others appear to have withdrawn, probably just until the local star quiets down. They will almost certainly be back." He sighed. "Yarlocke and her jackals are gong to be all over this one."

"I believe, General," Cara told him, *"that you are being too pessimistic."*

"Time will tell. Meanwhile, we need to get the rest of those Battle Damage Assessments turned out. I need something to show SecDef."

"Will you be transmitting that via CQQ, sir?"

He thought about that. "No. We'll translate *Hermes* back to Earth's L-3. We can take a few of the more badly damaged fleet elements back with us, and bring back a load of supplies. Maybe take the *Barton* back as well, if we have serious casualties who need treatment at NMH EarthRing. And I think I'm going to want to talk to both General Dorrity and Wilson in person."

Wilson was SecDef, the Commonwealth's secretary of defense, and ultimately Alexander's boss, at least underneath the supreme command of President Stiner.

The balance of political power within the Commonwealth had swung back and forth over the years. Theoretically, the legislative, executive, and judicial checks and balances were supposed to preserve that balance in a system that went back over a thousand years to the original United States of America. In practice, though, there was a constant ebb and flow of political power. During the dark years of the mid-27th Century, the Commonwealth Presidency had evolved into the Office of the Chief Executive, with almost dictatorial powers during the first interstellar conflict with the PanEuropean-Chinese Alliance. Since then, things had shifted the other way, and the President now was widely seen as a figurehead only, with the *real* political clout vested with the Commonwealth Senate.

Someday, Alexander reflected, things would swing back to the President . . . or to the Supreme Court . . . or even the wagging tail of the Legislative House. As a military man sworn to uphold the constitutions both of the United States and the Humankind Commonwealth, he by law could have no *public* opinion on the matter.

Privately, he thought the demagoguery of the Senate was a piss-poor way to prosecute a war . . . almost as poor as having the war run by one civilian with delusions of grandeur. That was why there *had* to be a balance, to keep *any* one group or individual from acquiring too much power and misusing it through misplaced ambition or ignorance or both.

The problem of the moment lay with the Senate—in particular with the senior senator from Maine, Cyndi Yarlocke . . . *the Warlock,* as he thought of her in strict privacy. The woman hated the military, hated the Marines, and hated him. She was worse than Senator Devereaux of a few years back in her determination to shut down both 1MIEF and the Corps. Through Dorrity and the Defense Department, a fair-sized cadre of senators still supported 1MIEF's efforts against the Xul, but Alexander knew they were fighting a constant rear-guard action against the Warlock and her misguided personality cult.

He also knew that the Warlock's minions were going to hammer at what they would perceive as a failure out here in Cluster Space—huge losses, the less-than-complete destruction of a Xul node, and the escape of a *very* large number of Xul ships. They would be seeking political advantage in the outcome of Operation Clusterstrike, of that he was certain. Alexander would need to marshal every positive aspect of the op to defend himself and his people.

"It does look like we have one piece of solid and useful intel, General. From the Penetrator teams."

"Really? What?"

Cara opened a window in his mind. Alexander found himself looking into a vista filled with stars, swarms of stars, stars gathered in teeming millions, like the inside of a globular cluster . . . no, like the Galactic Core itself. The vista was so filled with stars and a hazy, red-hued light it was difficult to make out individual details, but in the center of the vista was . . . *something*. Something strange, and very large.

"What the hell is that?" he asked.

"It's the center of the Galaxy, General," Cara told him. *"The Galactic Core. And it just may be the core, the very heart, of the Xul Empire. . . ."*

8

Freeport Tower
Bahama Banks, Earth
0914 hrs, local

Garroway stepped out onto the open concourse, enjoying the rush of salt-laden breeze, enjoying the feeling of un-linked openness that simply was not possible on board ship. Gravity tugged at him more strongly than usual; most ships maintained internal fields of one G, but they'd kept the gravity at a comfortable Martian one-third on board the *Barton*.

The docs had warned him to take it easy during his leave Earthside, clucking and fussing over his decision to go there straight off the hospital ship. No matter. He was here, and even standing up to Earth's one standard gravity felt great with his new legs.

In fact, the pair of legs he'd left on board the Xul fortress in Cluster Space had not been entirely organic. Nine years ago, at the Battle of the Nova, he'd been exposed to a killing blast of radiation from an exploding sun. They'd had to pare away a lot of organic tissue after his rescue; what they replaced it with had been neither purely organic nor purely machine, but a closely woven blend of the two grown from his own cells and from MAT, or medinano-derived artificial tissue.

They acted, looked, and felt like the legs with which he'd been born, with the same neural responses, the same strength and sensitivity to touch, temperature, or pain. But they also responded directly to controlling impulses from his implants, and that was especially valuable to a combat Marine. For short periods he could boost their strength and endurance, letting him run farther and jump higher. He could deliberately shut down feelings of pain or of exhaustion. And they worked automatically to shut off excessive bleeding.

For some time now, he knew, the Corps had actually been debating whether or not to encourage *all* Marines to have their arms and legs both replaced with new ones grown from MAT, but the very idea was controversial, and had several times brought the Corps under the fire of heavy criticism from various civilian quarters.

So far as Garroway was concerned, he doubted that he would have been able to cut off his own legs inside that fortress if they *hadn't* been artificial. It had still hurt like hell until the overrides kicked in, and he'd been in serious danger of decompression until his armor had sealed itself, but he'd known that his Corps-issued legs, as he'd referred to them, could be replaced once they got him back to a hospital facility like the *Barton*.

He flexed his legs, then did a couple of deep knee bends. They felt *good*.

And it felt good to be alive. . . .

"It's okay, Gare," a voice said behind him. "We're on leave. No morning PT!"

He turned, grinning. Nikki Armandez had just emerged from the terminal. Like him, she was wearing her Marine dress blacks.

"So?" he told her. "You can take the Marine out of the Corps, but you can't take the Corps out of the Marine."

"How are the new legs?" she asked.

"Good as new."

"That's because they *are* new." She stepped closer, moving into his embrace. "Have I thanked you, lately, by the way?"

"Only about a dozen times so far this morning." He kissed her.

They were not, strictly speaking, a couple in the usual

sense of the word. They'd been squadmates and friends before the Cluster Space op, but hadn't become close until they'd found themselves in adjacent recovery quarters on board the *Barton*. By that time, they'd already made the transit back to the Sol System, the hospital ship tucked away within the cavernous hold of the immense HQ ship *Hermes*. Nikki had been recovering from pulmonary damage caused by explosive decompression when her suit had been breached in the fortress, and Garroway was learning to use his new legs. They'd started taking walks together in the *Barton*'s arboretum. One thing had led quite naturally to another, and several days ago they'd become lovers.

Garroway hoped it wasn't *just* gratitude for his having dragged her out of the fortress in Cluster Space. He liked to think that he would have done as much for *any* fellow Marine.

The fact that she was smart and fun to talk to, easy on the eyes, and a rambunctious delight in bed didn't hurt at all, however.

They stood side by side on the concourse halfway up the side of Freeport Tower, leaning against the safety railing and looking out across translucent azure waters. Some patches of green and clusters of white buildings to the northeast and to the south marked dry land.

"Why the hell would anyone build a spaceport way out *here*?" Armandez wondered. "It's the middle of the ocean!"

"Damfino, Nikki," Garroway replied. "Maybe just for the view."

He did a quick check of the local datanet. There was a lot of history stored there, but access was clumsy and primitive, requiring nested layers of menu selections rather than a simple mental request. Earthside datanets were more primitive than up on the Ring, or anywhere in the fleet, for that matter. He would have to sort through the local library later.

"I gather there were a lot of islands around here pre-Armageddonfall," he volunteered. "Pretty big ones. Those islands out there on the horizon would have been the high ground. Freeport Tower is supposed to be built atop a drowned city."

"Oh, like Miami?"

"Yeah. And parts of Washington, D.C., and London, and a lot of other low-lying coastal cities all over Earth. Maybe the locals just refused to evacuate after the sea levels rose."

"It *is* gorgeous," she said. She pointed. "Think we can rent one of those?"

"Those" were a flotilla of sailboats slicing through the water to the east, low, lean hulls of various designs topped by colorful, triangular sails. Garroway and Armandez had just arrived at Freeport on one of the regular EarthRing shuttles. It was interesting to step from one of those silvery agrav transport pods, representative of the very highest transport technologies, and see people engaged in one of the most ancient of all forms of travel, skimming the water with the wind alone as motive force.

"Not this time through," he told her. "We're scheduled on a skimmersub for Miami. Departure at 1130 hours. We won't have time."

"Maybe this trip, though?" They had two weeks' leave, two glorious weeks, to explore ancient Earth.

"Maybe." Garroway wasn't entirely sure about the whole idea of tricking the wind to take you where you wanted to go. He knew modern sailing craft had their own on-board AIs to do the actual sail handling, but it still seemed an unlikely way of getting from point A to point B.

Aiden Garroway had been born in the 7-Ring orbital complex up in EarthRing. Until he'd joined the Marine Corps and gone to Noctis Labyrinthus on Mars for boot camp, he'd never been out of EarthRing.

Since that day nearly ten years ago, now, he'd been to quite a few other places—to special training facilities on Luna, at AresRing, and out at Europa. He'd served a tour at Ishtar, the habitable moon of the gas giant Marduk orbiting Lalande 21185, some eight and half light years from Earth, and a year ago he'd made E-7—gunnery sergeant—at the orbital complex over Eostre, the fourth planet of Epsilon Indi, eleven light years out.

His *first* tour, though, had taken him to Puller 659, several hundred light years from Earth, then to Aquila Space, twelve hundred light years out, and finally to Starwall, estimated at eighteen thousand light-years from Sol.

And his last mission, with Operation Clusterstrike, had taken him outside of the main body of the Galaxy entirely, thirty thousand light years, more or less, from the spot where he was standing now.

So since becoming a Marine, Garroway had been around. But never, in his twenty-nine objective years of life, had he been to Earth.

As a Ringer, he'd grown up with certain preconceptions about the blue-and-white globe hanging eternally in the star-dusted sky. The technologies used on Earth—especially computer and information net technologies—were primitive by Ring standards. From a Ringer's perspective, the people were . . . dirty. Not quite civilized, not quite educated, not quite culturally attuned. The unspoken assumption was that you had to be just a little crazy to *prefer* living on Earth.

Garroway doubted that the differences, if any, were all that pronounced. Sure, Earth's Globalnet might not be up to spec compared to the Ring's electronic data informational services, communications, entertainment, and so on, but it was still part of the electronic web spanning the entire Solar System. It worked. It wasn't as if Earthers sat in caves, grunting at one another over half-gnawed mammoth bones, whatever the jokes to that effect might claim.

As for the people, Garroway knew that a lot of Earthers preferred a low-tech life, that some even refused cerebral implants and the other necessities of modern existence. From his perspective, or from the perspective of *any* citizen of a space hab or colony, that made them a little weird. Garroway had been forced to live for three months without any implants or cerebral enhancement at all during his recruit training, and doing without had been like kicking an addictive drug. How anyone could *want* to live like that . . .

But he tended to be easygoing about the strangenesses preferred by others, and he was at least intellectually prepared to accept that his prejudices were not necessarily based upon fact.

Leaning against the railing overlooking the surging blue-green of the ocean, he drew a deep breath. The air seemed clean enough, though it tasted strange. Salty, with an undercurrent of what he supposed was seaweed or rotting vegetation, perhaps. It wasn't unpleasant. Just . . . *different.*

And the people. Most were tourists on their way up- or down-Ring. They wore a bizarre mix of fashion, from high-tech jumpsuits to sheaths of liquid light to gleaming bits of technological jewelry incompletely merged with their flesh to complete nudity save for an oily sheen of solar-protective nano. Hair styles varied as well, from the elaborate and brightly colored decorative to complete depilation. Local people, though, were easily picked out from the crowd, wearing simple textiles, their skins sun-bronzed almost to black. Most wore broad-brimmed hats woven from some local plant fiber. They moved among the tourists like shadows; the tourists, Garroway noticed, tended to move aside to avoid them without really *seeing* them.

"So . . . are your folks Earthside, Gare?" Armandez wanted to know.

"Uh-uh. They're up in EarthRing. The Giangrecos line family."

"Giangrecos? I thought your name was Garroway."

"It is. My birth mother was Estelle Garroway. She's dead now, but like most folks she kept her family name after marrying into the line. And on my naming day, I chose Garroway for myself."

She shook her head. "Naming day? I don't . . ."

"When two people get married, and they each keep their last names? A child of the marriage gets to choose what his last name will be—mother's or father's. Usually around his twelfth birthday."

"Where I come from, the woman takes the man's last name."

"They used to do that on Earth. That, or hyphenate the two names. Most cultures on Earth and in EarthRing nowadays have a naming day ceremony, or something like it. Sort of like a bar mitzvah. 'Today I am a man.' 'Today I choose who I am and how I shall be known to others.'"

"It must be confusing."

"Nah. I think things drifted that way to get away from the old idea that marriage meant ownership. Where are you from, anyway?"

"Ishtar, originally."

"Ah." That explained a lot. A sizeable human colony had been established in the Lalande 21185 system, consisting of both emigrants from Earth and the descendents of human slaves taken to that tiny, tide-locked world thousands of years ago by the alien An. They'd been forcibly emancipated only seven centuries ago, in the mid-22nd Century, when U.S. Marines had arrived and beaten the An in a sharp, short war. Today's human population on Ishtar consisted of a blend of transplanted humanities, of cultures ancient and modern.

"My family came to EarthRing a few years ago, though," she went on. "Talk about culture shock! I'm still getting used to it!"

He laughed. "So that's why you joined the Marines, right?"

She punched him in the shoulder. "You!"

"Ow! But it's true, isn't it? The Corps has its own comfy little microculture. We have our own way of doing things, our own way of thinking."

"Everyone's different, I guess," she said, sounding defensive. "On Ishtar, we don't see a woman taking the man's name as a mark of ownership."

He shrugged. "Different cultures. On Jana women don't even *have* last names."

"On Jana women *are* property, almost."

"It's that way on a lot of the worlds in the Theocracy." He thought about it a moment. The varied microcultures of EarthRing all possessed a strong cultural bias toward the ethic of diversity. Different was *good*, in other words, a principle that encouraged social experimentation throughout the medley of Ring cultures and among the human colonies on other worlds.

But from a Marine's point of view, that principle could sometimes be taken too far—as it had with support for the Islamic Theocracy, a product of cultural diversity that itself tolerated diversity about as well as it tolerated free speech. "Just because a culture is different doesn't mean it's good or healthy," he added after a moment.

"Of course. 'Good' is a value judgment imposed by the culture of the person making the judgment."

"I didn't know you were a philosopher."

"There's a lot you don't know about me, Gare. . . . *At least not yet.*"

"Mm. I'm looking forward to the download. Anyway," he went on, "you were asking about my family name. The Garroways have been around for quite a while and both the male and female carriers of the name have kept it going. There've been Garroways in the Corps for God knows how long, going way, way back. At least, that's what the family histories say. How about you?"

She shook her head. "Politicians run in my family, I'm afraid, not military." She didn't volunteer any further information, and Garroway didn't press.

"So you said your family is up on the Ring?" she asked. "Did you get to see them yet, this time back?"

"Um . . . no." He decided not to tell her that the Giangreco patriarch had kicked him out of the family when he'd enlisted. Delano Giangreco had been a member of the Reformed Church of the Ascended Pleiadean Masters, and a committed pacifist. None of *his* kids would be military.

"Oh, but you *have* to drop in and see them!"

"Why? Last time I was there, the Giangreco family had twenty-five spouses and a hundred and eighty-three kids and grandkids, plus a small army of cousins, in-laws, and hangers-on. I doubt that some of them even know I'm gone, ten years later." He looked away, watching sunlight beam and dazzle between the towering white mountains of cumulous clouds above the turquoise sea. "Besides, the Corps is my family now."

Another shuttle was coming down from EarthRing, a brilliant, silver speck drifting in from the southwest, then growing into a mirror-bright sphere as it approached Freeport Tower's upper deck landing platform.

"So," Garroway said, jerking himself back to reality. "You feel like getting something to eat?"

She nodded. "Sounds good. I could go with a bite of something. My stomach's still on Ring time."

He consulted his inner timekeeper. EarthRing kept time according to the ancient GMT standard, so his stomach was insisting that it was now mid-afternoon, even though the local time was just past 0930 hours.

"Let's find a place then, before the hungry swarms in that shuttle that just touched down get the same idea."

Senate Committee Deliberation Chamber
Commonwealth Government Center,
EarthRing
1422 hrs, GMT

"What you're saying, General," Cyndi Yarlocke said quietly, even sweetly, "is that you failed. Despite serious losses in ships and personnel, Operation Clusterstrike failed to make the target star explode, and left the Cluster Space system vulnerable to Xul exploitation."

"If you prefer to put it in those terms, Senator," Alexander said evenly, "yes. I would add that the operation is still under way, and that we have several options open to us, including—"

"The star that your expeditionary force was *supposed* to blow up," Yarlocke said, interrupting, "either did not explode, or did so with far less force than you anticipated. As a result, the massive Xul fleet in Cluster Space escaped. I believe that pretty much sums things up?"

Alexander bit back a sharp response. *Patience*, he told himself. What was it Tolstoy had written? "The strongest warriors are these: Time and Patience."

Tolstoy had never met Cyndi Yarlocke.

The Senate Deliberation Chamber had been chosen, Alexander was certain, so that his debriefing would be held on the Defense Committee's home ground, a bit of symbolism giving them a psychological advantage. It created and reinforced the illusion that 1MIEF was answering directly to this small group of powerful—and disapproving—men and women. Their public e-personae glowed with their coronae flammae, streaming auras of white and golden light projected as emblems of status and power. Alexander was authorized to wear the electronic emblem as well—indeed, regulations required it in certain circumstances—but he hated image and power games played in virtual reality even more than he disliked them in the real world. He'd chosen to make his appearance before the subcommittee in his Marine dress blacks, with only the rows of service ribbons on his chest glowing.

The virtual meeting chamber had been kept deliberately austere, perhaps to better show off the glow from all those high-level coronae. The five senators of the Defense Appropriations Subcommittee appeared to be hanging in a semicircle suspended in empty space, with a face-on view of the Galaxy shining behind them.

"Our science and battle damage assessment teams are still in the Cluster Space system," Alexander told them. "According to their initial reports, CS-1, the target star, did, in fact, blow off large portions both of its photosphere and of its outer convection zone, creating a shell of high-energy plasma expanding out from the core. The effect was more pronounced than a flare, but not as violent as a typical nova. Given that CS-1 was only about fifteen percent the mass of Earth's sun, the results were . . . satisfactory. As good as could be expected, let's say."

He flashed a quick mental request to Cara, his personal AI, who brought up a window displaying planetary data.

"According to our BDA teams," he continued, "CS-1 possessed a single planet, which we named Bloodlight I. Tidally locked to the primary. Diameter less than eight thousand kilometers. Rock and ice surface. Subsolar temperature in the 200-degree Kelvin range. Atmosphere primarily methane and nitrogen. Not exactly prime real estate.

"The Xul had a fairly large complex on the subsolar portion of the planet. That base was completely destroyed by the star's detonation, which stripped away the atmosphere and melted the rock and ice on which the base had been anchored. There is now very little of the structure left."

"The Xul fleet escaped, General," one of the senators said. His electronic ID gave his name as Senator James Witter, of the Commonwealth state of North California. "The idea, as presented to this subcommittee months ago, was that the Xul presence in Cluster Space would be eliminated."

"With respect, sir, the op plan we submitted to this subcommittee suggested that we might be able to deny Cluster Space to the enemy, and that we might cause considerable damage to his assets there. That's not the same as 'eliminated.' Our best estimates suggested that the Xul maintained an operational fleet in Cluster Space of around one thousand starships of various masses. The expeditionary force possessed fewer than one hundred fifty vessels, not counting fighters, drones, and minor combatants. We destroyed fourteen enemy vessels—"

"At a cost of thirty-three of our own ships," Senator Alan Connelly interrupted. "A loss ration of more than two to one. That is an unacceptable ratio, especially when some hundreds of Xul ships escaped the battle unscathed."

Alexander refrained from pointing out that, in terms of tonnage, at least, 1MIEF's losses were insignificant compared to those of the Xul with their kilometer-long monster hunterships. In any analyses of a battle's success or failure, everything depended on how you looked at it, on what statistical factors you chose to emphasize. These sharks were determined to paint Operation Clusterstrike as a failure. They would accept only those data that supported their preconceived worldview.

"You realize, General," Yarlocke went on, "that 1MIEF contains a majority of *all* Commonwealth military ships. The destruction of your command would leave Earth and all of Commonwealth space terribly vulnerable . . . not only to the Xul, but to other human interstellar nation-states not yet allied with us."

She meant, of course, the Chinese Hegemony and the Islamic Theocracy. A number of wars had been fought with both states over the past few centuries, and since the Alighan War of nine years ago, things had been simmering with the Theocrats—no open war, but no armistice, either.

Not for the first time, Alexander wondered if Humankind would ever get its house in order. Even the PanEuropean Republic, theoretically now an ally, couldn't be completely trusted, though they'd recently sent a contingent of heavy warships to reinforce 1MIEF. The South American Union had not yet committed either. The Russians, Japanese, and Indians supported the Commonwealth, but all of them had problems of their own right now—most of them involving the Chinese Hegemony—and were unlikely to be able to lend much in the way of support, either in fighting the Xuls or if another intra-human war broke out.

Any long-range military strategy formulated by the Commonwealth needed to take into account the possibility that they could be facing another war at any time, with the Chinese, the Theocrats, or both.

She appeared to be waiting for an answer. That much, at least, was encouraging. They might still hang him, but he'd be allowed to speak in his own defense.

"Senators," he said, "I'm very much aware of the current delicate political situation. My command constellation receives daily briefs from Commonwealth Intelligence. Believe me, I am as eager as any of you to preserve 1MIEF as a viable force, both against the Xul and against possible Islamic or Chinese threats. I submit that the mere existence of a hundred or so Commonwealth warships manned by crews with near constant combat experience over the past decade would give any other star nation pause before starting a war."

"Yes. Secretary of Defense Wilson has presented us with the same argument," Yarlocke said, disapproval tugging at her mental voice. "However, many of us in the Senate believe there is another way."

Here it comes, Alexander thought, masking the words carefully against unwanted transmission.

"What's coming?" Cara, his personal AI, asked.

The reason they dragged us in here for this asinine light show. "And what would that way be, Madam Senator?" he asked.

"It is time," Yarlocke said, "*past* time, in fact, to end this useless and dangerous confrontation with the Xul once and for all. The Galaxy is an enormous place, three to four hundred billion stars, tens of millions, even *hundreds* of millions of earthlike worlds, and we've seen no evidence whatsoever that the Xul even use planets like Earth. It's big enough that we can share."

"Uh-huh. And does the Commonwealth Senate believe it can convince the Xul of that?"

"That," Senator Ralston said, "is obstructionist thinking. Typical militarist thinking. We can't know until we've tried."

"I would have thought, Senator," Alexander said quietly, "that the Fermi Evidence was conclusive by now."

Eight centuries before, the physicist Enrico Fermi, according to a well-known anecdote, had asked the pregnant question, "Where are they?" He was referring to non-human galactic civilizations, conspicuous, at that time, by their absence. In the decades before spaceflight, there'd been only statistical probabilities suggesting that earthlike worlds, that life, that *mind* should be common in a Galaxy of hundreds of billions of suns, in a universe sixteen billion years old. The sky, Fermi reasoned, should be filled with the evidence of teeming civilizations far older than Humankind, with their radio signals and infrared leakage from titanic construction projects, with their starships, with evidence of engineering projects on an interstellar, even on a galactic scale.

Even if magical FTL drives remained forever impossible, technologies easily envisioned by 20th Century physicists suggested that, in the course of billions of years, the entire Galaxy could be explored and colonized many times over by civilizations only slightly in advance of Man.

And yet, Earth's skies of eight centuries past had remained eerily silent. The conclusion, that Humankind was the *only* technic civilization in the Galaxy, perhaps in the entire cosmos, seemed untenable simply and purely on statistical grounds. Hence, Fermi's Paradox: Where are they?

As humans had begun venturing off their birth world and into their own Solar System during the following century, the answer had begun to surface, fragmentary and incomplete at first, but chilling in its implications. Ruins and artifacts discovered half-buried in the sands of Mars and on the surface of Earth's own Moon had revealed ancient colonizing efforts by at least two different extraterrestrial civilizations—the Builders of half a million years earlier, and the An of ten to fifteen thousand years ago.

The first Xul artifact, the huntership lost beneath the ice of Europa and called "The Singer," had been uncovered late in the 21st Century. The first explorations beyond the Solar System, to the worlds of Chiron at Alpha Centauri, Ishtar at Lalande 21185, and elsewhere, had demonstrated that waves of interstellar colonization occurred across interstellar distances in regular cycles. Each time, the colonizing civilizations had been destroyed, abruptly and with xenophobic thoroughness.

Repeated encounters with the Xul over the past centuries had reinforced the self-evident conclusion. The Xul, for at *least* the past half-million years, and possibly for ten to twenty times longer than that, had maintained their dominance across the Galaxy by systematically destroying any species, any world which, to their way of thinking, represented a threat. Xul xenophobia had been confirmed by numerous intelligence-gathering probes into their ships and fortresses. Accepted xenosophontological theory suggested that the original precursor species to modern Xuls had possessed a kind of hardwired Darwinian imperative: *any* non-Xul life form was a potential threat, and the only rational way to deal with it was to destroy it before it was strong enough to become an actual threat.

Slowly, Fermi's Paradox became Fermi's Evidence. The skies were silent because noisy civilizations were detected and destroyed early in their phases of off-world growth. The few other cultures contacted so far—the An, the N'mah, and the Eulers—had survived by being inconspicuous, or by occupying planetary environments so far outside what the Xul considered to be the norm that they'd been overlooked

All of which meant there was no way to reason with the Xul . . . or to peacefully co-exist with them. Grim as the equations might be, either Humankind would wipe out the Xul, or the Xul would wipe out Humankind. There would be no middle ground, no basis for cooperative rapprochement, no peace short of the final peace of genocidal annihilation.

And that was something that a lot of humans simply could not or *would* not accept.

"General Alexander," Senator Tillman was saying, "some of us feel that the Commonwealth's military leadership is simply too, ah, reactionary politically. You look to the past, rather than to the future. You are locked into old patterns of thought that preclude your seeing future potentials."

"With damned good reason, Senator. It was the 20th Century philosopher Jorge Santayana who said that those who cannot remember the past are condemned to repeat it. The Xul have not exactly given us reason to trust them. And the experiences others have had with them—the Builders of ancient Mars and Chiron, the An, the N'mah . . . We need to pay attention to what they're telling us across the millennia."

"What history teaches us, General," Yarlocke said sharply, "is that military solutions do not work. Not the way their proponents suggest or intend."

"Indeed? That might be news to the Franco-UN leaders

of the 21st Century. Or the warlords of the Japanese Empire and the Nazi Reich a century before that. Or the British Empire faced with the loss of its American colonies. Or to the empire of Darius. Or the Carthaginians. Military solutions might be destructive and they might be expensive, but they *do* work."

"Again, a typically militarist response," Senator Ralston said. "I wouldn't expect a military leader to understand."

"Senator, I *am* a military leader. For thirty years, now, I have done my duty as I believed it was required of me. If you—"

"General Alexander," Tillman said, interrupting, "no one is questioning your dedication, your honor, or your sense of duty. We simply don't want militarist training and attitudes to . . . to *harm* Humanity by overlooking alternatives to war."

"Senators," Alexander said, "I suggest that this is something best taken up with SecDef and with the President. If you're looking for my resignation, I'm afraid I cannot and *will* not accommodate you . . . not like this. My understanding of the chain of command is that your committee provides oversight, advice, and can argue over my budget . . . but that only Mr. Wilson and President Stiner have the right to fire me. If you disapprove of the way I've been carrying out my orders, I suggest that you take it up with them."

"General Alexander," Yarlocke said with a frustrated shake of her icon's radiant head, "we didn't ask you here to criticize. Earlier, you invoked the words of Santayana. He also said, 'The wisest mind has something yet to learn.' We, the elected representatives of a sizeable percentage of Humankind, are facing the prospect of the interminable continuation of an endless, brutal, expensive, dangerous, and useless war, one that has dragged on now for centuries, off and on, with no promise or hope of an ending. We wish to explore alternatives."

"I can tell you what the alternative is, Madam Senator. Senators Ralston and Tillman will probably tell me that it's militarist thinking, but the alternative presented by both ancient and recent history is that Humankind will either be driven to extinction or so badly hammered by the enemy that only Stone-Age primitives are left. The Commonwealth military is dedicated to avoiding that alternative . . . assuming our progressive leadership allows us."

"That will be *quite* enough, General," Yarlocke said, and there was no missing the hostility in her mental voice. "Remember your place!"

"I am a Marine, Madam Senator," Alexander said. "*That* is my place. My cause is duty to the Commonwealth, which I serve, and to my Corps."

"Your *duty,* General, is to the civilian leadership of the Commonwealth, as directed by the President, true, but with the consent of the Commonwealth Senate. You would do well to remember that!"

"Yes, ma'am," Alexander replied. There was, he thought, no point in further antagonizing these people. They were looking for political witches to hunt, and had found a convenient one in him and in 1MIEF. They would tell him, no doubt in exquisite detail, exactly what they thought of him and of all "militarist" thinking, and all he could do was listen and let it wash over him.

But he was going to need a thorough shower afterward. He felt . . . unclean.

He wondered though if the Commonwealth's civilian government was going to allow 1MIEF to save it, or if they would succeed in so hamstringing the military that failure was inevitable.

It was a situation faced by democratic societies throughout history—the knife's edge balance between democratic freedoms guaranteed by the military, and military rule. Only rarely, however, had failure in that balancing act carried such a high ultimate cost—extinction.

That was an alternative Alexander would fight—bitterly and with every weapon at his command—to the very end.

9

Skimmersub Shuttle
Bahama Banks, Earth
1110 hrs, local

Just less than two hours after their arrival at Freeport, their
stomachs pleasantly filled with a somewhat spicy local con-
coction called conch chowder, Garroway and Armandez sat
together in the passenger lounge of the submarine shuttle
from Freeport Tower to Miami, a sleek undersea passenger
craft with large transparencies giving them an exceptional
and unobstructed view into the undersea realm between the
Bahamas and the Florida Peninsula.

The lounge was fairly crowded both with civilians and
with military personnel, all coming Earthside like a colorful
invasion from space. The orbit-to-surface space elevators
like the one at Quito took three days to reach Earth from the
Ring. That was fine for cargo and people on a tight budget,
but most tourists preferred the two-hour descent on board an
agrav shuttle.

Garroway looked out through the transparency—yes, a
real transparency, and not a viewall screen—and wondered
if he was dreaming, or caught up in a particularly rich and
detailed sim. The sheer beauty, the peace and tranquility of
his surroundings, were spectacular. It didn't seem possible,

in fact, to imagine a bigger leap—from the galactic vistas and savage bloodshed of Cluster Space to . . . *this*.

Inner space, someone once had called it.

The surrounding water was a crystalline glow of transparent, brilliant sapphire blue, with shafts of sunlight shifting and flashing from a ceiling as dazzlingly bright as liquid mercury. Ten meters below, a variegated landscape drifted past at fifty kph, mountains and ridges of brilliantly colored coral interspersed with vast, flat prairies of current-sculpted white sand or waving, green fronds of seaweed. Schools of bright-colored fish flashed and turned, reflecting dazzling flashes of silver in the shifting light. Larger creatures, sharks, rays, and others, moved and circled as silent shadows in the distance.

"I never knew it could be so beautiful!" Nikki was sitting in the seat next to Garroway's, leaning forward, holding his hand as the shuttle glided swiftly through the marine shallows.

"It is pretty," Garroway agreed. "Glad we came?"

"Definitely!" She started, then pointed aft. "Oh! What's that?"

Garroway consulted his implant, linked at the moment to the submarine vessel's AI. It was slower than he was used to, but the data came through in a moment. "Dolphin," he said. "I think there's a pod of them trying to follow us."

" 'Trying?' "

Garroway grinned. "Dolphins are fast . . . but not as fast as we are right now. They're going to have a hell of a time catching us."

"How fast are they?"

"Check your implant. There's a download available from the local AI. Thought-click the dolphins header."

She closed her eyes. "Oh . . . right . . ."

"Ten meters a second for sustained swimming," Garroway added reading his link. "Faster dashes over shorter periods of time. Say about thirty-six kilometers per hour over the long haul. And right now we're doing fifty."

"Yeah?" She nodded toward the transparency. "*They* seem to be keeping up pretty well."

Garroway turned, and saw a pair of streamlined gray shapes just off the submarine's starboard bow. They appeared to be matching the vessel's speed perfectly.

"Son of a bitch," Garroway said. "They're not supposed to be able to go *that* fast!"

"They're riding the bow wave," a Marine lieutenant said from his seat just behind them. "They're surfing on the pressure wave created by the sub."

Garroway turned, startled, then grinned at the man. "Good God! Have you become an expert on dolphin physics since your, ah, elevation to godhood, *sir*?" His emphasis on the word "sir" was deliberately insulting.

"Fuck you, Marine," the lieutenant said.

"Fuck you, too, sir."

Armandez looked confused. "Gare! You can't say that to an *officer*. . . ."

Lieutenant Ramsey laughed. "It's okay, Private. *This* time. I knew this snot-nose back when he was a lowly PFC."

"And *he* was a lowly Marine gunnery sergeant," Garroway added. "Private First Class Armandez, may I present to you Lieutenant Charel Ramsey, USMC."

"Nice to meet you, sir," she said.

"A pleasure, Private."

"This . . . this officer and *gentleman* happens to be the Marine who first established direct mind-to-mind contact with the Eulers, out in Aquila Space," Garroway explained. "Then the SOB went mustang on us. Became a fucking officer."

Ramsey shrugged. "Hey, seemed like the thing to do at the time."

"You don't usually see such old men running around as lieutenants."

"Now you're getting personal, Marine."

"So, which shuttle did you come down on? I didn't see you on the zero-seven-twenty drop."

"I was right behind you, Marine. Left Ringport Quito at zero-eight-hundred."

"Ah. We came out of Ringport Macapá. Welcome to Earth, sir."

Ramsey looked through the transparency. "It's kind of wet down here, isn't it?"

"Yup. Looks like we need to talk to the environmental department about the rain."

"Or at least submit a climate revision request to the proper departments. So what are you doing these days, Garroway?"

"First Platoon, Bravo Company, sir. One-Four Assault Recon. How about you? They stuck you in N-2, didn't they?"

Ramsey glanced around the lounge at the other passengers. None appeared to be listening. "I *could* tell you . . ." he began.

"But then you'd have to shoot us. Yeah, yeah, I've heard it before. What are doing planetside? Not scouting for an invasion force, I hope."

"Visiting my folks," Ramsey said. "They live in a beachtower near Orlando Beach. How about you? I seem to recall you didn't have a family groundside."

"You remember a Marine named Warhurst?"

"Gunny Warhurst? Sure as hell do."

"He's retired. Living under Miami."

"Son of a bitch. You got contact info on him?"

"Sure. Or tag along with us. Assuming you have time in your crowded sched, *sir*."

"Maybe I will. I haven't seen Gunny Warhurst in God knows how long. I thought the bastard was dead."

"*He* thinks he is," Garroway said. "I don't think he's been happy since he retired." He turned to Armandez, who was looking more and more confused. "Gunny Warhurst was my DI in boot camp, on Mars. Later on, he rotated to 1MIEF, just in time for the Aquila Space op. He, um, saved my ass. Big time."

"Really? Where was that?"

"Nova Starwall," Ramsey said. He grinned at her. "Did you realize, Private, that this butt-ugly character you're sitting with is a genu-wine hero?"

She smiled. "As a matter of fact, I did. He saved my tail in Cluster Space. Cut his own legs off so there was room for both me and him in his assault pod."

Ramsey's eyebrows crept higher on his forehead, and he looked down at Garroway's legs. "Oh, they're coming along fine," Garroway said, answering the unspoken question before it was asked. "They grew me a new set on board the *Barton*, after this last dust-up in the Cluster. My second pair, in fact." He slapped his thigh. "Good as new."

"Shit fire. Don't make a habit of that, okay?" Ramsey shook his head in mock sadness. "Cutting off your own legs . . . that's destruction of government property, you know? They'll bust you back to recruit private and have you scrubbing out the head for the rest of your tour."

"I got the lecture already, sir. There was this shrink-AI on the *Barton* who was sure I had some kind of self-destructive impulse."

"Well, hell, yeah. You joined the Marines, didn't you?" Ramsey looked at Armandez. "Anyway, I'm glad this character saved your tail, but that's not why he's a hero." Ramsey reached across and tapped a blue ribbon riding above the colorful rows of ribbons on his chest. "Didn't he ever tell you how he got *this*?"

"His Medal of Honor? No. He didn't. Every time I ask, he changes the subject. Do you know?"

"Battle of the Nova, at Starwall. Nine, ten years ago, now. This mental case volunteered to fly a Euler triggership FTL through a star. Blew up the star, and wiped out a major Xul base."

"Lieutenant Ramsey, here, was the guy who figured out how to use combat drones to find me," Garroway explained. "When the star blew, I was on the other side from the stargate, and the triggership was junked, going slower than light just ahead of the heavy particulate crap from the nova. But thanks to him, they found me, just ahead of the heavy stuff. And Gunny Warhurst, the guy we're going to visit in Miami? He's the one who spacewalked over and pulled me out."

Damn. Garroway remembered now why he didn't like telling the story. For just a moment, he relived the memory—including the flash of terror that always accompanied it. It had been so fucking *close*.

Even nine years later, he could see that exploding star reaching toward him, filling the sky with white fire.

"As you can see, Private," Ramsey was saying, "we have an extremely tight-knit little community here. Gunny Warhurst saves Garroway, Garroway saves you. . . ."

"So some day you can pull some young Marine's ass out of the fire, Nikki," Garroway said. "Look, can we change the subject? You two are making my head swell."

"Which one?" Ramsey asked.

"Fuck you. *Sir.*"

"Your family's in Orlando Beach, you said?" Armandez asked him.

"Yup."

"I thought most of Florida was under water since Armageddonfall."

"A lot of it is. Tidal waves from the Xul attack took out most of the eastern coastal areas. That was followed by the mini-ice age, Armageddon Winter. The climate control satellites and orbital solar mirrors reversed that after a century or two, but things swung back too far the other way. People didn't really know what the hell they were doing, and it was tough finding the right balance of insolation and ice. When global temperatures finally stabilized, ocean levels were about fifteen meters higher than they had been. Of course, a lot of coastlands had been slowly sinking already before the Xul strike . . . what they used to call global warming melting the ice caps. By the time the climate was balanced, some cities had vanished. Others had been built over even when the original was under water. Like Freeport. Or Miami."

"I'm looking forward to seeing Miami," Armandez said. "Especially the coral gardens."

"It's a dump," Ramsey said with a shrug. "Like most of the planet."

"I take it you visit out of family obligation?" Garroway said.

"I suppose so. I have a few friends here. And my parents. I used to have a wife and a husband, too, but they decided I was gone too much and kicked me out. Just like Gunny Warhurst, in fact. That was a long time ago." He grimaced. "Ancient history. The Corp's my family now."

"Amen," Garroway said. "A-fucking-men."

Senate Floor
Commonwealth Government Center,
EarthRing
1637 hrs, GMT

"We must," Senator Yarlocke thundered to the assembled crowd, "*must* learn the lessons of history! If we fail, we risk the survival of Earth, of the entire race of Humankind in its diaspora across the stars!"

Alexander was seated in the visitor's gallery of the Senate Deliberation Chamber, a huge room with seats arranged in semicircular ranks about the speaker's dais, listening to Yarlocke with growing amazement. Did loyalty, duty to her office, even common sense itself mean nothing to the woman?

Was that what politics did to a person? Or was she a politician because of some basic and ultimately fatal flaw in her character?

He recognized his own anger. He would have to watch that. . . .

"The history I have in mind," Yarlocke went on, "is the history of our relations with the Islamic Theocracy.

"Now, the Commonwealth has fought numerous wars with the Theocracy over the past centuries . . . eighteen major wars and literally hundreds of minor clashes and border incidents. Before the Commonwealth, the United States of America fought several major wars against the Theocracy's predecessors, what was once loosely termed 'Militant Islam.' Some historians would point out that America's struggle with Islam went back to the early nineteenth century, in a series of clashes known as the Barbary Wars.

"A thousand years of warfare against . . . not a state, not a country, but a religious and sociological idea. A thousand years of warfare . . . and it accomplished nothing save for making adherents of that idea our eternal and implacable enemies.

"Fellow Senators of the Commonwealth of Humankind . . . the lesson is painfully clear. *Direct military action accomplishes nothing,* nothing, *save to foster hatred and more bloodshed! . . ."*

"Yarlocke is in rare form today," the voice of General Dorrity whispered in Alexander's mind. The Senate-Defense liaison was seated among the senators in the auditorium below—Alexander could see him from his gallery seat, a tiny figure seated next to the two representatives from Ishtar—but a private channel let them speak as though they were sitting side by side.

"The Warlock is *always* in rare form," Alexander replied, bitter. "Give her an audience, and she'll play to it."

There was seating on the Senate floor for hundreds; fewer than a quarter, though, were physically occupied. According to the proceedings link in a window open in his mind, eighty-one Commonwealth senators were present physically for this session, while another one hundred seventy were linked in from elsewhere, attending the session via the Senate Net. The total represented just over half of the total Senate membership—enough to establish a quorum if Yarlocke called for a vote.

The unpleasant meeting with the appropriations subcommittee had ended an hour and a half ago, when Yarlocke had informed Alexander that she was delivering a speech to the full Senate at 1600 hours. She'd actually grinned at him when she'd told him that she would be presenting a new motion today, one calling for the immediate recall of 1MIEF to Solar Space and an end to the Xul War. She'd told him that he could watch, if he wished, from the Senate Gallery overlooking the floor.

She'd made it sound like she was doing him a special favor. This session, however, was open, meaning that it could be accessed by anyone throughout the Solar System with the appropriate download codes and addresses. According to the figures running in an open window to one side of Alexander's mind, some six hundred million people were watching, most within EarthRing, with a few watching on Earth, Luna, and—with a twenty-minute time-delay due to the limitations of the speed of light—Mars. If she hadn't given him the invitation, he could have tuned in and watched just the same.

His physical presence in the chamber, however, gave an immediacy to what he was hearing, an immediacy, he was fully aware, that was largely psychological, but nonetheless quite real.

So far, however, all he'd heard had been more of the same—a recitation of the need for peace, of the need to reach out and understand the alien, the unknown, the need to find common ground and mutual comprehension. There'd been nothing yet about Operation Clusterstrike being a failure, not exactly, but she had continued to hammer away at her old theme, that sending ships and Marines to unimaginably distant corners of the Galaxy to kill the Xul a few at a time was not working, *could* not work. Nine years of war, of raids by 1MIEF, and there was no indication that Humankind had even gotten the enemy's attention.

She continued to speak about the Commonwealth's ongoing war with the Islamic Theocracy, and was managing a rather blatant rewriting of history as she did so.

"Wait, wait," Dorrity said after a moment. "*What* did you call her?"

"Hm? The Warlock?"

"Yeah. Isn't that a male witch? Why do you call her that?"

"No. The entertainment conglomerates use the word that way in horrorsims and so forth, but it originally meant an oath-breaker, a traitor. It's from Old English, I think." He pulled down a dictionary page in his mind and double-checked. The word "warlock" was English, but not changed in the transition to modern Anglic over the past few centuries. "Yeah. Old English *Waerloga*. A covenant-breaker."

"Okay . . . so how do you figure her to be one of those?"

Alexander shifted uncomfortably in his seat. "I was just playing with her name," he said. "Helps me dismiss the creature without blowing a pressure seal. But . . . think about it, General. She swore an oath, a covenant, to the Constitution of the Commonwealth and, by extension, to the people she represents. The Constitution is a direct extension of the Constitution of the old United States. *To provide for the common defense. . . .*

"Now, we can sit here and argue until the heat death of the universe whether our Xul policy is right or wrong. Sometimes, I wake up in the middle of the night and wonder myself whether what we're doing is right. But *that* one . . ." He shook his head. "She twists words and theories and ideas and history itself in ways that would make a hyperdimensional topologist's stomach turn. She's Lewis Carroll's Queen of Hearts, making words mean exactly what she *wants* them to mean . . . and formulating policy based on *her* definitions, and to hell with what anybody else thinks."

"That, I thought," Dorrity said, "was what politics is all about."

"Maybe. But she does it to reinforce her own power base, to build up her own political authority, and trash her opponents."

"Again, politics in a nutshell."

"But she's doing it to the detriment of that common defense I mentioned. Can anyone truly believe the Xul *aren't* out to wipe us off the Galactic map?"

"Marty," Dorrity said, with an unexpectedly familiar use of his first name, "you've been out on the front lines for the better part of nine years. In all that time, the Xul have not launched a single attack on Earth, or against one of Earth's extrasolar colonies. That, my friend, is a remarkable achievement. But maybe you've done too good a job."

Alexander was shocked. "Good God, you're not serious! You can't be! If the Xul *had* managed to launch another Armageddonfall, do you think Earth would still be here? They won't send a single huntership next time. It'll be a fleet, like the one they had in Cluster Space."

"I know. My point is, though, that there's something like . . . what? Sixty billion people living in Solar Space, now. A couple or three billion on Earth, maybe a billion more on Luna, Mars, and the Jovians, the rest in EarthRing, AresRing, and the solar habs and planetoids. And except for those few actually in the military and their stay-at-home families, not one of them really *knows* we're at war. The fleet and your Marines have managed to keep the Xul at arm's length. They allow those billions to enjoy a quality of life that would seem downright magical to people living just a few centuries ago. They don't *know* the real horror of war."

"I thought," Alexander said quietly, "that that was why we're here, why the fleet is here."

He felt the other's shrug. "It is. Of course, it is. But that's also the reason that she can rewrite history to her liking in order to further her own ambitions."

Alexander listened to Yarlocke for a few moments. "In all those years of conflict with Islam," she was saying, "what was the benefit? What was the *point*? Great cities vaporized worldwide . . . Haifa . . . Tehran . . . Karachi . . . Moscow . . . Paris . . . New Delhi . . . Detroit . . . cities today that are names of horror and infamy because of the hundreds of millions incinerated in those holocausts. Holocausts, I might add, generated by religious intolerance, prejudice, and by a preposterous unwillingness on both sides to accept that there are *always* alternatives to war. . . ."

She did not point out that most of those cities had been nuked by the militants, not by their enemies. Tehran had been incinerated in retaliation for the attack on Haifa, and Karachi had been taken out by India in exchange for New Delhi, but the others had been random terror bombings through the troubled years of the 21st Century.

Nor did she point out that the bombings had stopped after the Western Alliance had unilaterally forced the separation of church and state, literally at gunpoint, in thirty-two countries from Morocco to Uzbekistan to Indonesia. Six centuries later, the resolution of the Islamic Wars was still a controversial matter. Did any government or alliance of governments have the right to shape or to dictate the religious beliefs and practices of a sovereign nation?

Alexander firmly believed the answer was no . . . *unless* a government-sponsored religion called for the wholesale destruction of other people, cities, and nations in the name of their god. The only controversy, so far as Alexander was concerned, lay in why the Western nations had waited as long as they had. If they'd acted sooner, and with less internal dissent, a number of cities and some hundreds of millions of people might have lived.

And in a twisted way, Yarlocke was right about one thing. The Islamists, beaten on Earth, had taken their absolutist beliefs to the stars. Militant Islamists had at last succeeded on colony worlds like Alighan, New Mecca, and 'Adali, overthrowing the secular governments of a dozen extrasolar worlds colonized by Islamic refugees and creating the Theocracy. After a thousand years, Militant Islam endured.

But *not* on Earth or in the Rings, where freedom of religious belief was at the heart of every constitution and popular covenant. It had taken military force to achieve that small miracle. Against the black-and-white, convert-or-burn theology of Islam's more fanatical advocates, nothing less would have sufficed, not in ten times ten thousand years.

"After a thousand years of bitter warfare between Islam and the so-called West," Yarlocke was saying, "an entire civilization still holds all non-Muslim peoples in utter contempt, hatred, and fear. And can we truly say that their attitude, their pain is their own fault? When it was we who made war on them over the centuries? . . ."

"God," Alexander said over the private channel. "Now she's rewriting history."

"A specialty of hers," Dorrity replied.

"And is the same pattern to be repeated with the Xul?" Yarlocke continued. "You've all heard the arguments, I know, that the Xul are psychologically unable to interact with other species in any way other than with wholesale genocide . . . but I ask you now, can we *truly* be certain of this? Just because the Xul are alien does *not* mean they are hopelessly irrational. . . ."

If Dorrity was right, the citizenry of the Solar System didn't care about Yarlocke's casually revisionist history. They would go along with what was convenient, or let themselves be swept along by the emotions raised by speeches, slogans, and news site downloads.

How long, he wondered, after 1MIEF's attacks ceased, would it be before the Xul found Sol once again and wreaked their inevitable retaliation? The city holocausts of the 21st Century would be snuffed candles by comparison.

"My proposal before the Senate now is a binding resolution calling for the immediate cessation of hostilities against the Xul, and the immediate recall of the Navy-Marine expeditionary force to Solar Space. It also calls for the creation of a *new* expeditionary force, to be called the *Pax Galactica,* as an emissary to the Xul. Their sole mission would be to establish peaceful contact with the Xul, and to lay the foundations of a lasting Galactic peace."

Yarlocke's words provoked an explosion of noise from the Senate floor, accompanied by an even noisier flurry of electronic exchanges over the Senate Net. Gavin Fitzgerald, the Senate Speaker, pounded on his gavel for silence. "Order! The chamber will come to order! Senator Yarlocke, will you yield for a question?"

"Yes, Mr. Speaker. I yield for a question."

Fitzgerald recognized one of the raised hands on the floor.

"Senator Yarlocke!" Janis Gallagher, a representative from the state of Nova Scotia said, rising. "The Xul could be the most peaceful and inoffensive civilization in the Galaxy, and they might still refuse to treat with us. As you've just pointed out, this war with them has been going on for a long time. There is bitterness on both sides. How do we know this *Pax Galactica* force you propose wouldn't be destroyed as soon as it entered Xul space? *The Wings of Isis,* remember, back in 2148, was also unarmed, and the Xul destroyed it, apparently without provocation."

"Remember that we still don't have a clear idea of what happened to that vessel," Yarlocke replied. "There may well have been unintentional provocation.

"In any case, however, we know far more now than we did then. The *Pax Galactica* expeditionary force would make extensive use of AI programming and of the information gleaned from Xul sources over the years to ensure peaceful electronic contact before humans ventured into Xul-occupied space. We now know how to enter Xul electronic systems. Our military does this routinely during their encounters with them. Specially programmed AI representatives would be sent into Xul space ahead of the main Pax force to initiate negotiations. Our military forces would, of course, be ready to provide back-up if, despite our best efforts, the *Pax Galactica* came under attack. . . ."

As the discussion continued, Alexander could only sink back into his padded gallery seat and let out a heartfelt sigh. Did the Warlock seriously think it was possible to negotiate with the Xul? That the Xul in any way, shape, or form thought like humans?

Alexander wondered, though, if Yarlocke was right, if there *was* another way. The trick was in finding it without exposing Humankind to a devastating attack.

"General Dorrity?"

"Yeah?"

"As a member of the Appropriations Committee . . . are you allowed to address the Senate?"

"I'm a non-voting member of a Senate subcommittee," he said. "I can address them, not the full Senate."

"Damn. Do you have an ally in the Senate who might be willing to speak for you?"

"As a matter of fact, yes. Senator Armandez, of Ishtar, right here beside me. He's a defense hardliner, and he has no love for . . . what did you call her? The Warlock."

"Have you seen the intel our people brought back from Cluster Space? The stuff on the Core."

"Yes, I did. Scary stuff."

"It occurs to me that we might use that."

"How?"

"Well, we need to know what the Xul are doing in there, anyhow. And our initial analysis of the data we brought back suggests that what we're looking at is the closest thing we've seen yet to a capital or military headquarters for the whole Xul empire."

"Jesus! You're thinking of taking 1MIEF in *there*?"

"Why not?"

"Cluster Space will seem like R&R by comparison."

"We'll need to formulate an ops plan," Alexander said, thinking with a quick, sharp ferocity. "And it's a hellish long shot. But if you can get Senator Armandez to propose something for you. . . ."

"Here," Dorrity said. "I've just brought the Senator on-channel."

Alexander felt the new presence on the e-communications line. "Hello, Senator."

"General. I've heard a lot about you. What do you have in mind?"

"I wonder if you could suggest *this* to the Senate. . . ."

10

Seaview Gardens
Lost Miami, Earth
1250 hrs, local

"So where is the lost city of Atlantis?" Nikki Armandez wanted to know.

"Lost," Garroway replied, grinning.

"You know what I mean. . . ."

"The Bimini Ruins?" Ramsey asked. "We probably zipped right over those in the ekranoplan phase of our trip."

"Damn. I was hoping to see those."

"Not much to see," Garroway told her. "I've been there in sim. Big flat rocks piled in long, straight walls and barricades, all pretty deep underwater. Besides, that wasn't the *real* Atlantis."

Mysterious ruins, apparently pieced together from slabs of local beach rock, had raised speculations for centuries about Plato's fabled lost city just off the now-sunken island of North Bimini, in the Bahamas. The actual identity of Atlantis—a Bronze Age superpower in the eastern Atlantic destroyed by a volcanic eruption around the time of the Trojan War—had not been confirmed until the 2500s.

The Bimini structures, most likely, had been part of a breakwater and port system built by Atlantis as part of their North American copper-mining franchise. When first discovered, the ruins had been located in shallow waters, less than ten meters down. With the melting of the polar icecaps five centuries ago, the water over that region was now nearly thirty meters deep, but archeological research continued from a large, seafloor complex raised over what had once been the island of North Bimini.

There was a possibility—little more than speculation even now—that the Bronze Age trading federation of Atalan had been deliberately destroyed by the Xul in around 1200 B.C.E., plus or minus fifty years. The Xul had a penchant for dropping large rocks out of space onto emerging civilizations across the Galaxy. Ancient myth and legend originating with hundreds of disparate peoples around the globe hinted that the famous lost continent's demise had been a deliberate act—a divine punishment for sins of arrogance and hubris.

If, in fact, this was true, it had far-reaching import for modern Humankind. It was already certain that the Xul had annihilated the An slave colonies on Earth sometime around seven to eight thousand years B.C.E., but the An at that time had been starfarers, with FTL drives and a highly sophisticated computer technology. If the Xul had bothered to bombard a Bronze Age civilization, still planet-bound, with no technology more advanced than sailing vessels and chariots, it suggested a xenophobic drive on their part much stronger than had previously been imagined.

It also suggested that the apparent Xul complacence of the past few millennia—the fact that they'd sent only a single huntership to Earth in 2314, for example, instead of an entire battlefleet—was temporary at best. Possibly Xul militancy ran in cycles. Possibly they'd possessed a different form of societal organization in 1200 B.C.E.

Possibly . . . no, *probably* . . . Humankind simply didn't have the full picture, even yet.

Garroway checked the skimmersub's data link just to be certain. In fact, they'd missed the North Bimini ruins by a good twenty kilometers, and they had been flying at the time. Only the beginning and ending portions of the skimmersub shuttle's course were under water. Twenty minutes after departing from Freeport Tower, they'd risen to the surface, flattened out the hull below and aft of the torpedo-shaped passenger section into something looking distinctly like a large stingray, and lifted gently above the waves on surface effect, skimming above the sea at nearly 150 knots. Just a few minutes ago, the skimmersub had settled back down into the water, gently submerged, reassumed its elongated egg form, and continued the voyage at a slower pace beneath the surface.

"According to the downloads I've seen, there's not a lot to see out there, anyway," Ramsey put in. "Like Gare said—flat rocks marking out some walls and breakwaters. The underwater ruins at Aguna, west of Okinawa, are a *lot* more impressive."

"Yeah," Garroway said, touching her shoulder and pointing ahead. "You know, if you want to see a *real* lost city, take a look at *that.*"

Armandez looked up, and gasped. Ahead, through the transparent hull, immense ruins were rising from the sea floor, shadowy masses slowly resolving into walls, towers, and buildings.

Since the 19th and 20th centuries, Earth had been struggling with the effects of a gradual global warming trend. In 2314, the Xul attack had sent titanic waves smashing into coastal areas around the planet, demolishing cities worldwide. The attack had thrown vast clouds of dust and water vapor into the sky, blocking off sunlight at the surface and plunging Earth into a brief, mini-ice age. Solar mirrors constructed in orbit had helped raise temperatures again and melt the ice, but no one had ever tried to manage climate on a planetary scale before, and *control* had been a problem. Eventually, things had balanced out, but by then the polar ice caps had vanished, and sea levels had risen some twenty meters above their pre-Armageddonfall depths.

"It's beautiful!" Armandez exclaimed.

"It's an underwater junkyard," Ramsey said. "But the marine growth does pretty the place up, doesn't it?"

Tangled wreckage—iron gratings, the shapes of ancient

vehicles, piles of broken stone, glass, and steel—everywhere
emerged from a smothering blanket of silt banked and
shaped around the submerged bases of those titanic buildings. Coral had taken root, and in places the wreckage had
been all but swallowed by colorful masses like living, flow-
ering rock. Schools of fish wheeled and turned above what
once had been city streets. They could see humans out there
as well, wearing black breathersuits as they worked among
the ruins. Genegineered dolphins, *Tursiops habilus*, sport-
ing muscular arms and hands, assisted them. They appeared
to be clearing a foundation for new seabed construction.

The skimmersub slowed as it entered a region of deep
shadow. External lights switched on, spearing ahead into
blue-green shadows.

"Those buildings are huge," Garroway said. "I saw some
of them in sim, but I didn't realize they were this big in
life."

"Hotels, most of them," Ramsey said. "Miami Beach. This
was supposed to be a tourist hot spot five hundred years ago.
It was pretty much trashed by the tidal waves in 2314, but the
buildings remained standing, most of them. After the ice
melted, they were sticking up out of the ocean a good 200
kilometers from the nearest large land mass, so people turned
the buildings into pylons and built platforms up above the
water. Some of them are a couple of kilometers high, now."

"Is that where Gunny Warhurst lives?" Armandez wanted
to know.

"Nah. He's in a hab called Virginia Key Reef. Actually, I
think that may be it up ahead."

The shuttle had passed through the looming pylons of the
partially sunken city and into a region of dazzling, shifting
light playing across brilliantly reflective sand. More ruins
loomed up out of the shadowy waters ahead, however . . .
storage tanks, forests of tangled piping, and more buildings,
most of them engulfed by mountainous reefs of coral.

In places, the coral had taken on oddly symmetrical and
geometrical shapes, due to the structure of the artificial
structures beneath it. A series of seafloor habitats had been

anchored to the sea bed just above one particularly large coral-encrusted amphitheater. The skimmersub was angling now toward the lock mounted on one end of the huge, semi-circular structure. The transport drifted above the vertical docking sleeve, settled onto it, and nanosealed with the facility.

Ten minutes later, Garroway, Armandez, and Ramsey were walking along a long, curving corridor, following downloaded directions to the Warhurst apartment. They found the right hab halfway around the curve, and Garroway palmed the announce panel.

The door slid open a moment later, and a pretty, young, blond woman admitted them. She was quite nude, save for a clinging flicker of holographically projected rainbow light. "Hi!" she said brightly. "I'm Traci. Mike's busy screaming at the viewall right now. C'mon in! Can I get you guys anything?"

"Not right now, thanks," Garroway replied as they entered the hab. Curving, transparent walls looked out into the sunlit waters of the coral reef. The ceiling was also transparent, and the apartment was brightly illuminated by the shifting patterns of azure-tinted sunlight flashing down from the surface some ten meters overhead.

"Damn it, I think we're overdressed, Aiden," Armandez whispered to him as they followed Traci into the living room.

Garroway recalled that some of the colony worlds were a bit on the prudish side when it came to casual social nudity. "Don't worry about it," he told her. "Lots of folks here and in the Rings go around in their skin all the time. Doesn't mean sex, or anything like that."

"On Ishtar we'd've been eaten alive by bitewings and drilleribbons," she told him. "There's a *reason* the gods created us with clothing!"

Garroway was about to ask her about that, but was interrupted by a shout from the entertainment well on the far end of the living area. "God *damn* those assholes!"

The E-center was curiously antique, featuring a large,

slightly curving viewall within which an illusion of three-dimensional reality was projected. Michael Warhurst was on the sofa with another young woman, both of them nude, the former Marine shaking his fist and shouting at the screen.

"Hey, Gunny!" Garroway called. "What's got you so riled up?"

Warhurst turned in the couch, then jumped to his feet. "Garroway, you son of a bitch! Welcome to Earth!"

"Thank you. Good to be here."

"And it's Lieutenant Ramsey now, is it? Welcome to my humble abode. *Sir.*"

"Thanks, Gunny. What the hell are you watching?"

Warhurst waved at the viewall dismissively. "Fucking politics. They're about to vote on whether or not to bring you guys back home."

"Oh, really?" Garroway said, intrigued. "What about the Xul?"

"That's just it. It's uni-fucking-lateral retreat. Declare victory and go home . . . and pray the SOBs don't decide we've gone soft and drop a few rocks in our laps."

"So where's it stand?" Armandez asked.

"Hard to say, yet. Things kicked off when that *über*-bitch Yarlocke called for a vote."

"On what?"

"The usual. The Xul aren't so bad. Bring the boys and girls home. Make kissy-face with the Xulies, and everyone'll be happy. But then the Senator from Ishtar dropped a bomb on the assembly a little while ago."

"Yay! That's my daddy!"

"Really?" Warhurst looked surprised. "Senator Armandez?"

"I'm Nikki Armandez," she said.

"Well, I'm delighted to meet you! Your dad's really something, let me tell you! A real ball of fire."

"He's a former Marine," she told him. "When he gets into speech-maker mode, he can be . . . formidable."

"I know. He was great! He told how the last MIEF op discovered a link to the Galactic Core, and how we needed to go there—in force—to find out what the Xul are really all about. He's calling for a compromise—send in the Marines and Navy, but include a peacemaking team as well. Madam Senator Über-bitch and her puppies have been fighting the proposal tooth and nail, but I think it's going to carry. At least it was. One of Yarlocke's people just raised a motion to delay."

"Is that why you were screaming 'assholes' a few minutes ago?" Ramsey wanted to know.

Warhurst grinned. "Yeah. I guess I got a little riled."

"What good would a delay do?" Garroway asked.

"I'm not sure what her idea is. Maybe Über-bitch wants some time to do some private arm-twisting."

"The motion was just defeated, Mike," said the other woman in the apartment, still seated on the sofa.

"Oh? Great! Shit, you gotta excuse me. Manners. You've met Traci, there. And this is Kath."

"Hi!" Kath said. She was a striking redhead. "Mike's told us all about Aiden! Why don't you guys shuck your skins and get comfortable?"

Armandez elected to keep her underpants on, a concession to deeply ingrained Ishtaran modesty taboos, but Garroway and Ramsey stripped down to match their hosts. Their uniforms and shoes vanished into a hopper that would disassemble them into component atoms and grow them anew, without travel grime or wrinkles.

"There's going to be a public vote!" Traci called out. "You want to chime in?"

"Oh, good," Warhurst said, taking his seat next to Kath. "About fucking time! Binding?"

"No. But I guess the Senate wants to know who's going to be pissed off by what decision."

Warhurst sighed. "The Net. The best *and* the worst thing ever to happen to Commonwealth politics."

"How do you figure, Gunny?" Garroway asked.

"The best because it allowed a true representative democracy. The entire electorate—whoever happens to be linked into the debate, anyway—can cast their votes and have them tabulated immediately. The Senators up there in the Ring can see in a few minutes which way the political winds are blowing."

"Wetting their fingers and sticking them into the wind," Ramsey suggested.

"That's about it. But it's the *worst* thing because a few hundred years ago it got so slick they decided they didn't need the House of Representatives to balance out the Senate. That happened, oh, gods. Long time ago. Twenty-five, twenty-six hundreds? Back when it was the United States of America running things, the legislative branch of the government was divided between House and Senate. A law passed by one might get shot down by the other, so there was a great balance of power going on . . . and they acted as a check against the power of the executive branch, right?"

"If you say so," Garroway replied. "I've never really figured out how they got anything done in pre-Commonwealth times."

"Yeah, well, once the citizens could vote on any resolution, they decided having a two-house legislature was redundant. The House split off and became a regulatory body just for the individual states, while the Senate passed laws concerning the entire Commonwealth. Over the years, the Senate became *way* too powerful. Hell, there's talk about the President being little more than a figurehead now, kind of like British royalty, back when they still had them."

"You think things would be better with House and Senate still battling it out with each other?" Ramsey asked. "Making back-room deals, that sort of thing?"

Warhurst shrugged. "Maybe. So far as I'm concerned, *anything* that paralyzes the government, keeps it from passing new laws and raising new taxes, is good!"

"Mike is a bit of a reactionary," Traci put in.

"Yeah, but he's my kind of reactionary," Garroway said, laughing. "How do we vote on this damned thing? And what are we voting on, again?"

Warhurst indicated a palm contact on the arm of the sofa. "Slap your hand down there. Your AI will access the Net for you. The vote is on . . . let's see . . . 'Should 1MIEF be sent to the Galactic Core, together with a peace envoy in an attempt to end the current state of hostilities? Yes, no, or protest.'"

Garroway was used to voting through a full-immersion e-connect, rather than this antique viewall connection, but when he placed his hand on the palm connect, a window came up in his mind, just as it would have with a full-sim link. But the thought-click key that would register his vote was blocked.

"Wait a sec," he said, reading the message scrolling past his awareness. "There's another motion up."

"Yeah, I see," Warhurst said, eyes narrowing. "*Damn* the bitch!"

"What?" Armandez asked.

"She's calling for a motion to block all votes from active-duty military. That means you guys."

Ramsey chuckled. "Well, it wouldn't do to have active-duty personnel vote on whether or not they're going to go into battle, would it?"

"Yeah," Garroway said. He laughed. "'Do you jarheads want to charge up that fucking hill and take it away from some very nasty and well-armed customers, yes or no?'"

"Yeah, except that the *über*-bitch knows the military would vote a resounding yes," Warhurst said. "She's hell-bent on shutting down 1MIEF, one way or another."

"Well, sure," Ramsey said. "The military knows how happy the Xul at the Core will be to see our peace envoy."

"And how long the peace would last afterward," Garroway added. "Whatcha guys think? Twenty minutes?"

"If that," Ramsey replied.

"Okay," Warhurst said. "That measure passed. So you guys don't get to vote. Sorry."

"Well, you vote for us," Armandez said. "Five or six times apiece!"

"Wish I fucking could." He put his palm down on the connector, then motioned to the women. "C'mon, girls. You get to vote, too. Civic duty, and all that."

"If we vote 'yes,'" Traci said, "does that mean you'll be going back out there?"

"No, honey, it doesn't." He sighed. "I wish to hell it did. But I put in my twenty, and I'd need a special waiver to re-enlist."

Traci, then Kath registered their votes. A recess for dinner, meanwhile, had been declared on the Senate floor.

"This'll take a while," Warhurst told them. "Hey! Let me show you around the place!"

The tour of the apartment didn't take long, since they'd already seen all there was to see except for the bedroom, bath, and storage areas. When they returned to the main living area, which included the entertainment center, a small galley, and sitting and eating areas, Armandez walked into the center of the room, looking up at the ocean surface visible through the overhead transparency. "This is simply gorgeous!" she said. "Is it expensive?"

"It's free. Veterans' benefits." He shrugged. "Anyway, the expensive real estate is up on shore."

"Tell me about it," Ramsey put in. "My parents are at Orlando Beach."

Warhurst winced. "Ouch."

"They're rich. They can afford it."

"Well, they're putting up more and more of these complexes out here at sea, especially on places flooded after the icecap melt. The individual apartments are grown as single units ashore, hauled out to a submerged platform with pontoon ballast tanks, and fastened down." He waved a hand at the transparent wall, and a vast, shadowy depression in the sea floor lined with coral. "Like the view?"

"It's certainly not what I thought of as *Earth*," Armandez said.

"There's a hell of lot more ocean on Earth than there is dry land," Warhurst told her. "*This* view is more typical of the place than, oh, central Iowa, say."

"Is that a crater out there?" Garroway asked, pointing. "Maybe a souvenir from 2314?"

"Nah. This area used to be an island right off the southern tip of Miami Beach proper. There was a seaquarium here . . . kind of like a theme park with trained whales. The historical downloads say that that pit over there used to be a public amphitheater for performances."

"Ha!" Ramsey exclaimed. He pointed to a cloud of colorful reef fish descending past the transparency. "So now it's a terrarium where fish watch *you*."

"Never thought of it *that* way," Warhurst said, "but, yeah. Exactly."

"We saw them building something on the sea floor outside of Miami," Armandez said. "Was that more living habs?"

"You probably saw where they're building the new big fish-farm complex up at Fisher Reef. The ocean's still recovering, you know, not only from Armageddonfall, but from what humans did to it in the centuries before. They say something like eighty percent of all marine species had been wiped out or were on the point of extinction when the Xul attacked, and the mini-ice age that followed must have killed a lot more. Nowadays, they're using sea farms more for reintroducing genegineered species than for food. Most of our food comes from nanufactories now, just like up in the Rings."

After a light meal, they ended up in a hot tub. Kath elected to stay in the entertainment center, watching the Senate channel, but Nikki finally overcame her modesty enough to lose the last of her clothing and join Garroway, Warhurst, Ramsey, and Traci in a large tub of scalding hot water.

"I just can't get over how gorgeous all of this is," she said, leaning back and looking up through the ceiling at wheeling fish and dancing light. "I never knew Earth was like *this*."

"First time down?" Warhurst asked.

She nodded. "I got as far as EarthRing when my father got elected a few years ago. Then I joined the Marines, boot camp on Mars, and duty stations all over this part of the galaxy ever since."

"Well, this is how the other half lives."

"Gare said you don't like it here."

He shrugged. "It's pleasant enough, I guess."

"He misses all of his old Marine buddies," Traci said,

moving close to him and taking hold of his arm with a play-ful pout. "*We're* not good enough for him!"

"Fuck, it's not that, baby," he said, putting an arm around her shoulders. "You know that. But I *do* miss the Corps, yeah." He grinned at Garroway and winked. "Screaming at maggot-recruits like *this* guy."

"Fuck you, Gunny."

"Ah. You turned out okay. Medal of Honor? Yeah, you're doing all right."

"If they bring 1MIEF home," Garroway said, "maybe we'll *all* be retired."

"You know that won't happen," Ramsey told him. "This peace initiative of Yarlocke's has about as much chance of success as making peace with a gorgonette."

"A gorgonette?" Traci asked. "What's that?"

"Oh, a little critter that lives on the major southern conti-nent of Nu Columbae IV," Ramsey told her. He held his hand out, palm down, half a meter off the deck. "Stands about yea high. All tentacles, muscle, claws, and teeth. A dozen feeding mouths, each on a separate neck, like a bundle of snakes. When they're migrating, a pack of 'em will shred a man down to bare bones in a minute or two."

"They're herbivores, actually," Garroway added. He'd never deployed to Nu Columbae IV, a marginally Earthlike world out on the fringes of the Chinese Hegemony, some 72 light years from Sol. Experiencing sims of the vicious local ecology, however, had been part of a Corps survival training program he'd gone through in boot camp. "They don't *eat* you so much as grate you into little bloody bits if they feel threatened."

"Lovely."

"Right," Warhurst said. "Just like the Xuls. A hyper-developed xenophobic protective reflex. And a *very* short temper! I hope that peace envoy they're talking about is wear-ing decent armor!"

"You think that's how the Xul started out, a few million years ago?" Ramsey asked. "Kill everything else before it kills you would be a reasonable survival strategy on Nu Columbae, and on a few other worlds I've seen as well."

"That's what the Excesses think," Garroway said. The name was derived from "XS," which in turn came from xenosociology, the science of nonhuman species, how they thought and acted, and why. "If they took that kill-or-be-killed mindset to the stars, maybe they never got rid of it. The Fermi Evidence, y'know?"

"If so, this peace initiative isn't going to go very far," Ramsey said.

"Sure it is!" Warhurst replied cheerfully. "It'll go all the way to the Galactic Core! And die there! . . ."

"Hey, wet people!" Kath called from the entertainment center. "The vote is being announced!"

"Okay," Warhurst said, standing up, dripping, stepping out of the deck-level tub. "Let's go check out the fucking BDA."

"Yeah," Garroway said. "This I've got to see."

Senate Committee Deliberation Chamber
Commonwealth Government Center,
EarthRing
1925 hrs, GMT

Cyndi Yarlocke watched the tabulation figures flickering into a window opened in her mind, and scowled. *Damn* Armandez and his short-sighted, disloyal interference. And damn Alexander. She turned and looked up, searching the visitor's gallery. Yes, there he was, sitting alone, leaning forward, fingers steepled in front of his chin, staring straight back at her. This was *his* doing. It had to be.

Armandez had a daughter in the Marines, in 1MIEF, in fact. Didn't the short-sighted bastard *want* to see her safely home from the stars, from constant warfare with the Xul?

But then, Armandez was an ex-Marine himself, and the bond between Marines sometimes seemed to transcend that of family. Yarlocke didn't understand that, but she recognized that it was true. Alexander must be using a back-channel communications link with Armandez, must have suggested the bare bones of the Armandez Proposal.

The hell of it was, Armandez's conservatism was being reflected by the electorate, apparently. The votes were still coming in, but, so far, nearly a billion citizens from the inner Solar System had electronically registered their votes on the issue. So far, it was running over seventy percent in favor of the Armandez Proposal, and just twenty-five percent against.

She could dismiss the lopsided tally easily enough. Many of those seven hundred million voters were most likely confused, thinking that by supporting the *Pax Galactica* going to the Core with the MIEF, they were voting for peace. They didn't realize that, if the Marines went along, there would be no peace. Alexander, the militarist bastard, would find a way to continue his war.

More crucial by far was the Senate vote. Two hundred fifty-one senators were present, either physically or in sim—a quorum. Twelve had abstained, a surprisingly small number, actually, given how politically charged this issue was. She'd thought a greater number would hesitate to associate their names and public voting records with either side of the question.

Of the rest, 121 had voted in favor of Senator Armandez's proposal, and 118 had voted against it. The measure had carried by three votes.

Three votes! . . .

It was frustrating, yes, but it was also, she was beginning to realize, encouraging. A three vote difference, with twelve fence-sitters? There were plenty of ways she could use that to her political advantage—calling in favors, twisting some arms, and a bit of simple, old-fashioned, out-shouting of the opposition. She could use the closeness of this vote to bring pressure to bear on the Appropriations Committee, and maybe find a way to further hamstring the MIEF's logistical support, or the fleet itself. . . .

And there was the matter of non-Commonwealth stellar nations, and their participation in anti-Xul operations.

Yes. *That* would do the trick.

It was clear that the electorate simply didn't understand what was truly at stake, here . . . nor did they understand just how enormous, how complex the Galaxy actually was. There was no way Humankind could grasp the size of the thing, much less rule it.

Yarlocke was ambitious, but she was also a realist. With just a little more support within her party, she would be able to take the final steps to eliminate the Presidency of the Commonwealth. The Senate would rule . . . and she would rule the Senate. With the battle-hardened Marines of 1MIEF under her *direct* authority, she would bring the other star nations of Humankind into line.

Let the Xul have the rest of the Galaxy. Humans would reign supreme within their own small, comfortable pocket of colony worlds . . . and Cyndi Collins Yarlocke would reign supreme over Humankind. It *would* happen.

For a moment, across the gulf of the Senate floor, her eyes locked with Alexander's. *I'm going to bring you down,* she promised him in her thoughts. *I'm going to bring you down, the electorate will side with me, and there* will *be a new way of managing this tired, old planet, I swear to you!*

No, it wouldn't be much longer. . . .

11

Orlando Beach
Florida, Earth
2225 hrs, local

A week later, under a dazzlingly star-filled night sky, Gar-roway lay with Nikki on the beach, holding her, tasting her, savoring this time with her. Towers ablaze with lights lined the northern skyline two kilometers away.

Much of the seacoast metropolis of Orlando was raised on networks of pylons extending far out over the ocean. Once, five centuries before, the Florida Peninsula had been twice its current length and breadth, stretching into the Gulf of Mexico for another full 350 kilometers almost all the way to the Commonwealth state of Cuba.

Numerous Floridian cities, including the surface portions of Miami, St. Petersburg, and Jacksonville, had been built up atop broad, nano-grown pylons anchored in shallow wa-ter, usually on the foundations of the long-sunken buildings of earlier cities. Orlando had the distinction of being built both on solid land and over the water. A region once occu-pied by a sprawling entertainment complex was now given over to public housing, and glowed against the skyline to the north. The narrow knife of the Glades Peninsula stretched to-ward the southeast, once the highland spine of South Florida and now given over mostly to mangrove swamps and isolated sand dunes facing the boom and rumble of the surf. High in the southern sky, the lights of EarthRing looked like a dusting of stars compressed into a slender thread stretched up and over from the western horizon to the east, a gossamer strand impossibly remote and delicate.

Garroway and Armandez lay on the sand above the lap of the waves and gently explored each other's bodies.

It had been a good week. *Expensive*, but a good week . . . and they still had another week to go before their leave expired. They'd spent most of the time at Gunny Warhurst's place, with side trips to see some of the more spectacular sights on old Earth.

Together, they'd stood atop the Verrzano Dike, the 25th-Century engineering marvel holding back the cold waters of the Atlantic from ancient, sacred Manhattan, and they'd visited the even more ancient Great Wall, stretching through the heart of the Hegemony's homeland. They'd played tourist and purchased a lowest-highest tour package, exploring the Marianas Abyss in a submarine, and, later that same day, flying to the visitor's pavilion at the top of Everest, where glaciers still gleamed beneath a dazzling, empty blue sky.

Three days ago, Nikki had finally talked him into renting a sailboat. They'd been in Egypt, visiting the Commonwealth Protectorate that included the awesome stone monuments on the Giza Plateau, and they'd taken a side trip to Siwa, on the shores of the Sahara Sea. The experience, Garroway thought, had been as close to flying as it was possible to come without an aerospace craft or being in zero-G. The waters of the manmade sea were crystalline, the bottom a surreal landscape of sculpted banks and dunes racing past beneath the AI-controlled vessel's keel.

Politics—even the ongoing cold war with the Islamic Theocracy that still embraced the rest of Egypt—had seemed remote indeed on that crystal sea. The citizens of the Theocracy in Egypt had been only too happy to sell the off-world tourists overpriced tour packages, exotic food, and expensive trinkets. The same in North China. Off-world, ancient political stresses still lay just beneath the surface, but the ordinary people continued to do business with tourists coming down-Ring.

As for the Xul, politics had seemed impossibly distant. For the first time in a long time, Garroway had felt himself relaxing.

There'd not been a flight direct from Egypt to Miami, so they'd flown in to Orlando Beach instead, arriving just yesterday and getting an invitation from Lieutenant Ramsey to come see him at his folks' place. They were staying in a guestroom there now, and planned to stay for another couple of days before choosing their next tourist destination. Peru, possibly . . . or maybe the huge, undersea ruins at Aguna, off the coast of Okinawa. Garroway was fascinated by Terran archeology as it related to the long history of Humankind's interactions with extrasolar civilizations—Sumeria and the An, Atlantis and the N'mah, the Xul strikes against Earth scattered across the planet's prehistory. Baalbek, Tiahuanaco, Titicaca. This seemed like a great opportunity to see at least a few of these legendary places for himself.

But best of all had been getting to know Nikki better. . . .

Sexual liaisons between Marines of differing ranks and experience—in this case a private first class only recently out of boot camp and a gunnery sergeant who'd been in for ten years—were not encouraged within the Corps. There was the very basic issue of an imbalance of power, where a junior might sleep with a senior either out of fear, or for purposes of manipulation. Either could seriously disrupt the cohesion of a unit.

Still, it was acknowledged that liaisons did happen. Service personnel were urged to use common sense and to avoid entanglements that put a strain on morale, good order, and discipline.

It would have been simpler, perhaps, simply to exclude women from combat duty, or, at the very least, to maintain sexually segregated units. Simpler . . . but impractical.

No one questioned the right of women to fight for their

nation or to serve in the military, but the presence of women in combat units had been an issue for debate for the past eight centuries. The advent of nanotechnic enhancements and prostheses and the widespread use of power armor in combat had long ago torpedoed complaints that females lacked the upper body strength or the endurance to compete with males. Reliable contraceptives for both sexes had long since ended the inconvenient need to discharge women who'd become pregnant; deliberately allowing pregnancy while on active duty was a violation of the enlistment contract and grounds for dismissal or even legal action. And within Commonwealth society as a whole, the widespread acceptance of casual social nudity had long ago ended privacy issues on board cramped transports or space-limited bases.

But one issue remained, and it was the one issue that science and technology could not address without changing people into something other than human. In Garroway's experience, men in the military, especially *unattached* men in the military, tended to focus on just two things—*fighting* and *fucking.* They were trained to be proficient at the first; they inevitably preferred the second. When they were engaged in the first, it was often at least subconsciously a route to the second; one's exploits in combat, told with suitable embellishment in mixed company around a table in a bar or in the squad bay after hours, might easily lead to a happy partnering with a comely squadmate . . . or at least it was perceived that way by the "no-shit-there-I-was" story-tellers in question.

In point of fact, men's behavior *changed* when women were around in what appeared to be a basic and incontrovertible fact of human sexual psychology. Training tempered the change, to be sure. Professionalism could overcome the instincts of basic biology. Concepts like honor, duty, and dedication to the Corps were deeply ingrained in every Marine, and guided every thought.

But always there were Marines, men and women both, who managed to overcome training and conditioning and act like idiots in their constant search of a good lay.

In the Corps' history, there'd been plenty of attempts to alter the sexual equation, from draconian regulations to drugs to suppress libido to using a Marine's cerebral implant to monitor his behavior. None worked well or consistently. Regulations could be ignored; drugs tended to suppress the very qualities in combat personnel the Corps needed; technology was susceptible to ingenious tampering. Garroway had done his share of that sort of thing back when he'd been a PFC, learning the codes that shut his personal AI monitor down when he wanted to break or bend the rules.

Control issues came and went in cycles. Ten years ago, when Garroway had joined the Corps, there'd been a lot of effort put into using platoon AIs to observe and report the behavior of individual Marines; now, Marines were simply warned not to screw up, to be careful, and to be discreet. No doubt it would come full-circle again some day, as yet another technological fix was applied to the problem.

Most individual Marines of both sexes and all ranks felt, however, that the issue was self-correcting. Hell, Marines didn't like micromanagement to begin with, and attempts to use technology to control the way they thought and acted and, especially, how they interacted with their fellow Marines would simply lead to more and more clever attempts to circumvent whatever strategy the powers-that-were had in mind.

None of this particularly mattered to Garroway as he drew Nikki Armandez close and kissed her, his left hand holding the back of her head, his right gently cupping her buttocks. Rules didn't matter, not here, not now. They were on leave and what they did with one another during their down time was their own damned business. The kiss deepened . . .

"Attention, all 1MIEF personnel!"

The voice, transmitted through his implant, sounded like a shout in his ear. He jumped, releasing Armandez at the same moment she pushed back from him. He saw her widening eyes, and knew she was receiving the same transmission.

"All leave and liberty is hereby cancelled. Effective immediately, all 1MIEF personnel are to return to the transport Hermes, *currently at Dock Three, SupraQuito Complex, EarthRing, by the most expeditious transport available."*

"Shit!" Garroway exclaimed.

"And double shit," Armandez added, her chest heaving, her face flushed. "They can't *do* this to us!"

Garroway sighed. "They can and they will, love. Let's see what the hell's going on."

Using his personal AI to initiate an uplink, he tapped into the platoon net back on board the *Hermes*. Orders, he saw, had just come through. The expeditionary force was returning to Cluster Space. And then . . .

"My God," he said aloud.

"What is it, Aiden?"

"We're going to the Core. Xul Central. . . ." Eyes closed, he continued to scan the posted data. "The damned idiots want us to make peace! . . ."

She was linking in now. "Debarkation in two more days," she said.

"Yeah. But they want us on deck as soon as we can get our asses up to the Ring. Wait a sec. . . ."

He opened another window and pulled down another page . . . a listing of departure times for Ringport shuttles.

"It'll have to be a transport," he told her. "The elevator takes three days. Let's see what's available. . . ."

There were, in fact, a steady stream of shuttles bound for the Ring from various sites all over Earth. There was nothing from Orlando Beach, he saw. No Ringport. But a shuttle was leaving in two hours from Freeport, and in three from Atlanta. Passenger bookings were already starting to fill them both up as other Marines logged in.

"Looks like a lot of service personnel are all reserving Ringbound seats in a hurry," he said. "It's going to be a zoo." He wondered just how many Marines were ashore right now, on leave from the *Hermes*. Eight or ten thousand at the very least, he guessed. He skipped ahead through the listings. The next Freeport shuttle was scheduled to leave in nineteen hours . . . at 1820 hours tomorrow. They could catch a local flier down to Miami, then take the skimmersub back to Freeport. That meant leaving Orlando Beach . . . he did a quick back-calculation . . . by 1200 hours tomorrow.

No problem. He entered data into the reservation pages, waited for confirmation, then relaxed.

"Okay, Nikki. We're booked for an up-shuttle to the Ring tomorrow."

"Damn, it, Aiden! We had another week coming!"

He shrugged. "Hey, that's the Corps. We belong to them. They say 'jump,' we say 'aye, aye,' and 'how high?' In this case, all the way up to the Ring."

It was just as well, he told himself. Booking that passage had just pulled a lot of credit from his financial storage. The Corps would reimburse him for expenses, but he was running just a little tight right now; that Marianas-Trench-to-Everest-Peak tour had been a bit on the expensive side, as had been the sailboat rental. His personal credit was boosted automatically by 150 points each day—his particular service pay grade—and Nikki's by 55, but neither of them had much saved up for big-ticket items like taking a suborbital out to Okinawa to see the underwater Aguna ruins.

In fact, the two of them would have had to put themselves on a pretty tight leash to make their credit reserves last for another week, even if they stayed with Lieutenant Ramsey or Gunny Warhurst.

He looked up at the stars overhead. Yeah, and truth to tell, he didn't like Earth all that much. The people didn't even know they were at war, though they were happy enough to drain a serviceman's credit. It was time to get back to *his* world, the Corps.

Nikki seemed to be reading his thoughts. She reached for him, sliding her hand along his side, from ribs to thigh. "At least that means we don't have to go back *right* away. We have some time for us."

Again, he drew her close. "My thought exactly, Marine. . . ."

3006.1111

UCS Hermes
Dock Three, SupraQuito,
EarthRing
0805 hrs, GMT

"They're starting to check in," Cara told General Alexander. *"It may be a while before they can all book passage back, though."*

"And lots of them will try to squeeze in a few more hours of freedom." Alexander thought for a moment. "You may need to establish a muster-aboard time."

"We could also send some aerospace transports down, and pick them up directly."

"True. If I know my Marines, though, they'll be spread all over the planet right now, seeing the sights, getting into trouble, and drinking and simming themselves senseless."

An image of Earth, minus the swaths and swirls of cloud cover, opened in his mind. Thousands of green pinpoints appeared, scattered across the globe. *"The majority of our personnel are in time zones Zulu minus five through minus eight,"* Cara said, *"which means it's the middle of the night for most of them."*

Briefly, Alexander considered the link-simmed globe. *Damn*, he thought. *A little leave time . . .*

He dismissed the thought, as though slamming a door. It had been . . . how long since he'd set foot on Earth's surface, on the surface of *any* world, for that matter? He knew he could check his personal log and find out in an instant, but chose not to do so. Electronic simulations and virtual realities made it possible to feel as though he'd left the labyrinthine passageways and compartments of the *Hermes* and was walking the open surface of a planet, but the illusion, he knew, was not, could never be, reality.

Someday, perhaps . . .

"We'll give them twelve hours," he told Cara, "and see where we are. I don't want to send the transports down unless we have to."

"Aye, aye, General."

Alexander felt the AI depart from his consciousness.

Cara had been with him for decades, first as his personal AI secretary, and later as personal aide within his command constellation, the group of humans and AIs who ran 1MIEF. Currently, she—he'd always thought of the genderless program as "she"—occupied what amounted to the MIEF's Executive Officer billet, handling all of the internal details of his command. AIs were good at the routine and picky details.

In some ways, Alexander preferred AIs to people. Their logic, their clean rationality, their essential lack of random emotion coupled with their programmed commitment to such concepts as *loyalty* and *duty* made them ideal both as subordinates and as companions. The thought brought with it a pang of memory, of the sort that people said faded with time . . . but never swiftly enough.

He took the memory out once again, examining it, feeling it. For over two decades, he'd been partnered with a lovely and keenly intellectual woman named Tabatha, but she'd left him five years back. That had been just after the Battle of Krulak Space, and the destruction of a Xul base in the firestorm of a double star nova. *Hermes* had translated back to Sol Space for replacements and supplies . . . and Tabatha had simply packed her things and shuttled down to Earth. He'd tried to find her, but his attempts to link with her had been blocked. Her own personal secretary, imitating perfectly her voice and mannerisms, had told him only that she needed time and space to grow on her own . . . and to have a relationship with someone who would *be* there for her.

Well, they *said* the memories would fade. He'd seen precious little evidence of that as yet.

Five years. . . .

He shoved the memory aside. The trouble with artificial intelligences, he thought, lay in the deeper moral implications. They *were* nothing more than complex software, epiphenomena arising from the interplay of positive and negative charges within the networks interconnecting massively parallel sets of hardware.

But they certainly acted as though they felt—the more advanced ones, anyway—and most cyberneticists believed that they did possess a genuine sense of self, of self-awareness, and that they were sentient within any reasonable meaning of that still poorly understood word. It brought into question a lot of attitudes and assumptions about AIs that had existed since their first, crude incarnations eight centuries ago—programming them to accept self-immolation, for example, which was routine now in the case of the AIs piloting Euler Starbursters into the cores of stars to detonate them.

As a Marine general, Alexander had given countless orders that had, one way or another, meant death for men and women under his command, but those Marines were volunteers, all of them, and often they were asked specifically to volunteer a second time for particularly hazardous missions. Giving human beings orders that might result in their deaths seemed quite different from accessing the mind of a being every bit as intelligent and self-aware as a person and writing in lines of code that made it accept suicide as a right and proper action.

The orders being prepared now for what was evolving into Operation Heartfire were like that. The AIs that would precede 1MIEF and *Pax Galactica* into the Core would have no choice in the matter. Lines of code would dictate their choices, and they would choose to enter the Xul fastness at the Galaxy's center in a mission at *least* as suicidal as diving an FTL starship through a sun. The humans in Heartfire would at least be able to make a more or less informed choice freely. . . .

Maybe he simply envied the emotionless aspects of artificial intelligences and their relationships with humans.

Damn it, why had Tabatha left him? The two of them had shared so much together for over twenty years. It just didn't make logical sense. *Why?* . . .

There did not appear to be any answers.

He was still studying the simulated image of Earth moments later. "General?" a familiar voice said in his thoughts. "Am I interrupting?"

"Of course you are, Liam. That's your job, isn't it?"

Admiral Taggart's icon unfolded in Alexander's mind, dress Navy uniform, medals, and corona. He wondered what the admiral really looked like at the moment. With icons and simulated realities, Liam Taggart could be in his bathrobe and slippers at the moment, and Alexander would never know it.

"I wanted to know what you think about this Pax thing."

Alexander gave a mental shrug. "Hardly matters what we think, does it? We have our orders. . . ."

"The hell with that. Yarlocke is playing politics with you and the MIEF, and she's going to get us all killed."

"I think she has her own agenda."

"Yeah. Big surprise. What is it?"

"Damned if I know. I think the important point, though, is that she has a lot of people on her side. Most of them well-meaning, whatever her issues might be. We're on the front lines, you and I, and we tend to look at things in a rather black-and-white way. We exterminate the Xul, or the Xul exterminate us."

"Isn't that the way it is?"

"Maybe. Probably. But a lot of people in the Senate, and the people they represent, think that peace is the best option."

Taggart snorted. "Peace *is* the best option . . . when it *is* an option. Do you think the Xul are going to go for this?"

"Frankly, I don't think we know the Xul well enough yet to know what they'll do. But the evidence of the past few centuries suggests that . . . no. They literally don't know what 'peace' or 'co-existence' are. Hell, the xenosophontology people can't even make up their minds about whether or not the word 'sentience' applies to the Xul. Did you see that last downloaded report?"

Taggart nodded. "Yeah. They think the Xul mentality may be a hive mind, intelligent, but without conscious volition. I don't see how nonsentient beings could build starships, though."

"It's a matter of definitions. Semantics."

"Like . . . how do you define intelligence?"

"Exactly. Or self-awareness. Ants, bees, and termites perform incredible feats of engineering and design, but as far as we know there's no consciousness to it. Hell, we think *we're* self-aware, but what does that mean, precisely?"

"I've heard the arguments," Taggart said. "There's still debate as to whether our own AIs are truly self-aware and sentient, or just putting on a very good act through their programming."

"Right. And if that's the case, if we only imagine our AIs are self-aware because we've made them to act that way, maybe the Xul are the same. Acting on programmed guidelines laid down millions of years ago, like an anthill or a termite mound, but not truly conscious in the same way we are."

"In the way we *think* we are," Taggart said, and he chuckled. "Some of the mind mechanics don't think we're truly self-aware, either. We just imagine we are. This whole mind thing is just an illusory epiphenomenon arising from our neurochemistry."

"Too deep for me."

"So . . . do we have an AI for the initial core probe?" Taggart wanted to know.

"Yes. Pappy."

"The primary 1MIEF AI?"

"That's the one. We've been reconfiguring him by merging him with Thoth, the Spymaster AI that brought back that intel coup from the Xul Nightmare."

In fact, Thoth had been derived from Pappy in the first

place, a copy of the original administrative software updated and expanded to meet the special needs of his Penetrator mission in Cluster Space. He'd returned from that mission with a great deal of specialized knowledge—experiences from within the Xul virtual environment—and that data could now be folded directly into Pappy's expanded matrix. Thoth's penetrator algorithms had been incorporated in the update as well, as had everything learned from the Spymaster mission in the way of Xul operating frequencies, data channels, and security routines.

"Pappy-Thoth?" Taggart asked. "Sounds like some sort of culinary masterpiece."

"Well, at the moment we're calling him Pappy 2.0. But the upgrade is serious enough that N-2 is suggesting a whole new persona."

"A new name?"

"Yeah. Athena. The Greek goddess of wisdom."

"And with a bit of a martial air as well. I like it."

"We're readying a new Spymaster probe." He opened a new link window for Taggart. "Here are the specs. We're hoping to send it through as soon as we translate back to Cluster Space . . . say, in another week."

"Sounds good. What do our friends in the Senate think of this?"

"Why should they even know about it?"

"I don't know. This whole idea of treating the Xul *nice*. I presume being nice to the sons of bitches doesn't include spying on them."

"Our op-plan—the general op-plan we share with Congress, at any rate—includes site reconnaissance and gravitometric readings," Alexander said with studied indifference. "We have to know about the area we're entering. Gravity and radiation readings. Local stellar populations, planetary positions and masses, presence and locations of local technic infrastructures. *Not* knowing all that stuff before we send humans through is not an option. Hell, that's one reason we have military AIs in the first place."

"Scout recon then."

"Standard operating procedure. And if the Warlock doesn't like it, the whole operation is off. We have to know what the local picture is before we barge in there."

"Don't preach to me. I'm one of the choirboys. What happens if Yarlocke doesn't like it and the mission is scrubbed?"

"We send the Spymaster through anyway. This is too good an opportunity to fill in the blank pages. We know so damned little about the Xul, about what they are and how they think. Liam, that Xul node at the Galactic Core may be able to provide us with a hell of a lot of answers."

"And the *Pax Galactica*?"

Another mental shrug. "Hell, they can tag along if they want. Just so they don't get in the way when the shooting starts."

"You assume there will be shooting then?"

"Assume? I'm *counting* on it. We've been fighting the bastards for a long, long time, and others have been fighting them as long or even longer. The Eulers. The N'mah. The An. The Builders. We might not understand how they think, or even if they think . . . but one thing we do know is that *peace* is not a part of their philosophical worldview. When we step through that gate in Cluster Space and appear at the Core, it's going to be like jamming a stick into a hornet's nest. All hell is going to break loose." He expanded the image of Earth, still hanging in his mind. The pinpoints marking personnel on shore leave were gone. What was left was Earth as it appeared now far beneath the SupraQuito Ring Complex, a bit less than half-full, city lights dusting the continental areas of the night hemisphere, sunlight glaring off streaks and swirls of cloud on the day side.

"I just hope we have what it takes to see it through, to end the threat, the *break* the Xul, once and for all."

"Well, one thing's sure," Taggart said. "One way or the other, Yarlocke will get what she wants. Peace, or . . ." He broke off the thought.

" 'Or?' "

"I was going to say peace, or an end to 1MIEF. But I'd hate to see Earth trying to hold out against what the Xul could send out this way, once we kick over the hornet's nest."

"No," Alexander said, still looking at the impossibly beautiful, infinitely delicate blue and white apparition of the Earth. "No, I wouldn't like to see that at all. . . ."

12

Atlantis Grotto
Sunken Miami, Earth
0125 hrs, local

"Hey!" Garroway said, startled as the realization hit him. "Do you guys know what the date is?"

"Oh-four-oh-seven," Armandez told him. "Why? You having a problem with your internal timekeeper?"

"The Fourth of July," Warhurst said. He lifted his glass. "Happy birthday, United States of America!"

"United States?" Kath said, wrinkling her nose. "What's that . . . like the Commonwealth?"

"Not quite," Lieutenant Ramsey told her. "The original United States was the forerunner of the Commonwealth, yeah. After it grew to sixty, seventy-some states, though, it was getting too big and unwieldy to be easily governed. The Commonwealth was created as a kind of over-government for the old U.S. and for the new states and territories that were coming in, especially out-system. Eventually, the sovereignty of the U.S. kind of faded as the power of the Commonwealth grew."

"The Marines still remember, though," Garroway said. The alcohol was wrapping itself around his brain, he realized, bringing feelings normally deep-buried to the surface. If this continued, he thought, he'd have to kick in the sobering circuitry pretty soon. "The Fourth of July . . . and the Tenth of November."

"What's the Tenth of November?" Traci wanted to know.

"You're hanging out with this character," Garroway said, nodding toward Warhurst, "and you don't know?"

"It's the anniversary of the founding of the U.S. Marine Corps," Warhurst told her. "The Corps' birthday."

"Yup," Ramsey said. "This coming November the Corps'll be eleven hundred twelve years young. So there, Mr. Forrestal!"

Garroway and Warhurst both chuckled. Nine hundred forty-one years before, during a fiercely contested battle on a volcanic scrap of an island in the Pacific Ocean called Iwo Jima, five Marines and a Navy hospital corpsman raising the U.S. flag atop a mountain named Suribachi had been immortalized in the act by a chance-snapped photograph. Secretary of the Navy James Forrestal, then on the beach at the base of the mountain, had turned to Marine General Holland Smith and told him that the raising of that flag meant that there would be a Marine Corps for the next five hundred years.

The incident, experienced in sim by all Marine recruits, was a point of Corps pride. Five hundred years? The Corps had endured over twice that, now.

One hundred eleven years ago, there'd been a mammoth party throughout the Corps celebrating the Marines' one thousandth birthday—a thousand years since the Marine Corps had begun signing up recruits at the Tun Tavern in Philadelphia, in the year 1775. There was talk of an even more enthusiastic Corps-wide celebration in fifty-nine more years, one thousand years after the raising of the flag on Suribachi.

Garroway wondered if he would still be here to join in the festivities. It was distinctly possible; he would only be eighty-seven then, and with nanoanagathics most people nowadays lived to be two hundred or more.

Most *civilians*, he thought, correcting himself. Unless he

followed Gunny Warhurst's example and retired, he stood a good chance of taking the Long Orbit—burial in space, assuming they'd recovered his body.

Of course, with the Xul threat, the same could be said of any one of the civilians here in the Atlantis Grotto. Earth and its delicate deep-space infrastructure and far-flung colonies remained horrifically vulnerable to a Xul strike.

He shook himself, thrusting the sudden and unexpected flow of gloom aside. He wondered if he should use his personal med implants to adjust his brain chemistry, then decided against it. Good friends and a pleasant evening out on the town should provide all the attitude adjustment he needed. He was actually feeling pretty good, though his new legs were sore. A full Earth gravity dragged at him, wore at his leg muscles, as the artificial gravity on board ship— usually set to around a half-G compromise between Earth and Mars—never did.

The six of them had come to the Grotto for a final evening together. Up-Ring transport had been so thoroughly snarled for the past thirty-six hours that there was no way they were going to make it to SupraQuito before noon tomorrow. They'd dressed up for the evening. Garroway, Armandez, and Ramsey were in Marine full-dress. Warhurst wore a pattern of fluorescent, animated tattoos, while Kath and Traci wore complementary, sensually shifting patches of liquid light.

The Atlantis Grotto, in keeping with the dinner, dance, and sex club's theme, was murkily lit by shifting patterns of undersea color. The main dining area was a domed transparency, some ten meters beneath the surface, on the coral-encrusted sea floor southeast of the central Miami pylons. Faux-Greek architecture had been erected around the dome— huge marble columns and pillars, many of them collapsed, and the eerie shadows of sunken temples, all lit from below by colored lights. By daylight, Garroway understood, the place looked quite different; at night, the light show was spectacular, but the subdued illumination meant that the light worn by the civilians was all the more brilliant. He could have read printed text by the silvery glow streaming off of Traci's breasts.

High overhead, within the cavernous space beneath the dome, a focused and self-contained agrav field had been set up within a shifting, boiling sphere of green light. Couples, trios, and larger groups danced to the sensuous background music inside the sphere, or swam, or engaged in enthusiastically public sex. The figures twisted and turned and moved against the background of the aquatic glow.

Technically, Garroway, Ramsey, and Armandez were stranded. They'd tried to catch the up-Ring shuttle as scheduled on the 30th, and found the civilian transport had overbooked and they'd been bumped. Miami and Orlando, both, were crowded with Navy and Marine personnel trying to get back to the *Hermes* at Ring SupraQuito.

Yesterday, the *Hermes* had left the dock at SupraQuito and moved to L-3, a gravitationally stable zone at Lunar orbit, directly opposite the Moon from Earth. From there, she was beginning the time-consuming process of shuttling 1MIEF warships and transports back out to Cluster Space, three and four at a time tucked into her cavernous cargo bay.

"So . . . you think we're going to get into trouble for being AWOL?" Armandez asked.

"We may get an ass-chewing," Garroway said. "Captain Black has been known to chow down on green Marine tail from time to time when they pushed recall too close to the wire."

"Hell," Ramsey said. "There must be three thousand Marines in the same fix right now, all trying to get back up-Ring at once. We all checked in on the Net. It'll be all right."

"Maybe if you're lucky," Warhurst growled, "they'll leave without you!"

"I wouldn't call that lucky," Garroway said. "We could be looking at a captain's mast—maybe even a general court."

"Again, us and three thousand other Marines," Ramsey said. "They won't leave without us."

"Why do you say we'd be lucky, Gunny?" Armandez asked Warhurst.

He shrugged. "Jesus. Dropping in on Xul Central? That's not my idea of fun. It's more like suicide, especially if you're on board the first ship into battlespace. Have you seen an op-plan yet?"

"No," Garroway replied.

"You think they'd tell us?" Ramsey said, laughing. "The grunts are *always* the last to know!"

"A couple of days ago I linked with a guy I know in Personnel," Garroway said. "He said the plan was still holding on getting data back from our AIs. They're supposed to send a bunch of probes through to the Core from Cluster Space. When they come back, if they come back, we'll better know what to expect."

"Makes sense," Warhurst said. "Assuming this peace initiative of the Senate's doesn't get in the way."

"It already has," Ramsey said. He sounded bitter. "That ship should have been *ours*."

"I heard the *Pax* is almost complete," Armandez said. "She's a sister to the *Hermes*. Just as big, with FTL capability *and* she can translate."

Translation was the big advantage possessed by *Hermes*-class transports. Originally, a decade before, *Hermes* had been an immense military facility called Skybase, designed to lurk unobserved in the little-understood hyperdimensional realm variously called paraspace or the Quantum Sea. She had station-keeping drives and agravitics just powerful enough to nudge her slowly through normal space.

With a solid enough understanding of the metrics of local space and of those of a desired destination, however, *Hermes* could phase-shift—translate, in mathematical terms—from one point in normal space through paraspace to another point, even if those points were separated by tens of thousands of light years. The maneuver was called a Quantum Space Translation, or QST, and it had proven to be the most efficient means to bridge intragalactic distances, bypassing the usually guarded choke points of the stargates.

Enormous amounts of Zero-Point energy torn from the Quantum Sea were required for each translation, and only truly huge mobile facilities like the *Hermes*-Skybase could manage the feat. *Hermes* massed two million tons, a face-to-face double saucer structure measuring over five hundred meters from rim to rim, with an enormous, open docking bay giving the appearance of a deep bite taken from the edge. Similar to some of the mining bases and colonies used in Sol's planetoid belt and out in the dark, cold reaches of the Oort Cloud, the UCS *Hermes* possessed ZPE power taps massive enough to manage QST travel.

A major upgrade eight years ago had installed an Alcubierre Drive module as well, so she was no longer a tug-towed hulk with translation capabilities. All things considered, *Hermes* gave the Commonwealth one of its few advantages in the war against the Xul.

The trouble was, 1MIEF needed more such monster ships. *Hermes* could tuck three or four warships into her docking bay—more if they were as small as escorts or patrol vessels—and make the translation to a battle zone. She would drop her ships off as though she were a titanic fleet carrier, then translate back to her origin point to take on another load of warships.

But there were currently 135 vessels of all types in 1MIEF, so each full fleet translation required twenty or more separate trips to transport the entire fleet, an operation that could take several days. The requirement sharply limited the fleet's tactical options. Those first three or four drop-offs would be all alone in hostile battlespace once *Hermes* phase-shifted out for the second load, so long-range fleet ops had to be staged through secure rendezvous points.

And no Marine enjoyed the thought of being in that first combat drop.

Ever since the first use of QST transport ten years before, the Corps had been urging the Senate to approve the construction of at least ten more fleet transports, of *Hermes'* mass or better. Six years ago, the Senate—after lengthy battles in the Appropriations Committee—had approved *two* new hulls, to be named *Brynhldr* and *Anubis*.

The ship names were those of mythological psychopomps

or "guides of souls"—deities or angelic beings, like the Greek Hermes, charged with conducting the souls of the dead to the afterlife. The *Brynhldr* had been scheduled to enter service this month, but, just weeks ago, the Senate had announced that she would be launched under direct senatorial command, and that her name would be changed to *Pax Galactica*.

Like Ramsey, most Marines felt bitter about what seemed to be a betrayal by the government. As Ramsey had said, that ship should have gone straight from the AresRing shipyards to service with 1MIEF, to cut translation times for the fleet in half.

"Tell me something, Gunny," Garroway said to Warhurst.

"Shoot."

"Why'd you get out? I mean, I hear you griping about the *Pax* shit and the government and all of that, but that's no different from just about every other Marine I know. Back when I was in boot camp, you seemed to me to be about the most gung-ho Marine ever spawned, *the* official image of a fighting Marine. I just can't picture you retired."

"Jesus, Gare!" Armandez laughed. "He's sitting there naked between Traci and Kath and you ask him *that*? The guy might be a Marine, but he's not crazy!"

"Hell, I thought being crazy was part of the Marine job description," Ramsey put in.

"You don't have to be crazy to join up," Armandez said, taking a sip of her drink, "but it sure helps."

But Warhurst was looking thoughtful. "I guess you could say it was a crisis of faith," Warhurst said after a moment. "Living the Corps life, I was . . . I don't know. Falling out of touch with the people back home. We have our own little microsociety in the Corps, you know."

Garroway noticed Warhurst's casual use of the present tense, but said nothing. An ancient adage had it that there were plenty of former active-duty Marines, but no *ex*-Marines.

"I found I don't have much use for the Ringers," he continued. "The fucking down-Ring tourists. Native Earthers, though, they're something different."

Garroway looked up at the illuminated air overhead. Fifteen or twenty dancers had apparently abandoned the music and were engaging in a mass orgy. "Different how?" he asked. "These people seem as much in love with themselves as any Ringer."

"Who . . . them?" Warhurst said, indicating the tangle of limbs and smooth bodies writhing overhead. "Those *are* Ringers. Most native locals can't afford a tourist Mecca like the Grotto."

"Figures," Ramsey said. "Business and capital has been flowing off-planet ever since Armageddonfall."

"Right. Earth's whole population now is less than . . . I don't know. Two, three billion? Five hundred years ago, before Armageddonfall, it was something like sixteen billion."

"I heard the people left on Earth are called *The Caretakers*," Armandez said.

Warhurst snorted. "As if they could do a damned thing to protect Earth if the Xul showed up tomorrow. The Belt and the Rings are where most of the system's population lives, now, and that's where the money and the major corporate facilities and the big population centers all are."

"Stands to reason," Ramsey said. "Commerce follows opportunity. The Inner Belt is where things are happening now."

"Yeah, there, and more and more out in the Kuiper Belt and Oort Cloud. If the Xul ever do show up, they'll have their job cut out trying to track down millions of individual habs and orbital colony complexes."

"Do you think they couldn't?" Garroway asked.

"Of course they could," Warhurst said with a shrug. "Next time won't be 2314. They'll be here in force."

"Which beings us back to the question. Why are you here?"

"Maybe I'm trying to remember Earth the way it was. Before all the damned tourists started coming down-Ring. Or maybe I just figure the natives need someone to speak up for 'em. They're not as wedded to high tech down here as up in the Ring, and sometimes the techie-toys from orbit tend to drown them out."

"Our savior," Traci said with mockingly overstated gratitude, like a stereotypical damsel in distress.

"What would we *ever* have done without him?" Kath added, putting her head on his shoulder.

"Aw, knock it off," Warhurst growled. "Happens I like Earth and Earth locals, okay?"

"It's the Ringers he can't stand," Ramsey said.

"Well, speaking as a Ringer," Garroway said, grinning, "fuck you very much."

"You're not a Ringer, Garroway," Warhurst told him. "You're a Marine. There's a difference, or hadn't you noticed?"

"Oh, I've noticed." Garroway continued to watch the erotic show overhead. "Those people don't even know they're at war."

"When it comes down to it," Ramsey observed, "isn't that why we're here? To keep them safe enough that they can enjoy at least the illusion of peace?"

"That's one way of looking at it, I suppose."

"What the hell?" Ramsey said. He looked around the room. "Someone's snooping."

"Interrogator?"

"Yeah. I think I see him. Over there."

Every person with an implant and a personal secretary possessed a cache of public data, which could be accessed by anyone else through an implant function called an interrogator. If you saw someone you were interested in, you could interrogate their cache electronically without approaching them, learning a name, a contact code, or anything else you didn't mind giving to strangers on the street. Most Marines kept their caches empty or nearly so. Garroway's read GNY-SGT. GARROWAY, UCMC and the legend SEMPER FI. If anyone wanted to know more, he reasoned, they could come up and ask him in person.

Ramsey fed him a targeting cursor marking the source of the interrogation, one of two young men seated at a table on the far side of the Grotto.

"Hey!" Armandez said. "He just pinged me, too."

"Curious civilian, you think?" Warhurst asked.

"More than that. He just sent me an e," she said.

"What does he want."

"Me," Armandez said. "In bed with him. I've locked him out."

"Mm. Maybe we should call it an evening, folks," Ramsey said.

"I'll be damned if I'll have my dinner and a pleasant evening interrupted by a damned snoop," Warhurst said. "Uh-oh. He's coming over."

"Low profile, people," Ramsey said. "We don't want trouble."

"And if that character does?" Garroway asked.

As he strutted toward them, the guy made an impressive display. He was essentially nude, but with most of the left side of his body, from scalp to boots, covered by implanted decoration, nanotechnically grown whorls and loops and filigree in gleaming silver, like liquid metal, and ebon black. The style, Garroway had heard, was called technorg, and emphasized the blend of the natural organic with the artificial.

The effect was somewhat clumsily highlighted by the size of the man's penis, genetically enhanced so that, in its flaccid state, it hung nearly to the guy's knees. The organ was purely for show, of course. No human female could have accommodated that thing sexually. When aroused, the outsized member was actually designed to *shrink* to more normal, though still generous, proportions. At least that was the theory.

This casual biological reworking of the human body was something Garroway found vaguely disturbing. His own body possessed hundreds of upgrades, of course, from his cerebral implants to his partly machine, partly biological new legs, to artificial pigments in his skin that helped shed ionizing radiation, to buckytube carbon weave grown around each of his bones to make them stronger. Every one of those enhancements, however, was Marine Corps issue, designed to make him a better Marine—faster, smarter, stronger, harder to kill. This guy's hardware—not to mention his grotesquely oversized software—were purely for ego gratification and for show.

"Well, well," the kid said as he approached the table. "What've we got here . . . pretty-boy marines? And a *very* pretty girl Marine!" He reached for Armandez. "How about you and me blow this hab and find us some privacy, baby?"

"Get lost, civilian," Armandez said. Garroway was amazed at how much disinterest mingled with nitrogen ice Nikki could pack into those three words. As his hand reached for her shoulder, she shifted slightly, and pushed it aside.

"Don't be like that, baby! I can show you a *real* good time!"

"Back off, kid," Garroway told him. "You don't know what you're messing with."

"Don't I? Fuck off, jarhead. This little gyrene slut deserves to find out what a *real* man is like!"

Garroway sighed, stood up, and turned to face the civilian. He'd run into this kind of testosterone-sodden display before, and always with the same outcome. There were civilians who just felt they had to prove their machismo by taking on a Marine. The surprise was that each time one of the idiots was shown the error of his ways, three more seemed to pop up and try the same nonsense.

"Don't, Gare," Armandez told him, standing up as well. "I need the practice."

"You?" The civilian snickered, leering at her. "What's a pretty bit of fluff like *you* gonna do?"

"Well," she said thoughtful, "I *could* jam that ugly thing dangling between your legs so far up your ass it comes out your nose, then tie a knot in the end to hold it in place in case you need a blow job. But I really don't want to get your slime on my hands. . . ."

The civilian's leer turned to a snarl, but before he could move, Armandez snapped her arm out too fast for the eye to

follow, two slim fingers thumped against the civilian's forehead, above and squarely between his eyes. The weiji-do
strike, backed by the Marine's augmented physiology, delivered the energy of a hammer's blow. The civilian, who out-
massed Armandez by at least two and a half to one, staggered
backward, arms flailing, and collapsed across a nearby table
with a crash. The two elegantly clad diners at the table
screamed and knocked their chairs over trying to get back.

Stooping next to him, Garroway touched his left palm to
the man's wrist. Public access data flowed—name, address,
health status. Lennis Tarwhalen. SupraSingapore Complex,
EarthRing 1.

"He's just unconscious," Garroway told the others. "Nice
targeting, Nikki."

"Thanks."

"The little shit's from EarthRing!"

"You sound surprised," Warhurst said.

Garroway shrugged. "I figured he was a local."

"In case you hadn't noticed, the locals are pretty laid back
and, like I was saying, most of 'em don't have the money for
fancy electronics. Look at that metalwork. That guy has
tribal affiliations. He's down-Ring slumming."

"Slumming?" Garroway had not heard the word before.

"Some of the tribes like to come down-Ring and play
tourist," Warhurst said. "They get kicks making trouble, going after targets of opportunity. They cruise joints like this,
pick up girls for some fast sex, pick fights, bust places up,
and they know their tech is far enough ahead of Earth standard that it'll warn them if the local police are on the way."

"So what's the idiot doing rousting Marines?" Garroway
asked.

"Interesting," Ramsey observed, "that the little SOB ze-
roed in on Nikki. Not Traci or Kath."

"That display wasn't about sex," Warhurst pointed out.
"The jerk was cruising on ego and testosterone. If he could
put the moves on Nikki, he'd have bragging rights with his
tribe. He's bound to have visual and physiological recorders
worked into that fancy metalware. He was either recording

for later playback, or transmitting to his buddies. Most likely both."

Garroway scanned for the kid's companion, but the table was now empty. He did see another civilian, however, a powerfully muscled civilian in black armor, bearing down on them like an incoming hovertank. "Heads up," he warned. "Trouble! . . ."

"What do you jarhead grunts think you're doing to my place?" the man screamed, his face a bright red. "You think you can just come in and bust it up like it was nothin'?"

"The guy was getting out of line with one of my people, sir," Ramsey said. "He started it. We finished it."

"What are you, some kind of smart mouth? Who's gonna pay for the damage? Eh?"

Garroway saw three other men in armor moving in from different directions. The speed of the response and the fact that they were wearing a civilian grade of light combat armor both were interesting. It suggested a set-up, probably a deliberate plan to shake credits out of the Marines. A quick interrogation of the Grotto owner identified him as Jerard Usher, and indicated that the florid-faced man was, indeed, the owner of the Atlantis Grotto. His address, however, was listed as an apartment in Ring 5.

Music and conversation in the Grotto had ceased. Even the orgy overhead had, momentarily, at least, come to a halt as the revelers peered down at the confrontation on the main floor.

"We're going quietly," Garroway said. "We don't want any trouble."

"Yeah? Well, you got trouble, gyrene! You owe me five thousand for that busted table!"

"What . . . for this cheap crap?" His leg moved, a blindingly fast side kick into the central support of the table they'd been sitting at. The material was a tough, nanopolymer, but it tended to shatter under a strong enough impact. It shattered now, toppling the table and sending their drinks crashing to the floor.

Warhurst stepped up close to Usher, grasping the front of

the man's armored vest and lifting him off the deck one-handed. In his other hand, he brandished a shard of black plastic from the table. "Perhaps you weren't aware, *sir*, that while this stuff looks like mahogany, it is, in fact, a kind of plastic easily and cheaply grown from landfill mines. See? No splinters. At a guess, I'd say your table is worth no more than, oh, five newdollar creds or so."

The two Grotto employees, tough-looking bouncers, approached the tableau, but they stopped as Garroway, Armandez, and Ramsey dropped into weiji-do combat stances, facing them.

"Now, I can understand your trying to take advantage of some simple Marines visiting your establishment on liberty," Warhurst went on, his growl loud enough to carry throughout the listening room. "Watered-down drinks, the meat nanoconstituted from seaweed and scraps . . . and maybe you figure your hired help can pick a fight with 'em and shake 'em down for a few newdollars, right? But I'm a civilian, and I live right here in Miami. I know you, Usher . . . and I know the local law enforcement monitors."

"Hey, boss?" one of the bouncers said. He evidently didn't like the cold look he was getting from Armandez. "Whatta we do?"

"Uh . . . maybe . . ." Usher gurgled. "Maybe there was . . . a misunderstanding? We . . . uh . . . we thought the Marines here had started a fight."

"No, the Marines did not start a fight. As the lieutenant there told you, they finished it, but they didn't start it. Now . . . do you want to start a fight with us?"

"N-no."

"What?"

"No . . . sir."

Warhurst dropped the plastic shard, then slapped his free hand across a data pad on the man's left arm, triggering a credit transfer. "There's ten creds," he said. "To pay for two tables. I suggest you take it out of Mr. Tarwhalen's paycheck. He is one of your employees, yes?"

"Uh . . . no . . . I mean . . . I don't know . . ."

"We're leaving, now," Warhurst told him. Gently, almost lovingly, he lowered the man back to the deck. "We'll be passing the word to our friends that the Grotto doesn't care for service personnel as clientele."

"But . . . wait! No!" Usher's eyes went wide. "I . . . uh . . . told you, there was just a misunderstanding!"

"Well, there won't be any more of those, will there? C'mon, people."

Warhurst led the others out of the club.

"I think he really wanted to apologize," Armandez said.

"Of course he did. When the fleet's in, half his revenues must come from Marines and Navy personnel down-Ring on liberty. He can't afford to lose us."

"So why the shake-down?"

Warhurst shrugged. "Hell, it's always been that way. Navy towns, Army towns, they grow up outside of bases like weeds, and their main source of income is military. Some treat their guests good. Others figure they can roust you because you don't want trouble, don't want the SPs hauling your ass off to the brig, don't want to maybe face a captain's mast for conduct prejudicial. Damned civilians . . . what? What's happening?

Garroway, Armandez, and Ramsey all had suddenly frozen in mid-stride, far-away looks on their faces. Garroway listened for a moment to a message streaming in through his implant.

"Sorry, Gunny," he said. "We're getting a special recall."

"Yeah," Ramsey said. "A transport is touching down outside of Miami. They want us aboard *now*."

Warhurst nodded. "Sent you an official ride, did they? Well . . . thanks for coming down and looking me up, Marines."

"Thanks for your hospitality," Ramsey replied. "Gunny . . . ladies . . ."

"Hey, come back next time you rotate through," Traci told them. "Please?"

She sounded . . . not scared, exactly, but very, very earnest. Like she genuinely wanted to see them again, but knew there was a chance that they would not be coming back.

"We'll take you up on that, Traci," Ramsey told her. He grinned. "Right now, we have some Xul to take down. After the Atlantis Grotto, it should be easy!"

They boarded a local commuter submarine that would get them to Miami proper in ten minutes.

And Garroway wondered if he would ever feel the tiring drag of Earth's gravity again.

13

Combat Center,
UCS Hermes
Cluster Space
0810 hrs, GMT

"A probe's coming back through, General," a technician reported. "The first one. Athena is coming on-line. We have a
data stream."

Alexander was standing in *Hermes'* battle command center, a cavernous compartment dominated by large display
screens, and by the ranks of couches occupied by men and
women linked into 1MIEF's computer net. Most of the
screens showed views, from various angles, of Cluster Space,
where *Hermes* drifted amidst a cloud of smaller warships.
The local star, now a slow-dimming nova, still burned fiercely,
bright enough to banish into invisibility the pale glory of the
galactic spiral far beyond, but it was shrunken now to an
arc-brilliant pinpoint of harsh light imbedded in the twists
and shining folds of its own atmosphere, shells of gas blasted
into space by the star's recent detonation. The light, cold and
blue-white, gave a sharp edge to the nearest stargate, a vast
hoop of tarnished gold.

On the far side of that ring lay the Galactic center.

He considered linking in. Generally, he preferred to be
on-line for raw feeds such as this one. The incoming data

were cleaner that way, more coherent, better ordered, and with full access to ancillary data as it was required. Still, it was good to appear in person once in a while, rather than solely by virtual presence icon.

But to get a good understanding of the incoming data, he would need to link in, at least superficially. There was simply no other way to understand even a fraction of what would be coming through. In pre-network days, of course, scout/recon data would have been compiled by an intelligence team, analyzed, then condensed into a report delivered by staff officers—an excellent way to lose the subtle nuances, or for the commanding officer to be fed only that information he wished to hear.

"I'm going to take this," he told Liam Taggart.

"You want full-im?" the admiral asked. "We can scare up an extra couch."

"Not necessary." For full-immersion, he would need a couch, entering what amounted to unconsciousness as he stepped into the link's virtual world. "I just want the overview."

Taggart grunted. "I think I'll wait for the briefing." And there *would* be briefings, of course, after the data had been thoroughly analyzed. But Alexander had been waiting for this moment with growing anticipation. To hell with command patience. He wanted to see what the Spymasters had found. *The Galactic Core*. The expeditionary force's astronomers and physicists would be waiting for this feed even more eagerly. The realm at the Galaxy's center was still largely mysterious, holding riddle upon riddle, enigma upon enigma.

On a nearby console was a palmlink. Placing his hand flat against the smooth plastic, he brought the myriad threads interlaced through the skin of his palm into contact with the link network. A password and automatic DNA check opened the security gate, and the data flooded through.

A window opened in his mind, showing a picket ship's external camera view of the incoming Spymaster, a blunt torpedo drifting in front of the nearest stargate. He repressed a start at the sight. They'd sent the probe through fewer than forty hours ago; it was returning worn and battered, the once pristine blue and white paint of the Commonwealth logo on its hull sandblasted almost completely down to bare metal and plastic, the black surface beneath burnt, scored, dented, and even peeled away in places as though it had been through a savage firefight.

Perhaps it had been. He would know in a moment.

"Looks like it's been in a fight," Admiral Taggart said in his mind. "Could mean they know we're here."

"We'll keep the fleet on full alert," Alexander told him. He didn't add the words *of course.* "But that might not be battle damage. We know that conditions at the Galactic core are . . . extreme."

"Gas and dust, high radiation levels," Taggart said. "Yeah, if we go in there, we'll be using everything we've learned in the past ten years dealing with novae. But if the Xul *did* spot it . . ."

"I know. And they'll have tracked it, and know where we are."

The Spymaster had been designed to slip into an enemy-occupied system and remain undetected, using various stealth-cloaking technologies as Athena, the on-board AI, probed local computer nets and virtual realities.

But the environment existing at the center of the Galaxy, as Alexander had suggested, was extraordinary, still largely unknown and unmapped, but definitely not conducive to life as Humankind understood it. It was a realm of hot gases and plasmas, powerful magnetic fields, and peculiar objects unlike anything found elsewhere in the Galaxy.

There might be other dangers to spacecraft within the Core besides lurking Xul.

At the moment, Athena—or a copy of the program, at any rate—was being downloaded into *Hermes'* computer network, where it was being assimilated by Pappy. Essentially, Athena was a smaller, more compact version of one aspect of Pappy, but with large quantities of matching code that were now being compared, line by line, with the incoming information. Data acquired in the Core—Athena's memory, basically—could be stored and analyzed as it came through. Thousands of subroutines, called code spiders, were going through the data now, cataloguing it and marking the most critical bits for immediate study. Although the data were raw—meaning only another AI could read and understand them at the moment—some of them consisted of camera and sensor imagery, which could be split off from the main stream and sampled by humans.

Alexander let himself enter one of those side streams . . . struggling to understand just what it was he was seeing.

At first, all he could make out was a bewildering wash of red and blue-white.

The human brain actually needs to learn to see, and seeing, of course, takes place in the brain, not the eyes. If the image being transmitted from the eyes is so strange, so alien as to be outside of human experience, it can take time for the brain to interpret the image in any meaningful way.

Gradually, though, Alexander was able to pick meaning out of the blurred and confused tumble of color.

He appeared to be looking into the center of a hollow shell, with shining walls composed of myriad stars and interwoven strands of soft-glowing dust and gas. The stars were as densely packed, it seemed, as the beehive stars within a globular cluster, like the one dominating the skies of Cluster Space. It looked much like the vista of another realm he'd seen—a region called Starwall just outside the vast, flattened sphere of suns and nebulae comprising the Galactic hub.

It was tough to judge distances by eye. Those stars were hundreds, perhaps thousands of light years away, but there was no way to judge that from the image in his mind. But the star-enclosed volume *felt* huge, intertwined by glowing nebulae and bathed in soft light.

Over all, that light held a distinctly reddish hue; the stars of the Galactic Core were old, old . . . red giants, among the most ancient suns of the Galaxy. Once they'd been thought to have been spawned in an epoch before supernovae had scattered transmuted elements across the heavens, and, therefore, metal poor of the type known as Population I. Later research had proven, though, that many generations of stars had come and gone within the Galactic Core, with barrages of supernovae flooding the region with heavier and heavier elements from which new generations of stars had been born.

How many of those massed red stars, Alexander wondered, had planets, had *life*? The entire galactic hub was bathed in intense radiation fields—they'd proven that with a military operation at Starwall a decade ago, just outside the Hub—and most xenobiologists assumed that life could not evolve under such extreme, such *violent* conditions.

But he knew that Life always was stronger, more surprising, more unpredictable, and less amenable to being stuffed into a box for easy categorization than humans ever were able to credit or accept.

So very many suns.

So many possible worlds. . . .

At first, that curving wall of stars was all Alexander could really see, and much of that was lost in a distinct haze that filled the star-hollow. As he adjusted to the scale and scope of the strange panorama, however, he began to notice other things, things that helped put the scene into perspective, helped reveal its true size and depth. As he kept looking, other features began to separate from the background, to make themselves known. He could pick out the gas-delineated bubbles of ancient supernovae, and several rings of gas clouds encircling the very center.

That central region of the image was dominated by a number of objects. Distance and scale made them all seem tiny, almost toy-like, and Alexander had to employ a zoom function in the download window to better see. Brightest and most obvious was a tight-packed but ragged cluster of brilliant, diamond-hard stars emerging from the tatters of a blue-lit nebula. Several of the stars were particularly bright, so bright that Alexander found himself mentally squinting at them, trying to see through their glare. Assuming that all had been born from the same nebula at about the same

time, they should all be of about the same mass and brightness. Those most brilliant of the stars were exploding supernovae. He could see the delicately sculpted folds and hollows
of the nebula, where radiation pressure from the exploding
stars were working the clouds of dust and gas like sculptor's
clay.

Nearby burned a bright red star, its crystalline ruby color
sharply contrasting with the blue light of the cluster; a tail,
like a comet's tail, streamed from the red giant directly
away from the hot glare of the cluster. And a few degrees
from that was something so strange that Alexander kept trying to focus on it, and kept failing, as though his eyes were
sliding right off of it. He had to focus sharply to make himself see the thing, which appeared to be imbedded in a
three-armed spiral of gas like a miniature galaxy.

Elsewhere were other objects—things like comets smeared
across light years, and something, well off to the side, that
looked like another, smaller miniature galaxy, its spiral
arms tightly wound into a flat accretion disk, and with brilliant shafts of luminescence, like searchlight beams, extending out from the poles of its central hub. That peculiar
object, at least, had been known to Earth astronomers for
many centuries. The searchlight beams were streams of
positrons emerging from a black hole; their interaction with
normal matter hundreds of light years from the singularity filled the Core with radio noise—the 511 keV shriek of
positronium annihilating its normal-matter counterpart—
electrons. That particular object, Alexander knew, had been
dubbed "The Great Annihilator" by Earth astronomers, but
it remained one of the deeper mysteries of the galactic Core.
Measurements of the velocity of gas within the accretion
disk showed that the singularity—probably originally a collapsed star—was equivalent to about ten to fifteen solar
masses. Astronomers had been looking for a black hole at
the Galaxy's center . . . but the Great Annihilator, paradoxi-
cally, was nowhere near massive enough to power all of the
strange goings-on in that eldritch region, and it was also
offset a bit—by perhaps 350 light years—from the actual

center of the Galaxy. In other words, the Great Annihilator was a black hole, but not *the* black hole, the one that scientists expected to mass at several *million* solar masses and to occupy the exact dead center of the Galaxy's gravitational system.

And there were other strangenesses as well. Perhaps weirdest optically were a number of streaks of light arcing across the gulf, where gas or dust had been smeared into vast, curving, and inter-nested bands or ring segments. Looking at these, Alexander was reminded forcibly of demonstrations he'd seen as a child of the existence of magnetic lines of force, using a magnet, a piece of paper, and iron filings to make the invisible fields of force visible. He had no doubt that he was looking at the effects of powerful magnetic fields here, as they reshaped clouds of ionized gas.

Alexander was still having trouble with scale as he studied the image, but the hollow within the central star cloud appeared to be filled with a faint mist, thin to the point of invisibility in some areas, so thick as to appear solid in others. Like a planetary atmosphere, the Core's haze shrouded things in the distance, like the far wall of Hub stars, and the curious artifact near the red sun was also blurred slightly by the haze, making it feel distant, and therefore titanic.

"I'm having some trouble with the scale," Taggart's voice said in Alexander's thoughts. "Just what the hell are we looking at?"

"The Galactic Core," Alexander said, speaking not so much in answer to Taggart's question as to release some of the pent-up awe he was feeling at the sight unfolding within his mind. He shook himself, then added, "What we're seeing matches the old radiotelescopy data. But it's different seeing it all by visible wavelengths, isn't it?"

"Amen to that. The question is, how much of that stuff is natural, and how much artificial? It looks to me like we may be seeing some evidence of engineering, but if so it's on a galactic scale. If that thing in the spiral is some kind of huge Xul base or fortress, how the hell can we hope to fight something that damned *big*?"

Alexander gave a wan grin, though Taggart couldn't see it in the sim. "We're not supposed to fight them, remember? Peace. That's the watchword now."

"Peace . . . with something so big and so advanced we're like insects by comparison? You know, Martin, I really don't like this."

"Me, either," Alexander replied. "But we're in the chain of command. Since when did whether or not we *liked* something have anything to do with what we did?"

"Yeah. Let's have a full three-sixty, okay?"

"Right."

The image data stream included information to reconstruct the view in all directions. With a thought, Alexander rotated their shared point of view, allowing the vista ahead to swing to the right. The Spymaster's vantage point, apparently, was in close to the center of the vast, empty hollow within the starclouds of the Hub. The wall of close-packed reddish suns extended in all directions, more or less equally blurred everywhere by the gas filling the central void. Behind the Spymaster probe, a stargate orbited in slow majesty, a golden hoop twenty kilometers across, the doorway leading into the Galactic Core from Cluster Space. Nearby, like tiny, metallic toys suspended in space, several structures hung near the Gate—the flattened sphere of a Xul fortress, and several tinier objects that were probably Type I or Type II hunterships.

Alexander never thought he would use the word *tiny* when thinking of typical Xul structures.

He studied that Xul outpost. Strange. Alexander had been expecting a much larger Xul presence here. The data gleaned from a Xul ship in Cluster Space had seemed pretty specific, indicating some sort of major complex here, something bigger than anything Humankind had yet encountered. One fort and a few ships might serve as pickets for the stargate, but not much else.

Taggart and others, though, believed the real Xul presence here lay much closer to the center.

There was an uncomfortable possibility, though, and that-was that some of what they were seeing at GalCenter was artificial, structures built by the Xul.

A chilling possibility. The ancient enemy of Humankind tended to build on a truly massive scale. But here, within the Galactic Core, against that staggering vista, even the largest Xul complexes appeared reduced to near insignificance.

If, however, Taggart was right, if the enigmatic structures near the Galactic Center were in fact Xul artifacts, then the Xul were capable of building on a titanic scale that Humankind had never before even imagined was possible.

They would need to study the Spymaster data closely if they were to have a chance in hell of understanding just what it was they were up against here.

He found himself dreading the experience, dreading what they would actually find.

                                                      0414.1102

Combat Ops Center,
UCS Hermes
1545 hrs, GMT

Charel Ramsey entered the COC with Lieutenants Cosgriff and Shea. Their boss, the head of 1MIEF N-2, was waiting for them, already in a couch but not yet linked into the system. He was Navy captain Felix Pollard, a rough-edged son-of-a-bitch who'd been in the Navy for almost three decades now, but who'd passed on a number of promotions to flag rank because his love was intelligence work. Informal, even rude to the point of eccentricity in a service that tended to emphasize uniforms, decorum, and appearance, Pollard was perhaps the one man in the entire Commonwealth who best knew the Xul and their capabilities.

"Gentlemen," he said with gruff acknowledgment to Ramsey and Shea, then added, "and Lieutenant Cosgriff. About damned time."

"We came down as soon as they passed the word for us, sir," Shea said.

Pollard grunted. "Strap in. You three need to see this."

The three junior intelligence officers took link couches side by side, settling back in their embrace as connector grips grew from the couch frameworks to embrace hands, arms, and heads. Ramsey felt the familiar tingle at the back of his skull, then the flare of light and sensation as data began flooding through.

The COC briefing center was wiped away, and he was immersed within the spectacular, mind-bending vastness of the Galactic Core . . .

"We're still analyzing the data," Pollard told them, his voice a growl in their minds. "Enough came back to keep an army of analysts busy for the next few centuries. But we have to move on this, fast. General Alexander wants to begin fleet ops in here within the week. And we're going to need you three to bring us back some specifics first."

All three of them had seen "rushes," the unedited and unannotated images sent back by the first Spymaster to return to Cluster Space. What they were looking at now was far cleaner, more detailed, and more highly interactive. A thought would call up blocks of data describing a particular object—or at least best-guess theories about what it might be—as well as hard data such as distances, size, and mass. The four officers—three Navy and Ramsey, the lone Marine in the group—could move through the simulated volume of space quite freely with a simulated velocity many times that of light, observing and examining everything. It was much like immersing within one of the interactive planetariums he'd seen and enjoyed as a kid.

Their briefing tour began, however, not at the Galactic Core, but from a vantage point high above the Galactic spiral, looking down on the Hub from some tens of thousands of light years out. Every Marine who'd been out to Cluster Space had seen this view with his own eyes, and not just in downloaded sim, and the basic structure of the Galaxy was comfortably familiar—a flattened, central mass of dense-packed suns perhaps ten thousand light years across and six thousand thick. From here, the central bar of the nucleus was clearly visible. Like many others scattered across the cosmos, the Galaxy of Humankind was a barred spiral, with a central core about twice as long, nearly 20,000 light years, as it was wide, imbedded in a glowing, flattened-sphere, beehive swarm of red-hued stars.

Out from the Hub, past banked cliffs of fast-moving dust and light-obscuring molecular clouds, the galaxy's spiral arms stretched out into the intergalactic Gulf, two major arms—the Sagittarius Arm and the Norma-Scutum Arm—coming off the ends of the hub bar, and three lesser arcs and arms—the Scutum-Crux Arm, the Perseus Arm, the Local or Orion Arm—in between. Those arms were strikingly distinct against the velvet black of the background space. The appearance, Ramsey reminded himself, was an illusion. The number and density of stars within the spiral arms was actually only about ten percent higher than in the apparently empty voids between. The effect was due to the density pattern moving out through the interstellar medium from the central Core, triggering star formation delineating standing waves. The arms, where interstellar material was being bunched up into stellar nurseries by those waves, were rich with young, hot, and therefore highly visible stars, and the brighter stars in turn illuminated vast fields of interstellar nebulae, which together gave the appearance of distinct spiral arms.

But the illusion was powerful and compelling.

It was startling to see just how dramatically *thin* the overall galactic disk actually was. The entire disk of stars stretched nearly 100,000 light years from one side to the other, yet the main portions of the spiral arms were never more than about two thousand light years thick, even in toward the Core.

"We've had a general idea of the topology of GalCenter for a long time," Pollard said. A point of green light winked on within the Orion Arm, between the Sagittarius and Perseus Arms, marking the solar system of Earth. "From Earth-Sol Space, of course, the Core region is blocked by the intervening clouds of dust, gas, and stars. Astronomers estimate that for every one hundred billion photons coming toward us from the Galactic Core, one actually reaches us. We've been hampered in our studies of just what's in there by the barrier presented by thousands of light years of obscuring dust and gas."

As Pollard spoke, the angle of view changed, so that it seemed as though the quartet of viewpoints were zooming in on the spiral arm toward the microscopic point of light representing the Sol system, then flashing in toward the star clouds of Sagittarius, piercing vast, high-banked clouds of light, of myriad shining stars, of streams and blobs and masses of obscuring dust hundreds of light years long on the way in toward the Hub.

"Back in the 20th Century," Pollard continued, "we couldn't see the Galactic Center optically, but we were able to kind of peer through all the crap and into the core region using radio telescopes and devices sensitive to infrared and X-ray wavelengths. Even from twenty-six thousand light years out from the center, out in the galactic suburbs, we could manage a resolution of objects as small as twenty astronomical units across—say, the size of Saturn's orbit.

"Since then, we've been able to get a better look at things in there from new vantage points, like Cluster Space. But until now, we've never actually seen the central region at optical wavelengths."

Their viewpoints emerged from a vast, curving wall of stars. "The innermost core of the Galactic Hub," Pollard went on, "is hollow. The gulf in here is about fifteen hundred light years across. Turns out it's filled with gas."

"Are you saying there's an atmosphere in here, sir?" Ramsey asked.

"It's still a pretty hard vacuum by Earth standards, Lieutenant, but the gas is denser at the Core, more concentrated, than in any other region of the Galaxy we've been able to measure. They estimate there's enough hydrogen here to form a hundred million new stars. Look there. . . ."

Ahead, a vast ring of nebula stretched across the center of the inner gulf, a thousand light years across and tilted some twenty degrees to the galactic plane, broken and lumpy in places, but giving the impression of great velocity even though it was visually frozen by its sheer scale. Data readouts showed Ramsey that the ring was expanding at 150 kilometers per second. The cloud was cold, at about ten degrees Kelvin; Ramsey's readouts began describing the cloud's composition—simple carbon monoxide and hydroxyl molecules, as well as more complex compounds, formaldehyde and formamide, acetaldehyde and ethanol . . .

"That ring, the astrophysicists say, must have been generated by an incredible explosion in the Galactic Core about one million years ago," Pollard explained. "It's a witches' brew of organic molecules."

"Ethanol, I see," Ramsey put in. "At least the fleet will have a great liberty when it arrives."

"Well, the Galaxy *is* a barred spiral," Lieutenant Shea added. "I think we just found the bar."

"Quiet, you two," Pollard growled. Their viewpoints continued to descend into the Galaxy's heart, flashing past the rapidly expanding smoke ring of nebulae. GalCenter was now five hundred light years ahead.

At four hundred light years from the center they passed an even thicker mass of molecular clouds, a vast and far-flung doughnut shape, dark on the outside, brilliant with shining nebulae and handfuls of bright, new-born stars within. Masers—lasers at microwave wavelengths—howled birth pangs into the cosmos.

"That expanding ring," Pollard told them, "which is passing outward through the hydrogen gas in here, is triggering massive star formation. The radio noise was part of the original radio source discovered at the Galactic Center back in the earliest days of radio telescopy. It's called Sagittarius B2."

Closer to GalCenter, now. Though still relatively empty, the gulf was occupied by numerous infrared sources and objects that defied description. Off to one side, 340 light years from the center, was the Great Annihilator, a fiercely white-burning accretion disk spewing antimatter searchlights into the void. A hundred light years above the center, the Arc reached up like a solar prominence, a streamer of gas smeared into parallel arcs by unimaginably powerful magnetic fields and magnetic flux tubes. The ungraspable scale of what he was seeing continued to surprise Ramsey. Each of those lines, according to his readouts, was half a light year wide.

Farther in still. Gas clouds concentrated and twisted, with velocities ten times higher than would have been expected from gravity alone. Stars swarmed in hot, young clusters.

Within the embrace of the Arc, the gas was denser still, dense enough that even the tidal forces here could not disrupt it, but there was no evidence of new star formation. Possibly the storm of energies here was so great that stars *couldn't* form. Or perhaps something else was in control. . . .

Twenty light years from the Center, the gas organized itself into a massive accretion disk, circling an innermost void. The young stars were thicker here, clumped in blue-white swarms. A soft glow of X-rays and cosmic rays filled radiant space.

The mechanism at the center was a complex one, its pieces identified centuries ago by radio telescopes but never well understood. The radio source at the Galaxy's precise center was called Sagittarius A. Sag A East was off to one side, a bubble of hot gas marking a supernova that must have exploded thousands of years ago. Sag A West was that spiral-shaped, twenty-light year cloud of warm but non-ionized gas at the center, while Sagittarius A* marked the exact center. Close by—just one light year out from GalCenter, a supergiant star, ruby-hued and streaming a comet's tail into emptiness—cast a bloody hue over surrounding streamers and curtains of gas. The tail was stretched out and away, not from Sag A*, but from a nearby cluster of intense, blue-white stars newly emerged from a tattered nebula. That nebula was extremely close to the exact center of the system—a tenth of a light year, perhaps, and the gas and dust comprising it were twisted into bizarre swirls and fragments that gave mute testimony to the violence of what was going on in there.

Ramsey tried to understand what he was seeing. The program he was using supplied labels for the various objects at his request, as well as data like mass and velocity. The cluster of intensely blue stars near the center was IRS-16—for "Infra-Red Source." Gas speeds within the cluster approached 1,000 kilometers per second. The red star was IRS-7.

Closer in still, a tortured red star labeled S-2 appeared to be hanging at the very edge of the central object.

"S-2," Pollard told them, "has been known for a long time. Its orbit was first tracked from Earth seven or eight hundred years ago, and it provided the first hard data proving that there was a supermassive black hole at the Galaxy's center." Which made sense, Ramsey thought. That was the beauty of Kepler's laws of motion. Know an object's orbit and its velocity along that orbit, and you knew the mass of what it was orbiting. "S-2's orbit is highly eccentric," Pollard went on. "But at perigalacton, at its closest approach to the center, it's only seventeen light *hours* out, and traveling at better than 5,000 kilometers per second.

"The math works out to something like two million solar masses in the surrounding stars, gas, and accretion disk, and another two million to three million suns inside that thing at the center. It *has* to be a black hole . . . given that much mass in such a tiny volume of space."

"So what's the problem, then?" Ramsey asked. "We've known about black holes for centuries."

"Right," Cosgriff added. She'd studied to be a theoretical cosmologist, Ramsey knew, until she'd decided to join the Corps. "Once a star just a few times more massive than Sol goes into gravitational collapse, *nothing* can stop it from falling into a singularity . . . a black hole. Two million solar masses? Yeah, that would make a nice, fat one."

"The problem," Pollard told them, "is that whatever we're seeing there at the exact center, it isn't a black hole. We ought to be seeing something like a much larger version of the Great Annihilator, which is over there. What we're seeing instead . . . well, here, look . . ."

Pollard zoomed the simulation in even closer, and Ramsey peered hard into the veils of tortured gas and dust. Unfortunately, the program linking him into the simulation appeared to have reached the limit of its resolution. He would have expected to see something at the center matching his expectations of a typical, if very massive, black hole—a spot of emptiness, perhaps, at the center of that swirling, three-armed spiral of gas just outside.

What he saw, what little he could make out, was quite . . . *different.* Its shape overall appeared vaguely spherical, but details eluded him in strangeness and in the shroud of mist. Eventually, though, he could make out shadows and interpenetrating geometric shapes which gave it a decidedly *artificial* feel . . . and yet the thing must be enormous, some millions of kilometers across.

"What the hell are we looking at?" Ramsey asked.

"We're not entirely sure, Lieutenant," Pollard replied. "We know from S-2's orbit that there're about two million solar masses packed into that tiny, central volume, and, as Cosgriff pointed out, that means it must be a galactic black hole. But if so, then the reason we're not seeing something like the Great Annihilator is that this black hole is shrouded or surrounded by something, as though it's walled up inside an artificial shell.

"We think—and this is quite tentative at this point—but we *think* that what we're looking at is a kind of Dyson sphere. Nothing else we've been able to come up with would explain the facts.

"And if we're right, it means that the Xul may be a lot further along technologically than we ever dreamed, and *that* means that we, all of Humankind, may be in very serious trouble indeed. . . ."

14

Company Office, Bravo Company
UCS Hermes
Cluster Space
0910 hrs, GMT

"What the hell is a Dyson sphere?" Garroway wanted to know. Even as he asked the question, he was already opening a channel to *Hermes*' computer net and beginning to download the data.

"Named after the pre-space physicist who first thought of it," Captain Maria Loren told him. "Freeman Dyson. The idea was that an advanced civilization, one trying to create a lot of living space for itself, or one that wanted to utilize every erg of energy from its sun, might do so by disassembling its planets and building a hollow shell around the local star."

"Got it," Garroway said as he followed the downloaded information streaming through his awareness, scanning rapidly through reams of data. "The shell would capture most of the heat, light, and other radiation from the star for industrial purposes. People could live on the inside of the shell if they had a means of generating artificial gravity. Or instead of a solid shell, it might be a Dyson *cloud*, with trillions and trillions of separate habitats and industrial complexes enveloping the star."

"I wouldn't want to be the AI that had to keep track of that many separate hab orbits," Lieutenant Ramsey put in.

The meeting was taking place in Captain Loren's office on board the *Hermes*. Two entire bulkheads plus the overhead had been set to display a view of outside. The local star continued to dominate the sky, an intensely hot, arc-brilliant pinpoint encased in shells of rapidly expanding nebula. The Galaxy hung in the far distance, the subtle tones and shadings of its spiral arms nearly lost in the glare from the nova. In a different direction, outward, a nearby globular cluster hung against Night Absolute, a frozen swarm of red-hued suns. More remote galaxies were lost in the novalight, but the nearest stargate spanned a quarter of heaven.

Present were Captain Black and his command constellation, including Garroway and a dozen other Marines, volunteers for a secret op, a sneak-and-peek, that had been dubbed Operation Heartfire. The N-2 contingent, Ramsey and six other men and women from 1MIEF's intelligence division, including Captain Pollard, had joined them, as had Captain Loren and several members of General Alexander's command group.

Maria Loren was a naval officer with fifteen years' experience, a member of 1MIEF's senior command constellation, and the officer in charge of the expeditionary force's Tactical Operations Division. She'd summoned the others to her office just abaft *Hermes*' combat center to brief them on Heartfire.

Also present were the artificial intelligences Smedley, Cara, Thoth, and Athena, though these last were necessarily invisible, and spoke to the humans present within their minds. A large viewall at the far end of the chamber displayed an image of the Galactic Center, a swarm of teeming suns, a spiral of gas and dust, and the enigmatic, vaguely spherical structure at the precise center of the Galaxy's heart.

"The Dyson sphere or cloud at GalCenter," Athena pointed out, *"cannot be enclosing a star. Studies of mass distribution force the conclusion that it encases a black*

*hole of two to three million solar masses, and with an event
horizon radius of approximately 7.8 million kilometers."*

Eight million kilometers—between five and six times the
diameter of Earth's sun. Large, perhaps, so far as pipsqueak
dwarf stars like Sol were concerned, but a pinpoint alongside giant stars like Antares, which had a diameter fifty
times greater.

And within that relatively tiny volume of space, compressed by the inexorable laws of gravitation, the mass of
two million or more stars warped the laws of space and time
into bizarre and wildly twisted new shapes.

The external shell, the Dyson sphere, appeared to span
some ten million kilometers, just large enough to accommodate the super-massive object inside.

"Okay, so why a Dyson sphere around a black hole?"
Garroway wanted to know.

"That's the question, isn't it?" Loren told them. "One
idea, going way back, suggests that an advanced civilization
might build a complex of cities and factories around a large
black hole in order to solve all of its energy problems. By
dropping mass into the black hole—whether that mass is
pieces of planet, stray asteroids, or their household garbage—
they generate a flash of energy, X-rays, mostly, that could be
captured and stored."

"I don't buy that," Captain John Black said. "Not in this
case. They have QPT technology, probably better than we
have."

Garroway nodded. "Exactly. They wouldn't need something that elaborate just to raise energy."

QPT—the acronym stood for quantum power tap—had
been the preferred means of generating large amounts of
energy, both on and off-planet, for centuries. The so-called
Quantum Sea, a kind of base state for all matter and energy,
was envisioned as a froth of elemental paired particles constantly coming into existence and immediately annihilating
one another. Artificially generated micro-black holes were
used to capture a fraction of these particles before they

could snuff out their mates, a process that appeared to liberate large amounts of free energy out of apparently empty vacuum.

"Don't be too sure of that, gentlemen," Pollard told them. "A two-million-solar-mass black hole might raise vacuum energy on a literally astronomical scale. And that's what has the brass worked up into a lather. Here. Check this."

Pollard opened a window for them, containing a brief historical file. Centuries before, it seemed, a physicist named Richard Feynman had estimated that within every single cubic centimeter of empty space lurked energy enough to boil all of the oceans of Earth. John Wheeler, one of Feynman's colleagues, had disagreed, suggesting that the actual amount of energy was something like 10^{80} times greater . . . enough, perhaps, and if a way could be found to apply it, to annihilate the entire *Galaxy*.

Perhaps, Garroway thought, it was just as well that Humankind hadn't yet learned how to generate or wield that kind of power. By harvesting a tiny, tiny fraction of the vacuum energy theoretically available in an empty cubic centimeter of space, he could accelerate ships to close to light speed, phase-shift into quantum space or bypass normal space at FTL velocities, and generate antimatter by the metric ton . . . all very useful, and all deadly on a planetary scale.

Garroway thought about the Commonwealth Senate with the power to destroy hundreds of millions of stars, and suppressed a shudder.

But if humans weren't to be trusted with that kind of power . . . what about the Xul?

"Sir, you're saying the Xul are using the Galactic black hole to generate really *big* amounts of energy?" Garroway asked. "Like . . . enough to destroy the Galaxy?"

"It's a distinct possibility, Gunny," Pollard told him. He opened another explanatory window. "Another possibility is that they're trying to access the base-state reality for the entire Galaxy."

The second window shocked Garroway even more deeply. In the 23rd Century, physicist Alaina Mauldin had pointed out that it might be possible to tamper with the Quantum Sea in such a way as to literally change reality . . . or to erase it. Within the froth of virtual particles that made up the Quantum Seas, she'd argued, were standing waves—regions where particle-anti-particle pairs came and went with a persistence that preserved *information*, if not material reality. Those information waves represented mass and energy in the more familiar universe of human experience—electrons and protons and photons and everything else that was. What humans were pleased to call "solid reality" was, in fact, an illusion; electrons, neutrons, and protons were not fundamental pieces of matter so much as they were persistent patterns of information.

Given enough energy, Mauldin had suggested, it should be possible to cancel out large numbers of those standing waves . . . and in so doing simply blink civilizations, worlds, stars, even entire galaxies out of existence.

Certain mental disciplines—notably the weiji-do martial arts discipline practiced by Marines and some other elite units—could shift reality on a small scale, guiding Marines through the maze of a Xul huntership, for example, or meshing together the individual members of a combat team for greater efficiency. What Pollard was suggesting was far more deadly and far-reaching than that. Given control over the black hole at GalCenter, perhaps the Xul could control reality on an infinitely greater scale, deleting worlds, suns, and civilizations at a whim.

The thought was chilling.

"Sir," Staff Sergeant Ivan Tomlinson said, "the xenosoph people have been saying for years that the Xul have a kind of hard-wired fear or hatred of anyone or anything who might be a competitor. If that's true, if they have the power to change reality on that grand a scale . . ."

"Precisely," Captain Loren said, nodding. "We don't know exactly what the Xul are doing in there, but any of the possibilities we've been able to imagine would be bad, very bad. It might be a doomsday device, and if the bastards get paranoid enough, they blow up the entire Galaxy, themselves with it, just to wipe us out. Or they might have a way of targeting just our planetary systems, and vaporize them all at once from twenty-five thousand light years away. Or they have a way to push a button, and Earth and all of Earth's colonies and all humans everywhere simply cease to exist."

"The hell of it is," Pollard added, "we don't know what they're up to." He sounded unhappy with the situation, as though it were a personal affront. Intelligence officers were supposed to *know*—or at least be able to make a good guess about—what the enemy was up to.

Pollard gestured toward the viewall, and the image of the Galaxy's center. Newborn stars, some of them supernovae, gleamed in blue-white splendor. With a thought, he shifted the frequency of the displayed light, sliding down into the infrared. Blue stars glowed orange, then in somber reds; the background of gas and dust became sharply visible, a thick mist almost obscuring the enigmatic objects at the center.

Starkly visible, now, were a number of beams of light stretching out and away from the Dyson sphere. At infrared wavelengths, they took on a solid appearance, rigid, straight, and extending across tens of light years in a complex spider's web of energy.

"The images brought back by Athena suggest they're building something enormous in there," Pollard went on, "something utterly beyond human comprehension. But we'd damned well better learn how to comprehend it and figure it the hell out . . . because if and when they get it working, whatever it is, we're *not* going to like it!"

"That . . . that structure," Lieutenant Ramsey said. "The beams of light? It looks like it covers a pretty large area."

"Almost seventy light years," Pollard told them. "And we think those energy beams are anchored somehow in the Quantum Sea." The view zoomed in on the Dyson object at the center, fuzzy behind the thick haze. "Our best guess is that the sphere, or whatever it is, is locked in place. It's actually in two halves. You can see the accretion disk—that spiral of dust and gas—circling in from the outside. It passes through that gap between the two sections to reach the black hole inside. The Xul probably control the infall of matter somehow, so that they can feed that monster at a steady rate."

"How in the hell do we fight something like that?" Garroway wanted to know. "The entire MIEF would be a dust mote next to that thing!"

"We're not going to fight it," Captain Loren said. "A least, not at first, and not unless we absolutely have to. There's the Senate's peace mission to consider, after all."

"Why do I get the feeling," Sergeant Carl Gonzales asked with grim humor, "that we're going to be in the position of fleas trying to bargain for peace with a Great Dane? If they decide to scratch, there won't be much we can do about it."

"Right," Captain Black agreed. "If we're lucky, they won't even notice us!"

"Actually," Loren said, "we're hoping that that is literally true. . . ."

Black raised his eyebrows. "What, going in under their radar?"

"More or less," Pollard told them. "The environment inside the Core is . . . unusual. And extreme. We're looking at ways in which we can take advantage of it."

"Here," Loren added, "is the plan so far as TacOps has worked it out for Operation Heartfire. . . ."

The plan, Garroway noted, was both complicated and daring. Essentially, a Navy-Marine ITF, an intelligence task force designated Group Henderson, was to be inserted into the Galactic Core. The insertion would be covert, requiring the unit to slip in past numerous Xul bases, ships, and fortresses to reach S-2/I, where they would dig in and establish a long-range observation post.

Heartfire incorporated three mission objectives. Their first would be to take a close look at Sag A*, in hopes of determining exactly what the Xul were building there. At the same time, they would be taking very precise gravitometric and radiation readings of Core Space, providing the data necessary to allow the *Pax Galactica* and her escort to translate into the area.

Their third mission would begin as soon as the *Pax* appeared, providing back-up support for the peace mission just in case the Xul decided to attack. If they encountered anything in the deep core that would preclude *Pax*'s mission, they would warn the Senatorial ship off.

Or try to. Garroway and the other enlisted Marines hadn't seen much of General Alexander in the past couple of weeks, but the scuttlebutt was that he was locked in an ongoing battle with elements of the Commonwealth Senate over the supposed peace mission. Senator Yarlocke, in particular, was rumored to be pushing the general hard.

The details didn't matter, and the politics, thank the gods of battle, were up to others higher in the Corps hierarchy. Fighting the Xul, Garroway reflected, might be preferable in some ways to facing the demons of Commonwealth politics.

Of more pressing concern was how the ITF was going to carry out its mission.

"Just how the hell," Garroway asked, "are we supposed to get to S-2/I without being spotted by every Xul huntership in the Core?"

"Yeah," Ramsey said. "Does this have anything to do with our new toy parked alongside the *Hermes*?"

That "new toy" had been the object of speculation and scuttlebutt for days now, ever since Navy tugs had brought it alongside. Almost one kilometer long and less than eighty meters abeam at its widest point, it was a Type I Xul huntership, one among some hundreds of enemy vessels found adrift within Cluster Space after the MIEF had detonated the local star. The ship appeared to be relatively intact, but was quite dead, its computer network burned out by the radiation wave front blasting out from the nova, its Xul crew—once resident patterns of data stored on that network—gone to wherever it was that data went when a system crashed so completely that the data were irrecoverable.

The captured huntership, with a typical Marine sense of history, had been named the *Intrepid,* but so far, details of what was intended for the prize, as well as an explanation for the repair yard now embracing the derelict, had been kept a close secret.

"Obviously," Loren told them, "we're going to have to approach the deep core in stages. We can't translate the *Hermes* or the *Pax* into the area until we have detailed readings on the local grav metrics."

A window opened in their minds, displaying a schematic view of the principle Core structures, the view pulling back until Sagittarius A* and the various objects in the deep Core had dwindled to a single, distant point.

"That means," Loren continued, "that we have to go in through a stargate, but the closest gate to the center of which we're aware is *this* one, designated Gate Hub-1. It's connected to at least one of the stargates here in Cluster Space, so we have a straight shot in to the galactic hub. However, it's still over seven hundred light years from Hub-1 in to Sag A-Star. Hub-1, of course, has a Xul fortress nearby, and is heavily defended."

Garroway struggled to maintain in his mind the scale of what he was watching. The gulf between Gate Hub-1 and Sagittarius A* was more than twice the span of the entirety of Human-colonized space. The most distant Commonwealth colony was a research outpost on Madoc, two hundred fifty light years from Sol. The Islamic Theocracy was thought to have some colonies even farther away, out in the direction of Scorpius and Libra, but for obvious reasons they tended not to share galactographic details of their empire with the Commonwealth.

The scale of the spaces and objects they were dealing with at the Core was *huge*.

"As Lieutenant Ramsey has suggested," Loren said, "the *Intrepid* is going to be our ticket past the outer Xul defenses. The shipfitters are going through her now, hollowing out a portion of her interior and wiring in life support for a human crew. They're also installing a carrier bay for a squadron of AV-110 Tarantulas."

"Our penetrator missions have recorded extensive sequences of Xul ship-to-ship communications," Cara added over their internal link with the ship's net. "We believe that we can enter the stargate, inform the Xul fortress at Gate Hub-1 that we are damaged and experiencing communications difficulties, and proceed under FTL to the deep inner core. Once there, we can approach S-2/I and debark the Marine and Navy OP personnel."

"What do we know about this planet?" Black wanted to know.

"Very little, so far," Pollard told him. "We haven't seen it at optical wavelengths, and inferred its existence from anomalies in the background radiation. S-2/I itself is a red giant trapped in a close and highly elliptical orbit around Sagittarius A-Star. The planet, we can assume, will be hot in at least two senses of the word . . . with a daytime surface temperature above the boiling point of water, and a background radiation count high enough to fry any unprotected life forms or circuitry. That whole inner core region is bathed in high-energy cosmic rays and X-ray radiation, both from frequent supernovae and from the effects of all of those black holes."

"Wait a second, sir," Black said, interrupting. "There's Sag A-Star and there's the Great Annihilator. What do you mean by 'all those black holes?'"

"Ah," the intelligence chief said. "Yes. We're just starting to work up a complete survey from the data Athena brought us. Athena? Can you address the question?"

"Of course," the AI replied. *"It has long been theorized that solar-mass black holes created elsewhere in the Galaxy would eventually move to the Galactic Hub as their orbits degraded over time. In addition, the large number and high density of giant and supergiant stars within the Hub suggests that large numbers of black holes would form as those stars reached the end of their life spans on the Main Sequence and exploded. By some estimates, there may be as many as ten thousand black holes between one and ten solar masses within the inner hundred light years of the Galactic Core. We have identified a number of these by means of radiation released as they move through the inner core dust*

clouds, but we believe many remain uncharted. That, in fact, will be another requirement for Heartfire—locating and tracking black holes that may pose a threat to the Pax Galactica."

"Frigging wonderful," Black muttered. "As if this joy ride wasn't already complicated enough."

If Loren or Pollard heard the comment, they ignored it. Garroway could understand Black's anger. In any military operation, the simpler you could make it, the more concise its objectives, the *fewer* its objectives, the better the chances of the op succeeding. Unfortunately, there was always the tendency to piggyback mission upon mission, especially when politics were involved. The admonition to KISS—Keep It Simple, Stupid—was the ideal in military planning . . . but it was an ideal rarely realized in practice.

"This is starting to sound pretty damned iffy," Ramsey said. "I mean, we're going in there to find a flat metric for the *Pax.* So far, so good. But now you're saying that we've got ten thousand unmapped black holes flying around in there. You *do* know that all those loose singularities will play hell with the metric, right?"

It made sense. Black holes—tiny pockets of gravitational distortion—would play havoc with the local space-time metric, and the fact that everything in close to GalCenter would be moving quickly as it orbited Sag A* wouldn't help. The operation was beginning to sound more and more unlikely.

"Of course, Lieutenant," Loren replied. "And if things prove too hairy in there, we just might be able to scrub the *Pax* mission."

"That's the first sensible thing I've heard all day," Black said. "This op is a cluster fuck waiting to happen. Wrapped up in ribbon and tied with a bow."

"We answer to the civilian authority, Captain Black," Loren said coldly. "Not the other way around."

And that, of course, was basic to the Marine Corps' mission. For over a thousand years, the Corps had done what the civilian government had commanded, without criticizing that government, and without attempting to set policy. That fact was one of the absolutes that maintained Humankind's oldest modern democracy.

"I meant no offense, ma'am," Black said. "But you gotta know . . . this op is a damned long shot. And our chances of coming out of there alive are somewhere between slim and nonexistent."

"Why did you volunteer, then?" Loren asked. "All of you are volunteers, correct?"

"Yes, ma'am."

"If it's hopeless, why did you sign up?"

Black shrugged. "Because we're Marines. Because even if the *Pax* mission is complete nonsense, we might be able to bring out some good, solid intel about the Xul. And the more we know about the enemy, the better our chances of beating him."

Because we're Marines . . .

Garroway thought about what Black had said later, after he'd returned to the platoon squad bay. Nikki Armandez had met him there, and the two had made their way aft and starboard to the mess hall for some chow.

Over nano-grown sliderloaf, he told her what he could of the meeting. Parts of that briefing had been security sealed, which meant that Garroway's own implants would block him if he tried to talk about them, but other parts were already general knowledge.

Like the fact that an intelligence team was about to be inserted into the Galactic Core, ahead of the *Pax Galactica*.

"Is it hopeless, Gare?" she asked.

He shrugged. "The skipper seems to think so," he said, meaning Black. "I think the brass is going through with it because of the intel we'll be able to bring back."

"*If* you can bring it back." She sounded bitter.

Both of them had volunteered for Heartfire days ago. Garroway had been accepted, but not Armandez. She'd been angry at what seemed like senseless discrimination.

"You still mad that they didn't take you?" he asked.

"I don't know. I just don't want you going in there alone."

"I won't be. It's a big op—a regimental strike team, almost three hundred Marines. And you'll be coming through later, with the *Hermes.*"

"Yeah. *If* everything goes right for you."

They faced, Garroway thought, one of the basic dilemmas of military romances—the fact that two lovers could not be paired up all the time and, sooner or later, one would go into harm's way while the other remained behind.

"To tell you the truth, Nikki, I don't think it's going to be as bad as all that. Intelligence thinks the Xul are all but blind in the Core. We should be able to set up our OP and transmit back everything the MIEF needs to complete the mission. If anything, you're going to be the one in the Xul crosshairs. *Hermes* and the *Pax* are pretty juicy targets, y'know? The Xul are bound to concentrate on them because they can rotate in and out of normal space."

"Maybe the Senate will call off the mission," she said.

"Maybe. Though where that one senator . . . what's her name? Yarlocke. Where she's concerned, I wouldn't count on it."

She looked at him, clearly hurting. "Why did they pick you?"

He grinned. "Because I'm a bad ass with ten years of bad-ass experience. Because my legs are more metal and plastic than they are regrown flesh. Because—"

"I'm serious, Aid!"

"So am I. Radiation levels in the Core are hot enough to fry any carbon-based life form silly enough to waltz in there. Our ship shielding is pretty good . . . and the new armor is supposed to be able to shrug off anything short of a thermonuclear explosion. But they still want rad-resistant Marines in there."

"Bullshit. Ramsey isn't a walking spare parts store like you are. Neither are any of the others."

"Mm. But they have had experience in hot zones, in high-radiation environments. Maybe it's as simple as that. They cross-indexed all volunteers with Marines who'd played tag with novae or places like Starwall. My name checked. Yours didn't."

"Maybe . . ." But she didn't sound convinced.

Later, after hours, the two of them made their way to a suit locker overlooking the ship's main hangar bay. The cavernous space, over eight hundred meters deep, was kept perpetually in hard vacuum, but transparent sections of the travel ways along the towering bulkheads looked down into a gulf of shadows and blackness, where brilliant work lights and the pinpoint dazzle of welding arcs cast wavering glows against the hulls of two ships currently in the bay grapples— the light cruiser *Ludwigson* and the destroyer *Plottel*. The area was kept in zero gravity, and the space throughout the chamber was filled with drifting motes and lights—the service craft and work modules used by *Hermes'* maintenance crews.

Halfway along one vast and curving bulkhead, a travel-way tube gave access to a compartment filled with vac suits and stored maintenance robots. There, they shed their uniforms and clung together, making slow love at first, but with an intensity and an urgency that built and built and built again to the final, gasping climax. Surrounded, then, by a tiny galaxy of sparkling droplets—drifting beads of sweat and other body fluids—they clung together in a drifting embrace, silent and close.

"It'll be all right," he whispered against her ear.

"I know that," was her reply.

And both of them knew that both statements were well-intentioned lies.

15

Tarantula 04,
Regimental Strike Team,
In transit on board UCS Intrepid
Cluster Space
1235 hrs, GMT

It was the second time a vessel named *Intrepid* had set sail against the Xul.

Both the Navy and the Marine Corps embraced history, the panoply of tradition and the men, women, and vessels that had gone before. The very first *Intrepid* in the U.S. Navy had been a ketch, originally built in Napoleon's France and later sold to the Barbary state of Tripoli, who put her into service as the *Mastico*. Under that name, during the conflict known as the First Barbary War, she'd participated in the capture of an American frigate, the *Philadelphia*, when the latter ran aground off Tripoli in October of 1803.

Mastico had been captured in December of that year by the schooner USS *Enterprise*, renamed *Intrepid*, and brought into the American squadron then blockading Tripoli Harbor. In February of 1804, Lieutenant Stephen Decatur had taken the *Intrepid* into Tripoli Harbor, and with about sixty hand-picked men—including Sergeant Solomon Wren and a Marine detachment, eight in all—had boarded and taken the *Philadelphia* without firing a shot. In an operation lasting all of twenty-five minutes, Decatur's men had killed or driven off the Tripolitan crew, set fire to the frigate, and escaped without losing a man. The *Philadelphia*'s powder magazines had detonated a short time later, destroying the frigate before her captors could refit her and add her to their own navy.

No less a celebrity than Lord Admiral Horatio Nelson had called the operation "the most bold and daring act of the age."

There had been several *Intrepid*s serving with U.S. naval forces in the centuries after the Barbary Wars, but the next vessel by that name to become the stuff of Navy-Marine legend had been a transport commissioned in 2314—the year of Armageddonfall, the year the Xul had attacked Earth. After a nine-year passage at near-*c* from Sol to the Sirius system, this *Intrepid* had entered the stargate at Sirius and delivered her cargo—25,000 metric tons of sand lifted from the deserts of Mars—releasing it at a velocity just under the speed of light. The sand cloud had scoured the surface of a Xul-colonized world in a region called Night's Edge, and vaporized an enemy fleet. The strike, a first and partial payback for the devastation wreaked on Earth, had provided a much-needed psychological victory for a broken and discouraged Humankind.

And now a new *Intrepid* was taking a Marine scouting force into the very heart of the Xul realm.

Unfortunately, at the moment, Garroway could see very little of the outside world. Scarcely able even to wiggle, he was stuffed into one of the newly issued Type 690 power armor units, and that, in turn, was nested within the narrow troop bay of an AV-110 Tarantula along with twenty-three other Marines in Type 690s. A dozen Tarantulas rode in a hollowed-out space in *Intrepid*'s alien belly, mounted in four ranks of three. He had the Regimental Strike Team's netfeed, but at the moment that was showing nothing but static on the vid channels, and nothing but the terse conversation of the Navy bridge crew on audio. Nestled like Russian dolls, Marines in armored suits in landing craft in hastily converted troop carriers, not all of the communication amenities were working yet. From the sound of things there'd been another delay.

Typical.

"Always the same story," Sergeant Willem Shelby said over the platoon net. "Hurry up and wait."

"Welcome to the Marine Corps, Shelby," Captain Black said.

"That's right," Corporal Michael Fossey added. "For every minute you spend in the Corps, it's fifty-nine and a half seconds of unimaginable boredom . . ."

". . . and half a second of stark terror," Garroway said, completing the old joke.

"Watch it, people," Staff Sergeant Tomas Vincent growled. "That's *my* Corps you're putting down. Every day an adventure! Every meal a banquet! Every alien life form another opportunity for target practice! . . ."

Garroway listened to the banter, amused, but also feeling the tug of conflicting emotions. It had been a month since his aborted leave Earthside, but he was still digesting some of his experiences. Out here, existence, *life*, took on a harsh illumination, an interplay of starkest black and white. A Marine's entire being was focused on his fellow Marines and, on a grander scale, on the War. On Earth, and in the teeming hive of EarthRing, people were barely aware that there *was* a war . . . or that Earth and all of Humankind might be snuffed out at any moment.

At the moment, Garroway's view was limited to his suit's primary optical input, which meant that all he could see was the red-lit near-darkness of the Tarantula's troop bay, where a twenty-four-Marine section was packed in shoulder to armored shoulder, unable to move, unable to even see if the transport was under attack. They were still in Cluster Space, evidently, but any moment now they would be transiting across about twenty-five thousand light years, to emerge in what might well be the most heavily defended Xul stronghold in the Galaxy.

Damn it, how much longer?

Garroway opened a private channel. "Hey, Gunny?"

"Yeah?" Gunnery Sergeant Michel Warhurst replied over the link. Garroway's former DI was in another Tarantula, 08, elsewhere within *Intrepid*'s belly.

"Why the hell did you come back?"

Warhurst's return to the Corps had been a complete and utter surprise to Garroway. He'd seen how the man had been living Earthside—that beautiful undersea apartment with its view of Sunken Miami, two gorgeous and loving fuck-buddies, and a hot tub that stopped just two decimals short of absolute hedonism.

He also remembered what Warhurst had said about this Galactic Core op. *That's not my idea of fun. It's more like suicide, especially if you're on board the first ship into battlespace. . . .*

"Right now," Warhurst replied after a moment's hesitation, "I'm kind of wondering that myself."

Warhurst had re-enlisted less than forty-eight hours after Garroway, Armandez, and Ramsey had returned up-ring and reported back on board the *Hermes*. Still well under the Corp's mandatory retirement age of ninety, he'd been sent to the Corp's Camp Helicon on Luna's Mare Imbrium, where his implants and personal software had been upgraded to current military standards. A two-week physical refresher course had followed, during which time he'd put in a request for duty with 1MIEF.

Normally, an older Marine who'd been out of the Corps for that long would have received a planetside billet, possibly embassy duty, possibly at a recruiting office or logistical base. Since Warhurst had been a former drill instructor, with a skill-set much in demand, they'd intended to send him to a DI billet on Mars to train new recruits. The way Warhurst had told the story, though, he'd made a loud enough noise that the powers-that-be had assigned him to Delta Company, First Marine Assault Battalion, then seconded him to the newly created Regimental Strike Team.

The truth of the matter was that losses had been heavy, and new recruits hard to come by. Personnel was so happy to get another warm body—a *trained* warm body, no less—that Warhurst likely could have written his own ticket.

The question was why he wanted to when he'd already served his time, and more, and had had it so good as a retiree back on Earth.

"I guess," Warhurst said after another long pause, "I just couldn't stand the thought of you young puppies going out there without my sage advice and years of experience and getting yourselves killed."

"I think you didn't want to miss the big one," Garroway said. "The last op against the Xul."

Warhurst chuckled, but it sounded bitter. "You think this is the last?"

Garroway performed a mental shrug. "Isn't it? We're going in against what looks like their main base. Either the Senate's *Pax* mission will do its thing and we'll have peace, or we'll kick the bastards right where it hurts them most."

"You're full of shit, Garroway. There'll never be peace. Not with the Xul. *You* know that. The Senate doesn't, but anyone who's been up against the Xul knows better."

"Then we take out their cozy little nest at GalCenter."

"And what makes you think *that* will end the Xul threat? These . . . these critters have been kicking ass all over the Galaxy for at least ten million years, maybe longer. At last estimate, the Xul have major bases in something like half a million star systems, and control at least that many stargates. In the last five hundred years, we've investigated . . . what? Maybe two-tenths of one percent of that number of gates and systems. Jesus, Garroway! There may be tens of *billions* of hunterships in our Galaxy, as many hunterships as there are human beings! Do you think they're all going to stop working just because we shut down their operations in the Core? And that, of course, assumes we *can* shut them down. It may just be too big."

Garroway was silent for a moment. In the background, he could hear the low-voiced murmur of conversation from *Intrepid*'s bridge. *"Engage primary drive."*

"Engaged. We're moving. . . ."

"Gate interface in twenty seconds . . ."

"If it's hopeless," Garroway said at last, "why the hell did you come? You could be back in Miami right now, soaking in your hot tub and alternating turns with Kath and Traci."

"I didn't say it was hopeless," Warhurst told him. "After all, we're *Marines*. . . ."

This was the man, Garroway remembered, who'd come after him ten years ago after his flight through an exploding star, who'd risked everything to pull him out of a burning, radioactive hell, just because he was a fellow Marine.

Perhaps there didn't need to be any deeper explanation than that.

"Well, it's good to have you aboard again, Gunny. Even if I did hate your guts back in boot camp."

A shudder passed through Garroway's body. "Hey! I think we just went through the Gate!"

"Yup," Warhurst replied. "We're in the Core, now." With a fine sense of understatement, he added, "Here's where it starts to get interesting. . . ."

Nightstar 442,
Flight Deck, UCS Cunningham
In Transit aboard UCS Intrepid
Core Space
1252 hrs, GMT

Unlike the grunts on board the Tarantula transports, Lieutenant Ramsey had a full sensory link with *Intrepid*'s C³, or Combat Command Center. The slender needle of the captured huntership had just threaded through the twenty-kilometer-wide hoop of one of the Cluster Space stargates, with the soft, spiral glow of the Galaxy dominating the starscape, and was emerging now into a very different, very alien realm.

Cluster Space had been dark, the glow of the Galaxy just barely discernable against the vast and ultimate blackness of endless night. Core Space was very nearly a photographic negative of that, a universe of pure light, with very little darkness visible anywhere against that softly radiant background. From Ramsey's vantage point, it felt as though he was just emerging into the interior of an immense bubble, a bubble with walls composed of gleaming, red-hued stardust, and woven through and through with the pastel glow of streaming, clotted nebulae.

He could see GalCenter in the distance, a knot of nebulosity ablaze with hotter, younger, bluer suns, with streamers of gas looping through space along the force lines of powerful magnetic fields. Data streamed into his consciousness from myriad sensors, monitoring numerous wavelengths. Besides visible light, he could see the background glow of radiation at ultraviolet, X-ray, and cosmic-ray wavelengths, as well as the sullen glow of infrared and radio-source objects. The Great Annihilator was a dazzling, twin-beamed beacon, as lesser black holes left curving tracks of hard radiation against the dust clouds through which they were plowing. From here, seven hundred light years out, GalCenter was partially blocked by the expanding molecular cloud, which resembled a large, big-holed doughnut, black and brown-red on the outside, gleaming blue-white on the inside. Shafts of light glowed through the openings at top and bottom; what Ramsey could see of the center itself resembled a furball of dust, gas, stars, black-hole tracks, and point sources of radiation.

High and to one side, beyond the arc of the stargate ring, the Xul fortress kept watch, a flattened sphere five kilometers across, bristling with towers, sponsons, and turrets.

Ramsey gave his Nightstar a final diagnostic run-through, reassuring himself that all systems were powered up and combat ready. The F/A-4041 Nightstar was the most recent space-capable fighter to be added to the Corps inventory—a heavy, powerful, hard-hitter massing almost 120 tons, it was capable of an acceleration of almost two hundred gravities. Slots for weapons pods allowed it to tailor load-outs for every mission from planetary bombardment and close ground support to battlespace superiority and orbital-fortress suppression. Mounting the new generation of pocket on-board QPT generators, they could operate independently from quantum-entangled power transmission, the smallest spacecraft to do so.

All systems were go. Ramsey and fifteen other Nightstar pilots of Raptor Squadron waited in dark silence as the *Intrepid* slid clear of the Core stargate. In his mind's eye, he could see the fortress some fifty kilometers distant.

"We are being probed," a voice said—Athena, the AI running both *Intrepid* and the Marine assets hidden within *Intrepid*'s bowels. "I am engaging the enemy in dialogue."

Ramsey wished he could actually hear that conversation, but knew that it was beyond any merely human ken, a rapid-fire exchange of electronic queries and replies in Xul trinary code, and completely non-verbal. He found himself tensing, holding his breath, waiting for a high-energy fusillade from the alien fortress.

When nothing happened in the next fifteen seconds, he gradually allowed himself to breathe. Athena, he knew, would be presenting *Intrepid* as a Xul huntership caught by the nova in Cluster Space and badly damaged, its memory, weapons systems, and electronic population all but obliterated. The kilometer-long vessel's exterior certainly supported that story. The ship's normally gleaming gold surface was scoured, blasted, and blackened where the exploding star's touch had seared the incredibly tough Xul metal-and-plastic alloys. Some dozens of Xul derelicts had been recovered from Cluster Space, and were being converted into Commonwealth warships; *Intrepid*, though, had been marked for special duty.

Most Xul warships and defense structures were almost entirely solid, their interiors packed with the Xul equivalent of electronic circuits and processors and riddled by shafts and tunnels used for access by the ship's robotic maintenance and defense units. Most of that circuitry, apparently, was used to support the billions of individual patterns of data that represented uploaded Xul personalities.

In *Intrepid*, several hundred thousand tons of support circuitry had been gutted, replaced by a small command center occupied by the ship's human crew and its life-support module, plus the Marine light transport *Cunningham* carrying sixteen Nightstar fighters, a single Euler-derived starburster triggership, and twelve AV-110 Tarantulas with 288 combat Marines already packed on board. Xul weaponry, much of which was still not understood by human xenotechnologists, had been replaced by human weapons—mass drivers, high-energy lasers, and plasma cannon. If the fortress detected something amiss, if it opened fire on the disguised intruder, the *Intrepid* would be able to return fire.

Not that she would be able to engage that monster for very long. Estimates suggested that *Intrepid* might survive as much as two seconds in the holocaust that would ensue.

The feeling that he was being watched, personally and microscopically, became an intolerable itch between Ramsey's shoulder blades.

"The fortress appears to have accepted us," Athena said over the link. *"I am detecting no change in weaponry power levels or scanner frequencies."*

Past the first hurdle. One of the very few advantages Humankind possessed in the war with the Xul was in the speed and adaptability of human-designed AIs. With every successful penetrator probe, the human computer technologists and xenosoph experts learned a bit more.

Very gradually, under Athena's guidance, *Intrepid* began to accelerate. Pushing at nearly three hundred gravities, her speed increased enormously, as her inertial dampers shrouded the fragile flesh and blood on board, protecting it from the crushing acceleration.

Light exploded around *Intrepid*'s needle-slim prow, as the gas and dust filling the cavernous void at the Galaxy's core slammed into the ship's protective screens. At nearly eight-tenths of light speed, the massive vessel's FTL drive switched on.

The Xul had developed a faster-than-light technology that operated on a completely different principle from Humankind's Alcubierre Drive. Rather than encapsulating the ship within a highly distorted bubble of space-time, the Xul hunterships engaged in a rapid-fire sequence of jumps between normal space and the Quantum Sea, each jump bypassing light minutes of space in a timeless instant.

That, at least, was the theory. Commonwealth xenotechnologists were still unraveling the secrets of Xul FTL theory. Athena could operate the drive, however, even if the exact mechanism of the vessels' space-devouring jumps through the Quantum Sea were not yet fully understood. Ramsey had no particular qualms about this; he didn't understand how a viewall or an agrav lift engine worked, either, but he used the technology every day.

The Xul ship hurtled deeper into the Core. Hours passed, and the ship dropped through Sagittarius B2, the expanding molecular cloud interacting with the surrounding medium. Sensory input received each instant that the ship was in normal space was stitched together within Ramsey's brain, giving the illusion that stars, dust clouds, and other objects were drifting slowly past, like towering thunderheads viewed from the cockpit of an atmospheric flier.

Dark clots of nebulae slid past . . . and then, four hundred light years from GalCenter, *Intrepid* emerged from a shining wall of light into the inner gulf. Ahead, IRS-16, the cluster of blue suns at GalCenter, grew sharply brighter. *Intrepid*'s computer was adjusting the data pouring in through the sensory inputs, correcting for relativistic distortion. The interior of the Core, everywhere, gleamed in dazzling light.

And yet more hours passed. Slowly, the tangle of objects just visible at GalCenter began to sort themselves out, untangling from the central knot of dust and light and drifting apart. From Ramsey's technically enhanced perspective, thousands of black holes, ranging in size from one or two solar masses to the Great Annihilator itself, were marked by icons showing the position and relative motion of each. They formed a cloud about the innermost Core, like a globular cluster . . . but with each member invisible at optical wavelengths, detectable only by its individual signature of X-rays and harder radiations.

Ramsey sincerely hoped that *all* of those gravitational

singularities had been spotted and mapped. If *Intrepid* happened to strike one, or even simply skimmed too close to an unseen event horizon, this operation would be over almost before it had begun.

A sudden jar shuddered through the length of the *Intrepid*. Athena had just performed a sharp and unforeseen maneuver, possibly to avoid striking just such an obstacle as one of those black holes orbiting GalCenter. For the shock of the maneuver to be felt through the Xul vessel's inertial dampers meant that it had been a violent one. A moment later, one of the black-hole icons separated from the knot ahead and slipped past to starboard.

A close one. . . .

The stars of the central cluster were opening up now, and Ramsey could see the broad, flat spiral of the central black hole's accretion disk, like a whirlpool twenty light years across, red at the outer regions, brilliant blue at the heart. Several stars hung within that maelstrom, many showing cometary tails pointed away from IRS-16. A single bright red star burned just above the accretion disk, illuminating part of it like moonlight upon clouds. His mental software identified the star as the mission objective—S-2.

Deeper still. Athena was highlighting Xul ships and structures now, bracketing them in red within his mind. Gods, they were everywhere! None of them, however, seemed to be paying much attention to the *Intrepid* as she plunged deeper into the Core. Ramsey could see the tracks of other Xul ships as they moved at FTL through the dust clouds of the center. Each time a ship dropped into normal space, its screens slammed into drifting grains of dust and molecules of gas at relativistic speeds, with the result that starships here scratched contrails against the sky in X-rays and hard radiation. He had to remind himself that the nearest of those ship contrails was a good ten light years distant, and marked, therefore, a ship that had been passing ten years ago. Most of those contrails were even more remote in both space and time.

But it was a reminder of how crowded this region was with Xul ships and orbital structures.

S-2 was growing larger, now, showing a distinct disk as *Intrepid* slowed and moved closer.

Athena made some final adjustments to the starship's course, then dropped into normal space, dumping velocity. The AI's timing was perfect. In an instant, the planet S-2/I appeared, a slender, red-ocher-white crescent bowed away from the red glare of the star, swelling rapidly from tiny crescent to a red-illumined scythe slicing across heaven.

Relative velocities matched, *Intrepid* dropped into planetary orbit. Below, the world's night side blotted out half of the swollen glare of the red giant beyond, but the surface, Ramsey noted, was not completely black. The planet possessed magnetic fields, and there was a dazzling display of auroras playing about both poles.

This in itself represented a major planetological mystery. Auroras, as Ramsey understood them, occurred when solar radiation, channeled by a planet's magnetic fields, interacted with atoms of the planetary atmosphere at high altitudes, causing them to glow in the same way that the gas in a neon light tube fluoresced when electricity flowed through it.

According to the readouts coming through the link from *Intrepid*'s bridge, however, the planet below had no atmosphere to speak of, and its rotation was so slow—it was rotating retrograde at the rate of one revolution every three months—that it was difficult to understand why it had any magnetic field at all . . . or where the intense auroral glows were coming from.

Those glows, however, illuminated the planet's night side—it was probably bright enough down there to read by the glow in the sky—and the glow was amplified by periodic and frequent discharges of electricity, powerful arcs playing across the world's polar regions.

From low orbit, though, there didn't appear to be much to see beneath the auroras and the lightning. Planet S-2/I had for eons been sandblasted by a constant rain of dust and gas molecules as it moved through the cloudy haze of the Galactic

Center. The constant bombardment must have stripped away the atmosphere eons ago, laying the surface bare to the constant flood of cosmic radiation. There was no sign of craters below, and even the highest mountain ranges appeared to have been sculpted smooth by the steady celestial bombardment.

The planet was as far from its red giant primary as Jupiter was from Sol. At that distance, the mean substellar temperature should have been around the freezing point of water, while the mean temperature on the night side plummeted to nearly two hundred below. In fact, though, the surface appeared uniformly warm, ranging from minus twenty degrees Centigrade near the equator to well above the boiling point of water at the poles.

Again, physical planetary science couldn't address the observed data. The anomalously high surface temperatures were probably related to the high background radioactivity and to heat caused by the steady rain of cosmic dust, but there was nothing in human experience with which this world's surface environment could be compared. Those flaring polar lightnings and high temperatures probably, *probably*, had their origin in the interplay of the planet's magnetic field with those of the local galactic neighborhood—especially the powerful magnetic fields emanating from Sagittarius A*—but so far as terrestrial planetary science was concerned, S-2/I shouldn't even *have* a magnetic field of its own . . . to say nothing of auroras in the absence of an atmosphere.

But all of those questions would have to wait for a follow-on team of planetologists. The immediate concern was the local Xul presence. S-2 was nearing perigalacton—its closest point to Sag A*—now just thirty light hours distant.

Intrepid dropped into a lower orbit, scanning the alien world's surface closely. Ten minutes later, she released the *Cunningham*, and the two craft slowly separated, flying in formation. Clouds of remote sensors and battlespace drones began to spread through local space, gather data at all wavelengths.

On the third orbit, they spotted the Xul base.

Tarantula 04, UCS Intrepid
Core Space
1523 hrs, GMT

"How the hell are we supposed to fight it if we can't see it?" Sergeant Vic Maler complained.

"What's the problem?" Garroway told him. "We disembark . . . and if it's moving and not a Marine, we kill it."

"Sweet and simple," Master Sergeant Clara Gardner added. She sounded nervous. "The Navy knows what the hell it's doing."

"Since when?" Sergeant Milo Huerra said, challenging her. "It might be sweet and simple, but Mal's right. Someone fucked up with the data link. What else did they miss, eh?"

"Quiet down, Marines," Lieutenant Cooper called over the link. He'd been promoted from one bar to two back at EarthRing, and he'd been slamming his mass around ever since. "Attention to orders, damn it!"

"We should have a decent picture once we drop from the *Intrepid*," Captain Black's voice told them. "Right now, all I can tell you is that the target looks like a small base on the surface of the planet, code name Objective Lima. There will be more extensive works underground, but we'll worry about that once we take the surface facility.

"I've just had word that our penetrator AIs have entered the facility and are coping with the local defenses. The idea is to kill the enemy's communications and control networks. Once they're down, the local Xulies won't be able to call for help, and the bad boys next door at Sag A-Star won't even know we're here.

"So move fast and keep moving. Remember . . . if you stand still the Xulies will nail you. Move fast—amphibious green blurs—and you'll keep the bastards off balance. We should be coming up on . . ."

There was a sudden thump, and a dizzying and disorienting feel of momentary zero-gravity. Tarantula 04 had just dropped free from the UCS *Intrepid*.

Garroway felt an instant's burst of static in his brain, and then his mind was flooded by incoming images fed through from the Tarantula's sensor net. Above, he could see the long, slender gold needle of the *Intrepid* slowly pirouetting against what looked like a solid wall of red-hued stardust and, to one side, the far smaller mote of the light carrier *Cunningham*. Ahead, the curve of the planet, red-ocher against the glare of a giant ruby sun. And below . . .

The Tarantula was hurtling forward and down less than one hundred kilometers above the surface of a sandblasted, alien desert. Blue and green curtains of light flared against the planet's poles, leaping like prominences to follow the world's invisible lines of magnetic force. Lightning flared, casting stark shadows for the instant of the flash.

Garroway could see other Tarantulas in the formation now—ungainly, bulbous machines with tightly folded legs that somewhat mimicked the landing craft's nickname. Terrestrial tarantulas, however, didn't mount ventral and dorsal particle-beam weapons, nor could they accelerate at an inertially damped one hundred gravities.

"Here we go!" someone yelled as the night-shrouded surface leaped toward them.

And Garroway and a dozen other Marines screamed back the ancient Corps battlecry.

"Ooh-rah!"

16

Marine Regimental Strike Team
Objective Lima, S-2/I
1540 hrs, GMT

The flight of AV-110 Tarantulas dropped to within scant meters of the dusty surface and skimmed at high speed toward a stark horizon. The vehicles spread out across a hundred square kilometers, each weaving in on a separate flight path designed to confuse enemy defenses.

The Xul defenses *should* be disabled . . . but Marines never entirely trusted tactical elements controlled by non-Marine assets. There was always the possibility of an unpleasant surprise.

Once clear of the *Intrepid*, sensory input had flooded through to the Marines packed into the AV-110s' squad bays. Garroway could see the crisp horizon ahead, with no hint of atmospheric haze to give it distance or depth. To his left, toward planetary south, auroras played against the star-dusted backdrop, curtains of yellow, green, and red-pink that wavered and shifted as though blown by the nonexistent wind.

Overhead, the sky had gone impossibly strange . . . dominated by a vast, three-armed spiral. Garroway was reminded of the spiral form of the Galaxy as seen from Cluster Space . . . but this one was more open, more distinct, and the colors were reversed—with sullen-glowing reds in the spiral's outer reaches shading to an intense blue-white near the center. To one side, the central cluster, a knot of carelessly spilled, radiant blue jewels imbedded in twisted nebulae; several nearby suns showed tails like comets streaming away from the fierce radiations of that central star swarm.

Garroway's eyes were drawn again and again to the spiral's brilliant center, in the sky halfway up from the northern horizon. He couldn't quite make out the details of what was in there, though it appeared to be . . . emptiness, a tiny disk of nothing at all. The Xul structure, the Dyson sphere or whatever it was, must be within that space, but still too distant to be visible to the naked eye, or even to a Marine's enhanced helmet optics and sensory feeds from the spacecraft.

Damn it, he thought, fiercely, *get your mind on the op! You can sightsee later, when the bad guys have been scragged!*

Reluctantly, he dragged his attention back to the horizon, then collapsed the feed window so that he could check his weapon—a Mk. VII pulse-plasma rifle. All weapons had been electronically disabled while the Marines were on board the transport, but once the suppressor field was shut down, the rifle would become fully operational.

"Thirty seconds to target, people," Captain Black's voice announced. "We've matched onboard gravity to local. Just remember to watch your rad counters. It's *hot* out there."

Garroway opened the download window again. The program painted brackets against his vision, marking the objective that was just now beginning to slide over the horizon. S-2/I, he remembered from his briefings, was a little larger than Mars, so the horizon at this altitude was . . . what? About twenty kilometers away? That felt right. Objective Lima was supposed to be a Xul base of some kind, but it was as large as a fair-sized city, easily twenty kilometers across, covering an area as big as a stargate, and consisting of hundreds of domes, towers, and blockhouses.

He felt a solid thump through the Tarantula's deck as the

landing craft took the objective under fire. On the download, he could see the flashes, like threads of quicksilver, flickering toward the enemy base.

A trio of savage explosions bracketed the area. In seconds, Garroway's download began feeding him an overlay showing tunnel systems and chambers under ground outlined in red, as sensors on board the Tarantulas picked up the seismic readings from the blasts. He suppressed the underground display. He wouldn't need the subsurface level maps until he was on the ground.

At first, there was no response of any kind from the target. The AI penetrator mission, Garroway thought, must have screwed up the enemy response enough to delay any return fire. The return came though, seconds after the Tarantulas began strafing the Xul base. Tarantula 06 exploded in a white flare of detonating antimatter and a burst of hard radiation. The Xul gun position, pinpointed by AIs, flared and vanished an instant later. Several awkward-looking Xul machines were beginning to emerge from the base, now—mobile gun platforms of some sort—but the Tarantulas burned them down as quickly as they appeared.

Then the incoming transports reached the objective, circling in from different directions, their deployment timed so that all arrived within a second or two of one another. Garroway's Tarantula settled in toward the circle of alien structures, main weapons pulsing with blue-white lightning, chewing through the enemy walls, domes, and towers with searing flashes of devastation. Drifting slowly, the Tarantula moved across the edge of the complex, where a nano-grown wall now lay in shattered, smoking chunks and the buildings beyond gaped open to the alien sky.

Six massive legs extended, grasping at charred debris and bare rock, and seemed to draw the craft down into the wreckage's embrace.

"Okay, Marines!" Cooper yelled. *"Go! Go! Go!"*

"Amphibious green blurs, people!" Captain Black added, as the clamshell doors in the Tarantula's rear lower belly slid open and the heavily armored Marines began spilling out onto the eldritch landscape.

Garroway was fifth out the gaping door, hitting the ground hard, but letting his armor's musculature absorb the shock with flexing knees. The Tarantula slowly raised its body on its widely straddled legs, continuing to lay down a heavy fire at any movement or flicker of energy within its sensors' range. A blast of plasma energy melted through a portion of molded wall just ahead, showering molten droplets on Garroway as he pressed forward.

He felt the drops splatter off his back and helmet, but suffered no damage. Type 690 Power Armor was the heaviest and newest battlesuit in the Marine inventory, designed after the first battles fought in high-radiation environments a decade before. Each unit massed over half a ton; a Marine could move at all only because of the direct neuromuscular linkage between his brain and the suit's actuators. Garroway moved his arm, and the firing of neurons in brain, back, and shoulder that would have raised it triggered instead the raising of the suit's massively gauntleted arm, and the heavy Mk. VII nanosealed to it. A piece of wall collapsed on his left. He swung his left arm in a block, and the massive chunks of rubble smashed and scattered, scarcely felt by the suit's occupant. When he jumped, his suit's computer made a fast calculation and triggered his jump jets, sending him sailing forward in a low, flat trajectory.

His landing sent up an explosive shower of dust and rubble. S-2/I's surface gravity registered about the same as Mars . . . a third of a G, or perhaps a bit more. It meant he had to be careful of the inertia he built up moving fast or when jumping. He might fall more slowly here than on Earth's surface, but he still carried that half-ton of battlesuit mass with him. Once he got moving, stopping could be a problem.

He brought up the underground map, noting several tunnel openings within a few tens of meters of his position. He started working toward the nearest one. The Marines needed to carry their assault underground as swiftly as possible . . .

and those openings were also the likeliest exit points for the
Xul combat machines that *would* be arriving on the surface
any second now.

"Heads up, Marines!" Staff Sergeant Vincent warned. "I've
got movement and energy leakage at Sierra one-niner-five!"

"Shit, there's movement everywhere!" Shelby replied.

"Watch it!" Sergeant Randy Douglas called. "They're
coming up outta the holes!"

The first Xul combot appeared almost directly in front of
Garroway, rising from the hidden tunnel entrance, high-
energy laser fire already snapping into his armor.

The black surface of his armor drank down the energy
and dissipated it in a blast of released heat. Garroway was
already dragging his Mk. VII into line with the enemy machine, triggering it with his mind. The weapon bucked, and
radio frequencies shrieked as the plasma bolt cracked through
vacuum and slammed into the Xul machine.

He heard it scream as radio circuits fried.

But more Xul combots were arriving every second, drifting in across the tortured landscape from several directions.

Garroway had encountered Xul warrior-types many times
before, both in simulation and in combat. Each was two to
three meters long, an elongated egg shape smoothly sculpted
with sponsons, swellings, and concavities, its ebon surface
imbedded with scattered lenses—some serving as eyes,
some as weapons. Each was unique, no two precisely alike
in form. Tentacles writhed, as few as three, as many as dozens emerging from random points on each smooth, black
shell.

After centuries of combat, Marine xenosophontologists
still weren't sure if the warrior forms were pure robots, or if
they were controlled by Xul uploaded intelligences, either
resident within the combat machines or teleoperating them
from somewhere within the base. Likeliest was a mix of the
three possibilities, with most of the machines operating under fairly simplistic programming, but with others piloted

directly by individual Xul. The machines appeared to use agravitic repulsion to hover, and maneuvered by interacting with local magnetic fields. In tight quarters, they could haul themselves along with sinuous, powerful flicks of their metallic tentacles.

Garroway pivoted left, burning down a second . . . then a third. Orange light geysered from the center of the base as *Intrepid*, ninety kilometers overhead, added her particle beams to the ongoing bombardment.

And then the fighters arrived. . . .

Nightstar 442,
Raptor Flight
Over Objective Lima
Core Space
1550 hrs, GMT

"Raptors, this is Raptor Leader!" Major Steve Treverton called over the squadron net. "Release by the numbers, in five . . . four . . . three . . . two . . . one . . . *go!*"

The sixteen F/A-4041s of Raptor Flight were lined up in *Cunningham*'s launch bay in four rows of four. The first four aerospace fighters slammed out of their launch tubes in rapid succession . . . and then it was Ramsey's turn, Raptor Seven.

His Nightstar dropped clear of the *Cunningham*, its massive, compact body unfolding to reveal weapons and drive pods, its vector already aligned with the night side of the objective planet, just below the brilliant ocher slash of the sunlit limb. With a series of practiced thoughts, he engaged the agrav, the inertial dampers, and, finally, the main drive, kicking the ship into a sharp, steep plunge toward the planetary surface.

"*Damn* the bastards," Ramsey snapped.

He wasn't referring to the Xul.

Since the earliest days of Marine aviation, back in the first half of the war-torn twentieth century, the primary purpose of military aircraft—and, later, of spacecraft—so far as the Corps was concerned had been close air support. The prime dictate of all Marines throughout history had always been that *every* man was a rifleman, whether they were front-line infantry, clerks, mess cooks . . . or fighter pilots.

Marines on the ground enjoyed a close and special relationship with the close-support pilots, who took pride in weaving in through heavy fire to place their warheads with devastating precision—often scant tens of meters from embattled Marine positions.

And that was why Ramsey was angry now. The squadron of F/A-4041 Nightstars should have been dropped an hour ago, should be over the target *now* reducing it to red-hot rubble. Someone, he thought, had screwed up. The aerospace strike fighters should have gone in first and leveled the place.

In fact, that had been the gist of the op orders; they'd been changed only hours ago, when word had come down from Ops Command that the Tarantulas would be going in first, without preliminary bombardment, in order to preserve the advantage of surprise.

Ramsey shook his head at the thought. *Surprise* in modern combat was a short-lived advantage, one measured in microseconds from the instant the enemy first detected incoming troop transports or strike fighters. He very much doubted that the advantage gained by rewriting the op plans would be worth the price paid in blood.

The dark landscape tilted wildly beneath his Nightstar. Symbols representing targeting pippers, angle of attack ladders, and scales for pitch, yaw, and roll drifted swiftly through Ramsey's vision, painted in his visual field by the ship's AI. Guiding the Nightstar with his mind, he brought the nose up, centering Objective Lima within the targeting cursor of his primary weapon and locking it on. As the landscape rapidly swelled larger, green pinpoints appeared, tiny emerald stars scattered across the alien base, each one marking friendly forces—the Marines of the Regimental Strike Team moving in from the periphery. Red points of light marked anything moving or giving off energy that didn't have a friendly IFF signal riding it.

There were far more red stars down there than green. . . .

Aiming for the center of Objective Lima, he mentally triggered his primary weapon, a massive GV-3662 Gatling fusion gun. Spinning barrels brought thumb-sized capsules of highly compressed metallic hydrogen into the firing chamber one by one, where each was further compressed, laser-heated, and magnetically accelerated to near-c velocities. Each charge massed less than a gram, but fired at that speed, thirty rounds per second, the recoil nearly overwhelmed Ramsey's inertial dampers, slamming against the hurtling strike fighter like staccato sledgehammer blows. Though silent in the airless sky of S-2/I, the vibration sounded like a thunderous howl within the narrow confines of the Nightstar's cockpit.

Flares of fusing hydrogen leapt from sky to ground in a solid-seeming stream, flashing into brilliant detonations within the central wreckage of the Xul base. He kept the fighter pointed at the center of the objective, hosing the area until the flashes merged into a burgeoning fireball engulfing several of the dome-shaped structures below.

Drawing back in his mind, Ramsey brought the Nightstar's nose up, cutting the Gatling's shriek. An instant later, the aerospace craft plunged through the rising fireball, climbing hard, now, as he fought for altitude.

Warning tones sounded. Xul defensive batteries were tracking him, snapping off bolts of white-hot plasma, filling the sky around him with deadly light. Above and behind him, other Nightstars twisted in from different directions, each weaving through the blossoming fire and past other Marine fighters in a complex pattern possible only to the squadron's directing AI.

A flash detonated above and behind Ramsey's craft; his data feed gave the grim news: Raptor 11—Lieutenant Randi Schactman—had taken a direct, 20-kiloton hit, the blast vaporizing half of the fighter and sending the rest hurtling toward the surface in a shower of white-hot fragments.

Ramsey took his fighter high . . . high enough that the red
sun burst suddenly above the western horizon, bathing his
craft in ruby light. His display showed the other fighters in
the sky around him, some completing their attack runs,
some just beginning to make their first pass.

He rolled hard left, bringing his nose around for his next
attack. . . .

Marine Regimental Strike Team
Objective Lima, S-2/I
1552 hrs, GMT

Garroway dropped to the ground as searing blasts of light
and radiation flared just ahead. Rubble, much of it half-
molten, showered over him, and he felt the ground hammer
at his armor as shock waves rippled out from the blast.

Modern combat presented fighters with *the* most deadly
environment ever encountered by living organisms, a searing storm of radiation and heat and hurtling debris that even
the best suit of armor couldn't completely block.

The close-support fighters of Raptor Squadron had hit the
center of Objective Lima with pinpoint precision, pounding it
with antimatter rounds, bolts of fusing plasma, X-ray lasers,
and high-velocity slugs. The attack had wiped out the first
wave of emerging defenders, but even as he started to rise, red
stars appeared on his in-head display, marking more of the
seemingly endless hosts of Xul combat machines as they
emerged from their holes and tunnel entrances. They moved
swiftly, seeking to close with the leading elements of advancing Marines. As Garroway stood, three of the gleaming, black
monsters closed with him, scrabbling across the broken rubble
with wildly lashing tentacles. He burned one . . . then another,
but the third slammed against him, driving him backward, too
close, now, for him to bring his weapon to bear.

Around him, other Marines were suddenly engaged in
savage hand-to-tentacle combat, the battle transformed into

a sprawling, deadly encounter at knife-fighting range. Perhaps the Xul had figured the Marine aerospacecraft wouldn't attack if they were mingled closely with friendly forces.

Garroway released the locking mechanism on his plasma gun, letting the useless weapon fall. In the next instant, he'd triggered both forearm-mounted slicers, extending the tough blades, each the thickness of a molecule at its edge. Snapping his left arm back, he severed three of the Xul machine's tentacles as it tried to hold him; his second slash gouged a chunk the size of his helmet out of the Xul combot's side.

At the same time, the Xul was firing bolt after bolt of high-energy laser light into his armor at point-blank range, rapidly overloading its energy-sink capabilities, and heating two patches on his front torso to red-hot temperatures. His armor's nano film began trying to cope with the damage, but the Xul beams were melting through the laminate faster than the armor could repair itself, and dangerously close to cutting through.

At last he'd sliced away enough of those whiplashing tentacles that he was able to shove the Xul machine back. It spun in the air, slowing to a hover, as Garroway raised his right arm and triggered the nano-D dispenser imbedded in the wrist cuff.

The stub-snouted weapon fired a slug that burst on impact, spraying a thin mist of nano-disassemblers across the outer shell of the damaged Xul combot. Programmed to devour the nano-grown plastic-metal laminates that made up Xul armor surfaces, the mist began condensing on the surface in white swirls. Complex molecules dissolved into component atoms, which boiled off the dissolving surface like steam. The Xul machine began writhing and twisting, almost as if in agony; in another moment, the nano-D ate through to the circuitry powering its agravitic lifters, and the machine collapsed to the ground, rapidly dissolving now like a snow ball floating in hot water.

Garroway had already stooped and retrieved his primary weapon. Other Marines around him were still struggling at close quarters with enemy machines, while others, their own battles won, were turning to help their comrades. Garroway put another nano-D slug into the Xul combot grappling Corporal Fossey, then swung his plasma gun to bring a group of enemy machines under fire as they emerged from a tunnel entrance.

Another barrage of explosions flashed and hammered across the ruined base as two more Nightstars slashed low across the star-dusted sky. Garroway ducked as his suit warned him of a hurtling chunk of debris the size of a small aircar tumbling toward him end over end. The slab missed him by two meters and slammed into a ruined wall behind him. He emerged from hot rubble, shaking the pieces aside and moving forward.

"C'mon, Marines!" he screamed over the platoon net. "*Drive* them!"

And all along the line, the Marines advanced.

Ops Center
UCS Hermes
Cluster Space
1550 hrs, GMT

Hermes remained in Cluster Space, overseeing the operation now unfolding some thirty thousand light years away, deep within the Galactic Core. Her Ops Center stayed in communication with the *Intrepid*—and, through her, with the Marines on the surface of S-2/I—by means of QCC field-entangled transceivers.

The equipment was still large and bulky, but ships the size of *Intrepid* could carry banks of Quantum-Coupled Communications gear matched to parallel units on board *Hermes*. Constellations of subatomic particles generated in pairs, separated, and captured in crystalline matrices remained linked through the quantum dynamics of nonlocality; change one particle, and its twin changed at the same instant, even if it had been transported to the other side of the Galaxy . . . or thirty thousand light years from the Galactic halo to the Galactic core.

General Alexander lay in one of the Ops Center link couches, immersed in the sensory flood coming from Operation Heartfire. One open mental window showed a computer graphic of the inner Core area, the spiral of the Sag A* accretion disk, and the orbit of S-2 in its dizzying plunge close around the central black hole. Another was an external camera view from one of the Tarantulas on the surface. He could see a line of Marines advancing with searing blue-white explosions in the background, hear the radio chatter as they moved, punctuated by the static shrieks caused by plasma gunfire. Marine Nightstars flashed silently past low overhead.

He turned his attention back to the simulated map. The Galactic Core, when reduced to graphic icons and symbols in a netlink display, felt small, almost cozy, with the various elements—Sag A*, the Great Annihilator, S-2, IRS-16, and all the rest—crammed into a volume of space equivalent to the C^3 Deck on board the *Hermes*. It looked as though the Xul garrison at S-2/I could call for support from the Gal-Center Dyson object by shouting.

But it was, Alexander knew, vitally important to maintain a sense of scale. The pinwheel of gas and dust circling Gal-Center, he reminded himself, was twenty light years across, almost five times the distance from Sol to Alpha Centauri. IRS-16. He fed data to his implant math processors, running the numbers. The cluster of hot, young stars close to the center, IRS-16, was one-tenth of a light year from GalCenter . . . 946 billion kilometers, or almost 1,600 times the mean distance from Sol to Pluto.

A *long* way.

And at the very center, at least according to the netlinked simulations, the star S-2 appeared to be right next to the mysterious alien structure at Sag A* . . . and twenty light hours *was* a mere stone's throw when compared with light years. But twenty light hours was 21.6 billion kilometers, or roughly 144 a.u.s, three and a half times the mean distance between Sol and Pluto. Unless there'd been active FTL communications links between Objective Lima and Sag A*—and there were decent intelligence reasons for supposing there were not—any Xul at the GalCenter Dyson body could not know that Marines had landed on S-2/I for at least twenty hours.

They had that long to stabilize the situation.

"General Alexander?" Cara's voice said in his mind. *"Senator Yarlocke wishes to link with you."*

Alexander suppressed a groan. He knew this was coming. Yarlocke's office had connected with him that morning, requesting a conference. But he'd not been looking forward to it.

"Conference room," he told his AI assistant. "Patch her in."

His viewpoint shifted to a conference room sim, one with large, curving viewall screens across bulkheads and overheads showing the view currently being received from the *Intrepid*. The planet below was in darkness as it eclipsed its red giant sun; the sky was dominated by the vast, glowing spiral of the Sag A* accretion disk, the backdrop of softly glowing star clouds, and the distant blue-white glow of the molecular cloud and its associated young stars.

"Why were we of the Senate not informed of this attack?" Yarlocke's voice demanded.

Alexander turned and studied the woman's icon. She wore a silver-white gown, with a personal coronae flammae gleaming in golds and silvers. Clearly she'd been going for the angelic look . . . but the expression transmitted through her face somewhat spoiled the effect. Behind her stood half a dozen men and women in more muted dress—her official entourage, he presumed, aides and staffers.

"You were, Senator," Alexander told her. "Yesterday, before they even went in."

"We were told you were conducting a reconnaissance, General! Not an invasion!"

"Reconnaissance in force, actually," he replied. "We're establishing a base close to GalCenter. From there, my people will map the local gravitational metric to the degree of precision necessary to allow the *Pax Galactica* to translate to the Core. They will also be standing by in case the *Pax* requires military intervention."

"You are determined to see the peace effort fail. . . ."

"*No*, madam, I am not!" He'd been working to control his anger, to remain diplomatic, but the charge brought a rising tide of white fury. Damn it, he had *had* it with these people. "No one would like to see an end to the Xul conflict more than me. But I have grave doubts that the Xul see things the same way we do."

He expected an argument from the woman, and was startled when she seemed to slump, then nodded. "I know," she said. "And I understand what you're doing, that you're doing what you think is best for the Commonwealth."

"Do you? Let me ask you . . . did you understand that when you attempted to cut off funding for 1MIEF a year ago?"

She hesitated. The other figures standing behind her abruptly winked out as Yarlocke cut their link with the two of them. They were now, effectively, alone.

"I think so," she told him. "I knew you thought you were doing what was right. I did think you were something of a warmonger, I suppose. But your heart was in the right place."

He frowned. "A warmonger, Madam Senator, goes out of his way looking for a fight. I haven't needed to do that since I accepted this billet." *Fighting the Xul, and fighting you,* he thought, but he kept the words carefully to himself. *I've had all the fighting I could possibly want.*

"I know. And . . . I know you probably don't believe me, but . . . you need to understand that *I* am doing what *I* think is right."

"I never thought otherwise."

"If we in the Senate thought that you were pursuing some agenda of your own—carrying on the war for your own glory or to build yourself a political power base, you would have been removed from your position a long time ago."

It sounded like she was reminding him of just where his

personal power lay. "The military arm of the Commonwealth," he told her, "answers to the civilian administration. It's been that way since the earliest days of the old United States. Military leaders can advise . . . but we do *not* dictate policy." He wondered what she was looking for, what she wanted from him, but he decided to let her come to it on her own.

"General Alexander, it's no secret that I will do anything . . . well, *almost* anything, to ensure peace. Our people, the Commonwealth . . . they're sick of war. Sick of going on decade after decade, knowing there's an enemy out there and never knowing when he's going to strike. They want an end to it."

"Do you believe me when I tell you that I want to ensure peace as well? You might not credit this, Madam Senator, but *no* one yearns for peace as much as the man or woman who has to actually engage the enemy in combat."

"I'll take your word for that."

"Good. My job, however, is not so much to ensure peace as it is to protect the people and the government of the Commonwealth. The Xul represent a very real, very immediate, very palpable danger to the continued existence of our Commonwealth. And I will do anything . . . *almost* anything, to protect it."

"So . . . tell me truthfully, General. About . . . this." She indicated the simulation displayed upon the viewalls with a sweep of her arm. "Not a last-minute attempt to circumvent the Senate's will?"

"Madam Senator," he said coldly. "I am a Marine. My oath is to the Commonwealth. And that means to the people you represent."

"Tell me why, *exactly* why, you sent your Marines in there, General. And why you did it without consulting us."

"As for sending the Marines into the Core, I told you. First, we need a base from which to map the gravitational stresses on local space in close to the Core. It's a highly chaotic, rapidly changing picture—very large masses moving very quickly. If *Pax* is to successfully translate into the

Core, we need detailed gravitometric mapping of the region. If we don't gather that data, the *Pax* does not make the trip. That's one."

"You could have sent remote probes."

"We have sent remote probes. Lots of them. Having Marines in there increases the chances of getting the data we need. Okay?"

She nodded.

"Two . . . we need a credible military force close by when *Pax* attempts to open negotiations. If the Xul want to talk, great. My Marines will sit tight and enjoy the show. But if the Xul perform the way they have in times past . . . we'll be in place to provide you with cover so you can get away. Three . . . well, this may be the warmonger talking, but in my experience it's *always* best to negotiate from strength. If the Xul see a well-armed party of Marines in their backyard when you arrive for your parlay, they just may be less inclined to be . . . adventurous."

"I actually hadn't thought of that one."

"It's true. We've delivered a number of sharp stings to the Xul apparatus over the past few centuries. They know we can hurt them. If it hasn't had that much effect, it's because the Xul apparatus is so big. It's like a cloud of stinging insects attacking . . . I don't know. An extinct mammoth or elephant. It hurts. They want us to stop." He shrugged. "And we may someday hurt them enough that they'll stop threatening our existence. The point is, if they see us in there, they'll know we can hurt them again, maybe worse than they've ever been hurt by us before. Whatever else they are, the Xul are intelligent. They may not reason the way we do, but they *do* reason. *Pax* will be in a much better position to negotiate if you have us in there providing you with some leverage."

She nodded. "I believe you. What about my other question?"

"Which one?"

"Why didn't you consult with the Senate first?"

"Tell me something, Madam Senator. If I'd linked through

to your office yesterday and explained all of this, just as I've just done, would you have authorized the operation?"

"Of course!"

"Really? Or would you have laid down conditions, tried to micromanage, tell 1MIEF what it could and couldn't do?"

"As you yourself pointed out, General, 1MIEF is ultimately under civilian control!"

"Agreed. But we're paid to know what the hell we're doing. Case in point. My office did inform you. We told you we were making a reconnaissance in force. That is exactly what we are now doing."

"I thought reconnaissance in force meant something like going in and scouting out the area."

"Which is what we're doing. The difference is that there are . . . nuances that you do not understand, because you haven't been *trained* to understand. You're not military. You're not a *Marine*. It is your job to make policy. It is my job to carry out that policy insofar as the military applications are concerned.

"In short, you have to trust me to carry out that policy to the best of my ability, according to my training and experience, and without pursuing any personal or warmongering agendas I might have. If you don't trust me, you need to replace me. Immediately.

"And I need to trust *you*, Madam Senator, that you will not try to micromanage my command, put unreasonable demands upon it, or leave my people hanging while you pursue *your* personal agenda. Have I made myself clear?"

She stared at him for a long moment, so long he could almost hear the thoughts turning behind her eyes. The woman wasn't used to being talked to this way. She could easily be on the point of dismissing him on the spot.

He was, Alexander thought, taking a fearful chance. If she dismissed him, he had a number of Marines fighting for their lives at GalCenter right now, and he would no longer be able to support them. If he lost his command, he would fight like hell to protect his people, but in the long run there wouldn't be much he could do. Take the whole affair to the news media and place it before an apathetic public? Appeal to a weak Commonwealth President?

His options would be sharply limited.

Possibly he'd let his anger and his frustration do too much of the talking. But there was no pulling back now. . . .

"You know, General," she said at last, "I don't think there is another person in the entire Commonwealth who would talk to me the way you are now."

"I am not a politician, Madam Senator. Or a diplomat. I am a Marine, the CO of 1MIEF, and the government pays me, among other things, to express my concerns and to give my advice."

"And I appreciate that. I appreciate your candor . . . and your willingness to tell me what you really think. And . . . I believe it would be best if we could work together, you and I."

"Aren't we?"

"Not as well as we might. You've spoken frankly. Now it's my turn. The Commonwealth is sick of war, and I, General, am going to give them peace. I have . . . certain ambitions. As the person who makes possible a Galactic peace, I will be able to realize those ambitions, to rise in power and in . . . in status within this government. And I can bring you up with me."

Alexander blinked. Was she trying to bribe him with a promise of power, for God's sake? "My oath is to the Commonwealth, Madam Senator. My first loyalty is to the Corps."

"Help me forge this peace, General. That's all I ask of you. Afterward, you will find me very grateful."

"I'll help you," he told her, trying to keep his mental voice neutral. "That's never been an issue. The question is whether the Xul will play along. *They're* the ones who will determine whether your peace plan has a chance in hell."

"The Xul, General? Or your Marines?"

He reopened the mental window showing images transmitted from the surface of S-2/I. Marines had reached the lip of a huge, circular crater and were pouring fire down into its depths, where thousands of black machines writhed, struggled, and died.

"The Marines, Madam Senator, have always been pretty

damned good at convincing the other fellow that they should play nice. That's why we're here."

For the first time, though, Alexander found himself wondering which the worse enemy was . . . the Xul?

Or the human behind the angelic image glowing in his thoughts?

17

0505.1102

Marine Regimental Strike Team
Hawkins Station,
Objective Lima, S-2/I
1612 hrs, GMT

Garroway led an ad hoc section of twenty Marines forward across broken rubble and steaming rock, an impossible sky overhead, silent flame and white-hot devastation ahead and below. He crouched behind a block of glowing rubble, pouring fire into the tangle of struggling Xul machines below.

To his right, one of the Tarantulas moved with them, two forward pods unfolding now as plasma blast heads, of the type used in large-scale asteroid mining. Other Tarantulas were already in place around the crater rim, playing the floor of the depression with blue-white plasma energy. As the huge machines hosed the tortured ground at the bottom of the crater, rock bubbled as black-crusted lava flowed and churned. Directly beneath the blast points of the plasma guns, rock didn't melt, but vaporized. As the vapor cooled in hard vacuum, it solidified as frozen flecks of white powder, like minute flakes of snow sifting down across the landscape.

Another flight of Nightstars streaked silently overhead, loosing weapons loads into the crater's center. There was very little return fire, now, and Garroway broke from cover, taking several steps forward to give him a better angle down into the half-molten pit. He was standing just inside the crater rim, on crumbling, heat-seared rubble.

Periodic explosions set off outside the Marine perimeter allowed ground sensors to continually update the images of underground passageways and chambers. Under the unrelenting assault from above, many of those chambers had been closed off or had collapsed.

A scream sounded over the Net, followed by another voice yelling, "Corpsman! Corpsman front!"

Corporal Tom Cushman was down, his right arm burned away, atmosphere gushing from his suit. In this hellish environment, there probably wouldn't be much Doc Scott could do. The automatic first aid features built into his Type 690 armor would stop the air and blood loss in seconds, but the repairs would not be enough to protect Cushman from the deadly and immediate effects of the high background radiation. Nevertheless, HMC Scott, one of the company corpsmen, was already bending over the fallen Marine, trying to drag him back from the abyss.

"First Platoon," Captain Black called. "Pull back! Pull back!"

That was Garroway's unit. Almost reluctantly, he stopped firing and backed his way up the crater slope, then joined the scattering of other Marines falling back from the firing line. The gas pack on his fusion weapon was almost exhausted. He thumbed the release to drop the empty, pulled a fresh pack from an external suit pocket, and snapped it home.

"We've got a fresh breakthrough in the making, people," Black told them. Fresh schematics flooded into Garroway's in-head situation sim. "Sector two-three-niner. Let's move it!"

On his download display, Garroway could see the indicated trouble spot, a large region a hundred meters back from the central crater, where tunnels and chambers crisscrossed underground. Movement and energy sensors were recording a lot of activity down there, just beneath the surface. Hundreds of red pinpoints appeared to be clustering in one vertical shaft that came up to within a few meters of the surface. As the Marines approached at a run, a geyser of rubble and debris erupted into the sky just ahead.

"Breakthrough, breakthrough!" one Marine called from farther up ahead. "They're comin' through!"

A dozen black machines emerged from the hole blasted up through the rubble, lasers and particle beams snapping into the Marine ranks. Two Marines went down, their armor holed. Garroway stopped, dropped to a crouch as he raised his Mk. VII, and mentally triggered a string of shots, slashing through the cloud of Xul robots. The cloud began to disperse, but he saw several large chunks of body and fragments of tentacles go flying, and four of the hovering machines collapsed, crashing to the ground.

"Don't let the bastards spread out!" Garroway yelled, still firing. Static blasted the radio channels and he wondered if anyone else could hear, but the other Marines were firing as well, plasma bolts crisscrossing through the Xul cloud. "Hit them! *Hit them!*"

The enemy combots were trying to organize into a formation, but were taking heavy losses. Marines closed in from three sides, pouring fire into the cloud of emerging Xul machines. The firefight continued for another ten agonizing seconds at near-point-blank range. Three more Marines fell, their armor breached in the deadly alien firestorm, but then the last of the Xul machines dropped to the ground, smashed and broken.

Garroway and a handful of others were the first to reach the newly opened entrance, a gaping tunnel mouth leading into darkness.

It was a darkness out of nightmare, a darkness haunted by terror and unseen demons. It was also a direct route down into the underground levels of the Xul city—exactly what they'd been looking for. The floor of the big, central crater was mostly molten, now, and there'd be no entrance there. But here . . .

"Ops just called and said we need a software probe down there," Black said over the Net. "Who's got an MSP-90?"

Garroway heard Black's words and shook his head inside his helmet. It was . . . inevitable.

"I do, sir," Garroway replied. One in every ten Marines in the RST was carrying one of the things, designed to connect with the alien data net. Reluctantly, he pulled the device from an external pouch, a softball-sized mechanism with LED lights in a band around the equator that would switch on when he mentally activated it. "Where do you want it?"

"As far down that hole as you can manage. Ops says they want it planted in contact with the Xul infrastructure, not just dropped randomly into a hole."

"Aye, aye, sir." Holding the probe in his left gauntlet, his plasma pulse rifle ready in his right, he moved to the rim of the hole. He hesitated, trying to pierce the darkness at infrared wavelengths. He didn't *want* to go down there. . . .

"Douglas! Gardner! Maler! Get down there with him and keep him covered!"

"Aye, aye, sir!"

Master Sergeant Gardner and Sergeant Maler went in first, weapons at the ready. "Okay!" Gardner called back. "We're on the bottom, in a large tunnel running east and west. It's clear!"

Garroway took a deep breath. "Coming down," he said. His helmet radar showed a drop of about ten meters. "Watch my boots!"

He slid from cold light into darkness, his helmet automatically adjusting to full-spectrum infrared as he entered deep shadow. A two-second fall carried him to the bottom, where he hit solid rock with both boots, absorbing the shock through his armor's heavily shielded boots and legs.

He'd come down between the other two Marines; the tunnel ran off in opposite directions, the walls smooth-polished and featureless. Gardner and Maler had already switched on the lamps mounted on their shoulders. Even at IR wavelengths, the tunnel was nearly black, and the lights cast weirdly clashing shadows across the smooth and somewhat shiny walls of the tunnel.

Sergeant Douglas arrived at the bottom of the hole a moment

later, landing heavily at Garroway's side. "Watch that first step," Garroway warned him.

"It's not the fall that kills ya," Douglas told him. "It's the sudden stop at the end."

Garroway held up the MSP and switched it on with a thought. The two halves popped apart from the equator, where green lights winked readiness.

Grasping the two hemispheres, he pulled the device apart, then, reaching high above his head, he pushed the flat face of one half against the wall of open shaft leading back up into the light. That flat, black surface, coated with a nanoadhesive, welded itself to the solid rock. A slender black tendril continued to connect the two halves of the device.

"Okay," Garroway announced. "Relay is in place. Let's find some circuitry,"

The MSP-90 had been designed after long experience with AI probes deployed on penetrator missions into Xul bases and ships. While such missions could be carried out over radio frequencies from a distance, things worked a lot better—and with less risk of discovery and blocking—if hardware could be physically planted in direct contact with Xul computer circuitry. The tunnel walls here were solid rock, smoothly polished and unbroken. They would have to go deeper to find a good place to plant the MSP's business end.

Guided by the seismic readouts coming through on the tactical channel, the four Marines began following one of the tunnels. It led down a steep incline, then leveled off. According to the seismic charts, this tunnel opened into a broad, subterranean chamber about fifty meters up ahead. The hemisphere in Garroway's hand continued to play out a single strand, unimaginably tough, of black thread, connecting it to its twin back at the entrance to this chthonic world. He held it over his helmet; that thread was dangerous, and could nick through armor as cleanly as his slicers if he was careless.

"Watch it, down there," Captain Black warned them over a radio channel increasingly fogged by static and break-ups.

"We're reading Xul activity in that big room ahead, moving into your tunnel fast!"

"Copy that," Gardner replied. "Watch it, people! Here they come!"

A dozen shapes appeared out of the darkness farther down the tunnel, illuminated by the Marines' lights, dragging themselves along the tunnel walls with almost lazy flicks of their metallic tentacles. Gardner and Maler opened fire immediately, while Douglas turned and kept watch toward the rear.

After several moments, it became clear that the Xul combat machines were not advancing, but appeared to have positioned themselves to prevent the Marines from penetrating more deeply into their sanctum. The two Marines on point continued burning them down, but more kept swarming in from the chamber beyond. They appeared to be locking themselves together, forming a wall blocking the way.

"I think they're trying to keep us out of the big room," Garner said.

"Might be a control center, or an important C³ node," Garroway suggested. "How about it, Skipper? Should we try to see what they're guarding?"

"Negative," was Black's reply. "Just plant the MSP and get the hell out of there! We're reading more bogies moving in on your position!"

"What do you say, Gunny?" Gardner asked him. She gestured with the hot barrel of her plasma weapon at the ceiling almost directly overhead. "That looks like an electrical feed up there."

She was indicating one of the organic-looking growths common to the interior of Xul bases and ships, like a slender black root or tentacle growing within living rock.

"That'll do," he replied. The ceiling of the tunnel here was low—just over seven feet. He reach up and slapped the flat face of the remaining hemisphere against the cavern roof, directly next to the electrical conduit.

Immediately, the hemisphere appeared to melt, reducing itself to what looked like a puddle of black tar adhering to the ceiling, reflecting Garroway's armor lights with a wet gleam. Myriad threads whipped from the viscous liquid and began to embrace the conduit, growing along it in both directions.

The Xul power distribution net, he knew, would be intimately entangled with the circuitry that carried both Xul data and their uploaded intelligences. Back at the tunnel entrance, more threads would be growing up the wall to reach the upper surface, where they would become an antenna. Athena or other, specially created artificial intelligences could use the MSP, then, to access the Xul computer network directly.

"Okay, people," Black's voice called to them. The static was quite bad now, his words almost unintelligible even after being filtered through their implant AIs. "We're getting a clear signal. Get the hell out of there!"

The Marines began pulling back toward the tunnel entrance, firing as they moved. More Xul machines were coming in from the other direction, now, and the four of them shuffled along in a small clump, two firing ahead, two behind. All of them had taken hits to their armor but, so far, damage was light. They waded on, burning down combat after combat, as more and more of the infernal devices swarmed in after them.

The MSP they left behind had begun eating its way into the electrical conduit's insulation and the surrounding rock, stretching itself out until each strand was only a molecule or two in thickness and impossible to remove without vaporizing the entire ceiling, conduit and all.

At last they reached the opening. This was the tricky part, since there was only room for two Marines in combat armor to move up the shaft at a time. Douglas triggered his armor's jump jets and rocketed up the opening first. Garroway prepared to follow, but then a fresh surge of enemy battle machines rushed in, firing wildly with every weapon they carried. Garroway took a hit in his left shoulder, a blow that slammed him back a step, but not enough to breach the suit.

"Maler's hit!" Gardner cried over the netlink. "He's down! There're too many of them!"

Garroway turned back, wading back into the melee. The fight was too close now for plasma weapons, so he locked his Mk. VII over his back, erected his slicers, and powered up the nano-D dispenser on his left arm.

For several nightmarish seconds, the two Marines struggled there in the darkness above Maler's collapsed form, surrounded by a jostling mob of black, metal-plastic shapes pressing in close. As tentacles fell across their armor, they used their slicers to cut themselves free, and both of them continued to pump nano-D rounds into the enemy at literally point-blank range.

Garroway was hit again. His helmet indicator showed he was losing atmosphere, and that the radiation levels inside his suit were rising. Fortunately, the background rad count was lower down here beneath the surface—still deadly, but not as immediately deadly as up above. His armor was pumping anti-rad nano into his bloodstream, so all he could do was keep fighting.

It was a more desperate, more immediate struggle, he thought, than that fight in Cluster Space a year ago, when he'd sacrificed his own legs. Garroway felt panic clawing at his mind . . . and then he was battling *two* enemies, the swarming Xul and his own terror.

He was screaming as he continued to pour nano-D slugs into the advancing mass of black shells, glittering lenses, and snapping tentacles. Laser beams struck his right leg, and his suit sealed the holes. He felt pain, and the shock of dropping air pressure, then a jolt as his suit sealed the holes over. Another beam struck him in the chest. . . .

Somehow, Gardner managed to drag the unconscious Maler back to the circle of light at the bottom of the shaft leading to the surface, as Garroway tried to cover them in all directions.

A line was dropped from the surface, and Gardner secured it to Maler's armor. "Okay, Gunny!" she yelled, slapping the back of Garroway's shoulder to get his attention. "Maler's on the way up! Let's get the fuck out of Dodge!"

Garroway pumped out a barrage of nano-D slugs as Xul

combat machines dissolved and crumbled all around him. Some of the nano-D, losing its programming, was starting to gnaw on his armor as well. He stepped back alongside Gardner, and together the two of them crouched, kicked off, and triggered their jump jets, vaulting up the shaft and into cold-frosted starlight.

The Xul machines did not follow.

Garroway collapsed at the top, trying to control a violent trembling. The air leaks in his armor all were sealed off; the shaking appeared to be purely an emotional reaction to the close fighting down there in the alien tunnels. He wondered if he could *ever* forget the dark and claustrophobic terror. . . .

"Garroway!" Someone was shaking him by one shoulder. "You okay?"

It was Black. Garroway nodded, then realized the skipper couldn't see his head behind his helmet's rad shielding. "Yeah. Yessir, I'm okay."

"Good job down there, Marine. Can you move?"

"An amphibious green blur, sir."

"Good. All of you, good work!" Black said. "Athena just uploaded a copy of herself into the alien net."

"Have the bastards found the MSP?" Douglas wanted to know.

"Of course they have, but there's nothing to grab hold of by now. They can't stop it unless they melt down the walls and ceiling of that tunnel."

The nanotechnic goo in the MSP would have started dispersing as soon as it was activated, individual molecules slipping into minute crevices within the rock wall and flowing along the length of the alien power conduit.

"Good news!" Black added. "We're getting word down from Ops! Looks like they're shutting down. . . ."

"Gods! You mean the bastards are surrendering?" Lieutenant Cooper asked.

"Negative. The Xul don't surrender. But Athena is isolating them."

It was a strategy that had worked before, but only in highly specialized situations. The Xul intelligences "lived"—if that was the appropriate word—on their equivalent of computer hardware; the dialogue between individual groups of Xul, like choruses echoed back and forth, served as a kind of democratic poll of intent and thought, and led to a consensus that resulted in specific actions. Athena, evidently, had managed to shut down the connections between separate Xul nodes, isolating individual units so that they couldn't chorus back and forth.

In essence, the Marines had just taken a large number of POWs.

"Hermes," Black called, "Hawkins Station is operational."

"Copy that," replied a voice. "Excellent work! I have members of the Commonwealth Senate with me here. We've been following the action closely. Congratulations, Marines! You've just made this whole thing possible! . . ."

The voice, Garroway saw on a com readout, was that of General Alexander himself, linking in from Cluster Space.

Well, it stood to reason. Heartfire might well determine the outcome of the whole damned Xul war. Garroway could feel the almost electric effect, however, as realization passed through the RST's ranks. *"Jesus and Buddha!"* one Marine whispered aloud. *"The Old Man himself's on-line! . . ."*

Garroway found it amusing that the Marines were more excited about having General Alexander looking over their collective shoulder than they were about the visiting senators.

But official notice or not, the Regimental Strike Team's work was far from done just yet. In some respects it had only just begun. Efforts to continue to root out the last Xul intelligences housed within the complex beneath the ruined base would continue, as would efforts to find any other Xul nests on the planet. At all costs, those had to be shut down before they could warn any other Xul assets in the vicinity—particularly those just twenty light hours away, at the Sag A* Dyson structure.

For the moment, though, those measures were largely electronic actions, carried out by highly specialized artificial intelligences within the nonphysical realm of cyberspace. In the world of knock-wood reality, the Marines and a small army of robotic devices armed with nano material processors began digging into the rubble-strewn surface of S-2/I, working around the heat-tempered rim of the central crater.

And new structures began to grow above the ruins of the old.

Hawkins Station had been named for another ancient hero of the Corps—Lieutenant Deane Hawkins.

In November of 1943, Lieutenant Hawkins had led a team of Marine combat engineers and scout-snipers ashore on the fire-torn coral sands of Betio in the desperate and bloody struggle for Tarawa Atoll. With his face badly scarred by a fire as a child, the Army had rejected Hawkins as "disfigured." The Marine Corps of the day, apparently, had had fewer scruples . . . or a quite different idea of what constituted disability. Hawkins had served with distinction at another Pacific island—Guadalcanal—where he'd earned a battlefield commission and transformed his scout-sniper unit into a deadly force.

On Betio's Red Beach Two, Hawkins had conducted a one-Marine offensive against the interlocking pillbox formations that secured the heart of the Japanese defenses. Armed only with a satchel full of grenades, Hawkins had attacked bunker after bunker, stuffing hand grenades through firing slits, down ventilator tubes, and through rear doors. Hit time after time, he'd continued his assault, until a Japanese machine-gunner put a Nambu round through his armpit and into his chest. He'd died ten minutes later, telling his scout-snipers, "I sure hate to leave you boys like this."

That one Marine had diverted enough enemy fire, however, to enable a battalion pinned down on the beach to move forward, cutting Betio in two and seizing the Japanese airfield in the island.

For his action, Hawkins won a posthumous Medal of Honor, and the captured airstrip became known as Hawkins Field—he'd been the only Marine infantryman to be honored in that way. The commander of the Marine assault regiment at Betio, Colonel David Shoup, credited Hawkins with winning the battle.

Garroway had been at Tarawa with Hawkins and his men in-sim, had run with him from pillbox to pillbox across fire-swept patches of beach littered with burning vehicles and dead and dying Marines. Modern Corps training sessions included hyper-realistic link simulations allowing personnel to experience historical battles, to *feel* as though they were present at key battles in the Corps' history. Derna and Chapultepec, Peking and Belleau Wood, Tarawa and the peak of Mount Suribachi, Chosin and Hue, Guaymas and Vladivostok, Mars, Ishtar, Sirius Gate, and Night's Edge—the blood-hallowed list of honor ran on for dozens of names, and all had been reproduced in sharp, bullet-snapping resolution for training simulations.

He wondered if future Marine recruits would one day link in and find themselves crawling down into that damned, black hellhole with him. What, he wondered, would they learn? That some Marines were dumb as rocks, he decided.

The Marines of the RST maintained a vigilant watch, but Xul resistance appeared to have collapsed completely. They dug in, established a perimeter, and did what Marines always did after taking a heavily defended beachhead.

They waited.

Ops Center
UCS Hermes
Cluster Space
1820 hrs, GMT

On board *Hermes*, General Alexander continued to monitor the situation on distant S-2/I. Yarlocke and her entourage had vanished several hours earlier, leaving him with reassurances that they would not interfere with the Heartfire operation, coupled with warnings that 1MIEF was expected to do all it could to make sure that the *Pax* mission *would* succeed.

Visible on the main screen in Ops Center, the *Pax Galactica* hung in empty space, bathed in the harsh light of the nearby exploded star. She was *Hermes'* twin, a pair of saucers joined hub to hub, half a kilometer across with what looked like a squared-off bite from the rim giving access to her cavernous docking bay.

Alexander had dealt with obtuse civilian authority more than once during his career, but the Warlock, he thought, brought new meaning to the term "clueless." He'd gone so far as to play for her a Marine training download, a sim of the first Xul encounter back in 2148, when a human exploration ship, *The Wings of Isis*, had approached the Sirius Star-gate. "Pure conjecture," Yarlocke had told him. "We don't know what *really* happened. . . ."

Years later, an AI penetrator probe had picked echoes of the *Wings of Isis* encounter within the data matrices of a Xul huntership . . . uploaded copies of the human passengers and crew of that vessel held in a kind of perpetual, virtual hell-sim. Human personalities, somehow read, copied, and uploaded into the Xul computer net, to serve as sources of data for their captors.

Whether those uploads were the literal, imprisoned members of the human ship's crew, or extremely sophisticated copies uploaded an instant before the humans were vaporized was immaterial, a question, perhaps, for philosophical sophontologists. Those copies thought of themselves as living, breathing humans, shrieking out their existence in unending pain.

Alexander had tried reminding Yarlocke of the fact. "Do you really want to risk ending up like the crew of *The Wings of Isis*?" he'd asked her.

"Didn't anyone tell you?" she'd asked in reply, apparently surprised. "I won't be there. Neither will any other senator. We'll be sending AI counterparts . . . like our personal assistants. There will be a Navy crew, of course, but the actual negotiations will be carried out with us linking through from EarthRing. . . ."

She apparently cared not a bit that there would be humans

on board the *Pax* . . . or that humans, the Marines of the RST, were already deep within the Galactic Core, where capture might well mean the same sort of virtual nightmare as that suffered by the *Isis* crew and passengers.

Was her attitude one, then, of simple self-centeredness? Or appalling ignorance coupled with a refusal to face reality?

Alexander didn't know . . . but he *was* sure that Yarlocke's fucking attitude was going to cost a lot of Marine lives.

18

Marine Regimental Strike Team
Firebase Hawkins,
Objective Lima, S-2/I
1945 hrs, GMT

"The way I heard it," Lance Corporal Phil Chaffee said, "is the Xul have a weapon, a machine of some kind, that eats your soul. . . ."

"Bullshit," Garroway said. "That's squad-bay rot-brain bull-session bullshit."

Four of them—Garroway, Chaffee, Sergeant Milo Huerra, and Master Sergeant Clara Gardner were sitting in a hole on the surface of S-2/I, passing the time in time-honored Marine fashion—exchanging scuttlebutt.

Behind them, Firebase Hawkins rose slowly but relentlessly from the plasma-baked rubble of the ravaged Xul base. Nanoconstructors, injected deep into the rock by the trillions, were devouring rock and reproducing, extruding as a by-product fast-growing shells of nanocrete. King-fisher heavy transports, massive and bulbous-hulled, had been descending from the *Intrepid* for the past several hours, bringing down heavy weapons and life-support equipment, turning the captured site into a Marine fortress. Numerous Xul caverns and underground facilities had already been converted into deep, well-protected bunkers. The word "invulnerable" had been floating around on the Net a lot.

There was considerable speculation within the ranks as to just how invulnerable the firebase might be. The Xul could bombard planets with asteroids, could annihilate worlds, detonate stars. Against *that* kind of firepower, the Marine base was just about as invulnerable as a stick of butter beneath the flame of a blowtorch. The only thing Firebase Hawkins really had going for it was the fact that it was *so* close to Sag A* that turning S-2 into a supernova wasn't a good option for the enemy . . . that and the fact, the *hope*, really, that the Xul didn't yet know the Marines were there.

In a nameless crater on the base perimeter, the four Marines had begun discussing Xul weaponry, and the chances that 1MIEF might be able to carry this thing off.

"But they were tellin' me back at the holding company after boot camp," Chaffee was saying, "that the Xul could just kind of reach out and . . . *snick*! Grab a ship and the souls of everyone inside!"

"Not quite, Lance Corporal," Gardner said, chuckling. "I think someone was having some fun playing with the new meat."

"That's right," Garroway said. "Soul-eaters? That's right up there with skyhooks and left-handed blivits. Stuff with which to haze the new kid in the platoon."

"But the master sergeant at the barracks said—"

"Look," Gardner told him, patiently, but with an edge to her voice, "if humans have something that answers to a soul, the Xul can't steal it, okay? What we *think* they do is electronically pattern or copy the state of every neuron, every electrical charge in a person's brain and nervous system. That gets stored inside a kind of computer subsystem that can translate things like language and memory. They can go in and question it, get information from it. It might even still think it's a whole person. But it's just . . . information. See?"

"But there was *The Wings of Isis* incident six, seven hundred years ago. . . ."

"Drop it, Chaffee," Garroway told him. "I don't think any of us want to think about alien soul-eaters right now!"

That drew some laughter from the others, but it was humor strained and on-edge.

The conversation had him wondering, though . . . and he imagined the others were thinking the same things. What was a human being, really, other than patterns of information? An organism made up of various organ systems and tissues, which in turn were made up of molecules, which were collections of atoms . . . and atoms themselves, according to the laws of quantum physics, were nothing more than standing wave patterns in the chaos of virtual particles filling the reality substrate known as the Quantum Sea. Human beings, so far as their individual molecules and atoms were concerned, were in a constant state of flux. Every cell in the body died—some in years, most in weeks or months—and was replaced. He thought he remembered having downloaded something once about even bone cells being replaced every seven years or so. The Aiden Garroway sitting here in a hole on S-2/I was a completely different being, in terms of his material make-up, than the Aiden Garroway who'd triggered a supernova a decade ago.

And yet he was still himself, still remembered cramming himself into the narrow constraints of the Euler triggership, still remembered the feelings of relief and trembling release when Gunny Warhurst had cut him free, as an exploding star filled heaven with radiant light. . . .

The individual molecules and atoms of his body all had been replaced, most of them many times over . . . and that wasn't even counting the fact that in those years he'd lost *two* sets of legs and had them regrown. All that connected the Garroway of today with the Garroway of ten years ago was . . . patterns of information.

A quietly disturbing thought. If there were such things as souls, they would have to be informational patterns as well, impressed somehow among those standing waves in the Quantum Sea. Patterns, perhaps, that survived the death and breakdown of the physical body.

Just what was it that the Xuls patterned when they took human prisoners?

He shouldered the thought aside, angry. Damn it, if the Xul *did* pattern him, copy him, it would be the *copy* that ended up in the Xul computers, right? Not . . . him, the quintessential Aiden Garroway. It would be someone else, someone with all the memories and feelings of Aiden Garroway, but a doppelganger, screaming out eternity in the depths of a Xul-manufactured cybernetic hell. . . .

Still, the thought that there would be an Aiden Garroway imprisoned on the Xul system, together, maybe, with thousands or millions of other such copies . . . the fact that they were copies didn't make it *right*.

"Okay, okay," Chaffee was saying. "But the records still say they could take something like *The Wings of Isis*—and she was a pretty big ship, remember—and break her down in an instant. Disintegrate her, I guess. And there have been a few other times that's happened, right? How do they do it?"

"We don't know," Garroway said.

"We think—*think*—they can reach down into the Quantum Sea and . . . change things," Gardner added. "Erase matter. But we don't really know."

"Apparently they can't erase whole planets," Garroway pointed out. "Ships, yeah. But not something as big as a planet . . . or a solar system."

"So they could come here to this planet and erase maybe just the firebase?"

"Maybe."

"The good news," Huerra pointed out, "is that, if they can do it, they don't do it often. They seem to rely on pretty conventional energy weapons most of the time . . . and on throwing asteroids around when they need to bombard a planet."

"*Very* reassuring," Gardner said. "They probably won't erase us, but they can drop rocks on us."

"The way I heard it," Garroway said, "is they only use their patterning technology when they need to gather intelligence about an enemy. And the Xul are, well, conservative in how they think. *Very* conservative."

"Stands to reason, doesn't it?" Huerra said. "The xenosoph people say the Xul are over a million years old as a race, maybe *ten* million. Once they uploaded themselves into their computers a million years or so ago, they stopped changing, stopped evolving at all. What worked for great-great-grand pap works for me, and if it ain't broke, don't fix it. I guess a race as old as theirs survives by becoming pretty static. No growth, and no new ideas."

"That may be our one big advantage over the Xul," Gardner said. "They may be millions of years ahead of us in evolution, but their technology isn't. *They don't change.*"

"Right," Garroway added. "You know, for a long time, people wondered why the Xul didn't just come in and stomp all over Humankind. At Armageddonfall, back in 2314, they sent one ship to destroy the Earth. We destroyed that ship, and then went nuts waiting for a follow-up fleet that never showed. On the one hand, the Xul have some kind of xenocidal hard-wired phobia of other intelligent species, to the point that they think any other space-faring species is a threat that has to be destroyed. On the other hand, they're damned slow in responding to a threat."

"Yeah," Huerra said. "If they'd ever invented FTL communications and wired the whole Galaxy into a comm network, they'd have figured out where we are and stepped on us eight hundred years ago. But information travels slowly from one Xul node to the next. Maybe it's by conventional radio, moving at the speed of light. Or maybe it's just carried by their hunterships, so it's FTL, but it only reaches a few of their nodes at a time."

"Right," Garroway said. "And each time we take out one of their nodes—Cluster Space, Starwall, Night's Edge—we screw up their internal comm system. They lose track of us and have to start over."

"A damned inefficient way to run a war of galactic conquest," Chaffee pointed out.

"Yeah," Garroway said. "Lucky for us. Thing is, they already own the Galaxy, so it's not a matter of conquest. We're more like . . . I dunno. Rats in the walls."

"Squeak," Gardner said.

"*Dangerous* rats," Huerra added. "Rats who've figured out how to blow up stars!"

Garroway laughed.

"What's so funny?" Gardner asked him.

"I just remembered something I downloaded once . . . an old image, maybe a frame from a short sim, I don't remember. Anyway, it shows this maze, right? Like they used to use to test the intelligence of rats? You put a lab rat in the door one side, and see how long it takes him to figure out how to get to the cheese."

"Yeah?"

"So the entrance is down in one corner, the cheese is in the corner diagonally opposite . . . and the rat has chewed a straight path from entrance to cheese, right through all the intervening walls of the maze. The image was titled 'Marine Corps rat.'"

"I've seen that," Gardner said. "It's *old*. Maybe pre-spaceflight. They haven't used lab rats and mazes in centuries."

"So what? I tell you, it's *us*."

"Ooh-rah."

"Anyway," Garroway continued, "most of the time, we're beneath the Xul's notice. They may honestly not even be aware of us, day to day, the way we are of them. When they sent that ship to Sol five hundred years ago, they were scratching an itch, a reflex, not trying to commit genocide."

"Well, Gunny," Gardner said, "you've certainly managed to step on *my* self-esteem for the day!"

"You're too ugly to have self-esteem, Master Sergeant," Huerra told her.

"Not true," Garroway said. "She has *esteem d'Corps*. What else do jarheads need?"

Gardner laughed. "*Semper fi*, Gunny."

Chaffee was leaning back, his opaque helmet visor turned skyward. Overhead, the vast, delicately colored spiral of

Sagittarius A arched across the night sky, glowing a sullen red out in the outskirts, but hardening to a definite blue toward the middle. A quarter of it was below the eastern horizon, but the rest dominated the entire sky, filling it despite the competing blue-white glare from the IRS-16 star cluster, and the overall backdrop of gas arcs, clusters, molecular clouds, and stars. A very *busy* sky, and yet, at the moment, impossibly serene.

Everything up there, Garroway knew, was moving one way or another at literally astronomical velocities, but the scale was so immense that you couldn't actually see any movement at all. According to the downloads he'd reviewed, the star S-2 was heading toward GalCenter at almost five thousand kilometers per hour, dragging the planet they were now occupying with it. Both would swing around the Dyson Sphere at the Galaxy's center in another thirty-some days.

By then, of course, the RST would be long gone, though he imagined they would leave behind robotic sensors to record and transmit S-2's actual close approach and passage. *What* a ride that would be! . . .

"That's it, isn't it?" Chaffee asked, pointing at a spot halfway up from the eastern horizon. "The Center?"

He was pointing at the place where the three vast, flat arms of the Sagittarius A spiral appeared to converge. You couldn't see a thing naked-eye, or even with IR imaging, but right *there*, twenty light hours away, was the Dyson Sphere enclosing the super-massive black hole at the Galaxy's exact center.

If the black hole was walled off behind some kind of shell, how did the infalling matter of the accretion disk, the Sag A spiral, reach it?

"That's the center," Garroway told him.

"You think they know we're here?"

Garroway shrugged, then remembered the gesture couldn't be seen through the embrace of his armor. "Who knows? Like Huerra said a while ago, they don't seem to have anything like faster-than-light QCC. We have to assume the bad guys here got off a radio message before their network collapsed . . .

but it'll be twenty hours before they hear about it at Gal-Center."

"More like seventeen hours, thirty minutes, now," Gardner reminded him.

"Okay, okay. But we've got time."

"A *little* time," Huerra put in.

"Right. And long before they hear, the *Pax Galactica* will be here starting the peace talks, right? And we either talk . . . or we fight. Either way, it doesn't matter whether they've heard we're here or not."

"What do you guys think is gonna happen?" Chaffee asked. "Peace or fight?"

"Fight," Gardner said.

"Fight, definitely," Garroway said. "The politicians don't know what the fuck they're dealing with here. They don't know the Xul like we do."

"I dunno," Huerra said. "We've kind of got the bastards by the balls, sitting here on their planet with an Euler triggership, don't we?"

The triggership had been brought down from orbit an hour ago, gentled in on its agravs into a deep and thick-walled bunker near the center of Firebase Hawkins. The idea was that a casual Xul probe might spot the triggership if it was still in orbit with the *Intrepid* and the *Cunningham*, but wouldn't notice it shielded and sheltered underground.

Of course, so little was still known about Xul technical capabilities.

"*That's* what's scary," Garroway said. "Up until now, we haven't been much of a problem for the Xul. Not on a big scale. Like I said, they were just kind of automatically scratching an itch when they hit us before. Now we're about to really bite 'em right where it hurts."

"It'll make them sit up and take notice, that's for damned sure," Gardner said. "You think they're going to roll over without a fight, Al?"

"A guy can dream, right?"

"It's a good dream," Garroway said. "But I wouldn't bet on it. Look at it from the Xul point of view."

"Is that even possible?" Gardner said with a laugh.

"Maybe not. But what I think their point of view is . . . is the rats in the walls get to scratching and squeaking every now and then. They go in, kill a few, watch the rest scurry back into the walls, and say, 'What the hell. It's only rats.'"

"Yeah," Gardner added, warming to the metaphor, "and that's just the Xul out on the back deck. The ones in the living room, the bedroom, the kitchen, they don't even know the rats are there."

"Right," Garroway went on. "Then one day, the rats show up with an AV-110 Tarantula, complete with a weapons pod load-out of K-772 particle beam weapons, programmed nano-disassembler dispensers, and a dozen tactical nukes, and say . . . 'Hi, there! Now that we have your full attention, please sign a peace treaty with us or we level your house!' What do you think they'll do?"

"I dunno," Chaffee admitted. "I guess it depends on what they have in the garage in the way of pest control."

"Exactly. We don't know what they have. We do know, though, that they don't seem to think the same way we do. They don't think in terms of surrender, or of taking prisoners."

"Except for the patterning thing," Chaffee said.

"Except for that, which we don't understand, and which they don't use often. They probably don't think of us as fellow sapient beings, certainly not as fellow sapient beings who are their equals."

"You have to be on a more or less equal footing to negotiate," Gardner pointed out. "Each side has to understand and respect the other. Not like them, necessarily, but know what they're capable of, and know that they're going to do what they say they're going to do."

"My point exactly," Garroway said. "All they know is . . . the rats have become a threat, and something has to be done about them, once and for all."

"Sheesh, Gunny," Chaffee said. "You sure know how to build up a guy's morale."

"Hey, it beats magic soul-eaters," Gardner told him.

"What religion are you, anyway, Chaff?" Garroway asked.

"You have one?" He was curious. There were so many religions among the teeming billions of Humankind. Their number and their diversity seemed to be defining characteristics of the species.

"RQH. Why?"

"RQH . . . Reformed Quantum Humanist?"

"That's right."

"So . . . no such thing as God, everything is wave-particle dualities, but the human intellect survives death in the Quantum Sea."

"I guess. We see God as what all Mind everywhere is evolving into, the Omega Transformation, we call it. The intellect—the soul, I guess—but we call it the personal omega, is the part of us in the Quantum Sea that survives death, and maybe inhabits a succession of bodies as it evolves. But while we're here, on *this* plane, we can't really see the whole picture."

"Fair enough. I see why you don't like the idea of the Xul stealing people's souls. Excuse me. Personal omegas."

"They're kind of like demons in my church," Chaffee said. "Other religions have the Devil, or Entropy, or bad God-aliens who fight the good God-aliens. We have the Xul."

"Jesus Christ, Chaffee," Gardner said, surprised. "If you believe *that*, why the fuck did you join the Corps?"

"To *fight* them, Master Sergeant. To stop them from devouring or killing every human everywhere. To stand between them and Home. Isn't that a good enough reason?"

"It'll do," Garroway said.

"Why?" Chaffee asked. "What god do *you* believe in, Gunny?"

"The God of Battles," Garroway said. "The Marine's God of Battles. . . ."

* * *

Ops Center
UCS Pax Galactica
Cluster Space/Core Space
2120 hrs, GMT

The *Pax* hung in empty space near one of the stargates in the Cluster Space system, actinic blue-white light gleaming from the smooth lines of her saucer hulls.

"Telemetry from the *Intrepid* is coming through, Madam Senator," the voice of *Pax*'s commanding officer said in her mind. "They have successfully mapped the gravitational matrix of an area in S-2 space. We are cleared to proceed with translation."

"Very well, Admiral," she replied. "Take us to the Galactic Center."

"It will take a few moments, Madam Senator. We're still coordinating with the other ships in the squadron."

"There's only the *Hermes*, damn it."

"There is the *Hermes*, Madam Senator, and there are eight warships loaded on both the *Hermes* and the *Pax*, which will be disembarking as soon as we complete the maneuver. There are also the *Cunningham* and the *Intrepid*, already in Core Space, along with a number of fighters and supply vessels. We need to be careful we don't translate into a volume of space already occupied by someone else."

She sighed. Another delay. These military types didn't know what the hell they were doing. Or maybe they did . . . and were being deliberately obstructionist. Well, they couldn't put it off much longer.

The QCC link with the *Intrepid* was transmitting to her mind the view at the Galactic Core—the twenty-light year spiral of the accretion disk, a point of ruby light marking the central Dyson sphere, other icons and symbols indicating S-2 and its planet, the positions of various Commonwealth ships and probes, gas clouds, debris fields, and black holes . . .

It looked damned crowded in there.

In reality, of course, and as she'd explained to General Alexander, Cyndi Yarlocke was not on board the *Pax*, was not even in Cluster Space at all. Physically, she was still in her private office in EarthRing, attended by machines and by a small army of human servants as her mind followed the unfolding of events at the Galactic Core.

The mastery of Quantum-Coupled Communications had been *the* technological advance of millennia, greater, even, than FTL travel itself. Originally, QCC instruments had been discovered on Mars, at Chiron, and scattered across a few of the other worlds so far visited by humans. They'd represented one of the great problems of modern physics—obviously linking together two points separated by light years with no time lag whatsoever. Apparently, they operated through the mechanism of entanglement, a principle of quantum mechanics dismissed by no less an authority than Einstein as "spooky action at a distance," yet one that had repeatedly been demonstrated in the laboratory.

It had taken centuries to unlock the secrets of those communicators, *ansibles,* as one pre-spaceflight author had called them. Not until the 25th-Century overthrow of the so-called Quantum No-Cloning Principle, which insisted that entanglement could not be used to transmit information because such would violate causality, had it become possible to build FTL communicators. Until then, humans had communicated faster than light only by borrowing the machines left behind and still working by the Builders of half a million years before.

As a politician, Yarlocke knew that if you controlled communications, you controlled the ultimate power in the universe. You could know what was happening on the far side of the Galaxy, could coordinate planning among your most widely dispersed forces, could even rewrite history to order, all by knowing the trick to instantaneous communications.

It was that, she knew, that would prove to be the eventual undoing of the Xul. Information exchange for them was slow, its dissemination limited to the movement of their starships, which appeared to happen randomly, rather than by plan. *Pax* would arrive at the Galactic Center, bypassing the bases, fortresses, and other defenses the Xul had erected farther out in the Core, and offer to deal with the Xul leadership directly. With a Commonwealth Navy squadron at the Core, the Xul would have no choice but to negotiate.

The peace, Yarlocke knew, would not last. It couldn't, because of the dynamic of History. The Xul, by all xenosophontological reports, were static, possibly even in decline, with no innovation, no growth, and quite possibly no social motivation to drive them forward. Humankind technology was constantly growing, changing, evolving; the Xul were advanced, but there was no sign that they'd changed at all. The Xul ships that had attacked Euler space some twelve hundred years ago, apparently, were identical to the ships they used today. Flat growth. *Stagnant.*

All Earth and her colonies needed was a little breathing room, and the Peace would ensure that. Within another century or so, Humankind would have developed so far in weaponry and engineering that the Xul would be left behind.

Cyndi Yarlocke, meanwhile, would use her new title as peacemaker to secure her own power in the Commonwealth, and go on to at last bring all of Humankind under the same government. That step, too, was necessary; General Alexander would be her principal tool in that, whether he agreed with her or not.

He was the revered leader of the Marine Interstellar Expeditionary Force, all but worshipped by every Marine alive.

And if she owned Alexander, she would own his Marine Corps. As simple as that.

"Madam Senator," Admiral Brooke's voice said, "we are beginning translation."

She pulled her awareness back out of Core Space, and watched from the bridge of the *Pax Galactica*. Young men and women sat at their consoles, while on the viewwall panels at the far end of the compartment, the vista of Earth's Galaxy shimmered, faded, and then was replaced by a new and quite alien backdrop.

There were no symbols or icons this time. She saw, as if with her physical eyes, the strange brilliance of the innermost volume of the Galactic Core, the red-to-blue spiral of Sagittarius A, the banked masses of star clouds in the remote distance, the nearer glow of dust clouds and arching jets of plasma within fiercely twisted magnetic fields.

Magnificent, she thought. . . .

The red-giant sun S-2 glowed sullenly to her left, close by the ocher-red crescent of S-2/I. The *Intrepid*, a red-gold illumined needle, was just visible between the planet and the *Pax*. On the other side of the sky, she could make out the shape of the *Hermes*, a tiny toy gleaming in red light.

The two transports floated silently in space for nearly three hours, as each unloaded the warships carried in their cargo bays—two light fleet carriers, the battleship *The Morrigen*, two battlecruisers, two destroyers, and a heavy transport. A tiny fleet, almost insubstantial . . . but a strong enough force to make the Xul think twice before attacking, surely.

Moments after *The Morrigen* completed her disembarkation from the *Pax Galactica*'s hold, Admiral Brooke announced their readiness to proceed.

"Do it, Admiral," she told him. Her viewpoint stood by him on the *Pax*'s bridge, watching as he gave orders powering up the Alcubierre Drive.

The process took some moments. The *Hermes*-class transport, originally designed not as a ship but as a semi-mobile base, had not originally been designed to travel FTL, save through its translation trick through the Quantum Sea. The Alcubierre Drive had been an add-on to the *Hermes*, and had been incorporated into the *Pax*'s design only belatedly, while she was still in the Ares Yard space dock as the *Brynhldr*.

But the drive was powered now by the full output of *Pax Galactica*'s banks of QPT generators, and space around her was bending inexorably as the power rose. She was moving. . . .

Then the star-clotted vista through the viewall panels blurred, then turned brilliant with unimaginable velocity. At several hundred times the speed of light, the *Pax* skipped in across the intervening light hours.

Abruptly, the view ahead cleared. Yarlocke was looking at . . . gods. What *was* she looking at? A cloud, perhaps, but in two halves, and dark as soot, but with an impossibly fierce white gleam peeking out from between. The soot, the cloud, whatever it was, appeared to have shape and substance, but in an oddly fluid manner. She was having trouble making out individual shapes; it was as though the eye kept resting on that . . . *thing*, then sliding off.

"Is *that* the Dyson sphere they've been talking about?" she asked Brooke.

"Yes, ma'am."

"I was expecting, I don't know. A shell or something."

"It's composed of some trillions of discrete . . . pieces," he told her. "Spacecraft. Worlds the size of asteroids. There may be whole planets in there bigger than Earth. They're in orbit around the central black hole, but they're held together in a semi-rigid structure by some sort of magnetic or energy-field network."

"But what—"

"Madam Senator, not now, please. We're . . . busy . . ."

She could see the other ship on the *Pax*'s screens . . . something that appeared to detach itself from the GalCenter cloud and move out toward the Humankind vessel at high speed. *Very* high speed. At first, she thought it was one of the big Xul vessels . . . one of the ones they called *Behemoth* class.

As the seconds passed, however, and the oncoming vessel grew larger, she realized that this was an entirely new class of Xul ship.

It was enormous. . . .

"Transmit the AI message," she ordered. An artificial intelligence programmed with everything Humankind knew about Xul language, technology, and computer net protocols would initiate contact.

"Already transmitted, Senator."

How big is *that thing?* she wondered.

Her personal AI, linked into the combat network, provided an answer. *"Approximately twenty kilometers across, Senator, and fifteen thick. We have never encountered a mobile Xul ship of this size."*

"It's too close!" Admiral Brooke said. "It's going to hit us!"

"Turn us around!" she yelled. "Back us off! . . ."

. . . but then something blinked, as though the universe itself had just winked out.

And Cyndi Yarlocke was awake on the link couch back in her office in SupraQuito EarthRing, as Reality itself twisted and tore within her mind.

She was shrieking mindlessly as machines and servants rushed to her side. . . .

19

Ops Center
UCS Hermes
Core Space
0040 hrs, GMT

"She's . . . *gone!*" a young naval officer seated at one of the Ops Center consoles said. She sounded shocked beyond reason.

"What do you mean, 'gone?'" Alexander demanded. "What's happening?"

"Sir! A large ship was coming out from that thing at the center . . . and then we lost all signal!"

Alexander watched over her shoulder as she replayed the image, transmitted back to the *Hermes* via *Pax*'s on-board QCC network.

"Damn. Looks like *The Wings of Isis* all over again, General," Admiral Taggart said.

"We have to assume so," Alexander said. "Do we have other viewpoints in the area?"

"*Pax* should have released drones, General," the communications officer said. "But they're not QCC. We won't get an image for another . . . nineteen minutes, twenty seconds."

"They must know what direction the *Pax* came in from," Alexander said. "They'll have FTL ships on the way by now. Pass the word, Admiral. Everyone stand ready, full alert."

"Aye, aye, General."

"Make sure our fighter screen gets the word. They'll be in line to spot incoming hunterships first."

"Right."

A minute dragged past. "Um, General?" Taggart asked at last. "Are you implementing Starfire?"

"Not yet. I want confirmation that the *Pax* is destroyed."

"Christ, what more confirmation do you need? That ship coming out of the Core must have been twenty kilometers across!"

"Right. And it might have swallowed the *Pax* and cut off her signal."

"May I remind the General," Taggart said carefully, "that there is no signal transmission in Quantum-Coupled Communications? No signal to be cut off, and it can't be screened or blocked."

"I *know* that, Admiral." The words snapped. "Damn it. Sorry, Liam. But everything is riding on this encounter. I don't want to start the shooting if what we have here is some kind of misunderstanding."

"Marty, you can't be serious. You can't believe that!"

"Not really. But we're going to be sure." He was still churning through the possibilities. Maybe *Pax*'s QCC gear had simply gone down. Maybe the Xul knew something humans didn't, something along the lines of how to screen off QCC communications. Maybe the *Pax* had been destroyed, but only because the Xul had been late in getting the AI peace message, and even now were composing an apology. . . .

Yeah, right, he thought. If the damned Xul even knew what the word peace meant, he'd be the most surprised Marine in the fleet.

But he had to *know*. Hell, Cyndi Yarlocke must be fuming back in EarthRing, wondering why she'd been cut off, maybe even suspecting the Marines of having pulled the plug. The QCC link with Earth was still open. They would be watching, watching and recording everything.

He didn't want to bring Yarlocke into this. As of a minute ago, this had become a purely military operation, and the responsibility to shoot or to stand pat was his.

But she should be in on this. "Cara," he said, summoning his personal AI aide. "Patch me through to Senator Yarlocke's private link channel, via QCC. She probably would like to know what's going down."

"Right away, General."

"Patience, Admiral," he said aloud. "We're going to wait until we see the bastards and know they're gunning for us. I don't want to give Cyndi Yarlocke ammunition for my firing squad."

"I hear you there."

"But pass the word to Starfire. Stand by to launch."

They wouldn't have long to wait now.

Marine Regimental Strike Team
Firebase Hawkins, S-2/I
Core Space
0043 hrs GMT

"Word just came down from Ops," Gardner said. "They're getting the triggership ready for firing."

"Shit!" Huerra said. "They're gonna do it! They're really fuckin' gonna do it!"

"What does it mean?" Chaffee asked.

"It means," Garroway said quietly, "that the Xul decided not to talk peace. There's a good chance the *Pax* just got vaporized, and that there's a major shooting war starting a few hundred kilometers above our heads!"

"God . . ."

"I thought you didn't believe in God."

"No such things as atheists in foxholes," Gardner told him. "You should know that."

"Yeah. Only too well. . . ."

The alert was spreading now throughout the regimental

command net. Behind the four Marines, several large, black spheres rotated smoothly in deep sockets, elevating the business ends of multiple hypervelocity mass cannons into line with the zenith. Elsewhere, smaller weapons—particle guns, plasma weapons, and high-energy lasers began powering up.

If the Xul came down on S-2/I, they'd find the Marines ready and waiting for them.

How long the Marines would be able to hold out, however, was anyone's guess.

Ops Center
UCS Hermes
Core Space
0043 hrs, GMT

"Here they come!" Admiral Taggart cried.

Alexander saw the Xul vessels on the main Ops screen, three of them decelerating out of FTL so abruptly they seemed simply to appear out of empty space. In the center was the monster glimpsed by the *Pax* seconds before her disappearance, a squat, flattened sphere that looked quite similar to Xul fortresses encountered in the past in both shape and surface structures, but which obviously had been improved by the addition of both normal-space and FTL drives.

"All stations!" Alexander snapped. "Hold fire!"

Technically, the squadron was commanded by Admiral Taggart, but as commanding officer of 1MIEF, Alexander had a certain amount of leeway in the orders he gave. Officially, he could advise, and holding fire until the Xul intentions were known for certain was the best advice he had to give at the moment. They could sort out the difference between a suggestion and a direct order later . . . if there *was* a later. . . .

The other two Xul ships were Type IV Behemoths, each a quarter the size of the monster they accompanied. The trio were moving toward the *Hermes* now, closing at a thousand kilometers per second, and still fifty thousand kilometers distant.

They were closer to the light carrier *Chosin*, released by the *Pax* just before she'd set off for GalCenter. One of the Behemoths was only ten thousand kilometers away as it drew abreast of the *Chosin*, and still the Xul held their fire. Maybe. . . .

And then lances of white plasma speared from the Xul ship, savaging *Chosin*. . . .

Nightstar 442
Core Space
0045 hrs, GMT

Lieutenant Charel Ramsey saw the Xul giants drop out of FTL only a few thousand kilometers ahead. *Gods*, they were close . . . and big! His orders were to observe, report, and hold fire . . . but to be ready for an attack at any second.

Then one of the Behemoths opened fire on the *Chosin*, spearing the light carrier with beams of starcore fury. *Chosin* returned fire, launching a salvo of high-velocity missiles armed with thermonuclear warheads. Most of those missiles were intercepted by the enemy vessel's defenses well short of the target, but three detonated within ten kilometers of the Xul warship's hull—one of them *very* close, at a range of perhaps half a kilometer—and white suns pulsed into harsh radiance, one after another flaring, brightening and expanding, then fading away.

"That's our cue," Major Steve Treverton, the Raptor's squadron leader, announced. The engage order was flooding through the squadron's tactical net. "Hit the bastards!"

Aerospace fighters operating in vacuum couldn't peel off and dive the way aircraft operating in atmosphere could. They had to kill their forward velocity by flipping end for end and applying full thrust in the direction of their drift, then align themselves with the target and accelerate again. Nightstars, however, with full inertial damping and GTE-5660 main drives, made ultra-high-G maneuvers appear nearly as effortless as those of any atmospheric fighter. Four of the Raptor Nightstars were traveling in formation within a thousand kilometers of one another. As the nuclear blasts hammered at the Behemoth's hull, all four began simultaneously killing their forward velocity and accelerating toward the Xul monster.

"Those explosions have thrown up a hell of a lot of space fluff," Treverton told the others. "We'll come in behind the blast screen where they can't see us."

"Shit, doesn't that mean flying through the rad zone, skipper?" Lieutenant Karl Mayfair pointed out. "We're gonna get cooked!"

"What's the matter, Mayfly?" Ramsey asked him, using his squadron handle. "Forget your radiation screening?"

"Nah . . . but the background count is redlining now."

"That won't be anything compared to what it'll read if *Hermes* or *Cunningham* get fried," Treverton told him, "and we have to *stay* out here."

"Point," Mayfair said. "*Sir.*"

The nuclear detonations from *Chosin's* salvo had thrown out huge, blossoming clouds of highly radioactive debris . . . most of it in the form of tiny bits of radioactively hot metal vaporized in the blasts and re-cooled as micron-sized flecks. As they thinned, the clouds became invisible at optical wavelengths, but they played hell with most sensors, especially those operating at radio or infrared wavelengths.

Ramsey's own sensors showed little ahead but a uniform haze of white-noise snow, as he navigated on the Xul Behemoth's expected position. The enemy ships were decelerating, which meant that the screening radioactive clouds would drift on ahead of them in another moment; the Raptors needed to hit the enemy ship before the screening effect was lost.

Linked in with the three other Nightstars, Ramsey accelerated at full boost.

Ops Center
UCS Hermes
Core Space
0046 hrs, GMT

"Battle has been joined, General," Taggart told him.

"Yes."

What else was there to say? Battlespace drones relayed intimate details of the struggle back to the *Hermes*' Ops Center—the *Chosin* adrift and foundering, her squat hull nearly cut in two by Xul high-energy weapons; the nuclear detonations alongside the nearest Xul huntership; the plunge of Marine aerospace fighters into the melee . . .

There was a horrid inevitability to it all—Yarlocke's peace offer, the instant and deadly Xul response, and now eleven MIEF capital ships, a handful of fighters, and a few hundred Marines faced utter annihilation.

Alexander was cycling through the options in his mind, even as the battle unfolded in strobing flashes of nuclear light on the Ops Center's main screens.

The destruction of the *Pax Galactica* had sharply limited his viable choices. *Pax* and *Hermes* together had brought eight smaller warships into the S-2 system, while the *Intrepid* had brought one—the *Cunningham*. Out of those nine transported vessels, four, at least, were doomed without the *Pax* if the battle in Core Space turned against them. While they could travel faster than light on their Alcubierre Drives, flying back to Commonwealth space under their own power would take years, and they didn't have the on-board supplies necessary for such a voyage.

They possessed, therefore, only two options for getting back home in less than decades; either they went out through a stargate—and the gates in Core Space appeared to be very well defended, or they had to leave as they'd arrived, translating out on board a larger, translation-capable vessel, like the vanished *Pax*. Now there was only *Hermes*, and she would require two jumps, at least, to take them all out.

As for *Intrepid*, her kilometer-long bulk would not fit on board the *Hermes*. She had to get out either through a gate, or by means of a long, *long* FTL voyage. She, at least, was large enough to be able to manufacture nanoassemblers in numbers enough to convert carbonaceous asteroids into food and water for the humans on board.

All of this had been anticipated in the planning for Heartfire, of course. Very few in the operational planning constellation had seriously believed that the Xul would agree to peace terms, and the possibility that *Pax* would be destroyed in the first few seconds of the encounter phase of her mission had always loomed quite large in their minds. The squadron's principle options were two . . . fight or run. If the choice was running, the plan called for losing any pursuing Xul vessels in the starclouds and nebulae of the Core, finding a place where *Hermes* or the *Intrepid* could carry out the delicate gravitometric readings necessary to measure the shape of local space. Once that happened, *Hermes* could make as many translations back and forth between Core and Sol as were necessary to get all of the ships except *Intrepid*—but including *Intrepid*'s crew—back to safety.

It was that or launch an assault on the fortress guarding the stargate through which they'd entered Core Space. With *Intrepid*'s firepower plus several capital ships, it might be possible to destroy the fort and allow the survivors to escape through the gate.

Might . . .

Alexander tried not to think about yet another alternative. In a battle with these gargantuan Xul vessels, not all of the Commonwealth warships were going to survive. *Chosin* was already crippled, leaking atmosphere and losing power. Much more of that and *Hermes* might be able to take all of the survivors back to Sol in one translation . . . *if*, of course, *Hermes* herself survived what was coming.

One of the Xul behemoths was reeling beneath an attack by Marine aerospace fighters. They still had a chance . . .

He considered ordering a full and immediate launch of Heartbreak, but shoved the thought aside. Patience. . . .

The ops plan as currently running had been worked out in long simulations back in AresRing over the past year. Dubbed "the Cometary Option," it offered the squadron a slender chance of survival, and promised to draw Xul forces away from the Marines guarding the triggerships on S-2/I.

It had been his suggestion, originally—drawing off any Xul ships in the system by directly threatening GalCenter, and, just incidentally, picking up some badly needed intel on the way. As the trio of Xul vessels continued approaching, it was becoming a better and better option . . . one on which he was going to have to stake his life, and the survival of the squadron, in one throw of the dice.

"General," Cara said in his mind. *"You have an incoming communication from EarthRing."*

"Right," he said. "The Warlock . . ."

"No, sir. Senator Yarlocke appears to be . . . indisposed. The communication is from George Stahl, her chief aide."

Curious. "Put him through."

"General Alexander?" Stahl's virtual icon appeared in Alexander's mind, a radiant nimbus with a lined, human face.

"Yes, Mr. Stahl. You must understand that we're a little busy out here right now."

"I understand that. General . . . the Senator appears to have been . . . attacked."

"Attacked? How? What do you mean?"

"She was linked with the *Pax Galactica* when a large spacecraft emerged from the GalCenter Dyson cloud. The connection was broken somewhat abruptly. The Senator appears to have suffered some sort of massive psychic trauma."

"I . . . see . . ." Alexander held back his initial, dismissive thought. *Massive psychic trauma* was a kind of popular catch phrase long common in entertainment sims and even the news media, but which had no place in real life. The assumption was that when a person was linked through their cerebral implants to a remote location, occupying a teleoperated sensory unit, for example, or jacked into a distant computer net, they ran a particular risk. If that connection

was suddenly snapped, the person could literally lose his or
her mind—as if the person's mind had actually been occupying the distant net.

Fictional sims made heavy duty use of the notion, but the
whole idea was nonsense. The optic nerves that brought sensory data to the back of the human brain were several centimeters long; the chains of neurons carrying information from
a person's left foot could be almost two meters long. Tele-
operation and cerebral linkage had long ago demonstrated
that it didn't matter how long the distance was between
sensor—whether eye or camera—and the brain that assembled the data into a coherent picture. A person who lost his
eyesight didn't also lose his mind; nor did a person who suffered an interruption in his sim-link with a teleoperated
submarine at the bottom of the Puerto Rico Trench or while
remotely probing the sulfuric, high-pressure hell of the surface of Venus. The remote explorer simply woke up back on
his or her link couch, confused, perhaps, but none the worse
for wear.

If it had been otherwise, of course, teleoperational technology would not have developed as far or as fast as it had
over the past eight centuries. Thanks to QCC links, people
could engage in sim-face to sim-face virtual conferences
across interstellar distances . . . or look over Admiral Taggart's shoulder as he commanded the 1MIEF squadron at
the Galactic Core. If people had actually risked insanity every time they virtually linked with one another, people would
still be communicating through the old-time media of tele-
phone, holovision, and electronic mail.

If Yarlocke's chief aide thought his boss had been injured
by some sort of psychic trauma, Alexander would have to
humor him. He didn't at the moment have time to persuade
the man otherwise.

"I'm sorry to hear that," he said. "But what do you want
us to do about it?"

"Break off the operation," Stahl told him. "Some of us
here believe the Xul have found a way to attack us through
you. Break off and return to near-Earth space!"

"That . . . is not possible at the moment." With a mental shrug, he disconnected the link. Commonwealth senators were one thing in the hierarchy of power, aides and secretaries something else entirely.

Could the Xul have established a link with EarthRing via the QCC? Worse, could they physically attack humans over such a link? It didn't seem credible but, until he had hard data on Yarlocke's physical and mental condition, he could not take chances. "Comm!" he said. "Switch off all QCC links with EarthRing!"

"Aye, aye, sir."

"All ships! Stand by to execute Cometary Option One-Alpha!"

It was the best, he thought, of a *very* poor handful of options.

Nightstar 442
Core Space
0054 hrs, GMT

Moving at nearly three hundred kilometers per second, Ramsey's Nightstar slammed into the tenuous blossom of one of the radioactive clouds. Minute bits of metal and debris flared as they were engulfed by his magnetic shields, shredded by the field's passage into energy and component atoms.

Ramsey had given the fire-at-best command thirty seconds ago. The fighter was moving too fast for merely human reflexes to pick out the best instant for loosing its weapons. The aerospace craft's AI, however, could calculate the best possible firing solution and release the weapons load at a precisely determined instant; Ramsey felt the ship kick, shudder, and jolt *hard* as its GV-3662 Gatling fusion gun howled, spewing thirty droplets of fusing hydrogen per second in a stream of blue-white fire.

For an instant, Ramsey saw the vast side of the Xul's hull looming huge, the surface coming apart beneath the caress of Gatling starfire. Large chunks of hull peeled back and spun away, as vaporizing metal-plastic laminate flared up in front of him.

The Nightstar slammed through, skin temperature soaring as the tiny craft threaded its way scant meters above the Xul ship's hull. Surface features flashed past like an alien landscape glimpsed in an instant . . . and then it was gone, falling away behind as Ramsey initiated full acceleration once more. Particle beams and lasers reached out after him; his AI was already jinking the fighter in random up-down-sideways bursts to frustrate Xul tracking and targeting.

And then he heard the recall. . . .

Ops Center
UCS Hermes
Core Space
0046 hrs, GMT

"General, it's going to take at least ninety minutes to get our fighters back on board *Cunningham!*"

"I know." The admission burned in his gut. "And there are the Marines on S-2/I. But we can't wait."

Taggart gave him a hard look. "I thought the Marines didn't leave their own behind. *Ever.*"

"Damn it, Liam, we *can't* stay. But we can come back. . . ."

"If there's anything to come back to."

Alexander stared for a moment at the main screen, where one of the Behemoths appeared to be drifting out of control, its drives crippled. "The idea is to get them to follow us. They will, if we're enough of a threat."

The display changed to a different image, one transmitted from a different battlespace drone. *Intrepid* had swung about and was approaching the largest Xul ship, coming up from astern. So far, there'd been no reaction from the large vessel; *Intrepid*, a Xul hull captured and with Commonwealth drives and weaponry installed, still looked like a Xul hunter-ship, whatever internal differences there might be now.

Intrepid's AI would be broadcasting on Xul frequencies, telling a story of communications difficulty.

The Xul monster abruptly accelerated, energy readings on board rising as she prepared to fire her weapons. *Intrepid* fired first. . . .

Explosions ripped through the larger ship, as inert, one-tenth-kilogram slugs accelerated to near-light velocities lanced from *Intrepid*'s mass drivers, shredding through the Xul vessel's hull and interior like bullets through tissue. With such weapons, and at such close range, size alone meant very little. *Intrepid* continued hammering at the Xul ship with every weapon that would bear. Enough damage would release the singularity at the enemy ship's heart and destroy her; the question was whether *Intrepid* could fire fast enough and hit hard enough before her opponent could get in a shot of her own. . . .

The Xul ship fired, a single bolt of plasma energy focused through intense magnetic fields until it was as bright and as hot as a piece of the Sun. The bolt burned through *Intrepid*'s needle-slender hull a third of the way forward from her aft end, devouring her QPT generators in a blaze of white light.

"Communications," Alexander said. "Make to all vessels and commands. Tell them that the squadron is going to execute the Cometary Option. Deployed fighters and any vessels that cannot initiate the Alcubierre Drive sequence due to battle damage are to drop into deep black mode and await our return. Forces on the planet will maintain their perimeter, and wait for a signal from *Hermes* to execute Heartbreak. Get me an acknowledgement from all commands."

"Aye, aye, sir," the communications officer replied. "Ah . . . General?"

"What?"

"EarthRing is attempting to initiate contact via QCC."

"Do *not* acknowledge. Our QCC is temporarily down. Understood?"

"Yes, sir."

"Good."

Once the squadron pulled back to Sol—even just back to Cluster Space—the chances were good to excellent that they would not be allowed to come back for the ships and men left behind at S-2.

And they *would* be coming back.

Somehow.

20

Ops Center
UCS Hermes
Core Space
0106 hrs, GMT

"Hermes is ready in all respects for Alcubierre Drive," Captain Robeson, the ship's commanding officer, reported.

"Very well," Admiral Taggart replied. "General? At your command."

Alexander gave his various data channels a last check. *Chosin* was badly damaged and unable to accelerate; *Intrepid* was completely out of communication and might well be dead. Thirteen fighters had survived the unequal battle against the Xul super-ships and were now en route to *Cunningham*.

Seven other warships, along with *Hermes*, had reported readiness for FTL drive. Moore, *Cunningham*'s skipper, had received and acknowledged his orders. He was to remain and recover his remaining fighters, attempting to avoid Xul notice by dropping into deep-black stealth mode, powering down all but absolutely essential power systems to remain unobserved by Xul sensors. If that didn't work, and the Xul spotted *Cunningham* and began closing, he was to break off and accelerate to FTL, attempting to reach safety within one of the surrounding molecular clouds.

Any fighters *Cunningham* was forced to leave behind would simply have to take their chances, either down on the planet's surface with the RST or powered down and adrift in stealth mode until Commonwealth ships could get back to S-2.

Of the three Xul ships ahead, one of the Behemoths was definitely crippled. The big one savaged by the *Intrepid* was damaged, but still maneuvering, still deadly, and the second Behemoth hadn't even been touched.

Worse, more Xul hunterships were arriving now, dropping out of FTL in a teeming swarm.

It was time to leave.

"Make a final call to all units remaining in-system," Alexander said. "Tell them, 'Stay low and stay out of trouble. We'll be back. Good luck . . . and *semper fi.*' "

"Message transmitted, General. We have acknowledgment from all units."

"Very well. Admiral? Initiate the Cometary Option."

"Aye, aye, General. *Hermes* to Heartfire Squadron. All vessels able to respond, engage Alcubierre Drive on my command . . . three . . . two . . . one . . . *initiate!*"

As the Xul armada closed on the eight Commonwealth vessels, those ships began accelerating. One by one, the images of those moving ships began to shimmer and distort, as bubbles of space around them warped.

And then they were plunging toward the Galactic Center at ten times the speed of light.

Nightstar 442
Core Space
0107 hrs, GMT

"Shit!" Lieutenant Mara Cosgriff shouted over the link. "They're leaving us! They're fucking *leaving us!*"

"Easy, Mar," Ramsey told her. "It's not like they have a hell of a lot of choice."

More and more Xul ships were dropping out of their equivalent of Alcubierre Drive, obviously attempting to corner the tiny squadron of Commonwealth warships. Those warships were winking out of normal space, now, in rapid succession, leaving energy trails of tortured hydrogen atoms pointing like arrows toward GalCenter. *Hermes*, requiring more time to power up her Alcubierre Drive, was the very last to flash out of normal space, and into the twisted realm of FTL.

Slowly, ponderously, the Xul giants began coming about, killing their forward velocity and aligning themselves on GalCenter. *Yes!* They were following the squadron.

Or most of them were. Five of the newcomers descended instead on the crippled *Intrepid*, and five more on the *Chosin*, which appeared to be completely dead now. They hesitated as they pulled alongside *Intrepid*, possibly fooled by her hull into thinking she was a damaged Xul huntership. *Chosin*, however, blazed into a blue-white glare of light as five Xul warships speared her with particle beams and high-energy lasers. The glare expanded, faded . . . and nothing was left of *Chosin* but coalescing particles the size of grains of sand.

And in another moment, the remnant fragment of *Intrepid* vanished as well, cleanly and instantaneously, a victim, apparently of the Xul patterning weapon. It made sense. If you didn't know whether a vessel was occupied by humans or Xul, copy them and upload them all, and let the Xul computer network sort them out.

"Stealth mode," Treverton told them all. "*Execute! . . .*"

And then the squadron net was silent.

At Ramsey's thought, his Nightstar powered down, leaving only a trickle of energy flowing from the batteries to his life support and to a few key external sensors. Massing just under 120 tons and sheathed in absorbing layers of active nanoflage, the Nightstar carried very little signature for the Xul monsters to spot. Even at close range, they were likely to dismiss one of the inert heavy fighters as a drifting bit of wreckage.

At least . . . that was the idea, and the hope that sustained the thirteen surviving members of Raptor Squadron now.

The fighter didn't have a transparent canopy, of course—not with the local background radiation count being what it was—but sensory data flowed through Ramsey's cerebral implants, giving him a magnificent, and supremely lonely viewpoint. With no links to the other Raptors, he felt completely alone.

Hell, at this point, he couldn't even see the Xul ships any longer. All that was out there was that impossible and surreal sky dominated by the spiral of Sag A, the ruby gleam of S-2, and the ocher crescent that was the planet, now some fifty thousand kilometers, low and on his port side, the entire vista slowly turning as his Nightstar tumbled.

Xul hunterships were large enough that some of those stars out there might be the enemy . . . but if so he couldn't pick them out from the millions of naked-eye stars that made up the distant walls of the Galactic Core. He would have to be looking in *exactly* the right spot to catch a glimpse of movement contrary to the background drift.

He checked his life support readout. His air generators would keep him going for a week or more—food and water about the same. His biggest limitation was his radiation shielding.

His magnetic screens were off. Those would be spotted by any passing Xul as easily as a flare. His Nightstar's phase shift was still engaged, however. Phase shift allowed him to occupy a hazy niche half a step out of the usual three physical dimensions. Since it leaked very little power, the system actually contributed to his invisibility, as well as greatly cutting down on the amount of radiation he was encountering.

More radiation was blocked by the active nanoflage on his outer hull, which absorbed all radiation, from radar to X-rays, and transmitted it to the chargers that kept his batteries going. Some radiation, though, was still getting through.

According to his med readouts, he would start getting sick within twenty-four to forty-eight hours, and that was allowing for the anti-rad nano already coursing through his blood.

He would have acquired a fatal dose perhaps forty hours after that.

Long before that happened, Ramsey knew, he would switch off his phase-shift unit entirely. There was enough background radiation out there now to kill him more or less instantly.

But he had time, yet.

He waited.

Marine Regimental Strike Team
Firebase Hawkins, S-2/I
Core Space
0110 hrs, GMT

"I don't believe the bastards went and left us!" PFC James Connors said. The young Marine had showed up a few minutes ago, wandering across the blasted plain toward the Marine perimeter, apparently lost. Gardner had ordered him into the hole. "What the fuck happened to 'no man left behind?'"

"They'll be back," Gardner told him. But she didn't sound hopeful.

"Hey, if it's a choice between a few hundred Marines buying it," Huerra said, "and those same Marines and the squadron getting scragged, I guess we know what the brass is going to do, huh?"

"Yeah," Chaffee added, "and tough shit if those 'few hundred Marines' happen to be *us*, huh?"

"Hey, welcome to the Corps," Garroway told him. "You volunteered. No one told you it would be easy. Or *safe*."

He looked up at the alien sky, at the silent, motionless pinwheel of Sag A. Word had been passed down the line moments ago that the squadron was leaving—promising to return, but *leaving*.

The Marines on S-2/I were on their own.

The perimeter seemed eerily quiet. Not that anyone was particularly expecting trouble out here. The biggest threat

right now was from undiscovered pockets of Xul combat
machines still buried somewhere beneath Firebase Hawkins, perhaps as deep as a kilometer or two. So far as any of
the sensor drones sent out around the planet had been able to
determine, this had been the only Xul outpost on an otherwise empty and lifeless world.

But Marine regs demanded a defensive perimeter for a
firebase on a hostile beachhead, and so half of the Marines
had been scattered along a broad circle surrounding the
center of the base. If the Xul *did* come from outside, they'd
hit the perimeter defenses first . . . and maybe, *maybe,* the
perimeter would hold long enough for heavier forces to arrive.

At least they would hold while the ammo held out. The
fighting earlier had drained everyone's expendables—slugs
for the mass drivers, hydrogen ice rounds for the plasma
guns, fresh power units for plasma guns and lasers. So far,
no one had bothered to issue fresh expendables, and that
meant a screw-up somewhere.

At the moment, though, the Net—which normally would
have allowed them to communicate their needs back to HQ
with a thought—was down, switched off to keep the Xul
from homing on it. Marines in the field were limited now to
their back-up suit comms, which had a range of only a few
meters.

He hoped the powers-that-be would remember to switch
on the Net if there was anything the Marines on the perimeter needed to know . . . like an immanent Xul attack.

Two hundred sixty-some Marines, not counting those
KIA and wounded during the landing assault, organized
into two companies—half a regiment—under a captain's
command.

If the Xul found them here, they wouldn't be much more
than a minor distraction.

Garroway just hoped to hell the squadron came back as
promised, and soon.

He was feeling a bit exposed out here. . . .

Ops Center
UCS Hermes
Galactic Center
0110 hrs, GMT

They dropped out of FTL, decelerating hard, their Alcubierre Drive clawing at surrounding space to reduce *Hermes'* headlong plunge into the Galactic Center to velocities that would let them swing around the supermassive black hole.

They could have stayed in FTL, of course, traveling in a straight line unaffected by the central black hole's gravity and finding a safe haven at which to rendezvous with the other ships of the squadron somewhere beyond, among those billions of Core stars. But Operation Heartfire had not been limited to support of the failed peace mission. It was also intended to gather intelligence—in particular, to get a truly close look at whatever it was the Xul were building in the Galaxy's innermost Holy of Holies.

Hermes was now just a few tens of thousands of kilometers from the outermost shell of the Dyson cloud, and moving closer every second, hurtling in on a tight, cometary path. The AI controlling the Commonwealth vessel's course had inserted them into an approach that would take them skimming just above that enigmatic central object, giving them a close look.

"Cara?" Alexander asked. He felt trapped—anxious, but unable to show it. "Is everything set?" It was only the third or fourth time he'd asked his personal AI that question.

"Affirmative, General," was her patient answer.

"Any sign of the rest of the squadron?"

"Negative, General. Even a slight amount of scattering would have put them well beyond visual range."

On the main Ops display screens, the central object had taken on a distinctly fuzzy appearance—a Dyson *cloud* as opposed to a Dyson *sphere*. The objects orbiting the central black hole must number in the hundreds of trillions, a vast and staggering swarm of artificial worlds and worldlets, each apparently pursuing its own independent orbit without coming close enough to one another to risk collision. Or did each object maneuver when an intercept with another object was detected? Alexander tried to imagine the computing power necessary to keep track of such complexity, and shook his head. The sheer scale of the engineering took it beyond human ken.

He was reminded, though, of what had been happening in Earth's Solar System over the course of the past few centuries. Already, most of Humankind resided within the rings of stations and habs circling Earth and Mars, and billions more lived in hollowed-out asteroids and cometary bodies terraformed into tiny, artificial worlds circling Sol in a haze of life and civilization. In another few millennia, Earth's sun might well look something like the Dyson cloud ahead, completely surrounded by shells of orbiting habitats in a cloud so thick that Sol himself could no longer be seen from the outside.

As *Hermes* hurtled closer, he could see that the polar regions were lightly occupied, a mere dusting of orbiting objects. Stranger, though, was the narrow and empty zone around the cloud's equator. That made no sense whatsoever in terms of traditional orbital dynamics. Since it was orbiting the center of the gravitational singularity, an object passing above the northern hemisphere of the central black hole *had* to cross the equator during its orbit and pass over the southern hemisphere, then cross the equator again back to the north; it couldn't simply circle above one hemisphere or the other, and yet that appeared to be exactly what was happening here.

"Most of the cloud components," Cara was whispering in his mind, *"are not in orbit."*

This was getting weirder and weirder. "How the hell do they stay put, then? Antigravity?"

However they were managing the trick, Alexander could easily see why they needed to do it. The equatorial area was clear to allow infalling mass—the gas, dust, and debris that made up the twenty-light year spiral of Sagittarius A—to pass through the cloud and enter the black hole's event horizon. From here, the gap appeared as a narrow line, illuminated from within by X-rays, bisecting the cloud and perhaps no more than a few thousand kilometers wide. This close to GalCenter, the spiraling matter of the accretion disk had been gravitationally compressed to a thin sheet of hot gas, invisible at optical wavelengths but aglow in the high ultraviolet, and no more than meters thick. The sheet streamed between the two halves of the cloud, whipping around the supermassive object hidden inside before vanishing into the event horizon with a high-energy shriek of X-rays and cosmic radiation.

"Analysis of the cloud components," Cara said, *"indicates that most of the individual objects are anchored to others. The Dyson cloud is essentially a very large and extraordinarily complex crystalline lattice arranged in two opposing hemispheres."*

Which explained how they kept the equatorial regions clear. There were two clouds, one above the black hole's northern hemisphere, one above the south. The two almost touched at the equator, but were rotating separately.

That didn't explain how they kept the system stable, however. If the cloud objects were not actually in orbit around the black hole, they *should* fall inexorably into the event horizon and be destroyed.

"There are energetic structures anchoring the cloud sections in space," Cara continued. *"The Xul appear to be manipulating strong, local magnetic fields both in order to link individual habitats and to anchor the systems in place."*

"Anchored how?"

"The engineering details are unclear, and likely represent a level of technology far in advance of anything with which we are familiar. The anchoring structures, however, appear to extend into the Quantum Sea."

The base state of reality. Suddenly, Alexander was reminded that everything he was seeing here represented only a tiny fraction of the whole . . . like a blind man touching a tree and missing the forest. The construction project ahead didn't exist in only a single set of spatial dimensions.

"Here we go!" an officer at a nearby console said. *Hermes* was picking up speed fast as she was gravitationally accelerated along her path. Alexander had a blurred and momentary glimpse of the cloud expanding. She slammed through the thin sheet of plasma at the equator . . . and for the briefest of instants, Alexander stared into the full radiance within the cloud.

And then *Hermes* was receding into space once more, its close passage so fast that human senses could neither see nor interpret what had just happened.

"We have Xul ships coming up off the cloud behind us," Taggart told him.

"Of course." The enemy couldn't allow this trespass of their inner space without at least an attempt at protest. *Hermes* was the slowest and most clumsy of the Commonwealth ships in the squadron, so the other seven vessels must already have completed their swing-bys.

The Xul defenses would be on full alert by now.

Alexander gave thought to ordering *Hermes*' weapons systems officers to open fire, but dropped the idea almost as soon as it surfaced. All of the warships in the Commonwealth's arsenals could not have caused serious damage to that vast and hazy structure at the center. The op planners had anticipated that, and combat was not a priority in this pass, save in self-defense. They would save energy for the escape.

Just possibly the fact that the Commonwealth ships had *not* attacked might convey a willingness to talk.

No one seriously expected the Xul to understand that message, however. Judging from the way their ships were wafting up from the Cloud, the close passage had only succeeded in giving the hornet's nest a good, swift kick.

And now the swarm was coming up after them.

"Tell me we got that passage," Alexander said.

"We did, sir," a bridge officer reported. "Athena is analyzing the images now."

"And did we get the Spymasters away?"

"Yes, sir. Two hundred of them."

"That won't even begin to scratch the surface. But we'll get some data back, at least."

Hermes was again moving in a nearly straight line, her hairpin turn about the gravitational singularity completed. Taggart gave a mental command, and *Hermes* again began accelerating. Her Alcubierre Drive engaged, space warped around her, and she slipped into the ghostly otherworldliness of FTL.

Marine Regimental Strike Team
Firebase Hawkins, S-2/I
Core Space
0115 hrs, GMT

Garroway rose in the crater sheltering the five Marines on the Hawkins perimeter. In the distance, he could see a lone figure—a Marine in massive Type 690 armor—trudging across the rubble a hundred meters away. He was, Garroway decided, coming from one of the other perimeter positions, possibly the next one over, occupied by Bravo Company.

"Who do you think it is?" Gardner asked.

"Damfino," Garroway replied. "I'm going to go check him out."

"What, you think it's a Xul sneaking upon us in Marine armor?" Huerra asked.

"No, but it looks like he's coming from the next fighting hole over. I want to know who's over there."

Scrambling up out of the hole, he started to walk, making for a guestimated intercept point in front of the other Marine.

The other Marine saw him coming and turned to face him. "Hey, what's up?"

Garroway recognized the voice even before his implant identified the speaker. "Son of a bitch! Gunny Warhurst! Change your mind about coming back in, yet?"

"Days ago, Gare. *Days* ago. It's just a little late to change my mind now, y'know?"

"You're a rock, Gunny, you know that? As in 'dumb as a.' You could be back in Sunken Miami with two gorgeous naked women in a hot tub."

"Don't rub it in, Marine. That hot tub is looking better all the time."

"What're you doing out here?"

"Lieutenant Whitfield sent me out looking for fresh plasma charges. You guys got any to share?"

"You've got to be kidding, right?" Garroway said. He slapped the side of his weapon. "I'm down to my last hundred rounds."

"There should still be a bunch of ammo on the Tarantulas," Warhurst told him.

"Yeah, and right now they're as dangerous as the Xulies," Garroway replied.

The last he'd heard, half the Tarantulas were being employed as tunnelers, digging down into the crust of S-2/I in search of surviving pockets of Xul, while the rest were carving out battlements on the surface. Rock slagged down and became plastic, glowing a sullen, black-crusted red, where those monsters plied their beams.

"So who screwed up and sent the 'rants underground without offloading the goods?" Warhurst wanted to know.

"Good question."

"Captain Black?" Warhurst suggested.

"He's too smart for that," Garroway replied. "But maybe his constellation slipped on some code."

Modern combat, he thought, was entirely too fast and too complicated for any one man to keep track of everything that was going on in a battle zone. The command constellation of an officer at any command level was made up of both human aides and AI personal assistants. Ideally, the intersection of organic with electronic was seamless, but the ideal could rarely be achieved in practice. AIs were smart—brilliant, in certain applications—but they still were essentially nothing more than sophisticated software that did what the human members of the constellation told them to do.

Someone further down the logistical chain of command must have forgotten to offload that ammo.

"C'mon," he told Warhurst. "Let's go together and see if we can hijack some ammo. Let me tell my people where I'm going."

"Right."

Thirty minutes later, the two of them entered the center of the new base, which rose black and glistening from rubble fused into volcanic glass. A pair of Tarantulas, huge and ponderous, were gnawing their way down into solid rock thirty meters away, bathed in the arc-light glare of their plasma cutters and wreathed in the steam coming off of molten rock.

"What *you* two apes doin' here, sightseein'?" an armored figure bellowed from nearby. Garroway's receiver IDed him as Sergeant Major Dulaney, and he was the LZ master. "Get the hell out of my work zone!"

"We need ammo on the perimeter defense, Sergeant Major," Garroway told him. "Plasma pellets, slugs, missiles, everything. And as near as we can figure, everything's still on board the damned 'rants!"

"Tough shit. We're not stopping work for you people!"

Garroway sighed. The Corps was a brotherhood, closer than family. And sometimes he wanted to kick certain family members in the ass.

The Net came back on, data streaming in . . . an alert. *Shit. . . .*

"You there," Dulaney was shouting, pointing with one of his extended slicers. "Get those nano canisters in there *now!*"

Those canisters would inject assemblers deep into solid rock, growing the complex of bunkers and fortifications that had been programmed into them.

"Sergeant Major?"

"What the fuck! Are *you* still here?"

"You'd better let us get that ammo. *Now.*"

"Why the fuck should I?"

"*That's* why." Garroway pointed. In the sky, off beyond the perimeter at Dulaney's back, a hard-edged shadow was moving against the background stars . . . a flattened sphere, huge and menacing, growing slowly larger as it descended.

"*Jesus!*"

21

Marine Regimental Strike Team
Firebase Hawkins, S-2/I
Core Space
0125 hrs, GMT

Fire lit up the night.

Firebase Hawkins, bringing every battery to bear, loosed bolt after bolt at the incoming Xul huntership. Armored Marines raced toward the perimeter beneath the salvos, some skimming low across the tortured terrain on bursts from their jump jets. To either side, Tarantulas, huge and ponderous, drifted on straining ventral jets and agravitic lifters, moving apart to position themselves to lay down a crossfire on the enemy. Above the horizon, the Xul huntership looked as huge as a mountain, drifting slowly toward the surface.

Garroway triggered his jump jets and sailed in a low, flat trajectory, swinging his legs as he flew so that he came down with his boots well ahead of him, sending up a spray of powdery dust when he hit. The crater with his companions was just ahead.

Plasma bolts from the main firebase batteries were smashing into the descending Xul ship; Garroway could see the hits as twinkling sparkles flaring briefly against the artificial mountain of that hull. The Xul monster was injured; he could see craters and tears along its flanks. But he had no doubt that its weapons were still quite effective.

He found himself tensing against the anticipated strike of the Xul patterning weapon. What would it feel like?

For that matter, had they already fired the thing? People said that if you were patterned, you might not even know you'd been hit. The brain took *any* information fed to it as Gospel, whether from the real world outside your head or an imaginal world existing within a sophisticate computer. He could be living a virtual life already, an electronic prisoner, and never know it.

What, though, would be the point of capturing digital re-productions of humans and keeping them in a cage they didn't know existed? Reaching the fighting hole, he leaped in, landing heavily beside Gardner and Huerra. He had to assume this was real, and not try to second-guess the universe.

The other Marines had their weapons up, but weren't firing. The Xul ship was still fifty kilometers away, and the beams fired by man-portable plasma weapons tended to bloom and dissipate within a tenth of that distance—especially within the twisted magnetic fields here in the Core.

"How do you think they found us?" Huerra asked.

"Shit, does it matter?" Gardner asked. "They did . . . and they're gonna be damned sorry they did, too!"

Garroway charged his weapon. He could think of no finer epitaph for the RST.

Nightstar 442
Core Space
0131 hrs, GMT

"Okay, people!" Major Treverton called. "Stay dispersed, and let your AIs handle the approach! Unload every damned thing you've got, 'cause we're not going to get another pass!"

Ramsey felt the shudder as his Nightstar hurtled through

something . . . not atmosphere, not here, but a patch of hydrogen gas or drifting debris, something that slammed against his fighter's magnetic screens and vaporized, transmitting enough kinetic energy as it shredded into subatomic particles to shake the hurtling aerospace craft as it passed.

He'd drifted alone in silence for only about ten minutes before a Xul Behemoth had appeared, moving toward the planet below. Treverton had brought the squadron's net back on line, then. The Marines on S-2/I needed some close aerospace support, and the Raptors were the only fighters in the area.

One by one, the fighters of Raptor Squadron had boosted into an approach vector that brought them in behind the Behemoth. The Xul ship appeared to be damaged; defensive fire snapped out at the incoming fighters, but it was scattered and badly aimed. Off to the right, Lieutenant Jamison's Nightstar was hit by a sun-bright ball of blue-white light that struck him bow-on, turning his Raptor into a hurtling mass of flaming debris.

Ramsey kept his attention focused on the Xul huntership as it loomed larger and larger ahead and below. His AI brought up the target lock icon in his mind, and he triggered the Raptor's Gatling cannon.

Marine Regimental Strike Team
Firebase Hawkins, S-2/I
Core Space
0133 hrs, GMT

The optical feed in Garroway's helmet blacked out momentarily as light seared across the landscape. Marine aerospace fighters—where the hell had *they* come from?—stooped silently out of the sky, each in turn pouring streams of blue-white flame into the drifting Xul monster. As his vision cleared, he could see the Behemoth lurch to one side, hesitate, then begin descending more quickly.

It struck the planet's surface kilometers from the Marine

perimeter. Seconds later, Garroway felt the shock as it rippled through the ground beneath his boots. The Marines around him were cheering wildly, waving their weapons and shouting imprecations at the fallen giant.

The Xul ship continued falling even after it had struck, appearing to crumple in upon itself as its unimaginable mass kept moving, unstoppable. Pieces were flying off the top, and a tidal wave of dust was rushing out from the impact point.

Hunterships, Garroway knew, carried small gravitational singularities on board; human-designed quantum power taps did the same, using tiny, artificially generated black holes to harvest energy from the Quantum Sea. When the huntership began to crumple, the black hole inside was released, flying out of control through the heart of the giant ship, devouring everything it touched. The crumpling effect continued, the titanic mass beginning now to collapse upon itself, falling into a fast-growing rogue black hole.

The Marines continued cheering until the first Xul combots began swarming in across the plain, moving straight toward their position. "Here they come!" Captain Black called over the Net. "Commence fire!"

The last hundred plasma charges in Garroway's weapon went fast. When the tone sounded in his helmet indicating that he was dry, he dropped the weapon and scrambled out of the crater. "I'm going to go get more ammo!" he told the others. "Chaffee! Connors! You two come with me!"

"Make it fast, Gunny!" Huerra yelled. "I'm down to my last fifty!"

A half-dozen Tarantulas were still moving slowly across the plain toward the perimeter, their belly jets throwing up impenetrable clouds of gray dust and grit. Garroway triggered his jump jets and bounded for the nearest one.

For centuries, military strategists had argued pro and con on the usefulness—and the survivability—of the tank, a weapon that had first come into service back in the twentieth century, existing in one form or another throughout most of those intervening years. Once the deciding mobile factor of the battlefield, most strategists now deemed tanks irrelevant. A single Marine could pack enough firepower in his personal weapon to destroy any of the tanks of earlier centuries, and most human combatants no longer bothered fielding them.

What did exist nowadays, however, was an odd hybrid of spacecraft and tank—vehicles like the AV-110 Tarantula, a multi-purpose vehicle that could ferry troops and equipment down to a planet's surface from orbit, employ point plasma arcs to cut tunnels into solid rock, or deploy a variety of swap-out weapons mounted in external pods.

When military forces were deployed to other star systems, experience soon proved that *flexibility* was what was most needed in modern weapons systems, weapons that could serve a number of roles and fill a number of billets. Tarantulas served well as armed assault craft for planetary invasions, but were too slow and cumbersome to provide traditional close aerospace cover for ground forces. However, by hovering just above the surface on ventral jets and agravs, they could take advantage of concealing terrain, maneuvering like tanks—or like the far more ancient cavalry arm of the assault force—and provide much needed mobile armored fire support.

Critics—especially armchair strategists within the Corps—liked to point out that Tarantulas represented the worst of two worlds. They were a hell of a lot bigger than tanks, and therefore better targets, while not being as fast or as maneuverable as a Wyvern or a Nightstar when they were drifting along at an altitude of two meters or less.

Garroway didn't care about any of that at the moment. The Tarantulas were big, they were mobile, and they packed a hell of a lot of firepower, which was what the RST needed now more than anything else.

Except, possibly, ammunition. With Chaffee and Connors close behind, he jogged closer to the nearest of the Tarantulas, which hovered a few tens of meters away, almost invisible in the slashing storm of grit and jet-blasted dust. Through his implant, he linked in with the craft's pilot. Tarantulas generally had a crew of four—pilot, two gunners, and a loadmaster, but the pilot was the vehicle's commander.

Flying Pig was the name of this particular machine, and its pilot commander was Lieutenant Joash Grooms.

"Whaddaya want, Marine?" the man said when Garroway hailed him. "We're kinda busy!"

Plasma streamed overhead, directed toward the Marine position from a ball turret high up on the Xul Behemoth's hull. The shot lightly brushed *Flying Pig*'s dorsal surface, gouging out a long and molten groove.

"Yessir! But you've got ammo we need out here! You want close infantry support, you've got t'feed us! Sir!"

Flying Pig opened up with a double-pod fusillade directed against Xul weapons mounts. Had there been atmosphere, the noise would have been deafening. As it was, static shrieked inside Garroway's skull as tightly focused magnetic fields sent the plasma bolts slashing across the intervening space into the target.

"Okay! Master Sergeant O'Malley'll take care of you! But snap it up! I'm moving my ass just as soon—" The rest of the transmission was blasted into incoherence by static as the Tarantula's main gun fired.

The Tarantula lifted slightly, the blast from its ventral jets slamming at Garroway's armor and knocking him back a couple of steps. The rear ramp dropped open, spilling light into the moving dust, and the craft's armored loadmaster appeared on the cargo deck, waving them on. "You want it? Come get it!"

Garroway, Chafee, and Connors formed a human chain, passing crates of plasma charges, power cells, and other munitions down the ramp and into a tumbled pile on the ground. Warhurst and several other Marines appeared out of the flame-shot night, helping to unload the Tarantula and picking up crates to take back to their positions.

The Xul combots were moving toward the Marine position now like a tidal wave.

Ops Center
UCS Hermes
Point Diamond,
Core Space
0151 hrs, GMT

Hermes dropped out of FTL at the point designated Diamond, the primary rendezvous zone for the squadron. As transponder signals began bouncing back to *Hermes*' Ops Center, crawling in at the speed of light, other ships in the squadron began showing up on the tactical screens—the light cruiser *Ludwigson*, the destroyers *Ardash* and *Plottel*, the ponderous battleship *Morrigen*, the sleeker battlecruiser *Mars*, the carrier *Lejeune*, and the heavy fleet transport *Howorth*.

Hermes was the last to arrive. All of the squadron's vessels had come through the close passage of GalCenter intact, and Alexander felt a deep-rooted blossoming of relief.

They were such a long way from home. . . .

The sky appeared to be an eerie, almost sullen deep blue, a radiant nebula, the nursery of new-born suns. In every direction, imbedded in that cloud, stars glared, blue-white and hot. Point Diamond was located near the center of a young, hot, dense-packed star cluster, the object known since the early years of radio astronomy as IRS-16. Imbedded in the far-sprawling accretion disk circling GalCenter and only a tenth of a light year from the central black hole itself, the cluster was torn by violent cosmic winds. Those winds blasted through the nebula within which the newborn stars were imbedded, reacting with the cloud and loosing a sleeting storm of hard radiation.

The squadron's magnetic screens and their phase-shift technology would let them ride out the storm in relative safety, at least for a standard day or two. Each Commonwealth ship on the Ops Center visual display screens showed an eerie corona of light as the radiation fields and drifting nebula-dust interacted with the vessel's screens.

"Well, General . . . no sign of the opposition," Taggart

said. His voice was subdued, even awed. The vista outside was unspeakably beautiful . . . as beautiful, perhaps, as it was dangerous.

"We'll wait here for three hours," Alexander told him, "and see if the Xul show up. But this is a good place to lay low for a while."

IRS-16 was a veritable forest of closely packed stars—several hundred suns crammed into a volume of space only ten or twelve times larger than Earth's Solar System. The nearest star was less than half an astronomical unit distant—about seventy million kilometers—and a dozen more were less than a hundred million kilometers away. *Hermes'* outer hull must be baking by now as its active coating struggled to redirect the incoming heat. Between the fog bank of the nebula itself, the searing temperatures, and the cascade of deadly particulate radiation, Xul sensors were most likely completely blind within this tiny pocket of hell.

Of course, if I were the Xul commander, Alexander thought, staring into that blazing starscape, *and an enemy squadron buzzed my Dyson cloud and then vanished off my screens, this would be the first place I'd look. . . .*

How smart *were* the Xul, anyway?

The question was impossibly complex. There were many types of intelligence, many different ways of thinking and processing information. The Xul had shown how different, how alien their thought processes were from human many times over the past centuries. They had blind spots . . . and they seemed to have trouble thinking outside of a fairly narrow and tightly defined box. They tended not to think in terms of life evolving outside of the so-called habitable zone of a typical star, for example, which was why the An colony on Ishtar and the deep-benthic Eulers had escaped extinction.

Maybe they wouldn't think that organic life could find shelter in this searing radiation storm cloud.

"Cara?" he said in his mind. "Initiate gravitometric mapping."

"*Aye, aye, General.*"

Taggart heard the order over his link. "That's going to be a tall order," he suggested. "The gravitational tides inside this cluster are pretty fierce."

"I know. But if we can get a decent picture of the local metric, we can get the whole squadron out of here in two translations . . . either to S-2 or all the way back to Sol Space."

"Sounds good," Taggart replied, "assuming our AIs can solve the metrics in something less than a century or two."

"We've got eight platforms," Alexander reminded him. "That will cut down on the time somewhat."

But Taggart had a valid point. Quantum Sea translations required extremely accurate gravitometric maps of two volumes of space—where you wanted to end up, and where you were starting from. At first, it had been assumed that you needed as flat an area of space as you could manage—well out beyond the boundaries of the nearest solar system, for example.

But basic physics stated that it was impossible to get all the way out of any body's gravitational field. Theoretically, Earth's gravity exerted a small but non-zero tug on objects all the way out to the teeming galaxies of the Virgo Cloud, and well beyond. What was needed was not an *absence* of gravity, but an extremely accurate picture of how local space was bent and twisted by local gravitational fields. The AI navigators learned how to use areas that were in balance—such as the Lagrange points in the Earth-Moon system back home. The *Hermes* had used that Earth's L-3 point ever since her first deployment, over ten years ago, now—in Luna's orbit around Earth, but on the other side of the Earth from the Moon.

The metric of space here within the Core was anything but flat. Hundreds of millions of stars surrounded the center, itself occupied by millions of stars more, plus several hundred million solar masses' worth of black holes and millions of masses more of gas and dust, and *all* of that mass traveling at high velocity in all directions.

Alexander hoped, though—and Cara had informed him weeks ago that it should be possible—that the gravitational effects of the stars of the IRS-16 cluster would pretty much overwhelm everything else, at least within this one, tiny volume of space. The nebula, with the stars imbedded within it, was moving very swiftly indeed as it orbited GalCenter, and the gravitational tides of the central black hole a tenth of a light year distance were smearing the cluster out into an almost cometary shape. The distances involved, however, still were so large that local space, while badly warped by all of those conflicting gravitational fields, was not changing rapidly . . . not by human standards.

It should be possible to take a snapshot of the local metric and use it for starship translation before the picture changed significantly.

"General? Admiral?" Cara said, breaking into Alexander's thoughts. *"Captain Pollard has the first images from the Spymaster probes. You wanted to see them."*

"Good," Alexander said. "Link him in."

The expeditionary force's head of N-2 entered Alexander's shared command link with Taggart and the rest of their shared constellation. "General Alexander," he said. "Admiral. I think you're both going to be interested in this."

"Let's see it, Felix," Alexander told him.

"The data damned near flooded our system out," Pollard said. "A real overload. And we're going to be sorting this stuff for the next fifty years at least. But we have some preliminary results."

A window opened in Alexander's mind, and he felt himself falling through. . . .

At first, he thought he was seeing stars—clouds of stars massed together by the hundreds of billions, by the trillions. But the stars were gray and dark, and as he plunged into the cloud, he experienced a shift in his perception. Not stars . . . but *worlds*. . . .

As each of the eight starships of the squadron had rounded the central Dyson cloud, it had fired a barrage of some hundreds of K-794 Spymaster probes, spraying them more or less at random into the cloud's depths. As each probe accelerated at two hundred gravities, it started transmitting on a number of wavelengths, radio, optical, and ultraviolet, sending back detailed images of everything it encountered.

Many of the probes encountered Xul constructs and, engaging their nano-tunneler elements, plowed into the structures to connect with Xul electronics. Others, bypassing the Xul structures, plunged all the way through toward the event horizon of the monster singularity within.

As each Commonwealth ship had dropped out of FTL and rounded the Dyson cloud, it had sampled the returning transmissions from all of those myriad spy probes. Athena and various AIs under her command had sorted through that bewildering sea of information and begun piecing it together, bit by electronic bit, into a coherent whole.

Worlds. Trillions upon trillions of worlds. . . .

The largest, Alexander noted, were actually planet-sized, up to about 6,500 kilometers, roughly the diameter of Mars. The smallest, and there were billions of these, were the size of basketballs.

The vast majority, however, fell between these two extremes, measuring a few tens or hundreds of kilometers across and massing a few billion *billion* tons. Most likely, each was an asteroid transformed by the Xul equivalent of nanotechnology, though to have so many they must have been importing asteroids from thousands of far-flung star systems. As Alexander's roving viewpoint moved closer to one, he could see its surface was mingled black and dark gray in geometric patterns. In fact, it appeared identical to Xul fortresses he'd encountered guarding various stargates throughout the Galaxy, roughly spherical, flattened at the poles, with bulges, sponsons, blisters, turrets, and towers creating an artificial and highly geometric terrain of hills and straight-line canyons.

Within the outer layers of the cloud the sky was dark, heavily shadowed by thunderheads composed of drifting Xul fortresses in their massed billions. As Alexander's point of view fell farther and farther into the cloud, however, the sky ahead grew lighter, taking on sunset hues of gold, red, and blue as the intervening mists thinned.

Abruptly, the cloud turned ragged, then cleared away as if blown by a cosmic wind, and the central black hole of the Galaxy was revealed. The light, Alexander saw, came not from the singularity, of course, but from a constant sharp glow emanating from the blue spiral of the inner accretion disk. Flaring pinpoints like tiny, blue-white stars dropped in long, curving arcs into the event horizon in evenly spaced groups, each growing brighter as it neared the gravitational point of no return.

Those flares, he thought, were too evenly spaced to be natural. The Xul, operating through the Dyson cloud, were *feeding* the central black hole, sending in packets of debris and star stuff in neatly patterned and regulated streams.

He was witnessing, he realized, cosmic engineering on an inconceivably vast scale.

The point of that engineering remained elusive. Not the mere generation of energy, surely . . . though the steady pulse and flash of X-rays released by matter spiraling in past the event horizon was being absorbed by the cloud, according the readings from the Spymaster sensors. No wonder the astronomers of past centuries hadn't been able to confirm the existence of a super-massive black hole at the Galactic center; the Dyson cloud was effectively blocking all radiation from the enigmatic central object.

He thought back to the various briefings he'd attended or given. The possibility that the Xul were using the Core singularity for something extremely far-reaching indeed seemed more and more plausible. To be able to edit Reality across the Galaxy might justify such a gargantuan technological effort.

Whatever the Xul were doing here *had* to be stopped.

But the implementation was the problem. A direct attack on the cloud by the squadron was clearly and utterly impossible. A million, a *billion* starships wouldn't be enough.

But S-2 still offered them one slim hope. . . .

Marine Regimental Strike Team
Firebase Hawkins, S-2/I
Core Space
0220 hrs, GMT

Garroway found he was glad to be out in the open for a change. In ten years of fighting the Xul, the vast majority of his encounters had been below ground or within the close corridor-tunnels of their giant spacecraft and gate fortresses. That last underground fight in the buried city earlier had nearly pushed him past his limits with its claustrophobic terror. It felt *cleaner* out here, somehow, though he knew that distinction made no rational sense. He leaned up against the lip of the fighting hole and targeted the oncoming black machines as they drifted in from the downed Xul Behemoth.

Every Marine position was firing now, both along the perimeter and from the hard points grown in the city to the rear, hundreds of weapons pouring a devastating fusillade into the approaching black tide. The black sky above that tortured landscape flashed and sparked with hellfire volleys of Marine weaponry—rapid-fire plasma weapons, lasers, Gatling cannon, pulse rifles, high-velocity mass drivers, mortars, shoulder-launched missiles. Nightstar fighters continued to streak overhead in flights of two, scant tens of meters above the ground, strafing and bombing the sea of Xul machines. Plasma bolts from the Tarantulas snapped overhead between each fly-by, vaporizing oncoming Xul combots by the hundreds . . . by the thousands. . . .

And still there were enough of them to sweep past and through the Marine perimeter, firing wildly as they came. Garroway held his position, firing with cool, almost detached precision. When his plasma gun again showed empty, he dropped the weapon and drew his pistol. Xul machines floated into the fighting hole, tentacles snaking out. He fired into one point-blank as it grappled with Chaffee, then extended his slicers and began carving up a second machine as it tried to grab him.

Master Sergeant Gardner twisted and screamed as three Xul machines targeted her together, slamming bolt after bolt of high-energy laser fire into her armor, vaporizing a ragged emptiness in her left shoulder and the side of her helmet as her atmosphere blasted free and instantly froze into glittering crystals of blood-tinged ice.

Chaffee was dead a moment later, his armor holed squarely through his chest and out his back. PFC Connors crumpled and fell, shrieking. . . .

Breaking free of the enemy, Garroway dropped and rolled, snatching up Chaffee's plasma gun and pouring fire into the advancing mob. "This is Perimeter Three! Perimeter Three!" he yelled over the regimental net. "We need close support here! Perimeter Three!"

With no atmosphere, he couldn't hear the approach of the Nightstar fighters, but he felt the shudder traveling through the ground as it rippled beneath his boots. An instant later, he was tumbling across the rocky ground, as white fire engulfed the rim of the fighting hole.

"All perimeter teams!" an AI's voice said, speaking in his mind. *"Fall back to secondary positions!"*

"About fucking time!" Garroway snapped back. Standing, he cut down three more Xul forms as they drifted out of the haze of light and falling dust beyond the position. "Huerra! Grab Connors and let's get the hell out of here!" He was already checking Gardner and Chaffee. Both Marines were dead, but there was always the possibility of bringing them back if their brains weren't badly chewed up.

Half of Clara Gardner's skull was missing. Chaffee, though, had taken a small, high-energy slug through his chest, losing atmosphere and a lot of blood, but it might be possible to recover him . . . *if* they could get him to a hospital ship or facility in time. Stooping, he hoisted the Marine's body over his shoulder, then started sprinting toward the rear.

Behind him, another close pass by the Nightstars lit up the shadow-cloaked landscape for kilometers around.

22

Ops Center
UCS Hermes
Point Diamond,
Core Space
0445 hrs, GMT

"The astrogation department just checked in," Taggart told Alexander. "They should have the local metric nailed within the next couple of hours."

"Thank God."

"Commander Warnke didn't sound too enthusiastic about it."

"What do you mean?"

"I got the impression he would like to keep the AIs chewing on the data for the next ten years or so, before risking an actual translation, that's all. He didn't sound happy with the simulations."

"We don't have ten years."

"That's what I told him."

Alexander frowned, considering alternatives. S-2 was only about a tenth of a light year away from IRS-16—roughly the same distance as the Dyson cloud, or close enough. They could make the run under Alcubierre Drive, and be there within an hour or so.

But he didn't want to risk it. Ships moving under Alcubierre

Drive left wakes in the surrounding interstellar medium, as the space-distorting bubble of the drive field alternately compressed, then stretched space-time around the moving vessel. Xul instrumentation might well detect the little squadron as it made its way from the star cluster back to S-2.

Besides, every Xul ship within a thousand light years of GalCenter must be on alert by now, and half of them must be swooping in toward the Core's innermost realm—S-2, the Dyson cloud, and IRS-16. It was going to get very crowded around here, and damned quickly.

"So what do you have in mind, exactly?" Taggart asked him. His voice was patient, but carried a slight edge. Alexander could hear the unspoken question: *Just what do you plan to do with my squadron?*

And it was a fair question. Sure, Alexander might command the entire MIEF, ships and all, but Admiral Taggart still carried the primary responsibility for the naval vessels within the group. Liam tended to think of them all as his children, to be as fiercely protective as any parent.

"I want to load four of the squadron ships onto *Hermes*," he told the admiral. "*Ludwigson, Plottel, Lejeune* . . . and especially the *Howorth*. We leave the others here for now. When things quiet down, we can come back for them, or they can get to S-2 under their Alcubierre Drives.

"We translate to S-2 and drop the ships off. If there are Xul ships in-system, we neutralize them. *Howorth* goes down to pick up the RST, after they initiate Operation Heartbreak."

"You want to leave *Morrigen* here?" Taggart asked. "Her firepower would be damned useful if the Xul are occupying S-2."

"I know . . . but she's a big-assed bitch. And so are *Howorth* and *Lejeune*. We can't fit all three of them on board *Hermes* at once. We need *Howorth* to lift our Marines off the planet . . . and I want *Lejeune* so we can take our fighters on board, if *Cunningham* didn't make it."

"Of course. I should have thought of that."

"No, you're thinking in terms of concentrating firepower

where we need it, which is exactly what you *should* be thinking about. I wish we *could* have *Morrigen* along . . . but this is going to be a recovery mission, not a strike."

"Yes, sir."

"Cara? Pass the word to begin maneuvering *Howorth*, *Lejeune*, *Plottel*, and *Ludwigson* in for docking with *Hermes*. Admiral? I suggest *Mars*, *Ardash*, and *Morrigen* be deployed farther out, on perimeter defense."

"We call it picket duty in the Navy, General. But, yes. I concur."

Alexander ignored Taggart's gentle jab. Both the admiral and he were stressed to the limit at this point. An argument, a turf war, would serve no one, save, possibly, the Xul.

"So what are we going to do about Earth?" Taggart asked him. "And the Senate?"

"I don't know," Alexander conceded. "I was hoping to bring in the rest of the MIEF through the nearest Core stargate as support. At this point, I doubt the Senate will release them."

"The fleet's still in Cluster Space."

"It *was*." He checked his time sense. It had been roughly four hours since the *Pax Galactica* had vanished, and since *Hermes* had suddenly developed "communications difficulties" and cut the connection with George Stahl back in Earth-Ring. Yarlocke's people must be frantic by now, and sending QCC messages to every naval vessel they could reach. "If the Senate is panicking, they may have already ordered it back to Sol, and if we translate back, either to Cluster Space or Sol Space, we may find ourselves under direct orders not to return to the Core . . . even if we still have ships and personnel here. I don't want to see that happen."

"True," Taggart said. "But it takes time to get the MIEF ready to move. And without orders from you, well, prep time could be a lot longer . . . if you know what I mean."

Alexander gave a wry grin. "And *I* should have thought of *that*."

Taggart shrugged. "Remember, sir. You're Alexander the Great."

Alexander snorted, a dismissive sound. All military commanders, he was certain, picked up nicknames in the course of their careers. During the past few years, General Alexander hadn't so much acquired a nickname as he had a persona . . . an assumed connection with the historical figure of Alexander the Great.

The comparison, he thought, while distinctly flattering, had little enough connection with reality. Like the historical Alexander, he was leading his nation's military forces against a far larger empire that threatened that nation's very existence. Like the original Alexander, his campaign thus far had been remarkably successful, successfully striking node after node of Xul control just as Alexander of Macedon had taken on the individual Persian satraps.

But where Alexander of Macedon had ended up conquering a large portion of the known world, Martin Alexander had not been engaged in a war of conquest. Alexander the Great might have demolished Tyre and burned Persepolis, but he hadn't been in the habit of blowing up Persian star systems.

He decided that if he, Martin Alexander, ever began showing signs of acute alcoholism and mental instability—to the point of killing his closest friends and advisors—it would be time to retire. That would be pushing the absurd connection *much* too far.

"Your people adore you at least as much as Alexander's men loved him. They damned near followed him to the end of the Earth . . . they were willing, at any rate. And your people feel the same about you. Or were you aware of that?"

"I was aware that Alexander's men mutinied when he tried to push them too far," Alexander reminded the admiral. He'd experienced a rather lengthy and detailed entertainment sim on the life of Alexander of Macedon a few years before—at right about the time he realized the personnel of 1MIEF were making that comparison. "That's why he turned back from India." Alexander the Great had pushed the boundaries of his empire east to within the borders of India, only to turn back at last when his army simply refused to go farther. He'd died—probably of the combined effects of disease, drink, and dementia—at Babylon during the return.

"That's beside the point," Taggart said. "He also drank himself to death at the age of thirty-three, and you're well past *that* milestone."

Alexander grimaced, a good-natured jibe. "Thanks *so* much for reminding me."

"Any time. Point is, Klass is going to take his sweet time withdrawing the MIEF from Cluster Space if the order doesn't come from you. And if he did, he'd have a real fight on his hands with Pierce."

Rear Admiral Regin Klass was Taggart's exec, and had been left in command of the rest of the MIEF back at Cluster Space. Brigadier General Timothin Pierce was in command of the rest of the MIEF's Marine contingent currently stationed in Cluster Space.

Taggart, he knew, was right. The MIEF's personnel would follow him before they would follow the orders of anyone in the Senate hierarchy. The idea left Alexander somewhat uncomfortable. The Commonwealth military in general and 1MIEF in particular were *supposed* to answer to the Commonwealth Senate, not to any particular officer. Once, the ultimate command authority would have been the President, but the steady and long-term erosion of the executive branch's power had left the military solidly under the control of the Senate's Military Council . . . and that meant Senator Yarlocke and a handful of others.

He wondered again what the hell had happened to the woman.

He was facing, he realized, the ultimate crisis in any nation's hierarchy of command and control. The forces of 1MIEF answered to him, were loyal to him, and it was, therefore, up to him and to him alone to maintain the chain of loyalty with the constitutionally designated command authority. If he wanted to overthrow the Commonwealth government and establish himself as a military dictator, he could probably do it; 1MIEF constituted less than a quarter of the Commonwealth's total military might, but it was by far the best quarter and, properly led . . . sure. He could see several possible ways to seize the EarthRing government centers swiftly enough that the Army and other services would be presented with a *fait accompli*.

That thought made him even more uncomfortable. He'd sworn an oath to the Commonwealth Constitution and to the Senate. Hell, he didn't even *want* to be a dictator.

But what if he became convinced—absolutely and determinedly convinced—that to save the Commonwealth he would have to overthrow the Senate?

A new thought startled him. Was *that* why Yarlocke hated him so much? Why she kept trying to dismantle the MIEF? Because she was afraid of what he, Alexander, might do? He'd never even considered that possibility.

He realized Taggart was watching him, waiting for some comment. "Pierce and Klass had damned well better follow *any* legal orders they get," he said. "The Expeditionary Force is not my private army . . . and it's just possible that the Senate might have need of it some day."

"Maybe. But we only developed our 'communications problems' four hours ago. They'll try to get in touch with us with courier drones, if nothing else."

Which meant that they needed to get done what needed to be done quickly, before they found themselves in the position of having to directly and deliberately disobey orders.

Of one thing Alexander was certain. No matter what orders the Senate managed to transmit to the squadron, they would *not* be leaving personnel behind at S-2/I.

Nightstar 442
Surface of S-2/I
Core Space
0505 hrs, GMT

Lieutenant Ramsey pulled his Nightstar around and lined up for yet another pass over the battlefield. His plasma weapons were long since empty, but so long as he possessed power taps he could keep flying and keep his lasers charged. There were only two real variables in the equation—how long the Nightstar would hold together as hour followed pounding hour of combat, and how long the pilot could keep flying under the unrelenting punishment.

Flying an aerospace fighter in vacuum was utterly unlike flight within a planetary atmosphere, where the pilot could bank, roll, and use lift and drag to maneuver his craft. Even close to a planetary surface like that of S-2/I, the only constants of flight dynamics were thrust and gravity. Once he'd over-flown the target, he had to flip the Nightstar end for end and use his agravitics to decelerate, killing his forward velocity, then build up acceleration once more for another pass at the target. While he could jink a little with his lateral thrusters, his approaches and attack runs tended to be strictly ballistic, virtually straight-line and entirely predictable.

It was that predictability that was wearing down the squadron. With each pass over the Xul hosts, powerful pulses of laser light snapped across the sky, weaving deadly webs attempting to snag the onrushing fighters. Major Treverton had died an hour ago as he streaked low above a mass of enemy combots. Lieutenants Handley, Baker, and Smeth all had been killed since. Only three Nightstars remained in the sky now: Eva Grant, Karl Mayfair, and Ramsey.

Since the other two were newbies, only recently commissioned, Ramsey had taken command, leading each pass across the battlefield through ever-shifting three-dimensional mazes of deadly laser light. Each time, they came from a different direction, lining up on different sets of targets, always trying to keep the enemy fire controllers guessing.

Each time, their Nightstars took more damage—mostly through high-velocity collisions with bits of grit, rubble, and shrapnel flying above the battlefield. Ramsey's ship was failing rapidly, its magnetic rad shielding degrading with each pass, its phase-shift protection working now only intermittently.

Just a few more passes. There were so damned many of

the Xul combots. From up here they resembled black seas flowing out from the wreckage of the fallen Behemoth. The three fighters targeted the largest masses with their lasers, but also continued to hammer at the wreckage. There were gaping, town-sized craters in the alien's hull, now, and maybe, just maybe, they could yet score a hit that would stop the march of those black hordes.

He put his targeting cursor over one of the larger craters on the Xul hulk. Enemy laser fire flicked past him, made visible by his AI's computer graphics. Initiating the thought-code sequence that triggered his primary lasers, he directed a stream of invisible, high-energy fire into the depths of the target.

And then, shockingly, he was tumbling, half of his Night-star sheared away by a Xul weapon—probably a plasma bolt. Sky and ground merged in a wild, frantic whirl as he tried to trigger the cockpit eject sequence.

"Mayday! Nightstar 442 . . . I'm hit! I'm going in! . . ."

Marine Regimental Strike Team
Firebase Hawkins, S-2/I
Core Space
0507 hrs, GMT

One of the Marine close-support aerospacecraft was falling. Garroway watched it streak low over the battlefield, between his position and the distant mountain of the alien wreck. *Damn . . .*

There were only a couple of fighters left, and those wouldn't last much longer. The enemy's fire was too heavy, too accurate. Explosions flashed across Xul positions. The stricken fighter vanished over the southern horizon.

Garroway was exhausted. He'd been in combat now more or less nonstop for seven hours, and his armor had only limited supplies of the drugs used to keep faltering organics going under this level of stress. Somehow, though, he'd managed to keep going.

He could feel a slight tremor through his boots—another seismic quake. It felt like a heavy bombardment, but no one was shooting at the Marine position at the moment. Maybe the squadron had returned and was shooting up a Xul position somewhere over the horizon? It was a pleasant thought, but not one he could embrace enthusiastically. If the squadron had returned, they would have linked in with the RST's command constellation, and every Marine on the planet would be cheering right about now.

Possibly S-2/I simply went through periods of heavy seismic activity due to tidal stress, both as it orbited its giant red sun and as it continued to swing in closer toward GalCenter.

He keyed into one of the ubiquitous Marine combat drones drifting above the ground just in front of his position, using its sensors for a view of the battlefield rather than raising his helmet above the level of the nanocrete parapet. The latest Xul charge appeared to have tapered off, but there were still small pockets of Xul combots out there, and the things never gave up. Garroway wondered, and not for the first time by far, whether the Xul combat machines were literally piloted by the real Xul, the electronic uploads of once-organic beings, or if they remained safely hidden away on their Behemoth and operated the black combots by remote control.

The drone picked up movement, and its limited AI flashed a targeting cursor over the thing, whatever it was. Zooming in provided little additional detail; Xul combots were well shielded against heat loss and didn't show up well on IR. It was still night over this part of S-2/I, *would* be for several more standard days, and the combots' surface coloration and light-drinking surfaces made them almost invisible in the deep shadows of night.

Garroway had slung and locked his plasma rifle over his shoulder, and was holding instead a Man-Portable Variable Munitions Launcher, or MP VML-44. Stubby and blunt, with a pistol grip and shoulder-armor mount, it fired a 70mm projectile—in this case a smart antiarmor nano round known popularly within the Corps as a wasp nest. Raising the weapon nearly to the zenith, he linked the drone's target lock with the shell, then triggered it with a thought. He felt the recoil thump as the round left the weapon, traveling in a high, curving arc over the battlefield.

Within two seconds, its sensors had found the target and locked on directly. Falling, the round steered itself by using the local magnetic field; fifty meters above the target, the shell burst, releasing twelve submunitions rounds that spread out over a larger area, each seeking its own target. Xul machines on the ground opened fire with a deadly web of laser light, knocking out several of the incoming rounds, but eight, at least, got through, homing on the laser flashes, spewing deadly clouds of nano-disassemblers onto Xul machines as they floated just above the ground.

Garroway, meanwhile, was already moving, slipping farther to the left along his defensive trench, just in case the Xul had some sort of counter-battery fire working on backtracking the trajectory of the round. Seconds later, a Xul plasma bolt slammed into the spot where he'd been standing, shattering blocks of nanocrete and gouging out a ten-meter crater. Slowly, relentlessly, the nanocrete fortifications began merging, flowing, reshaping themselves, erasing the scar and returning the fortifications to their former shape.

Marines moved back and forth through those interconnecting trenches, shifting from position to position to deliver fire. Around them, surviving Tarantulas and fixed gun turrets along the firebase fortifications continued sweeping the blasted and devastated ground outside the base with white fire. The RST was down to fewer than 150, now, with another fifty incapacitated, either in the sick bay or frozen for later attempts at retrieval. The team's handful of "docs," the Navy corpsmen, moved back and forth endlessly, crawling up to fallen Marines, linking with their suit AIs, firing packets of medical nano into their armor ports, and dragging them back to the relative safety of the rear. Overhead, two surviving Nightstars continued their ceaseless sweeps. Both were out of plasma charges by now, but they still possessed lasers, and continued to strafe Xul formations as soon as they began gathering.

Eleven of the aerospacecraft had been destroyed in the past hours, victims of massed fire from Xul forces.

Garroway stopped to lob another VML round toward the enemy, then moved to yet another position. Another Marine was already there. An ID came up through Garroway's link: Warhurst.

"Hey, Gunny!" Garroway said. "Good to see you're still with us."

"So far," Warhurst said. He indicated the enemy with a movement of his plasma weapon. "Feels like we've broken the bastards."

"I hope so. I lost track after about ten or twelve mass wave-attacks. Think they're running out of machines?"

"I doubt it. Intel thinks they grow their own on the spot. Maybe we're managing to kill the drivers, though."

Garroway considered this. The Xul possessed a technology similar to and in many ways more advanced than Humankind's nanotech. Damaged ships were repaired by clouds of flying devices that fit together like pieces in a 3D jigsaw, and they always seemed to have inexhaustible supplies of combots. The best guess Intel had come up with was that they manufactured them as they needed them, with Xul software "pilots" controlling each until it was destroyed, then shifting to another, fresh machine.

If true, sooner or later the tiny pocket of Marines would be worn down and overrun.

But the good news was that the wave attacks had stopped, at least for now. There were still large numbers of Xul machines prowling about in the darkness, but they were in isolated and noncooperating groups, and they seemed unwilling to test the Marine battle line again.

"It would be nice to think we're doing *something* to them," he said. "I'm about dead on my feet."

"Me, too. You know what I think?"

"What?"

"When that Behemoth crashed, it lost control of its on-board singularity. I think whatever mechanism they used on board for creating new combots was destroyed, and what's left is an empty shell."

Garroway raised his helmet above the parapet, studying the distant fallen huntership. It had come down at a forty-five-degree angle, flattening much of its five-kilometer breadth into the landscape. The far end, though, still extended well over a kilometer above the ground. The upper surface was scarred and cratered now, after repeated bombing and strafing runs by the Marine aerospace fighters, and much of the structure appeared to be sagging, as though it were collapsing from the inside.

"You may be right," Garroway said. "Doesn't look like it has a lot holding it up. If that black hole got away, though, where is it now?"

"Think about it, Gare. A black hole—even one the size of an atom—breaks free of its restraining fields, it falls, moving toward the nearest gravitational mass, right?"

"Straight down into the planet."

"Exactly. Eating as it goes. It would pass through solid rock as easily as through air, almost. Momentum would carry it past the center of the planet almost to the other side, and then it would fall back."

"And repeat. And repeat. Shit, Gunny. The core of this planet must look like Swiss cheese by now." That explained the quakes he'd been feeling over the past few hours. A sub-microscopic black hole was bouncing around the core of the planet, eating rock, spewing radiation, and generating shock waves felt at the surface as small earthquakes.

"Hey, all a black hole like that can do is get bigger," Garroway said. "How long before it eats the whole planet?"

"A while, would be my guess. It's probably no bigger than a hydrogen atom right now, and the tunnels it's leaving probably close up behind it right away. It would take a *long* time to swallow the whole planet."

"Oh." Garroway felt a surge of relief. Xul he could fight against. A black hole, even a tiny one, was a force of nature with which no human could contend, not without some pretty sophisticated technology.

"So what's it like under General Alexander?" Warhurst wanted to know.

"Hell, you've served with him."

"Yeah, but that was nine, ten years ago. Men change."

Garroway shook his head. "Not this one. Scuttlebutt has it he's been standing up for us against the Senate the whole time, fighting them more than he's had to fight the Xulies, I think."

"So he's not going to leave us here on this rock."

"Huh? *Hell*, no! What makes you think he would?"

Warhurst didn't reply. Garroway knew the older man had been wrestling for a long time with personal issues—in particular, a line family that had kicked him out a long time ago. Things like that could shake a person's trust in other people. And in himself.

Maybe that's why he'd retired from the Corps.

What, Garroway wondered, had brought him back?

The simplest explanation, he decided, was that Warhurst had felt a need to stand between Earth and the Xul demons. Everything was at stake, after all, including all of Humankind's survival. In Garroway's experience, though, warriors rarely faced death for something as ungraspably vast as human survival.

In that moment, he realized why Warhurst had returned. Garroway, Ramsey, and Armandez had visited him in Miami, and a few days later he'd returned to the Corps. He'd come back for *them*.

"Gunny Warhurst?"

"What?"

"Thanks."

"Huh? For what?"

"For being here."

"Shit. I'm here to save Humankind, not *your* sorry ass."

"Right. But—"

"Shut up! We've got company! Bearing one-niner-five!"

One of the battlefield sensor drones had picked them up, a

long, ragged column of Xul combats moving out from the
fallen Behemoth. Maybe the machinery was still working
inside that hulk after all.

"Get ready to move," Garroway said, locking in on the
target. The Xul were getting smart, stringing their fighting
machines out in a long line instead of bunching them up.
But the VML submunitions rounds were smart enough to
counter. He triggered the first round, dropped the muzzle a
bit, and triggered another. "Okay!" he snapped. "Go!"

The two Marines crouched low and trotted to the right. A
dazzling light engulfed them, and the shockwave, blasting
through the floor of the trench, picked them both up and
flung them down.

And a fresh tidal wave of Xul combots surged toward the
Marine positions.

Ops Center
UCS Hermes
Point Diamond, S-2/I,
Core Space
0735 hrs, GMT

"All departments report ready for translation in all respects," Taggart said. "We are at battle stations, and with all
power taps generating at 105 percent. At your command,
General."

*How the hell do you ever get ready for something like
this?* Alexander thought, but he left it unspoken. "Very well.
I want *Lejeune* out of the docking bay first when we drop in.
I want her fighters out to screen us in case there are hostiles
in-system. And *Howorth* next."

"Yes, sir."

The big question was whether there would be a Xul fleet
waiting for them in orbit over S-2/I, or close enough to detect them when they dropped in.

They would know soon enough.

"Initiate translation," he said.

For a moment, the universe around him felt . . . blurred, and he felt the inward, sinking sensation he always felt when going completely out of phase. The *Hermes* and her cargo of four warships fell through the cracks between Reality, rotating through the eldritch continuum of the Quantum Sea, and emerging . . . somewhere else.

The blue clouds and dazzling beacons of the IRS-16 cluster were wiped away. In their place, the vast and awe-inspiring spiral of the outer accretion disk, Sagittarius A, dominated a sky once again filled with the distant wall of stars shrouding this inner pocket within the Core. Streamers of plasma flame, frozen by size and distance, arced high above and far below the Core, following lines of magnetic force. S-2 gleamed like a brilliant, ruby-hued beacon high and to one side.

There was no sign of S-2/I.

"Damn it!" he shouted. "Where's the planet?"

"Checking," Commander Warnke told him. The *Hermes* astrogational officer was linked in with the command constellation, and Alexander felt him following strands of AI input.

"Belay the launch order on *Lejeune*," he said. There was no point in releasing the carrier and her fighters if they were going to need to move again almost at once. For a long minute, *Hermes* drifted in open space, alone and vulnerable.

"It's the metric," Warnke announced a moment later. "I was afraid of this. It's changing too quickly! We're a couple of a.u.s away from where we ought to be!"

Two astronomical units . . . about three hundred million kilometers, or twice the distance between Earth and Earth's sun, a gulf of roughly sixteen light minutes. A small enough error when you were dealing with distances measured in light *years*, but potentially deadly in a game of cat and mouse at the Galactic Core.

"Put us back where we're supposed to be," Alexander told Warnke. "*Fast.*"

"It'll have to be under Alcubierre Drive," Taggart told him. "We can't recalculate the metric."

"Do it."

What had gone wrong? Through his link with *Hermes'*
navigational feeds, he could see the location of S-2 marked
by brackets, and a number of icons marking gravitational
anomalies . . . a few of those thousands of black holes orbiting GalCenter. The movements of the nearest of those singularities must have literally changed the shape of local
space, resulting in *Hermes* overshooting its target and coming out somewhere else.

They were lucky, Alexander thought, that they hadn't
popped out somewhere farther out, out there among those
teeming star clouds, for instance.

The starfield on the Ops Center display rotated, bringing
the red jewel of S-2 and the nearby bracket marking its single planet dead center. He felt the faintly queasy sensation as
the Alcubierre Drive field began gathering about the ship,
and then the red star swelled brighter, a slender crescent
growing out of invisibility close beside it.

As the *Hermes* dropped back to non-FTL velocities, Alexander snapped off another series of orders.

"Scans! If there are Xul ships in here, I want to know it!
Release the *Lejeune*. Any sign of *Cunningham*?"

Icons were appearing on the display . . . some of them
Xul vessels, but all of those, he was relieved to see, were
dead and aimlessly adrift.

"General! We have contact with the *Cunningham*! Captain Duquesne reports they left the system under FTL, then
returned an hour ago. He reports the S-2 system is clear of
Xul ships!"

"Excellent." It was better than he'd dared hope. "Liam? Close
with the *Cunningham*, please. As soon as *Lejeune* is away."

"Aye, sir." Taggart hesitated. "Sir, we're also in touch now
with Captain Black on the planet's surface. He reports his
command under heavy ground attack . . . but he's holding."

"Any sign of the enemy in space?"

"No sir," Taggart said, relief in his voice. "Lots of wreckage, but it looks like all the live Xul ships followed us when
we headed toward GalCenter!"

Which meant they had a time, a very *short* time, before

those ships, possibly, returned. There might be Xul sensor drones out there now, reporting on *Hermes*' arrival, or the Xul Black was fighting on the planet might see them and call for help.

Now was the time. Before the enemy regrouped.

"Pass the word to Captain Black," he said. "Initiate Heartbreak. I say again . . . initiate Heartbreak."

They would finish this. *Now*. And no matter what was about to happen to the MIEF squadron.

23

0605.1102

Ops Center
UCS Hermes
Orbiting S-2/I,
Core Space
0747 hrs, GMT

In close formation, *Hermes* and the light carrier *Cunningham* fell in low orbit about the barren ruggedness that was S-2/I. Scans of the surface had proven what Captain Duquesne on the *Cunningham* had already reported, that Xul combots were attacking the Marine firebase on the surface, but that, for the moment, at least, there were no other Xul forces within detection range.

Likely, the Marines of the Regimental Strike Team hadn't attracted much in the way of Xul attention directly. The attack being reported from the surface sounded like an afterthought—Xul machines swarming out of a downed Behemoth and attacking the Marine positions simply because they were there. For now, the squadron could operate freely within the S-2 system.

If they were going to launch the Heartbreak trigger ships, it would have to be now.

"Transmit navigational data for GalCenter space to the triggerships," Alexander told Cara. "We want the orbital mechanics just exactly right."

"Extreme precision will not be possible, General," his AI reminded him. *"There are too many variables, too many unknowns in regard to S-2's composition and dynamic equilibrium. However, the necessary data has been transmitted to Firebase Hawkins."*

Leave it to the AIs to be on top of things. The longer he worked with them, the harder it was to think of artificial intelligences as mere software. They were smart, they were responsive, and they acted alive.

And he was about to sentence twelve of them to the electronic equivalent of death.

In a window open in his thoughts, Alexander saw a schematic of the S-2 system, with twelve curving trajectories rising from the night side of the planet, swinging around to the day side, and accelerating under Alcubierre Drive toward the giant sun. The first ships in line would be transmitting data about stellar density, temperature, and dynamics to the ships following, allowing for subtle course changes to take advantage of the new information.

"Hawkins reports the Euler ships have been programmed and are ready for launch," Taggart announced.

Alexander drew a deep breath. Technically, he was required to consult with the Senate Military Council before firing the Euler triggerships . . . and there were unknowns enough here to pose a significant threat to Earth. If anything was guaranteed to generate a xenocidal Xul response directed against Humankind, attacking their complex at GalCenter must be it.

On the other hand, there was opportunity here . . . the opportunity to do the Xul so much damage in one blow that the war might, at long last, be brought to a close.

He could not let that opportunity slip away in bureaucratic wrangling or politics.

"Do the Xul on the planet's surface pose a threat to a triggership launch?" he asked in his mind.

"Conceivably," Cara told him. *"Individual Xul elements are battling within the Marine trenches, and are within a kilometer of the triggership silos."*

"Relay to Captain Black," Alexander said. "He is clear to initiate Sunrise in order to clear the area."

"Yes, sir."

"And as soon as the silo area is secure, he is to launch Heartbreak," Alexander said.

Marine Regimental Strike Team
Firebase Hawkins, S-2/I
Core Space
0747 hrs, GMT

The Xul combots had swept through the wreckage and into the Marine lines. His VML launcher out of rounds, Garroway had retrieved his plasma weapon and fired at the advancing black sea until they were swarming over the trench itself. For a time, he'd used the nano-D dispenser in his right arm, crouching at the bottom of the trench and firing straight up as the machines drifted overhead.

Then they were too close even for that, and he was using his slicers.

Combat became an endless dance of repeated movements, coordinated and executed through the mental discipline of his weiji-do training. Reach out with the left arm, hook into black ceramic-plastic and metal with one slicer, strike up and in and twist with the right, letting molecule-thin blades core and gut the struggling artificial monster.

Exhaustion dragged at Garroway. How long could he keep this up? . . .

"Listen up Marines!" Black's voice came through on his regimental channel. "We're implementing Sunrise, two counts, in fifteen seconds! Keep your heads down!"

Garroway gutted another Xul machine, shoving the wreckage aside in a tangle of writhing tentacles. Warhurst was next to him, almost against his back. "About fucking time!" Warhurst growled.

But Garroway was mentally running through a countdown. *Twelve . . . eleven . . . ten . . .*

Another Xul combot drifted overhead, its tentacles reaching down for him. He snapped out with his arms, right, then left, severing tentacles, then plunging his left slicer into what passed for the alien machine's belly. It tried to back off, and he felt his boots leaving the ground.

Eight . . . seven . . . six . . .

Warhurst fired his suit's nano-D weapon, the round snapping past Garroway's helmet and imbedding itself in the struggling machine. Clouds of nano-disassemblers began devouring the alien device, sparkles of blue light showing where molecular bonds were breaking.

Garroway wrenched his right slicer free and fell back into the trench as the Xul machine began to disintegrate.

Three . . . two . . . one . . .

"Down!" Warhurst yelled, and then the landscape outside of the trench lit up.

Sunrise indeed. The missiles had been fired from two of the surviving Tarantulas, each tipped with a ten-kiloton tactical nuclear warhead. Marines rarely used such weaponry—the chances of scoring friendly-fire kills, often irretrievables—was simply too great. But the nanocrete trenches grown into the fabric of Firebase Hawkins had been designed with tactical nukes in mind.

Twin fireballs expanded like deadly, spherical blossoms. With no atmosphere, of course, there was no mushroom cloud, but the firestorms of raw, hot plasma swept out from the target points, merged, and swelled. Xul machines caught in the open were shredded, melted, and whipped away in the seething maelstrom of heat and intense EM radiation. The sky above the trench went dazzlingly white as the plasma wall swept overhead, leaving the depths of the trench in shadowed darkness.

The shock waves arrived seconds later, blasting through solid rock and nanocrete, picking Garroway and Warhurst up from the floor of the trench and slamming them both against the back wall.

And then there was a long, black silence.

"All clear," Black's voice reported. "We have the bastards on the run! Pour it on, people!"

Unsteadily, Garroway got to his feet, retracting his slicers and extending a gauntlet to Warhurst to help the older Marine up. Beyond the trench, two hundred-meter craters still glowed white-hot in the aftermath of the strike. Picking up his plasma rifle, Garroway brought it to his shoulder, locked in with his implant, and began picking off individual Xul machines—survivors overlooked by the blast because, by chance, they'd been in shadowed corners, craters, or crevices where the nukes had overlooked them.

The few still afloat appeared to be straggling toward the fallen Behemoth, breaking off the attack at last.

A kind of madness had overtaken Garroway, lifting the exhaustion, giving him new, if momentary, strength. "Burn 'em!" he yelled. "Burn 'em! Burn 'em down!"

"All units," Black's voice said over the Net. "Heartbreak has been initiated and deployed. You people might want to see this. . . ."

"Hey!" Warhurst called from Garroway's side. "They're launching!"

Garroway turned, lowering his weapon. The nearest triggership's bunker was over a kilometer away, and there wasn't a lot to see, but Garroway and Warhurst stood in their trench watching as the slender craft rose above the nanogrown base. The tiny ship, curiously organic, egg-shaped, but with sculpted flutes and swellings and blisters, drove skyward on its agravitics and was rapidly lost to sight.

That explained the use of the nukes. Marine command constellations were super-cautious when it came to the nuclear option, simply because even a ten kiloton warhead was so damnably indiscriminate, but nothing less could have swept the battlefield clear enough of Xuls to allow the triggerships to get away.

He found himself wondering if any Marines or docs had been caught in the open just now. If they had been, their bodies would never be found for retrieval.

Elsewhere across the base, other black Euler vessels were rising and following, streaking toward the western horizon before vanishing into darkness.

Garroway dropped his gaze to the western horizon. The red sun would be rising there on this backward-turning world in another few standard days, but it was lost for the moment beneath the bulk of the planet. That was just as well, considering what was about to happen.

He watched the last of the Euler triggerships vanish into the western sky. He was devoutly, almost insanely glad that he wasn't piloting one. He never wanted to be in that position, that role, again.

His heart was racing, his respiration elevated. All too well he could remember being crammed inside an identical ship a decade earlier, plunging into the core of a star. The thought always brought with it a throat-clutching fear on the ragged verge of panic.

Memories of that close, confining interior of the alien starship mingled with other, more recent memories. For a moment, he flashed back to the nightmare terror of the fight underground hours ago. Damn . . . was he becoming a claustrophobic? Mental and emotional traumas could be as debilitating as physical injury, and frequently were a hell of a lot harder to treat.

He swallowed the fear. He didn't want to alert any of the Network AIs and have his name reported. That could get him pulled off the line in short order. Something like claustrophobia could get him pulled off of combat duty entirely.

For a moment, he let himself be teased by the thought. A psych downcheck might get him sent home. The thought was damned tempting.

And then he shook his head, angry again. What home? Where? EarthRing? He was home *here*, with his buddies. With his *Corps*. . . .

And he would *not* let them down.

● ● ●

Heartbreak Flight
S-2 System,
Core Space
0748 hrs, GMT

Accelerating hard, the first of the Euler-designed trigger-ships emerged from the planet's shadow, plunging into dazzling red sunshine. As it approached the speed of light, S-2/I vanished astern, swept away as if by some titanic, cosmic hand. Ahead, S-2 grew brighter, its edges distorting with the bizarre optical effects of supraluminal travel, then blacked out entirely as the Alcubierre field so completely warped the surrounding space that light could not penetrate to the tiny vessel within.

On board, a sub-program drawn from Athena directed the craft's course and speed. Normally, triggerships were designed to plunge directly into the heart of a star. As the Alcubierre Drive field moved into the high-density realm of the stellar core, a considerable volume of space ahead of the vessel was enormously compressed, vastly increasing that density. Astern, space was stretched out, and here the density of the star's interior dropped sharply. The result was a rebound that collapsed the star's core, creating a shock wave that blew the star's outer layers into space—a nova.

This time, though, the triggerships' AI pilots were aiming well to one side, arrowing in toward one limb of the blazing red star ahead. Each vessel had a slightly different target point, one calculated to cut a chord through a circular cross-section of the star.

Physics calculations and endless simulations had suggested the probable result. Still, with so many unknowns, no one could be sure of what the exact result would be, not until the string of triggerships had actually completed their passage, and Commonwealth ships and probes had had a chance to record and evaluate the data.

Moving at ten times the speed of light, the lead triggership plunged through the stellar photosphere and deep into the lower levels of the star's atmosphere. Not even the senses of the AI pilot could record that instant. Besides, the AI couldn't see out, and was piloting now entirely on programming that assumed the star would be where it was supposed to be at the instant of passage.

In the ship's wake, the predicted shockwave spread through the star.

The star designated S-2 was nearly two hundred times the diameter of distant Sol and, like other red giants, was correspondingly less dense, especially within its outer regions. The passage did not trigger a nova.

It *did*, however, cause a rebound effect that sent nearly a quarter of a Solar mass hurtling out ahead of the star, blasting up and out through the photosphere in a geyser of mass and energy that momentarily outshone the entire star. It was, in fact, a stellar flare, but of unprecedented size and force and volume. As that mass erupted from the red sun's deeper levels, the shock rebounded against the entire star, visibly flattening it along its direction of travel. The flare persisted, growing broader, longer, more powerful . . . in short acting like a gigantic rocket blast with power enough to slightly slow the onrushing star's velocity . . . and subtly change its course.

That first stellar flare would linger for hours . . . perhaps for days, swelling out into space like a fast-expanding pillar of fire. But scant seconds after the first triggership passage, the second triggership in line passed through the star, striking at a slightly sharper, slightly deeper angle.

A second flare, even larger than the first, erupted into space, merging with the first, strengthening it, burning so brightly now that the entire red giant's light output seemed sullen and subdued.

The third triggership increased the force of the stellar rocket even more, extending the growing prominence some forty million kilometers put into space.

Then came the fourth, the fifth . . .

One after another, the Euler triggerships dove into the

star's limb, each passage unleashing titanic and unimaginable forces from the star's depths. There was terrible danger here. Shockwaves were rippling through the star's photosphere and core, both from the explosions themselves and from the shock of deceleration, and the AIs had suggested that there was a chance that the huge star would tear itself into pieces.

Gravity, however, continued to hold sway. The star had a rotational period of some twenty standard days; had it been faster—some giants, younger, hotter, and without planets, rotated in a matter of a few hours—the star might indeed have disintegrated under that ferocious bombardment, though, of course, the individual pieces, the entire mass of the star, would continue moving on its original path.

The impact points had been precisely calculated. The geysering pulses of erupting star stuff were pushing against the star from the direction of its travel as it looped in toward GalCenter. The thrust of those jets acted to slow the star somewhat in its mad, five thousand kilometer-per-second plunge. As the star lost energy, its orbit decayed.

As the artificial flares continued to explode from the depths of S-2's atmosphere, they were acting like retrorockets on a titanic orbital spacecraft. . . .

Ops Center
UCS Hermes
Near S-2/I,
Core Space
1015 hrs, GMT

Alexander watched the savaging of the giant star.

Because of the scales of distance and size involved, everything was happening in slow motion. It had taken hours for the stellar prominence to develop, brightening as it grew until it outshone the rest of the star. From here, the jet appeared as a dazzlingly bright blue-white thread sticking straight out from the much larger sphere of the star. The star was visibly deformed, flattened somewhat, and concave in the region of the super-flares, with concentric rings of shadow showing against the sullen ruby glow of the star's photosphere.

"My God," Alexander said, whispering. "Cara, are you getting all of this?"

"We are recording the operation from the vantage points of over seven hundred remote battlespace probes, General," his AI told him.

"Of course. . . ."

It had been a needless question. Of *course* the AIs would be recording this for later study. And for replay back in the Sol System, as a historical record.

Cyndi Yarlocke and her crowd would make a lot of that record, he thought. For the past ten years, the MIEF had been blowing up entire stars in the war to keep the Xul at bay. Now, they'd refined the process somewhat, found a way, not to destroy the star outright, but to *move* it, to use an entire star as a colossal projectile weapon.

That, to Alexander's mind, seemed more obscene, somehow, than the mere destruction of a star with its attendant planets in an artificially generated nova. Yarlocke, he thought, would have agreed, would have seen this as a forbidden tampering with the natural order on a cosmic scale.

Besides, this was *really* going to piss off the Xul. . . .

A fragment of history nagged at his thoughts. *I am become Death, the destroyer of worlds.* Who had said that? He ran a search, and his link with *Hermes'* data banks brought back the result almost at once.

The quote, technically, was from the ancient Sanskrit *Bhagavad Gita,* the speaker the god Vishnu. The passage had become famous in the West when it had been quoted by Dr. Robert Oppenheimer, the physicist in charge of the Manhattan Project, in July of 1945, on the occasion of the first detonation of a primitive nuclear device. According to the download, Oppenheimer had first mentioned thinking that passage—he'd been fluent in Sanskrit and knew the *Bhaga-vad Gita* well—in an interview in 1965, twenty years after the event. According to Oppenheimer's brother, who'd been present at the time, what he'd *actually* said after that first, test detonation, was, "It worked!"

It would be some time before they would know if *this* had worked, using a giant star as a weapon. They'd been running calculations and simulations for months, now, trying to re-fine the basic idea. The Eulers themselves, that deep-sea race of superb mathematicians, had contributed to the calcu-lations.

According to the numbers, if the thing worked, if they were actually able to change S-2's orbital path about GalCenter enough, the star would reach perigalacton—and the super-massive black hole's event horizon—in thirty days more.

There was no way, no way at all, to speed things up.

"The Xul are going to get to have a crack at it," Taggart said. He might have been reading Alexander's thoughts. "They have fifty days to try to intercept that thing."

That thing. Not "star" or "sun" but "*that thing.*" Perhaps, like Alexander, Taggart was having some trouble with the sheer scale of what they were trying to do here, as well.

"It'll take time, Liam," Alexander replied. "Time for them to figure out what's happening here. And unless they are able to rewrite Reality on a pretty damned big scale, the only thing they can do is induce a nova."

"We know the Xul can blow up stars," Taggart pointed out.

"Yes. But they can't . . . just wink them out. As far as we know." He nodded toward the red giant with its brilliant, lead-ing thread of light. "If they explode that star, the pieces of it—all the gas and particulate radiation, and whatever is left of its core, all of it, will still be moving on the new course."

"True. But the Xul may have been detonating stars in here already. There's Sagittarius A East. . . ."

Alexander nodded. Sag A East was the vast, empty bubble marking an ancient supernova remnant close to GalCenter.

It was at least conceivable that the Xul had blown the star up deliberately, perhaps in such a way as to change its orbital path about the center, rather than allow it to get too close to their construction project at Sag A*.

Then again, supernovae were common occurrences, relatively speaking, within the crowded heart of the Galaxy's core. Sag A East might not have been artificially induced.

"The Xul are bound to hesitate," he said. "I'd think the last thing they would want in close proximity to their Dyson cloud is a nova. It's less than twenty light hours to GalCenter from here. Even if S-2 detonates *now*, it would cause terrific damage in there."

"I just hope it's enough," Taggart observed.

"General?" one of his human aides called over the net. "*Lejeune* is clear of the *Hermes*."

"Thank God. Tell *Lejeune* to launch fighters. And get the *Howorth* out into space and down to the planet. Fast!"

He hoped *that* would be enough, too.

Nightstar 442
Surface of S-2/I
Core Space
1020 hrs, GMT

Charel Ramsey struggled back to consciousness. He was surprised to find that he was still alive, that despite a variety of sharp aches and bruises, he even seemed to be more or less intact. His cockpit had separated from the crashing Nightstar, as it had been designed to do, and managed a landing on emergency thrusters.

Landing, he decided, surveying the damage, was probably too kind a word. His Nightstar had been moving fast when it had been hit—over eighteen hundred kph—and he'd been at keel-scraping altitude to boot. The cockpit's inertial dampers had cut in and spared him the worst of the impact, but he'd still hit fast enough and hard enough to knock him out. According to his implant timepiece, he'd been out for over five hours.

His instruments all were dead. He had no idea how far he was from Marine positions, or if they knew where he was. Without screens or phase-shifting, he must be taking a hell of a dose of radiation right now. He doubted that he had more than a few hours more to live.

And with radiation poisoning, they would be extremely unpleasant hours. Slowly, he raised his gloved hand to the latch on his helmet. He *could* end things quickly, by opening up his helmet to hard vacuum. The alternative was to tough out the inevitable pain and nausea for those few hours in hopes that someone was coming to get him.

His hand was on the catch mechanism for a long and trembling few minutes as he wrestled with the decision.

At last, though, he shook his head and dropped his hand. Marines tried always to recover their own, and if they found him out here and could get him to a Commonwealth military medical facility, he had at least a fair chance of recovery. Garroway had been more badly burned ten years ago, when he'd flown that first triggership mission at Starwall.

Besides, he wasn't feeling too bad just yet. The absorptive nano on the exterior of his cockpit was keeping the internal radiation levels to manageable levels, and his suit's medi-packs were injecting him regularly with anti-rad nano. If things got . . . bad, *really* bad later on, he could always open his helmet then.

The cockpit escape unit included a powerful automatic radio beacon, which was already beaming a distress message into space. The signals might not reach Firebase Hawkins, somewhere over the northern horizon, but any Commonwealth ships in orbit over S-2/I ought to pick it up.

Yeah, they might have someone on the way already.

Ramsey leaned back in his seat and closed his eyes, settling down for the wait.

• • •

Marine Regimental Strike Team
Firebase Hawkins, S-2/I
Core Space
1038 hrs, GMT

Howorth was easing her way down toward Firebase
Hawkins, her massive cigar-shape hanging dark in the sky,
silhouetted by the glow of the spiral arms of the accretion
disk far beyond. Garroway stood in the trench next to Warhurst, watching her come in. They were going to make it.
They were actually going to get the hell off this rock.

Five Tarantulas were still operational, and three of those
were already lifting off, carrying wounded up to the *Hermes*,
in planetary orbit overhead. The other two were parked
nearby, providing cover as the Marines came in off the perimeter. There'd been no new Xul attacks for some hours,
now, but the RST Marines remained on guard. Another Xul
ship could appear at any moment, arrowing in from the invisible monster *there*, halfway up the sky at the center of the
accretion spiral.

"Listen up, Marines!" Captain Black's voice cut in over
the regimental link. "We've got a situation!"

"Shit," Warhurst grumbled. "It's always something!"

"We've got a Marine pilot down, people," Black's voice
went on. "He's alive, but trapped in his ejection pod on the
ground 156 kilometers south of the firebase. I need volunteers to go pick him up."

Garroway keyed his own link, putting his name up on the
board back at RST HQ. A Marine down in that radiation-
blasted wasteland? Hell, *yeah*, he'd volunteer.

Other Marines were volunteering as well. Black had to
cut off the flood of responses. "Okay, okay. We've got all we
need." Garroway's implant put up an icon indicating that his
name had been chosen. He took a deep breath. They always
said never volunteer, but . . .

"I've tagged twelve of you," Black went on. "You'll board
Flying Pig, Lieutenant Grooms, and provide perimeter
security for the doc flying out there with them. From there,

you'll bounce straight up to orbit and rendezvous with the *Hermes*. Understand?"

"Aye, aye, sir!" Garroway, Warhurst, and a number of other voices chorused.

"We've IDed the downed pilot. He's Lieutenant Charel Ramsey. . . ."

"Shit!" Garroway said.

"Old home week, ain't it?" Warhurst added. "All we need now is your girlfriend, Gare."

"She's not here," Garroway said. "Thank God!"

"Then you have someone to go home to. C'mon. Let's go pick up the lieutenant."

They jogged toward one of the waiting Tarantulas. Nearby, *Howorth* had touched down, her vast bulk crushing nano-crete defenses and other structures that happened to be in her way. Marines were streaming up a ramp that had lowered from her belly. In another hour or two, this desolate little world would be empty of human life once more.

The twelve Marines trotted up *Flying Pig's* ramp and strapped themselves into the cargo deck seats. *Thank God Ramsey's alive*, Garroway thought as he activated the magnetic clamps. *This'll be simple. In and out. Grab him and boost to orbit. . . .*

He tried not to think about how the simple missions rarely turned out that way. The evil god Murphy was always all too ready to step in and change the situation beyond all recognition, and always for the worse.

The Tarantula was rising before the rear ramp had even cycled shut.

And the actual pick-up *was* simple, much to Garroway's surprise. The *Flying Pig* made a low, suborbital bounce over the southern horizon, coming down a few tens of meters away from the groove carved into the ground by the cockpit escape pod as it plowed into the surface and at last came to rest. An optical beacon winked from an extended antenna. The Marines raced down the ramp, spreading out, dropping belly-down in a broad circle facing out, weapons ready.

But there were no Xul here. The landscape was utterly

desolate, utterly empty and silent. At their backs, a couple of *Flying Pig*'s flight crew used a plasma cutter to slice into the cockpit. Hospitalman 1st Class Dan O'Neill was there, helping to pull Ramsey from the embrace of his cockpit, administering medinano and packing the man into a rad-shielded transport tube. Ten minutes . . . and at Grooms' order, the Marines began pulling back, reboarding the transport and buckling themselves in.

They began rising, accelerating to orbit. . . .

And then something struck the *Flying Pig* in the side, a savage, ringing blow that put the awkward transport into a wild tumble. Her agravitics were out, her thrusters firing madly in an attempt to stabilize her.

She'd not been accelerating long enough to build up to anything close to orbital velocity.

Helplessly, she was falling back toward the surface of S-2/I.

24

0605.1102

Ops Center
UCS Hermes
Orbiting S-2/I,
Core Space
1135 hrs, GMT

"Sir!" a Navy rating called from the comm board. "We've lost one of the Tarantulas!"

Alexander brought up the data, opening a new window in his mind. Cara pointed out the location, on the planet's surface. "What the hell happened?"

"We're still checking," Cara told him. *"But it seems probable that the Tarantula struck a piece of orbital debris."*

Space around S-2/I was filled with hurtling junk—fragments left over from the *Chosin* and the *Intrepid,* from a number of Nightstar aerospace fighters, and from the Xul giants hammered by the Commonwealth squadron. With no atmosphere around S-2/I to burn up the debris, some of those pieces could orbit at quite a low altitude.

"What were they doing that far south of the base?"

"Captain Black dispatched one Tarantula to recover an aerospacecraft pilot shot down by the Xul," Cara told him.

"General!" Taggart's voice called, interrupting.

"Just a minute, Liam." Alexander was checking the trajectories of other craft leaving the planet. The *Howorth* was boosting clear of the surface already, while the other Tarantulas were already en route. It would be risky to redirect one of them to go back and pick up the fallen Tarantula's occupants, but—"

"General!" Taggart's and Cara's voices sounded together.

"What?"

"We have hostiles inbound!" Taggart said.

Alexander's attentions snapped back to the primary link channel. Xul ships, *lots* of Xul ships, were materializing out of FTL a few tens of light seconds away. Radiation trails scratched through the hydrogen and dust cloud pervading local space showed they were coming from the direction of the Dyson cloud.

"Sensors have detected nearly one thousand Xul huntership," Cara told him, her voice maddeningly calm.

"General Alexander!" Taggart added. "We *must* leave!"

Alexander felt as though the operation were unraveling around him.

"How many people are on board that Tarantula?"

"Five Navy crew," Cara reported. "One Navy corpsman. Thirteen Marines, including the rescued man. We're also missing two other pilots. Twenty-one total."

Twenty-one Marine and Navy personnel.

We never leave our own behind.

But there *were* times when a few Marines had to be sacrificed for the survival of many. That was, in fact, the nature of warfare despite the fine-sounding words and principles— the need to pick and choose and make key strategic decisions, all the while knowing that those decisions would result in some Marines dying, while others lived.

We never leave our own behind.

But sometimes we have to, for the sake of completing the mission.

"Radio them," Alexander said. "Tell them we'll be back!"

"Aye, aye, sir."

"Admiral? Get us the hell out of here."

"Where to, General?"

It scarcely mattered. Back to Earth? No, the rest of the

fleet ought to be still at Cluster Space. "Rejoin the MIEF, Admiral."

"Make to *Cunningham* and *Howorth*," Taggart said. His words were leaden. "Order them to make their own way back to friendly space by the best means they can determine. Astrogation! Initiate translation to Cluster Space."

"Aye, aye, sir. It'll take a few. . . ."

"We don't have a few, Commander. *Do it*."

Alexander snapped his awareness back to the Ops Center. On the main display, the star still glowed a brilliant ruby hue, but the light was dimmed, somewhat, by the fiercely radiating white thread extending from its surface. The crescent of the planet bowed away from the star; at visual wavelengths there was no sign of the approaching horde of enemy ships.

Then *Hermes'* AI put up the graphic icons, red brackets each marking an invisibly distant Xul ship. A mass of intertangled brackets spread across the visual display, moving out from the focus of the accretion spiral. Range data appeared next to the mass. The nearest enemy ships were five light seconds away, and fast moving closer.

The MIEF squadron had done all it could—setting the star S-2 onto a new orbital path. Sensor drones in battlespace would record the star's passage fifty days hence . . . but there was nothing more the Commonwealth ships or Marines could do.

Including rescuing the nineteen people stranded on the planet's surface.

"We don't even know for sure they survived the crash," Taggart told him.

"No. But we should have checked."

"There's no time, sir," Cara said.

"I know." Alexander drew himself up a little straighter. *Cunningham* and *Howorth* were under full acceleration now, looping around the planet and engaging their Alcubierre Drives. They had a chance, at least, of making it back to human-occupied space, though the journey would take months, even years. Both were large enough that their onboard nanoprocessors should keep their crews well supplied with oxygen, water, and food no matter how long the trip. All they would need do is stop, occasionally, to harvest raw materials from comets or carbonaceous asteroids.

"I know," he said again. "But we will be coming back. . . ."

And then *Hermes* shifted phase, dropping into the Quantum Sea and translating through the dimensions and across a spatial gulf of twenty-five thousand light years.

Marine Regimental Strike Team
10 kilometers from Firebase Hawkins, S-2/I
Core Space
1210 hrs, GMT

Garroway pulled himself free of tangled wreckage. Broken power cables hung sparking from the overhead, and the deck was sharply canted. Other Marines were struggling to their feet as well. Their link feed from the Tarantula's cockpit had cut off with the crash.

"Anyone hurt?" Doc O'Neill called, moving down the cargo deck aisle, checking on the Marines. "Is everyone okay?"

The landing, clearly, had been a rough one, but the Marines, well padded within the cocooning embrace of their armor, had ridden out the crash without injuries more serious than bumps and bruises. Someone blew out an emergency hatch on the starboard side forward, and the Marines began scrambling out of the fallen transport.

"Where the hell are we?" Warhurst wanted to know. The terrain was the same as at the pick-up site—broken rock, radiation-baked dust, all beneath that impossible and dramatic three-armed spiral filling a sky of stardust.

"We're about ten kilometers south of Firebase Hawkins," a young Navy rating—one of the Tarantula's crew—told him. She pointed at the horizon. "*That* way."

"Yeah," Lieutenant Aviles, the craft's pilot, added. "I was

trying to make it back to the base. Damn it, we *almost* made it back."

"It looks like you're in command, sir," Warhurst told him. "We'd better get ourselves sorted out if we want to have a chance of getting rescued."

"Right, Gunny."

Garroway heard the conversation, but his attention was elsewhere—on helping Doc O'Neil get Ramsey's cocoon out of the crashed Tarantula. "How is he?" Garroway asked.

"One step above dead," O'Neill told him. "I dropped him into cyber-hibe."

Cybernetic hibernation had been the first means by which humans had gone to the stars, back when transports were limited by the speed of light and voyages to even the nearest stars took ten years objective. The cerebral implants grown within the brains of Marines and starship personnel could be set to take the man or woman into deep unconsciousness— as O'Neill had said, "one step above dead." Medical nano swarmed through the circulatory and lymphatic systems, slowing cell growth and metabolic processes to a near stop, removing toxins building up slowly over time, repairing cell damage as tissue inevitably broke down.

With the advent of Alcubierre FTL Drive and, better still, the quantum translation effect used by the largest ships, marines no longer had to hibernate across the gulfs between even neighboring stars. The medical department, though, still used cyber-hibe in serious cases, when a Marine was so badly wounded that he or she would die within hours or days, and the nearest hospital facility was too far away for an immediate medevac.

"Is he gonna be okay, Doc?" Garroway asked.

"I don't know, Gunny," O'Neill replied. "I've got him doped full of anti-rads, but there's been a lot of cell damage already. And it's still happening. Cyber-hibe doesn't stop radiation. I guess it depends on how long it takes to get him to a hospital. Here, give me a hand with him, okay?"

An hour later, the line of armored Marines and naval

personnel had left the crashed Tarantula and was making
its way north across the broken plain. They would have a
better chance of pick-up, Lieutenant Aviles had decided,
back at Firebase Hawkins—not to mention power, intact
communications gear, and functioning nanoprocessors to
provide water, air, and food. The Tarantula might keep
them alive for a few more days . . . but twenty-one people
could live indefinitely at the firebase, *if* they could reach it.

Garroway and a Marine sergeant named Jennings carried
Ramsey's cocoon, with Doc O'Neill walking alongside, keeping an eye on the cocoon's readouts. They'd laid a sheet of
metal cut from the Tarantula's hull over the cocoon; the active nano surface provided a little extra in the way of radiation protection for the unconscious officer.

Readings were high for all of them, though. Some of them
were going to be sick by the time they made it back to the
base.

"They *couldn't* have left us," Milo Alvarez said, his boots
kicking up small puffs of dust as he trudged along.

"They could and they did, Sergeant," Warhurst replied.
"The damned Xul must've jumped them about the time we
crashed."

"So . . . is that it?" Alvarez asked. "They're just gonna
leave us here to die?"

"Nah," Garroway told the younger Marine. "They *always*
come back for their own. We just have to hold on until that
happens."

But the sky overhead, the dramatic sweep of the accretion
disk spiral, the distant clotting of stars and nebulae, only
emphasized how very small and how very alone they actually were in a very large and very hostile cosmos.

. . .

1105.1102

Senate Committee Deliberation Chamber
Commonwealth Government Center,
EarthRing
1417, GMT

". . . and for those reasons," Alexander was saying, "I formally request permission to return to the Galactic Core immediately, with the full strength of the MIEF."

He was present at the Senate hearing in person rather than electronically, wearing his full-dress Marine blacks with the blue and red trim. He'd even allowed Cara to convince him to wear a personal corona projector, which imitated the radiant nimbus projected by people present in simulation. He disliked this concession to what he considered to be dim-witted fashion nonsense, but was willing to play along if the golden light playing about his head and shoulders convinced even one senator that he should be heard.

He stood at the speaker's podium; at his back, a three-story-tall visual display mirrored the downloaded images he'd just played for the assembly through their cerebral links—the red sun with its intolerably brilliant jet, the ocher curve of S-2/I's planetary crescent, the hundreds of tightly packed brackets marking the approaching swarm of Xul huntership.

He'd emphasized, of course, the need to recover the twenty-one people left on the surface of S-2/I as well as the starships left behind . . . but the primary thrust of his argument had been on the need to go back and see what was actually happening now at the Galactic Core. That the Xul had been responding to the squadron's close passage about Gal-Center there could be no doubt. That they knew that the star S-2 had been tampered with, slowed in its orbital passage of GalCenter in order to put it onto a new and closer path was certain as well. The question was how the Xul had responded to the decelerating star . . . and exactly what they'd been able to do about it.

He'd been trying to read the emotional presence of the Commonwealth Senate for the last three days as he'd delivered his presentation and, so far, at least, he had no idea where things stood. Senator Yarlocke, he'd learned, was still in a deep coma, her body kept technically alive in cybernetic suspension, but her mind, apparently, gone. Senator Gerrad Ralston was now head of the Senate Military Committee in Yarlocke's place.

Ralston, Alexander knew, was a member of Yarlocke's camp, one of the bitch's puppies, as he thought of her coterie of hangers-on, an ultra-liberal anti-militarist, and one of the authors of the misbegotten *Pax Galactica* peace proposal.

"General Alexander," one of the senators in the curving rows of seats before him said. His link IDed the man as Senator Jeofri Dunford, of South Michigan, and a political moderate. "You stressed just now the need to understand Xul technological capabilities, and gave that as a principal reason for returning to the Galactic Core. Could you elaborate on that, please? If the Xul are as technologically superior as you've been painting them, what chance would our fleet have against them?"

"A good question, Senator. I wish I had as good an answer. The best I can do is to say that, in military terms, we can engage a technologically superior enemy if we're careful about choosing the time and place of that engagement. History is full of instances where groups took on superior technology and won, or, at least, held out for long enough that they could win a political victory, if not a military one. The classic examples are Vietnam in the 20th Century, or the various Islamic terrorist groups of the 21st. And that has been our grand strategy against the Xul for some centuries, now."

"Indeed. But we don't seem to have much hope of a political victory, here. We're not engaging the Xul in a political dialogue."

"No, sir. And that is a problem, not being able to talk with them.

"But since we *can't* talk to them, it may be that military

actions of the type we've been employing—quick, sharp raids against targets small enough to give us a good chance of short-term success—that those give us our best long-term option in dealing with the Xul, and for protecting ourselves. We've been saying all along that to be able to talk with them, we need to get their attention. But, just maybe, we've been going about it in completely the wrong way. It may be that, so far as the Xul are concerned, there's no one there for us to talk to. The Xul, as a collective entity, are *not* intelligent. . . ."

Several senators came to their feet, shouting.

"What are you talking about?"

"What the hell does that mean?"

"General Alexander! Explain yourself!"

He'd already put his conclusions into a written report, but doubted that many here in this chamber had actually bothered to read it.

"For centuries," Alexander went on, "we've been dealing with the Xul on the assumption that they are intelligent, rational beings. We've learned, slowly, that they're quite different from us, that they think differently, that they react differently to various stimuli. But because they are a *technological* species, building spacecraft and colonizing worlds, we've assumed that they are intelligent . . . meaning that they are capable of reason and of rational discourse, the same as us.

"We now believe that we were wrong in making that assumption."

Alexander waited for a moment, as shouts echoed through the chamber. Gradually, the noise died away; he had their full attention now.

"Our most recent probes of Xul ships, and of their complex at the heart of the Galaxy, has convinced the xenosophontologists with the MIEF that the Xul are, in fact, a CAS."

There was a long pause. "Can you explain that term, General?" Senator Tillman ventured.

"A CAS, ladies and gentlemen, is a *Complex Adaptive*

System. We've known about them for a long time—since the dawn of our relationship with artificial intelligences, in fact.

"A CAS is any system made up of many independent operators, or agents. Each agent operates on a fairly simplistic level, doing one or two things independently. A good example is a termite nest."

"We've already determined that the Xul do not have a hive mind, General," Senator Ralston said.

"I'm not talking about a hive mind," Alexander said. "At least, not in the sense that most humans understand the term. Most people think that an ant hill or a termite mound are analogues of human cities . . . that there are soldiers to defend them and workers to build and, somewhere down inside the mound, there's a queen termite telling all of the other termites what to do.

"Termite nests *do* have queens—and kings as well, unlike ant hills—but their sole contribution to the colony is reproduction. They don't give orders or control the nest. In fact, no one 'gives orders.' Each termite goes about its daily life, doing termite things. Thousands of termites—certain species of them, anyway, together build incredibly complex 'cities' six meters high, which regulate the internal temperature to within one degree Centigrade over the course of a day. A colony of a million termites working together creates the impression of a single organized and intelligent mind.

"In fact, each termite is a CAS agent with a very simple set of behaviors. The termite colony has its own pattern of behavior—far more complex, interesting, and apparently intelligent than that of a single insect. One termite is rigid in its behavior, and it dies when its surroundings aren't appropriate for that behavior. The entire colony, however, is highly resilient and adaptive, can survive a wide range of threats and conditions, and in some ways mimics what we humans think of as intelligent behavior."

"General Alexander," Senator McLeod, of Ontario, said, "are you saying the Xul are *termites*?"

Alexander sighed. How to get through to them? Senators were as rigid and as predictable in their behavior, in some ways, as individual termites.

"No, sir. I'm saying they are a complex adaptive system. Nature is full of them. A hurricane is a CAS, with numerous chaotic agents that work together to create a storm that *appears* to have conscious volition. Individual agents can be anything. Termites in a termite colony. Humans in the Commonwealth. Machines. AIs or more simplistic software. Corporations spread across the Commonwealth and in other nation-states. Cancer cells are CAS agents. The Commonwealth economy . . . that's made up of hundreds of billions of individual agents, from banking laws and the rules of supply and demand to individual Commonwealth citizens earning and spending credit. We have government bureaucracies tasked with maintaining and regulating our economy, but no one is in charge. It just *happens*. City air traffic in a congested environment like New Chicago. Schools of fish in the Atlantic sea farms. Antibodies in the human body. They work together because they grew and evolved together, and what they do was streamlined along the way until it appears to be a seamless, an *intelligent* whole.

"Ladies and gentlemen of the Senate, we've been puzzled for a long time about Xul behavior . . . about why we couldn't communicate with them, about why they didn't seem to show curiosity about us or anything else in the cosmos. They seemed to react to us in a simplistic fashion—as radical xenophobes—but we couldn't understand why their efforts to hunt us down and exterminate were so sporadic and more or less ineffectual. We assumed they were a machine intelligence . . . and yet our own AIs show more intelligence than a Type IV huntership carrying billions of Xul uploaded minds.

"Now we understand. Or we're beginning to. Their behavior is starting to make sense. Individual Xul, we think, are the conscious minds of once-organic beings uploaded into computer networks. Maybe the original organic Xul, a few million years ago, were xenophobic and built starships and wiped out other species . . . or maybe those behaviors developed later when individual Xul stopped thinking for themselves.

"But they did stop thinking. Groups of Xul arrive at a consensus by echoing thoughts back and forth—what we call 'singing' or 'choruses.' But the evidence suggests that they are only rarely aware of what's going on in the larger world around them. They may have created the Xul equivalent of paradise-simulations inside their computer networks, and don't bother with what we think of as the 'real world' any longer.

"In our culture, we have people who are addicted to simulations—game sims, simulated sex, simulated relationships. I submit that the Xul, the *real* Xul, have taken this process several steps further. They interact with reality around them as rarely as possible. And the blind interaction of trillions of Xul ships and nodes scattered across the Galaxy takes on a life, a personality of its own."

"What are you saying then, General?" Senator Ralston asked. "That they're not a threat?"

"Oh, no. They're very much a threat. When buildings were made primarily of wood, termites could destroy them. The best-regulated national economy can react to market forces in unexpected ways to unexpected conditions and collapse. For millions of years, the Xul CAS has more or less systematically hunted down and exterminated emerging sentient species, star-faring cultures, alien intelligences. And there is a distinct possibility that the CAS is reacting in a startlingly high-tech way at GalCenter to erase Reality, thereby insuring that the Xul survive in their tight little electronic paradises. We can't permit that to happen, because to do so would mean our extinction . . . and quite possibly the extinction of every sentient species in the universe."

"Then what are you suggesting, General?" Ralston said, pushing. He spread his hands. "You're saying we can't talk to them, we can't fight them . . ."

"We can learn more about them, Senator. *Information*, right now, is our most precious asset. We have set events in motion at the Galactic Core that may well fundamentally change Xul behavior, because the Xul CAS has never in its existence faced a threat quite like this. If we're lucky, we're going to eliminate so many of the individual Xul agents that the total number may drop below some critical mass, some necessary level below which their CAS doesn't function. To continue the termite analogy, if you reduce the number of termites from a million to a few hundred, the mound will stop acting as though it's got a mind of its own. I can't promise this, now, but I do promise that Xul behavior is about to change.

"If we want to have it change in our favor, we need to be there."

"General," Senator Tillman said, rising, "we've seen the records you brought back. A thousand Xul hunterships were coming toward your squadron. The entire MIEF, a fleet consisting of every warship in human-controlled space wouldn't be enough to stop them all. You acted rightly in breaking off the action and returning here. To take our only defense against the Xul back into that . . . that cauldron would be to squander it, to throw it away. An unthinking militarist response is *not* what is called for now."

"No, sir, but perhaps a thinking militarist response is what's necessary. Let me go back in there, with enough ships to make a difference. We will recover our people from S-2/I before the world is destroyed . . . and we will be in place to take action should we see an opportunity to make a positive difference.

"Maybe, Senator, when the Xul stop reacting as a non-sentient CAS to external stimuli, maybe the real Xul intelligence will poke its head up, look around . . . and try to talk with us. Isn't that worth a try?"

The session, the questions, the answers, the pleading went on for another two hours, and at the end, Alexander, exhausted, left the podium and retired to a side chamber, there to watch the debate, the speechmaking pro and con by a number of individual senators. He listened for nearly another hour to senators urging an adoption of the proposal interspersed with others urging it be rejected. One senator—Alexander never caught his name—insisted that the Navy and the Marines were not in existence to destroy termites at the Galactic Center.

Eventually, it was time for the vote.

"General Alexander?"

He rose. "Senator Armandez! It's good to see you."

"Hello, General. I wanted to stop in and tell you . . . thank you. I appreciate what you've tried to do."

Alexander grinned, shaking the man's hand. "Shouldn't you be on the floor voting?"

"Already did, General. We gave it our best shot. I don't know what else we can do."

"You don't sound too confident, sir."

Armandez shrugged. "It's going to be close. As usual, things are divided pretty evenly between the established party positions, conservative and liberal, militarist and anti-militarist. I don't know how many of the antis are going to let your speech persuade them. They all have some pretty heavy political baggage, reasons to see the proposal fail."

The proposal was Alexander's suggestion, that the full MIEF be allowed to return to the Core and watch events transpire.

"I still don't understand what they think they have to lose, sir."

"Political face, in part. And a fair-sized minority would like to have your MIEF at its beck and call. You'd be posted here in the Sol System in case the Xul came here. Eventually, you might find yourself being used in little wars and land grabs elsewhere—in the Islamic Theocracy, or against the PanEuropeans."

"I thought they were *anti*-military, sir?"

"They are, General, whatever is convenient for the moment. Whatever serves their career, their political agenda, or their immediate need. If it scratches their itch, they want it. Doesn't matter what the words are. In a way, the Senate is a CAS, too."

"I was aware of that, sir." He hesitated. "May I ask why you're supporting me? I know you're considered pro-military—"

He waved the statement aside. "It doesn't have to do with pro or anti-military. Every man and woman in that chamber knows the military is necessary. They just disagree on how best to employ it. No . . . partly, I agree with you that if we're forced to fight this . . . this force of nature, it's best done as far from Sol as possible. And, there's a personal reason."

"What's that?"

"I have a daughter."

"Yes, sir?"

"A Marine."

"I remember, Senator."

"She's in love with another Marine. One of the men still back there on that planet. She . . . *we* would like him to come home safely."

"I . . . understand, sir."

"Ah! Here comes the tally."

A total of 321 senators were voting this evening. As the results came in, the numbers came up on the display above the image of the Senate Chamber . . . 151 in favor of Alexander's proposal, 165 against, with 5 abstentions.

The 1MIEF would be recalled to Sol Space. It would not be permitted to return to GalCenter.

"Don't worry, General," Armandez told him. "We'll find a way. We *will* find a way."

"Yes, sir."

But would it be in time to save the people still stranded out there within the Galactic Core?

25

2606.1102

Marine Regimental Strike Team
Firebase Hawkins, S-2/I
Core Space
0815 hrs, GMT

There weren't many of them left.

The five Navy personnel who'd been the crew of the Tarantula had died first, one after another just a few days after the march back to Firebase Hawkins. They'd been wearing the old-style armor during that ten-kilometer march, Type 664 suits, instead of the newer Type 690s. The old suits had not been able to handle the background radiation loads and all five people were desperately sick by the time they'd staggered into the firebase.

Two of them, including Lieutenant Grooms, had gone up onto the surface and opened their own helmets before the end. The other three had lingered a while longer, as vomiting and diarrhea and the rapid disintegration of their cellular structure had slowly killed them.

The survivors' numbers had been increased by two Marine officers early on—Lieutenants Eva Grant and Karl Mayfair, the pilots of the last two Nightstars. Over the course of the next month, however, four of the Marines had died of radiation sickness as well—Pettigrew, Davis, Grant, and Mayfair. The Marine pilots had been wearing light anti-rad protection on board their Nightstars, depending on the anti-rad nano covering their fighters for protection. They'd landed close by the ruins of Firebase Hawkins, but by the time they reached the base's underground shelters, both had received irreparably lethal doses.

Gunny Warhurst was the senior man present, now—not counting Ramsey in his cybernetic suspension inside the medical cocoon. There'd been some discussion about senior ranks and who should be in command. Warhurst had been a gunnery sergeant long before Garroway, but for the past ten years he'd been a civilian, and going by their actual time in rate, Garroway had been the senior by a matter of a few months. But if you measured from the actual date of enlistment, Warhurst had Garroway beat by ten years.

In fact, it didn't matter. The proprieties and traditions were observed because that was how Marines kept order in a small and isolated unit. Garroway had no particular desire to lead the little group of survivors, especially since it seemed more and more likely that they all were going to succumb one by one to radiation sickness and die, and there was *nothing* anyone could do about it.

But he would do his best to serve as Warhurst's exec, making sure the air, food, and water were doled out appropriately, as were Doc's dwindling rations of anti-rad nano.

For the past fifty days, they'd been surviving in a sealed bunker deep beneath the ruins of Firebase Hawkins. Excavated and nanogrown originally as a sickbay for the facility, it consisted of three rooms including sleeping quarters, a small nanoprocessing center, and a medical storeroom, though unfortunately most of the medical supplies had been taken by the rest of the RST when they'd evacuated. The quarters were crowded and utterly lacking in privacy. A single head provided basic sanitary facilities and a sonic shower, but the place stank with the accumulating miasma of unwashed bodies and the body gloves they wore under their armor.

An airlock led to the surface via a ladder up a vertical

tube; a display screen pulled from the communications center had been rigged to show scenes transmitted from the various battlezone sensors still moving about the surface, their one connection with the universe outside.

Through those sensors, the surviving Marines had watched as the sky, already strange, slowly shifted into a surreal and eldritch fantasy from the hallucinations of a brain-burned sim-addict. Eventually, S-2/I's slow, retrograde rotation had carried the central focus of the accretion spiral below the northeastern horizon, but three weeks later it had risen once more in the northwest; by chance, the point marking GalCenter was very nearly circumpolar, and dipped out of sight during the long diurnal cycle for only a relatively brief time.

By the fortieth day of their isolation, they could see the Dyson cloud, a fuzzy patch at the accretion spiral's center, partly obscured by the ripple and flash of enigmatic lightnings at S-2/I's north pole.

By the forty-fifth day, the cloud was much larger and more distinct, a dark and curiously regular spherical blot against the grainy glow of the background stars.

"It looks," Sergeant Huerra said with studied Corps aplomb, "like something puked by my girlfriend's cat."

"That's supposed to be a cloud of Xul ships?" PFC Lenny Delalo said, looking at the screen. "How come they haven't come after us, then?"

"Likely they don't even know we're here," Warhurst told him. "We've had some overflights, remember, but they didn't sniff us out."

Corporal Natasha Kaminski sniffed her own armpit and made a face. "If they couldn't fucking smell us, they don't have a sense of smell."

Twice, on Day 8, and again on Day 22, clouds of Xul machines had swept over the ruined base. They were like standard Xul combots—egg-shaped and mounting tentacles and glittering lenses—but larger, as large as Nightstar fighters. There'd been thousands of the devices, most passing over, a few stopping and poking around in the ruins below. The

Marines, their life support powered down, had donned their armor and crouched in darkness, weapons ready for a final and apocalyptic encounter.

But either the Xul hadn't detected them, or they'd decided the tiny party of buried Marines simply wasn't worth the digging.

"Maybe the smell's why they didn't bother," Sergeant Paul Willian suggested. "They got one whiff and decided there was something dead down here."

That brought nervous laughter, but Garroway thought it had been a little too close to the mark for comfort. Fourteen Marines left . . . and they *would* be dead before much longer.

Actually, the smell wasn't *that* bad. Perhaps they'd all gotten used to it by now or, as PFC Ted Bergen had suggested, their olfactory nerves had simply fried on Day 1. But, in fact, the nanoprocessors filtered the air constantly, removing water and excess carbon dioxide, along with the various organic aromatics. They were cycling their shit and piss efficiently enough, too—carbon, hydrogen, oxygen, and nitrogen were, after all, carbon, hydrogen, oxygen, and nitrogen. The processors rearranged the atoms, including those of the intestinal flora growing in the raw materials, into food bars, water, and air. The raw materials were supplemented by a dwindling stock of carbon and various trace elements but, sooner rather than later, supplies would run out. They couldn't live on their own waste products forever.

Garroway knew the numbers better than any of them. As exec, it was his job to keep track of their resources, and ration the consumables.

He estimated that within another three months they would be producing so few metabolic waste products that their daily rations would fall below the minimum necessary to keep them all alive.

There'd been some discussion early on about adding the seven bodies to the resource reserves, a kind of high-tech cannibalism that might extend the lives of the survivors by many months. Although no military unit can afford to be a democracy, Warhurst had taken a vote in order to end the morbid speculation.

The result had overwhelmingly favored leaving the bodies where they were, sealed in body bags up on the surface.

It was just as well. Those bodies were so radioactive that it was extremely unlikely that the nanoprocessors could have handled the decon without themselves becoming contaminated. Warhurst and Garroway hadn't mentioned that to the others, though. Those bodies would be returned to the Commonwealth somehow, some day, presumably along with the bodies of the fourteen still alive in the underground bunker.

The Corps always brought home its own.

And, in fact, none of that really mattered, not in the long run. Over the course of the past seven weeks, as the Dyson cloud first appeared, then rapidly grew larger in the northwestern sky, it became more and more clear that the planet itself might well not survive much longer.

S-2/I orbited its red giant primary at a distance of over six astronomical units, farther from its sun than Jupiter was from Sol. As week followed week, S-2 appeared to be dwindling, as though the distance between world and sun was growing larger.

When S-2's orbital path had been changed, S-2/I, gravitationally locked with its primary, had been pulled off course as well, but the planet had lagged behind somewhat, and its orbital velocity had been slowly tugging it farther and farther from its star.

The star's leading plume of flame had dissipated weeks ago, but some tens of solar masses had been funneled up that thread of white light, acting as a titanic rocket engine. S-2's close pass around GalCenter was now going to be a *very* close pass.

Exactly how close, no one—not even Athena$_2$, the small version of Athena remaining in the RST network—could predict. The chances were good, though, that the star would pass close enough to the super-massive black hole at Gal-Center to be disrupted, even torn apart. If that happened, S-2/I would likely be destroyed as well. Already, the mild seismic quakes Garroway had noticed seven weeks before were becoming stronger and more pronounced. If a micro-black hole *was* devouring the planet from the inside, it was going to have a lot of help soon from the gravitational tides of GalCenter.

Even if S-2/I survived the passage, though, its star would not. The planet's surface temperature was kept within toler-able limits both by the heat from its giant sun primary and by tidal forces raised by that sun. With S-2 destroyed, even if the planet was flung clear of the central maelstrom, tem-peratures would inevitably plunge. The background radia-tion might keep temperatures a few degrees above absolute zero, but the planet *would* freeze. When local temperatures dropped below about minus 150 or so, not even the base's small reactor would be able to keep them warm for long.

A choice of deaths, Garroway thought. Death by malnutrition—starving to death by centimeters. Death if their world was torn apart by the central black hole and de-voured. Death by freezing. Death by radiation poisoning.

The only real choice was which one would claim them first. No one was talking much about the possibility that the MIEF might come back for them. Not any longer.

"I'm going up on the surface," he said at last.

"What the hell for?" Warhurst demanded. His eyes wid-ened. "Wait a sec, Gare. You're not—"

"No," Garroway told him. "I'm not taking a walk."

Taking a walk had become the accepted euphemism these past weeks for what Lieutenant Grooms had done—going up to the surface and opening your helmet visor to vacuum.

"The rads'll kill you," O'Neill said.

"Kill me faster, you mean. I just want to look at the sky for a while, okay?"

With space at a premium, the Marines' armor had been stowed inside the airlock, at the base of the surface access tunnel. He had to take one of the suits on top, though, rather than finding his own, because 690s were heavy and tough to manhandle alone.

It didn't matter if he got someone else's suit, though; Marine armor, with nanotechnic appliances that adjusted the fit, was definitely one-size-fits-all.

Well, almost. The suit he picked had Kaminski's name stenciled on the chest, and the crotch had been configured for female plumbing. No problem. He didn't plan to be on the surface long enough for that particular need to assert itself.

Slowly, almost ritually, he donned the armor, letting it adjust itself to his size and shape, feeling the seals close, the connections with his implant open. He took a plasma rifle simply because a Marine would not go into a potential hostile zone without a weapon, cycled through the lock, and started up the ladder.

He was struck by the utter stillness of the surface, and by the eerie, icy light. The Dyson cloud hung suspended in the northwestern sky. In the west, the red-giant star S-2 was rising just above the horizon, blood red, appearing a little larger than Sol looked from Earth, though it was more than six times farther off. Pale lightnings played along the horizon, beneath a shimmering, almost invisible haze of auroral light.

According to Athena$_2$, S-2 was close to perigalacton, its close passage of the Galactic Core. S-2/I dutifully was tagging along, pulling away slightly from its parent sun, but still moving toward GalCenter at a velocity well above five thousand kilometers per second. S-2's speed had been slowed significantly by the triggership-induced stellar rocket effect, but it had picked up all that lost velocity and more as it fell deeper and deeper into the gravity well of the central black hole.

Athena$_2$ was unable to tell him just how fast the planet was moving now. There were no celestial landmarks, no rangefinders, no instrumentation that could make such a reading, not now, not from here.

But as Garroway stared up at the Dyson cloud, he could have sworn he could actually see it moving, see it *growing*, second by passing second.

"What the hell are you doing up here, Gunny?" Huerra said, clambering out of the open access tunnel. Garroway glanced at him, then turned back to face that awesome celestial panorama.

"Hey, if S-2/I is going to be eaten by that thing, I don't want to wait for it down a hole, know what I mean?"

"I hear you, Gunny. I think the others agree. They're all putting on their armor."

"Yeah, Gare," Warhurst said, climbing out of the tunnel. "You seem to have started a stampede."

"At least it looks like we're going to have a front-row-center seat."

Warhurst chuckled. "That it does, my friend. That it does. . . ."

The other Marines began spreading out on the surface. If there were Xul machines about, they might be spotted and attacked, but Garroway doubted that to be the case. Any Xul in the area must be as transfixed by that sky as the humans were . . . assuming they could react to wonder in a human manner.

Interesting thought. Could the Xul feel something like wonder?

Did they feel fear at what was metaphorically thundering down upon their cloud of habitations, there at GalCenter?

"Someone record this," he said. "They'll want to see, back home."

Ops Center
UCS Hermes
Core Space
0850 hrs, GMT

They'd made it through at last.

The Marine Interstellar Expeditionary Force had passed through the stargate in Cluster Space, emerging through another gate a thousand light years from GalCenter. There might be, must be other stargates closer to the super-massive black hole and its attendant Dyson cloud, but there'd not been time to locate them, or to map alternate gate routes among the stars. Alexander stood in the Ops Center on board the flagship *Hermes*, watching the passage.

Ralston and the other antimilitarist senators were going to be damned pissed, he thought. They'd given permission for a reconnaissance raid into Core Space, specifying that *Hermes* and "select support vessels and troops" could make the jump. The assumption had been that *Hermes* would translate from Cluster Space to the region close by S-2/I, with four naval warships on board. They'd not imagined *this*, some three hundred Commonwealth warships, passing through the Stargate almost *en masse*.

Well, Alexander thought with wry satisfaction, *I said* Hermes *and her supporting vessels would be making the passage at zero-eight fifty hours Zulu. I just didn't tell them how many "supporting vessels" were coming along.* . . .

Three of the new Navy heavy monitors were among the first vessels through the Gate, positioned to emerge with their primary weapons already aimed at the Xul fort drifting a few kilometers from the Gate's rim. *Derna, Chapultepec,* and *Tarawa* had been designed as Xul fortress-busters, with names drawn from especially significant battles in the Corps' history, with high-velocity mass drivers and turret-mounted antimatter accelerators augmented by massive 300mm cannon firing two-ton nano-D shells. As the three monitors emerged from the Gate's lumen, their weapons began hammering at the fortress with savage, rolling fusillades, the rounds smashing in with unerring accuracy, guided by the swarm of battlespace sensor drones that had preceded the fleet.

The Xul fortress opened fire with plasma discharges, but only the *Derna* and two of her accompanying destroyers suffered slight damage before the fortress dissolved in flashes of dazzling light from multiple hivel impacts, and the ragged disintegration of its thick outer hull as nano-disassemblers swarmed across its surface.

The rest of the fleet didn't pause to watch the destruction, but shifted to Alcubierre Drive within seconds of emerging from the Gate. *Hermes*, positioned near the center of the fleet, had only a glimpse of the destruction before accelerating out of optical range.

Ahead, the central reaches of the Galactic Core lay shrouded in dark molecular clouds and the gleam of hot suns.

Just for an instant, Alexander felt a surge of relief. The panorama of the central regions appeared unchanged from his last visit to the Core almost two months ago. *We haven't missed it!*

Then reality reasserted itself. Of *course* there was no change. The fleet was still a thousand light-years out; whatever might be happening in there, the light revealing it would not reach this Stargate for another ten centuries.

Then the darkness of the Alcubierre Drive closed around the *Hermes*, replaced, eventually, by an AI-created sim. The light years fled past. . . .

Marine Regimental Strike Team
Firebase Hawkins, S-2/I
Core Space
0858 hrs, GMT

The Dyson cloud filled half the sky.

It was growing visibly larger, though the scale of what they were watching was so vast, so tremendous, that the planet must be accelerating at an unthinkable rate for change to manifest in the sky so swiftly. Garroway tried to picture the geometry of the situation, based on schematics that Athena$_2$ had painted for him several days before, and failed.

It was enough, he thought, just to watch. To *experience*. . . .

The remaining lifetime of S-2/I might be measured now in only seconds. It didn't matter. *Nothing* mattered now but the unfolding view overhead.

"It's beautiful . . ." Sergeant Willian said quietly.

"Fucking gorgeous," was Kaminski's reply.

"I wonder if the Xul know that—" Warhurst started to say.

The star exploded.

Much later, it would be determined that the Xul had detonated S-2 themselves in a last-ditch effort to save the Dyson cloud. The red sun appeared to tremble, to begin to collapse inward, then, suddenly, to grow intolerably bright, shifting from sullen red to diamond-hard, crystalline blue-white brilliance as the star's outer layers suddenly rebounded outward, flying into space.

"Shit!" Sergeant Huerra said. "They blew the star up!"

"Nah," Warhurst said. "Look at it! The star's being torn apart by tidal stresses as it gets in close. . . ."

"We're dead," PFC Enewold said. "My rad counter is off the scale."

"What a way to go, eh?" Corporal Ann Croley said. And she laughed.

The detonation of the red giant, fewer than seven a.u.s distant, had bathed the planet in hard radiation—gamma rays traveling at the speed of light. Particulate radiation—protons and neutrons—would follow, though it would take time, as much as another day, perhaps, to reach the trailing planet.

"So . . . did the bastards save themselves?" Huerra wanted to know.

"Not hardly," Garroway said. He pointed. "Look at the star. . . ."

The brilliant star, now a dazzling white, was almost too bright to look at even with the heavy filtering by their visor optics. They could see enough of it, though, to see that it was stretching, growing ever more and more elongated as it neared the super-massive black hole at the Galaxy's center. It was impossible to see the Dyson cloud now, so brilliant was the dying star's light. Had the star struck the cloud, passing through it? Or was it still outside of the cloud? Even if the tortured star remained well beyond the Dyson cloud itself, surely even Xul technology couldn't save those trillions of structures from the heat and hard radiation of an exploding sun.

As minute followed minute, the star appeared to be

stretching. The fast-expanding outer shell of its photosphere appeared to have stopped, appeared to have been grabbed by some vast and invisible hand, crumpled, and pulled back away from the Marines watching just a few astronomical units away.

Garroway could feel his skin burning. The shredding star was vomiting massive amounts of X-rays.

Yeah. *What a way to go! . . .*

Ops Center
UCS Hermes
Core Space
1030 hrs, GMT

The joke was on the Senate, Alexander thought. They'd approved a recon probe by *Hermes* and the four ships she could carry, but assumed that *Hermes* would translate back to S-2/I. Somehow, the scientific niceties had simply escaped them. *Hermes* couldn't translate back to S-2/I, because the local metric had been steadily changing over the course of seven weeks. Alexander, his aides, and a host of AIs had explained the science time after time, but they never seemed to get it.

Their ignorance had played into Alexander's hands, though, and cleared the way for Senator Armandez's campaign to let the MIEF enter the Core.

The biggest problem was timing. Alexander knew in a general way that S-2 was due to make its close passage around GalCenter soon—fifty days after the induction of the rocket effect in the star's photosphere. The trouble was that there'd been no way to measure the exact effects on the star. Many solar masses had been expelled in that jet . . . but how many? How long had the effect lasted? How much had the star been slowed? Then how quickly had it accelerated in its plunge toward GalCenter? There were too many unknowns. It was possible that S-2 had swept into the Dyson cloud sometime yesterday . . . or that it was still a day out from perigalacton.

The fleet might be too late to save the Marines on S-2/I. The planet might have been swallowed by the monster hours ago.

They wouldn't know until they dropped out of FTL. *Hermes* and the rest of the MIEF were decelerating now, angling toward the spot where S-2/I *ought* to be, based on the best astrogational guesses possible.

The darkness evaporated, and the sky grew suddenly brilliant.

"My God! . . ." Taggart said at Alexander's side.

Together, the two men looked down into the annihilation of a star.

Marine Regimental Strike Team
Firebase Hawkins, S-2/I
Core Space
1104 hrs, GMT

The radiation was catching up with all of them. Garroway had vomited several times already, and was feeling the deadly weakness that he knew must mean a lethal dose of hard rad. Most of the others had been vomiting as well, despite the best efforts of the last of Doc O'Neill's anti-rad drugs.

The Marines had been spelling themselves in their vigil, either by clambering back down into the bunker, or by taking shelter on board an AV-110 Tarantula left behind by the evacuating Marines. This particular Tarantula, it turned out, had been damaged by a Xul plasma bolt and was immobile, but still offered a pressurized cabin and enough active nano on its outer hull to cut down on the storm of radiation sleeting across the planet's surface.

But after a few moments of relative comfort, each Marine found him or herself drawn again to the deadly ringside seats outside, staring up into a maelstrom of incandescent destruction. They were dying moment by moment.

But the view, all of them agreed, was worth it.

Ops Center
UCS Hermes
Core Space
1120 hrs, GMT

The view, actually, was better on board the ships of 1MIEF as they approached the hurtling planet. The starships' sensors were more sensitive, their optical screening filters more discriminating, their AIs more powerful than anything possessed by the handful of Marines still on S-2/I. As the fleet slowly adjusted its vector to close with the planet, they recorded everything.

Alexander remained with Taggart in the Ops Center, watching the drama unfold on the main display. The red giant had an overall diameter of perhaps thirty million kilometers—three times that of the Xul Dyson cloud. The exact size of the incoming star was difficult to determine, however, for the outer layers were expanding swiftly, a dazzling white shell of gas, as the star exploded. As that shell expanded, however, it was being warped by the insatiable gravity well created by the central black hole. As hour followed hour, what had been a red giant was being twisted and stretched into something entirely different.

The star had been, roughly, three times larger than the Dyson cloud, and it plunged through the near side of the Dyson cloud at something like ten thousand kilometers per second. As it passed the suddenly revealed black hole, it was drawn more and more into an elongated, curving sausage, then into a ribbon meeting itself and merging into a rapidly spinning torus, a doughnut shape melding with the accretion disk and spiraling into the black hole's bottomless maw.

There was too much stellar mass for the black hole to

consume at one sitting. The excess, well over half of the star's bulk, was funneled off the black hole's north and south poles as intensely brilliant beams of violet-white radiation. The Dyson cloud was swept away, as insubstantial against that onslaught of matter and energy as cobwebs. Soon, even the best of the MIEF's optical filters could perceive nothing but the intolerable glare.

Curious, Alexander had downloaded more of the *Bhagavad Gita* during the fifty days since the triggerships had first assaulted that star, searching for the verses that had inspired Oppenheimer all those centuries before. In the original story, Arjuna, a prince fearful of the outcome of an upcoming battle with a superior foe, had asked to see the god Vishnu in his full glory. Vishnu's reply had been recorded in Chapter 11, verses 32 and 33.

> *"The Supreme Lord said: I am death, the mighty destroyer of the world, out to destroy. Even without your participation all the warriors standing arrayed in the opposing armies shall cease to exist.*
>
> *"Therefore, get up and attain glory. Conquer your enemies and enjoy a prosperous kingdom. All these warriors have already been destroyed by Me. You are only an instrument, Oh Arjuna."*

The verses seemed especially fitting in the current setting, as Alexander watched radiance fill the Galactic Core. *I am death . . .*

Marine Regimental Strike Team
Firebase Hawkins, S-2/I
Core Space
1120 hrs, GMT

It would be determined, much later, that the planet passed within half an a.u. of the black hole's event horizon, slingshotted by that intense gravitational field to a velocity high enough to send it hurtling past perigalacton and out into the gulfs of empty space once more. Garroway wasn't able to even guess when the closest approach actually took place. The sky was twisting in an odd way as gravity accelerated the planet, twisting it into a tumble. The star, on a path that took it much closer, had smashed through the vaporizing remnants of the Dyson cloud, stretched like taffy, and whiplashed down the gravitational maw into the unknowable depths beneath the event horizon.

For just an instant, Garroway saw the black hole itself, twice as big across as the Sun appeared from Earth, but black, *black*, a bottomless emptiness drinking light, seated at the precise center of a vortex of blue-to-violet whirlpool of light, spiraling into oblivion. And then the brief vision was blotted out in exploding star-stuff.

The black hole was receding now, quickly. The planet was already far out beyond the Monster's reach.

Garroway heard cheering.

"What's going on?" he asked. He looked around for Warhurst. "Michael?"

"They're back!" Warhurst shouted. "They're fucking back!"

"Huh? Who? . . ."

"The Marines, stupid! *Now* who's a rock, as in 'dumb as a?' Huh?"

Garroway had tuned out his RST channel. As he brought it back on-line, he heard the radio chatter of dozens of men and women. In the sky overhead, a pair of Nightstars flashed past, blue Core-light gleaming from their flanks.

Despite his weakness, the dizziness, the wrenching nausea, Garroway joined in with the cheers, waving his plasma rifle above his head, shouting *"Ooh-rah!"* and *"Semper fi!"* as the lead elements of 1MIEF began descending from the sky.

And *still* no response from the Xul. They couldn't all have been killed, could they? Perhaps the shock of S-2's assault on their inner fastness had simply stunned them into immobility.

Or maybe other processes were at work.

Perhaps the Xul had been beaten after all.

The transport *Howorth* again hung in S-2/I's sky, gentling down on carefully balanced agravs. He would learn later that the MIEF warships left behind when *Hermes* translated back to Cluster space—*Howorth* and *Cunningham*—had rendezvoused with the *Lejeune*, *Plottel*, and *Ardash* at Point Diamond. Technically, they'd disobeyed their orders to return to human space, waiting there within the star cluster a tenth of a light year away until they'd received a QCC message from the MIEF, then joined the main body over S-2/I after the planet's hair-raising close passage of the black hole.

Semper fidelis. Always faithful. We don't leave our own behind. . . .

He must have lost consciousness. When he could see again, brother and sister Marines off the *Howorth* had crowded around, helping him stumble up the ramp and into the safety of the huge ship's belly. Radiation sickness tore at him, much worse than ten years ago.

At that moment, Garroway didn't know if he was going to survive the massive rad overdose he'd picked up in the past hours, but he accepted the not knowing with a calm equanimity. It wasn't that he didn't care if he lived or died. He *wanted* to live, there was no doubt about that. But somehow the events of those hours had left him utterly drained, until only a single thought, a single emotion remained.

Home.

He was going home.

Epilogue

In the outlying regions of the Galaxy's Perseus Arm, within the dense polar jungles of the warm, inner world of a class-G5 star, a race of brachiating mollusks swung from the interwoven branches of sessile thermovores not unlike Earthly trees. The species was young, as yet, but one of its best known musician-philosophers had just sung an important dream-song.

It spoke of other worlds, of other forests among the stars, of other singers who one day might join the race in new and alien harmonies.

They were closer now to the realization of that dream-song than they could possibly have imagined.

Closer in toward the galactic core, within the teeming star clouds of the Sagittarius Arm, on the rugged, tide-strained volcanic moon of a superjovian gas giant, a race of armored paraholothurids built water's-edge hive-cities of compacted excrement and composed palindromic epics celebrating their having been chosen as slaves of the sky-disk they saw as the eye of God. On this day, they recited a new palindrome, one announcing the revelation of a new messiah, latest in a long line of messiahs proclaiming the Vision of the Eye of God.

God's message was that there were countless other beings living on alien worlds scattered across the vastness of the sky, that some of these beings Knew the glory of God, and many did not.

But there might one day soon be a means of taking God's Vision to the stars.

Closer in still toward the galactic hub, near the merging of the Norma and Scutum-Crux Arms, a fiercely radiating Type A star blasted its unusual coterie of rocky worlds with intense radiation. Bathed in abundant radiant energy, Life had emerged on the innermost world and, borne by the local stellar winds, had seeded the other, outer planets of the system as well. On one of those radiation-baked worlds, sentient crystalline chemovores had just discovered the principle of the solar sail, and had now within their grasp the ability to reach other nearby stars. The voyages would take centuries . . . but what was that to a species whose member beings lived for millennia?

The race, perhaps, would survive, even if their increasingly unstable sun did not.

1507.1102

Warhurst Residence, Seaview Gardens
Lost Miami, Earth
1540 hrs, local

Garroway leaned back in the hot tub, savoring the blissfully scalding swirl of water across his shoulders. Nikki Armandez snuggled against his side, as naked as he was despite her Ishtaran upbringing. Opposite, Warhurst sat between the delightfully bobbing charms of Traci and Kath.

"Too bad Charel can't be here with us," Warhurst said. "You heard anything about him, Gare?"

"Only that he's doing well. The regrow's just taking longer with him. He was burned a lot worse than either of us."

"But he'll be okay?"

"Doc O'Neill said so." Garroway shrugged. "That's good enough for me."

All fourteen of the surviving Marines stranded for so long at the Galactic Core had made it, though it had been desperately close for a few of them. Seven, including Ramsey, were still in the Marine hospital in EarthRing. Garroway had been released only two days earlier. Much of his body had been either regrown from scratch or replaced by exotic nano-chelated materials. It was sobering to realize that less than a third of his total body now was organic in the traditional sense.

But he was alive. *Alive.* He could even still have sex, as he'd enthusiastically proved several times now both with Nikki, and in one memorable five-way last night that had included Kath and Traci. He would never have children of his own, not in the traditional way, at least.

It didn't matter to him in the least. Aiden Garroway had all the family he needed. He'd checked out on a two-week leave and come down-ring with Nikki to Miami. Warhurst had checked out of the hospital almost a week earlier, and was spending it back home with his partners.

"So!" Traci said brightly. "Have either of you boys seen the latest from the encyclopedia? It just came through this morning!"

"Hell, no," Warhurst said. "You three kept me up all night, remember? I've been getting my hard-earned beauty sleep."

"Which you definitely need," Garroway told him. "No, Traci. What came through now?"

"Have a look!"

With a thought, a large display rose from the deck behind the tub and switched on. She could have given him a direct link, of course, but apparently she wanted to see his reaction as he watched with his eyes instead of his mind.

"My God," Garroway said, looking at the image on the screen. "What *is* it?"

"According to the Translators, it's a living rock. A kind of complex crystalline solid that processes stellar energy on some planets around an A-class star maybe twenty thousand light years from here. The planet's surface is so bathed in radiation that—"

"Ah . . . I don't think I want to hear about that," Garroway said, holding up a dripping hand. "I've had enough radiation baths to last me, thank you very much."

"How many alien species does that make now?" Warhurst wanted to know.

"Two hundred seventy-three . . . and according to the Translators, more are turning up every day. Looks like the Galaxy's a pretty crowded place after all."

It had been an astonishing end to an astonishing adventure, Garroway thought. When S-2 had crashed through the Dyson cloud surrounding the central black hole, many of those trillions of structures had been vaporized outright in the heat of the exploding sun. Others, their magnetic support structure fatally damaged, had collapsed into the relentless pull of the black hole.

The Xul, the ancient Hunters of the Dawn, still survived, of course. There were, N-2 estimated, some tens of thousands of Xul nodes still scattered across the Galaxy. But the vast majority of their total numbers had perished in the cataclysm at the Galactic Core. There was some question as to whether the survivors could even function now, given the possibility that they'd needed a critical mass in terms of numbers in order to act.

Whatever had happened to the Xul, one startling change had manifested almost as soon as the Dyson cloud was swept away from the region encircling GalCenter. Someone, some thing, was using the Galaxy's black hole as a colossal communications and information storage device. The Xul cloud had been blocking the signals from that device. With the Xul gone from the Core, now, the signals had resumed.

Black holes, large and small, were doorways of sorts into the Quantum Sea, the base state of reality. Technically, nothing could escape a black hole, a gravitational singularity that held captive *everything* that passed its event horizon, even light.

And yet, it seemed now, black holes could communicate with one another, instantly, via the Quantum Sea. Fluctuations of their event horizons as matter fell through them created gravitational distortions that served as carrier waves.

Modulations impressed upon those distortions carried information. A *lot* of information.

The nature of those waves had been detected by the MIEF hours after the collapse of the Dyson cloud; nested signals, layer upon layer of them, were captured, recorded, and routed through powerful artificial intelligences programmed as translators. The surface data in those layers, it turned out, were mathematical formulae designed as a linguistic and technical primer, allowing for a relatively simple translation of the deeper layers of data.

In a month, the Translators had barely begun their work. Still, public fascination with the news had forced the government to release some data as it became available. Every so often, a description of a new and utterly alien race was gleaned from the ocean of electronic data, condensed into an entertaining format, and broadcast over the GlobalNet.

Centuries before, radio astronomers had speculated on the possibility of a Galaxy-wide network of stored information bearing data on myriad worlds and civilizations. They'd called it the *Encyclopedia Galactica,* and assumed it would be presented as information encoded into radio signals broadcast from star to star. The fact that in years of painstaking searching they'd never found such a thing had been part of the enduring mystery of the Fermi Paradox. Where was everyone?

And now the *Encyclopedia Galactica* had been found . . . its signals masked by the Xul cloud at the Galactic Core. No one yet knew whether the Xul had been reading those imbedded messages, or were so intent on their tinkering with Reality that they'd not even seen them. Another mystery. Another Unknown.

The primary broadcast center was the Galactic Core, but it turned out that *every* black hole was linked into the Network. While the central black hole was off-line, as it were, no signals had come through any of them. Now, though . . .

There were hints that the Network was more than Galactic in scale, hints that galactic black holes across the entire universe might be talking with one another . . . and in real time, not the crawl of eons endured by slow-paced light.

"Well, it's good to know the Xul didn't wipe out everyone in the Galaxy," Garroway said. "It was starting to feel a bit lonely, you know?"

Not as lonely, perhaps, as the surface of S-2/I. But every indicator suggested that the Galaxy should be humming with life, while Humankind's explorations so far had uncovered so few—the An, the N'mah, the Eulers.

And the Xul.

Within the titanic elliptical galaxy called M-87, located in what Earth astronomers described as the Virgo Cluster some sixty million light years from Sol, Mind considered the new data. For some millions of years, a particular modest spiral galaxy within the outlying reaches of the Virgo supercluster had been unaccountably silent, the singularity within its central core somehow shrouded and muffled, blocking Mind.

And now, the shroud had been lifted.

Mind considered the implications. Presumably, the inhabitants of that galaxy had chosen to isolate themselves from the rest of the cosmos. It happened sometimes, for religious or philosophical or emotional reasons. There were so many, many different types of mind, so many forms of thought.

The collective sentience that called itself Mind had not interfered, of course, but it was curious.

And it wondered now at just what had changed in that insignificant spiral, sixty million light years distant. . . .

Perhaps further investigation would be necessary.

Much later, Garroway awoke, cuddled between Nikki and Traci, while Warhurst and Kath snored gently nearby. The overhead had been set to show the star-clotted night sky. After the Galactic Core, the sky seemed dark and empty with its scant handful of bright stars, its almost nonexistent dusting of dimmer ones. The Milky Way stretched across the zenith.

I wonder if we really made a difference?

Sagittarius. In *that* direction, he thought, lay the Core. Energy shredded from the dying sun S-2 and from the infalling trillions of Xul habitats had been blasted outward in an explosion that would likely continue for millennia. Most of the debris had been swallowed by the central black hole, but much, too, had escaped. In a few centuries, the outrushing blast would intercept those molecular gas clouds ringing the center, and the shock wave would trigger a burst of star formation that in twenty-some thousand years would turn the Galactic center brilliant, even out here in the stellar suburbs.

Oh, yeah. The Marines had made a difference. No one knew, yet, if the Xul War was over. Probably it wasn't . . . but the balance of things had most certainly changed.

Things would be different. Changed. Perhaps in ways now unguessable.

As he drifted back into sleep, Aiden Garroway thought about the Marine Corps, and the difference the Corps had always made in the vaster scheme of things.

Semper fi. . . .